No Way Out

ALSO BY T.J. BREARTON

TITAN SERIES

Book 1: Habit
Book 2: Survivors
Book 3: Daybreak
Book 4: Black Soul

NORTH COUNTRY SERIES

Book 1: Dark Web
Book 2: Dark Kills
Book 3: Gone

TOM LANGE SERIES

Book 1: Dead Gone
Book 2: Truth Or Dead
Book 3: Dead Or Alive

STANDALONES

Highwater
The Husbands
When He Vanished
Her Perfect Secret
Her Husband's Lies
The Perfect Fiancé
The Bones In The Backyard
No Way Out

NO WAY OUT

T. J. BREARTON

JOFFE BOOKS

Revised edition 2025
Joffe Books, London
www.joffebooks.com

First published by Bookouture in Great Britain in 2017
as *Gone Missing*

Cover art by Nick Castle

ISBN: 978-1-83526-987-9

For my daughters, Tatum and Sabine.

CHAPTER ONE

Katie stepped onto the porch and laced up her sneakers.

In the Northeast, mid-August, dawn came at 5:30 a.m. Over the mountains, a smattering of salmon-tinged clouds heralded the sun.

She lunged to stretch out her calves, bent forward to loosen her thighs and lower back.

Today's target heart rate was 122. Target heart rate was 220 minus her age, 33, multiplied by 65%, since jogging ideally increased a person's heart rate by that amount. Or so *Runner's World* had told her.

She left the house, walking first. Her sneakers were springy and new, ready to launch her forward. She began her run, falling into her rhythm, feeling fit.

Running was one of life's secret pleasures. She'd run rain or shine, only warned off if the thunder was too close, or if there was lightning. This morning was pristine, redolent of pine and mown grass, alive with birdsong. The air was damp from a cool night, a nice change from the recent heat wave.

She turned down Everett Road, headed into Loop Three, tuned in to the beating of her heart. Always her heart, but then also this morning, memories of her mother.

There were three loops Katie alternated. Loop One was the shortest and stuck close to the small town. Loop Two widened out a bit and featured a steep hill. Three was the longest run. All of the loops wound up passing Footbridge Park, her way back home.

As her muscles warmed and her stride lengthened, her thoughts swung from her mother to David, her husband, and to the rest of her family. There was always gossip in the family, usually about Glo's financial troubles.

But the latest gossip seemed to be focused on Katie, and whether or not she was going to get around to having a baby. Her stepmother — who had no biological children of her own — thought that thirty-three was heading into "high-risk" pregnancy territory. Her sister just wanted to be an aunt. No one knew that Katie and David had actually been trying for months.

Her mind cleared the further she ran, thoughts dropping away at last. She stayed focused on her heart and imagined it doing its work.

The sun now painted a yellow smear above the rolling horizon and she ran toward it, picking up a little more speed, starting to break a sweat.

When she reached the park, she saw a vehicle alongside the road. A white minivan.

She slowed down a bit, staring at it from a distance.

Seeing vehicles at the park wasn't unusual — plenty of people who worked in town drove over to take their lunches while gazing at the river, sipping coffee from paper cups. But it was only six in the morning, too early even for breakfast.

She transitioned from jogging to walking and took her pulse while she watched the vehicle, wondering if it belonged to someone local. She thought maybe she'd seen one like it recently, parked at the grocery store. It was something — when you'd been in a small town for a while you came to recognize everyone's car. Just maybe not this one, yet.

Her pulse was at 128. Not bad. Pretty close.

The road dead-ended at the footbridge spanning the river. She continued walking toward the bridge, keeping an eye on the minivan.

It didn't look like it had been parked there overnight — no dew covering it. And she thought she caught a faint scent of exhaust in the air, like it had only just recently arrived.

Katie glanced behind her. The only other way home was to run the loop backward. But the thought of doing that — of turning around because of some minivan sitting by the quaint little park making her nervous — seemed irrational.

She blamed Facebook for filling her feed with stories about women attacked while jogging and clowns lurking in the woods. Or news sites like CNN with their gossipy, sensational reporting.

She longed for a headline which read: "Despite Recent Crimes Assholes Have Committed, Women Are Still 99.9% Safe Going for a Run."

It was like being afraid of flying. Everyone had heard it by now — the drive to the airport was 100 times riskier than the flight to their destination. Plane crashes were just more dramatic, better headlines.

She picked up the pace, jogging again, and was starting to pass it when she heard a sound coming from inside the vehicle.

An infant crying.

She stopped.

She listened.

Definitely a baby, squalling quite unhappily.

Maybe her ears were playing tricks, and the sound wasn't coming from the van. But the nearest house was too far away for it to carry.

A dog barked on a distant street. The river burbled nearby. The crying continued.

The park consisted of several picnic tables, a barbecue pit, a wooden swing set, and a climbing wall for the kiddies. Hiking trails threaded the woods for dog-walking and nature-viewing. Katie scanned the trees, but there was no one around.

Her phone was zipped into her running skirt. She always brought her phone on a run, even when her preferred jogging shorts were in the dirty laundry and the phone banged against her leg a bit, some old grocery receipt crunching around with it.

She withdrew the phone, then hesitated.

Would calling the police be an overreaction? What would she even say? *Hi, I'm jogging past Footbridge Park in Hazleton and there's a baby crying. Please send help — it may have a poopy diaper. I can't be sure, officer, but it might also need feeding, so please bring formula. If you can . . . make it organic.*

Her husband would still be sleeping. No need to disturb him. She opted to text.

> *On my run. A baby is crying near the park. Just checking it out. Call the cops if you don't hear from me lol.*

She put the phone away.

It could've been her imagination, but the baby's cries seemed to be growing more frantic.

Katie approached the minivan, hoping to catch a glimpse of an adult-sized figure moving around in there, tending to the child. But the windows were tinted.

Her mind flashed on another recent tragedy in the news — not as recent as the joggers, but still fresh enough in her mind — a man who'd left his baby in the car and gone to work.

Even though the vehicle was white and reflected the sun, it would be getting hot in there soon.

"Hello?" She raised her voice an octave. "Hello? Anybody in there?"

The side and rear windows were dark, but she was able to get a clearer look through the front. It wasn't a perfect view, but she saw a child's seat in the back with a small figure harnessed in.

"Hey, baby, shhh. It's okay, baby."

The baby was not soothed.

Katie tried the front passenger door first, found it locked. Her pulse quickened. What if the baby was trapped? Now she would have a real reason to call the police. But when she tried the side door, it opened.

Katie rolled the door back and leaned in. "It's okay. It's okay, little one. I'm here. I'll help you . . ."

Dark in the van. She put a foot up on the step and leaned in. Whoever these assholes were, they were going to get a piece of her mind when they showed up. Who put a baby in the very back seat of a minivan, so hard to access?

She stepped all the way in and stretched past the middle seats so she could at last get a clearer look.

In proximity, the infant's cries sounded a bit strange.

"It's alright, here I am, here I—"

Katie's words caught in her throat. She recoiled, pulling her arms against her chest. She started to back away, ready to turn and leap from the vehicle. Something was very wrong.

Hands reached in and shoved her back. She sprawled over the seats and landed on the floor, her thoughts a jumbled alarm. What was happening? She flailed and kicked instinctively, connecting with nothing. The silhouette of a man moved across her field of vision. When she tried to sit up, he smashed her on the head, knocking her back to the floor.

The door slid closed with a bang. The engine started.

Then she was moving, the van was moving, they were driving away.

CHAPTER TWO

Investigator Justin Cross had overslept and hurried out the door to work. He picked up coffee at the convenience store where he usually stopped in the morning. The clerk gave him a funny look.

"That color looks good on you," she said.

He had no idea what she was talking about until he glanced at his hand holding the coffee. Three of his fingernails were painted lavender, one of them light blue. His thumbnail was daubed with red.

"Ah man," he muttered.

The people behind him in line were having a good look. Cross tried to smile as the clerk pointed to a rack of household items near the register. "Nail polish remover, small bottle, right near the tampons."

He collected the item, and the other customers were gracious enough to admit him back to the front of the line. One of the customers was Laura Broderick, a forest ranger with the Department of Environmental Conservation, wearing a bemused expression. "Something you want to talk about, Justin?"

Cross paid for his coffee and nail polish remover. "Had my girls this weekend." He hurried out of the store, ignoring the impish grins.

Sitting in his car, he squinted at the tiny instructions on the bottle. He had no idea how to do this, but he was probably going to need paper towels. Cursing, he backed out of the convenience store parking lot and headed up the road to the state police substation.

It came flooding back along the drive — little Patricia (Petrie, for short), getting her fingernail paints out of her backpack and convincing him in her adorably squeaky voice to let her "do his nails." He'd compromised with the one hand, and she'd happily gone to work. They'd had to stop twice because of her sister, Ramona, who'd been getting into the lower kitchen cabinets. Twice, Ramona had gone after the bleach beneath the sink and Cross had to eventually barricade the cabinet doors.

Maybe the three beers and two glasses of Scotch after their mother picked them up that evening were what had caused the brief memory lapse. The hangover pulsed in his temples as he drove the winding country road to the substation.

He justified his drinking: For one thing, his heart ached each time the girls had to go back to their mom, Marty. The emptiness was so big, the silence so profound, he had to fill it or go crazy. For another thing, those girls, as much as he loved them, were totally overwhelming. Without Marty, he floundered around like a three-legged goat.

The substation was a simple little one-story building they called "the house." Cross had a plan as he pulled in: He was going to rush to the bathroom and use the nail polish remover. Let them make their jokes about him having a sensitive stomach — if he got caught with painted nails, he'd never live it down. They'd call him Boy George or something for the rest of his career.

Inside, though, the place was lively, and the only attention Cross was paid came when Trooper Billy Farrington put down the radio transmitter he was holding and said, "David Brennan just called 911."

"Brennan?"

"Yeah, you know who I'm talking about?"

"I think so. He has the place on Cobble Ridge?"

"That's the one. Wife is Katie Calumet. She kept her name or whatever. He's worried about her."

"Why's he worried?" Cross had the nail polish remover in his pocket and was eyeing the bathroom door. He kept the offending hand behind his back, coffee in the other.

"She was out for her morning run, stopped somewhere near Footbridge Park, sent him a weird text."

"What does 'weird' mean?"

"And then he says she never came home. Uhm, yeah, weird I guess because she said something about a kid crying. A baby."

"Where is Brennan now?"

The phones rang, but Cross ignored them.

"That's just it," Farrington said. "He went down to the park first, says he found something. Then he made the call."

"Found what? A baby?"

Farrington put on his duty belt, smirking. "Ah, no. Don't think so."

The second trooper in the substation was Maize, talking on one of the phone lines.

"Maize? What'd the guy say he found?"

"He said a toy," Maize said.

The other phone kept ringing until Farrington grabbed it. "Troopers."

Cross looked around. The two other troopers on shift were working road patrol. Cross stepped closer to Maize as she hung up. "Where are Crowley and Redford?" Cross asked.

"Crowley is halfway to Plattsburgh, running radar," Maize said. "Redford is holding the scene of a truck that swerved to avoid a deer and dumped its firewood across Route 9. Dispatch polled the call — the only posted deputy is in the middle of a pickup order. So, we're closest."

Farrington hung up the phone. Finished fixing his belt, he gave his pants a hitch and said, "Looks like it's you and me, Cross." He then hesitated. "Unless you need to talk to BCI first?"

"No," Cross said, thinking it sounded like an over-reactive husband and after a quick statement he'd be back in the office. "Let's go."

He grabbed some paper towels from the bathroom and followed the state trooper out.

* * *

Trying to drive and scrape nail polish off at the same time was a feat, but by the time they'd reached the park, Cross had gotten rid of most of the paint. He let the rest go for now.

The sight of David Brennan standing there by the footbridge was enough to wipe Cross's mind of any of his own petty problems.

Brennan looked like an anxious mess. He was pointing at something on the ground, his eyes wide, lips flapping even though no one was yet in earshot.

Farrington flipped on the deck lights and hopped out. Cross pulled his unmarked car beside the cruiser. They both walked over to Brennan.

"I didn't touch it," Brennan said.

Cross saw what he was talking about: A baby's rattle lay on the ground. He stuck out his hand and introduced himself and Trooper Farrington.

Brennan's eyes caught the flashing police lights. "I've been through the woods. I walked all the trails, I called her name. I've been here since seven thirty, called at eight. What took you guys so long?"

Cross nodded sympathetically. "Why don't you explain to me exactly what's happened. Let's step over here, okay?"

He led Brennan onto the harder blacktop, eyeing the soft shoulder. There were tire tracks there which could have now been muddled by Brennan.

The distraught husband lowered his head and spoke, as if to the ground, gesturing with his hands. He told Cross that Katie, his wife, went for a run a few mornings a week. She had three different patterns, but they all led past the park.

"And that's when she texted me. She was right here."

"Okay, do you know anyone who recently had a baby? Would it have been someone she knows?"

"We know the Harts, who just had twins, still in the hospital. Otherwise there's Megan Hasselbeck, but she's down in Schroon Lake. No, no one we really know. And she would've said so if she knew. Wouldn't have just said 'baby.'"

Cross put his hands on his hips and surveyed the scene. Farrington had set out a couple of cones. The good news was the park was away from the main roads. It was still early, just before nine, and a Monday. School wasn't in, so no kids were likely to have come through. Workers in the area came down to have their lunch, but that was a ways off.

"So, what do we do?" Brennan was growing more frantic by the second. He was a big man, over six feet, two hundred pounds. He wore his blond hair back in a man-bun, but his beard was threaded with gray — Cross thought he was forty or forty-five.

Cross didn't know much about the couple, only that they had some money, either on her side or his, or both. Rumor was they divided their time between Hazleton and New York City, where they also had a home.

"You've tried to contact her, obviously."

"About 100 times. Nothing. When I send a text, I don't get that little notification — 'delivered' — you know what I mean? And calls go straight to voice mail. So her phone is switched off, or . . ."

"Can I see your phone? Show me that text."

"Yeah, yes. Sure." He thumbed the screen then handed over the phone.

On my run. A baby is crying near the park. Just checking it out. Call the cops if you don't hear from me lol.

"And you were pretty sure she meant this park?" Cross asked.

Brennan scowled. "Well, yeah."

"Not the baseball park or anything like that."

"Like I said, she has one of three runs she takes; she's pretty routinized. But they all come right by here. It's the way back to our house, unless she wants to turn around and go back."

"I understand. But she could start in one of two directions, right? We're fairly close to your house. She could come by here first or wind up here near the end of her run."

"Yeah, sure. But she usually winds up here. Sometimes she takes a little break . . ."

"Who else would know about her running habits?"

Brennan gave him a sharp look. Then he softened with a sigh. "She's probably told Gloria. Her sister."

"Gloria live around here?"

"No, no. She's down in Brooklyn. Their parents are in Manhattan. That's it. That's the whole family. But, I mean, people see her. She's been running up here for two years, so . . ."

"Okay. And no way this is a prank or anything? She's not having you on? It's not your birthday or anything . . ."

"No, absolutely not. Nothing like that. Katie wouldn't do that. I mean she's got a sense of humor, but, no."

"And you guys are doing alright?"

Brennan narrowed his eyes, defensive again. "What do you mean?"

"Getting along. Your . . . you know, ah, relationship."

"We're fine. I know what you're doing — Katie wouldn't run off. Ever. We're solid. Even if we're having a . . . We always work it out. We've got a strong marriage."

Cross nodded and Brennan looked away, gazing over the river. He bit at his lower lip.

His hands were shaking.

"It's gonna be okay," Cross said.

Brennan didn't look convinced.

Regardless of the man's insistence, Cross had to decide how seriously to take the possible disappearance.

He still had Brennan's phone. They were going to need to look at it some more, but right now Brennan would consider it his lifeline to Katie, and so Cross handed it back. "Just hang tight for a minute."

He walked to Farrington.

The trooper had placed a dozen small cones around and was tying crime scene tape to a tree, getting ready to spool it out. "You want me to secure it, right?"

An area marked with cones and tape was going to draw onlookers and the press. On the other hand, if something untoward had happened to Katie Calumet, it was a necessary precaution to protect the integrity of the scene. "Yeah, go ahead."

Cross looked at the rattle lying in the dirt between the grass and blacktop. Maybe Katie had heard something and run off into the woods. He'd had a baby raccoon or porcupine in the woods outside his house before. Temporarily abandoned by a foraging mother, the baby animal's cries sounded eerily like a human's. Maybe Katie had seen the rattle left behind by someone, heard an animal, then run off into the woods, fallen, struck her head. It wasn't a big area, probably less than two acres. A quick search could resolve the question.

His gaze shifted to the tire tracks. People parked down here all the time; the tracks meant little. But together with the rattle lying beside them, the text message, the distressed husband . . .

Farrington stretched the tape across the narrow blacktop lane that led to the footbridge, Cross moving beside him.

"Do me a favor, trooper — when you're done, let's see if we have a tire tracks specialist on call. Or at least a CST trained in tire casting. If not, we'll have to recall someone."

"Got it."

Cross ran a hand over his face. Something in his gut said to act fast. Or maybe it was the hangover, still sitting just behind his eyes. He needed to call his supervisor.

CHAPTER THREE

Katie didn't dare move. Didn't want him to hit her again.

She'd lain still as he'd groped her, found the phone in her pocket. Then he'd ripped off the back plate and pulled out the battery.

Through the panic and the pain bleating in her temple, Katie had tracked the van's movement. She'd thought they'd made a left turn out of Footbridge Lane.

When they'd stopped again a minute later, they'd turned right. That would have put them on 9, a main route.

Then they had driven without stopping or turning for about ten minutes. Hard to be sure. But the final turn felt like a left. If her sense of direction was accurate, it put them on a path toward the interstate.

Or, she could be completely off. Lying sideways between the second and third rows of seats, perpendicular to the movement of the vehicle, it would've been easy to confuse her directions.

Breathe, she told herself. *Breathe*.

Twenty minutes of driving so far, at least, and no one had talked since telling her to *lie the fuck down and don't move* after hitting her on the head and taking her phone.

She risked a look from the floor, glimpsing the profile of the man beside her who was facing away, his hand on her knees. He wore a camouflage balaclava mask. She thought there were only two men — one driving, the other in the back with her — but she didn't know for sure.

They made another turn. It sounded like the engine was really working, the vehicle gaining speed.

As if merging with faster traffic.

She was right, and the thought of the interstate triggered a wave of fear.

The man turned to her, holding up another phone. Only his eyes were visible, but Katie thought he was smiling.

He tapped on the touchscreen and Katie heard a familiar sound — the baby's cries which had baited her. They sounded canned but still realistic.

"Pretty cool, huh?"

"Knock it off," said the driver.

The man tapped the screen again and the shrill cries stopped. "It's an app." He stared down at her, his eyes glinting in the dark.

"Carson," the driver barked. "Get up here."

Carson, the man in the mask, flicked a glance up front then stared down at Katie again. "I'll be right back. I don't have to tell you again to lie there and be still, right?"

Katie said nothing. Carson took it as her agreement. He moved out of her sight.

The driver spoke to Carson in low, urgent tones. Too quiet for Katie to hear over the roar of the road beneath her and the sound of the engine.

Carson. Obviously not his real name, unless they were complete morons.

She thought about the sliding door.

The door was probably locked. Even if it wasn't, a jump from a moving vehicle at this speed would either kill her or maim her for life.

She thought about banging on the windows, trying to summon help from a nearby driver.

Just as futile. The windows had been tinted. Even if someone was close enough, they likely wouldn't hear or see her.

The final option was to somehow subdue both men and take control of the vehicle.

It was probably the craziest of the three ideas, fueled by the adrenaline surging through her. She felt just angry and crazy enough to give it a try, but decided she'd have a better chance of surviving if she bided her time.

Carson came back and took his seat. The two middle seats were separate from one another, and the kind that could swivel. The rear seat was a bench.

Carson rotated around and put his feet up on the bench seat so that his legs were suspended above her. He had a bag of popcorn and started munching it as he stared out the back window, shoving the food up under his mask.

She glimpsed his beard-stubbled chin.

Her heart was racing, her body trembling all over, and her head ached. She couldn't overtake the men physically, or escape the moving van, but she could get information. "What do you want?"

Carson continued staring out the back window for a moment. "I want peace on Earth. That's what I want."

"Why are you doing this?"

The driver yelled, "Quiet back there!"

"See?" Carson said. "Leno says we have to be quiet."

Leno, Katie thought. *Carson and Leno*. The names of former *Tonight Show* hosts. For some reason, thinking about this made Katie nauseous and she turned her head to the side and gagged.

"She's gonna blow!" Carson yelled.

"What?!"

"She's gonna puke, man."

"She pukes, you fuckin feed it back to her," Leno said.

Katie kept gagging, but nothing was coming up, mercifully. Normally before a run she'd have something, if just a banana, but this morning she'd gone without.

She dry-heaved, tasting bile in her mouth, and she spit, despite the driver's nasty ideas.

Carson took his legs down and leaned over her. "Come on now, Katie. Don't do that. Here, you want a snack?"

He thrust the bag at her, popcorn crumbs tumbling, landing on her face. The spasms stopped and she rolled her head and faced upward again, taking deep breaths, crossing her arms over her breasts and stomach.

"No, thank you," she said between gasps for air.

"Suit yourself." Carson resumed his position. He started humming, still stuffing in the popcorn. The sound of his crunching was loud and Katie's stomach rolled with nausea again, clenching, but she forced herself not to gag. Tears slipped down her temples and pooled in her ears.

"What are you eating back there?" Leno called.

"I found it in the van."

"Well, take the fucking bag with you when we go."

"Yeah, yeah," Carson said. "Some people, Katie. Ya know?"

Katie, she thought. *They know my name.*

CHAPTER FOUR

David Brennan looked out the window of Cross's vehicle, wringing his hands together. "This is good." He was watching the searchers arrive. "I was worried about that twenty-four hours thing."

"That's mostly BS," Cross said, studying Brennan. "If someone is missing, they're missing. What was this morning like?"

"What was it like?"

"When Katie left for her run."

"I was sleeping."

"And everything is okay with you two?"

Brennan looked at Cross. "You already asked me."

"Okay. You're not fighting or anything. How about — is she under any sort of stress?"

"Under stress?" Brennan's forehead knotted and the tension grew palpable. "Everyone's under stress." He stared out the window again.

George Regan, a volunteer fireman on the search and rescue committee, was talking to a group of troopers and deputies in the safe area outside the cones, pointing at the river and the woods beyond the park.

"They're not going to find anything," Brennan said. "I was already out there. I walked the trails. She's not there. Somebody took her."

Before Cross could respond, another state police investigator knocked on his window. He rolled it down.

"Hey," said Investigator Dana Gates. "How's it going?" She flicked a look past Cross at David Brennan.

"Good," Cross said.

"Can I talk to you a minute?"

Cross turned to Brennan. "Can you sit tight for a minute, David? Just one minute, okay? This is my supervisor."

He stepped out and squared up with her. Gates was in her early forties, with high cheekbones and a short, dark haircut. Small, faint scars on her face, one just beneath her eye. "I get the sense things are a little hot in there," she said.

"He's torqued-up, yeah." Cross looked at the park while he spoke. "We're gonna deploy this attempt-to-locate . . . What about trampling trace evidence in the woods?"

"They know the drill. They'll mark anything they find, call out. It's good you cordoned off the shoulder. I called Bouchard to get the green light on CST and we've recalled Scott Fleming to go over the tire tracks."

Her gaze fell on the baby rattle, now sitting in the dirt surrounded by four sticks, which were wrapped with caution tape. Like a bizarre mini crime scene that made Cross's stomach feel cold to look at.

"Brennan thinks she was taken."

"Is he . . . Do you think he's . . . ?"

"I think he's on the level. They've been married for five years. I plan to pull his sheet, if there is one."

"Alright. I'm going to work the attempt-to-locate since we're a little understaffed at the moment. You stick with Brennan, okay? Get the personal info on Katie Calumet."

"I can do that."

"And . . . you know."

"Yeah. I'll keep him calm."

She hurried off to join the team about to comb through the woods.

He got back into the car and asked Brennan, "Why do you think Katie might have been abducted? Have you gotten any threats, anything like that?"

Brennan shook his head. "No. But someone might take Katie for the obvious reasons. My wife has money."

"I don't know her, personally. I don't know her background, I'm sorry."

Brennan sighed and looked away from the search party disappearing through the trees. "Katie's family owns a restaurant chain. Several high-end, five-star restaurants. They have other investments, too. She's worth quite a bit."

It seemed to pain Brennan to talk about it. He wrung his hands as he stared down at them.

"Who would know that?" Cross asked.

"Who would know? I mean, everybody, I guess. Except you, apparently."

Cross let the remark slide, and a moment later Brennan apologized. "This is really hard," he said.

"I know. It's okay."

"Are you married?"

"Separated."

"Sorry to hear that."

"I understand that a lot of people must be familiar with Katie's family, and their business. But can you think of anyone who stands out? Maybe someone who's brought it up before, maybe inappropriately or something? Or anyone you can think of who envies her. Openly, or even privately; someone you might suspect . . ."

Brennan was already shaking his head. "Everybody likes Katie. She has money but she's never acted like it. She works hard, she gives back to her community. She volunteers, she's on several boards, she works with Paul Smith's College getting school kids out there for nature walks at the VIC." Brennan gave Cross a heart-rending look, his eyes welling up. "She didn't ask for it, you know? We get what we get with family."

"Yeah, that's true," Cross said. "And what about her family — they get along?"

Something passed over Brennan's features, just a flicker. "They're like any family, I guess. People are different, but they're still family."

It was a cryptic remark, but Cross caught the gist of it. In his own family there were differences in religion, politics, and income, but they all gathered together around the Thanksgiving table and tried to make it work. Sometimes, it did.

"Okay, David. Here's what's next: I'm going to have Trooper Farrington take your statement, okay? We just need to get it all down on paper, now, while things are fresh. Things can get hazy with time, you know what I mean? Just tell the trooper what you've told me already, you know, you woke up, you got the text . . ."

"It was the text that woke me up."

"Okay. So the incoming text wakes you up . . ."

"Then I got up, did some normal stuff, went to the bathroom, and about twenty minutes later, I dunno, a half an hour, she wasn't back. She should've been back." He picked up the cell phone on his lap and stared at it. "So I texted her and asked her if she was going to want breakfast. No answer. I waited, I guess, another ten minutes and said, 'You there?' I got nothing. I waited about five more minutes, then I got in the car and drove down here."

"What were you thinking? I mean, was it unusual for Katie to talk about—"

Another scowl. "No — Katie's that type to jump in if something's wrong. I thought — when she didn't text back, when she wasn't home — maybe she was having a problem."

"You mean problem with someone she encountered?"

"Or a physical problem. I mean, I didn't think about that yet — someone she encountered. Not until I got here, saw the rattle, thought about the thing with hearing the baby."

"When you say physical problem, though — like, a cramped muscle or something?"

Brennan didn't take his eyes off the phone. He scrolled through the messages as he spoke. "She gets tachycardia."

"And that's, ah—"

"Irregular heartbeats; rapid heartbeats. She was a smoker for like fifteen years. We quit together a couple years ago and she started exercising more, jogging. But the heart thing runs in her family. Like I said, we don't get to choose, right?"

Cross smiled, but Brennan only looked at the screen.

Then Brennan seemed to snap out of it. "Anyway, so, like I said, I drove down. I didn't see her, just the thing on the ground, the toy. Went into the woods — I guess I spent a half hour looking for her. Those trails don't go very far. So I was back out here, and then I dialed 911."

He fell silent and they both gazed at the searchers heading into the woods. Cross heard voices calling out Katie's name.

"They're not going to find her out there," Brennan said.

CHAPTER FIVE

Katie stared up at the ceiling, still gripping herself in a protective hug.

It had been a half an hour, at least, of straight driving at high speeds. In the North Country, that only happened on the interstate.

The question was whether they'd gone north or south. If they'd gone north, then by now they'd be coming to the US–Canada border. But there was no way they'd make it across, not with her lying in the back of the vehicle.

It had to be south. And if she was right in her time estimate, that put them somewhere around Schroon Lake, or Pottersville. Maybe even as far as Lake George, but she doubted it. She'd driven I-87 many times on her way to the city.

"Get her ready," Leno called.

Carson had lapsed into silence for a while — she even suspected he was dozing at one point, his legs still up on the bench seat, head tipped back. He snapped to attention now and swiveled the seat a half turn, leaned out of her sight.

The minivan slowed and listed to one side as they curved down what was surely an exit ramp. It came to a stop and

Katie's pulse quickened. Stop signs and secondary roads meant she had another chance at escape.

Carson loomed over her with a plastic tie in his grip. "Hold out your hands."

She hesitated.

"Raise up your fuckin arms." His voice was muffled from the balaclava mask, but she knew a bridge-and-tunnel accent when she heard one — maybe Queens or Brooklyn, but possibly even Jersey.

Katie did as she was told and he cinched the plastic tie tight.

"Ow."

"Oh, tell it on the mountain. Sit up. Lean against the seat here."

It was difficult; her body was stiff from running, from all the adrenaline and tension, and from lying still for so long. But she was able to get on her butt and scrunch between the bench seat and the swivel seat. The baby doll was right behind her head. She couldn't resist a glance.

The doll looked back with a blank stare.

Duped by a toy. Some kid's Bitty Baby and an app that sounded like an infant's cries.

"Eyes front," Carson commanded.

With Carson distracting her, she didn't know if they'd taken a right or left from the stop sign, but they were moving again, albeit much slower than on the interstate. Probably back on Route 9, which paralleled the interstate down all the way to New York City.

For the first time, she could see Leno up front. Since he was driving he wasn't wearing a mask. He had black hair, a bald spot on top.

"I know what you're thinking," Carson said. He leaned down so his face was inches from hers. "I can read minds."

She could smell his breath through the mask — cheese popcorn and something worse. He laughed in her ear and then sat up straighter, reached away, and came back with something in his hands. She couldn't tell what it was at first. Then he unfurled it and slipped it over her head.

The instant she was plunged into blackness she started to panic.

There had been something that visibility had provided her — a sense of proportion, reason, even hope. In the stifling shroud, it all fled. Now she was in a directionless, timeless environment.

You can still hear, you can still sense things. Relax.

"Oh man . . ." Carson sounded aroused. "This is just fuckin . . . Oh man. Look at this, huh?"

She sensed him move closer and then his voice was in her ear again. "That shit turns me on."

When she felt his touch, she recoiled. But he grabbed her arm and yanked her close. His hand encircled her breast and gave it a squeeze. The hand moved to the other breast and groped that one, too, and the nausea rolled through her again. She felt revulsion, anger, and fear all at once.

"Carson!" Leno snapped.

The hand withdrew.

It was the worst thing to happen yet. She'd thought maybe — *maybe* — this situation was something which wouldn't turn sexual. She could still feel his hand on her, like it had left an impression.

No. Don't think about it.

She couldn't account for the certainty, but a pure, inarguable logic formed in her mind — if she gave in, showed fear, disgust, even anger, it would only feed Carson and make her situation worse.

He was dangerous. They both were, but she felt a particular malevolence from Carson, an impulsivity. Leno constantly yelled at him, like a parent trying to keep an unruly teenager in check.

She refocused on the driving. They were slowing again, perhaps nearing another intersection. Maybe they'd turned left at the last stop sign, crossed over the interstate, which would definitely put them on Route 9. If they made a right turn here, then it was highly likely she was correct about their proximity to Schroon Lake.

He just groped you.

They made a left turn.

What if he rapes you.

She felt her hopes sink again. She didn't know where they were after all. Pottersville? Okay, then it could have been a right turn first, when Carson was distracting her, and then this left . . .

Was that correct?

Stop. Forget it. You're somewhere off 87, that's enough to know for now.

But it didn't feel like enough. Everything was dark. She didn't know where they were. Her hands were tied. Carson had just molested her.

Why did they take you?

She was surprised she hadn't asked herself that earlier. Then again, it wasn't every day she was abducted.

Maybe they just want money. This is a kidnapping.

The thought should have brought her some relative comfort, but it didn't.

The minivan took an abrupt turn and hit a few bumps in the road. The sound of the road beneath the tires changed — that whine of rubber on asphalt was gone. A few seconds later, they came to a stop and Leno killed the engine, plunging them into silence.

Carson was in her ear once more. "Alright, Katie. We're getting out. Real quick, just real quick. You're going to do exactly as I say, when I say it . . ."

She heard Leno open the driver's side door. The van rocked slightly when he slammed it behind him.

". . . and we'll all get along just like peas and carrots, alright? Now, stand up."

She did, and he put his hand on the back of her head. She listened intently — no sound of nearby traffic, no voices, nothing. Then another vehicle door opened and closed. An engine started up. The van slid open in a loud rush.

They hadn't arrived at their destination. They were switching vehicles.

Carson pulled on Katie and her mind raced. Shrouded, her hands tied, running would be futile. The noise of this new engine was close. She was only going to be between vehicles for a few seconds.

Carson tugged on her, and Katie reached for the zip pocket on her running skirt.

He kept the hand on her head so she wouldn't bang the roof, pushed down, and bent her further as they stepped from the van. He guided her to the ground and she slipped her fingers into the small pocket.

The receipt was still there — she'd stuck it in after buying bottled water on a previous run and it stayed, went through the wash. She withdrew it using two fingers and let it drop, praying Carson wouldn't see.

Then she was being shoved into the second vehicle. Carson forced her onto her hands and knees, awkward because her wrists were bound.

She lost balance and sprawled forward, her face scudding across thick carpeting. Carson heaved her from behind, and she had to roll her shoulder to get further inside, ending up on her back.

She panted for breath, her skin tingling all over.

Calm down, calm down, calm down.

Then the door banged shut, a lock engaged, and the vehicle got moving.

CHAPTER SIX

Captain Lance Bouchard arrived at the scene. Bouchard was a tall, barrel-chested man in his fifties. His silver mustache sprouted fledgling handlebars. Cross had a word with him away from the commotion.

"David Brennan has called all of her friends," Cross said to Bouchard. "He called her family — her parents — and left messages. He put out a message on Facebook. I think we need a press conference as soon as possible."

Bouchard looked around. People were gathering beyond the tape, just a half-dozen or so. Cross knew there would be more, and the media would be there soon too.

"How long has it been?" Bouchard asked.

"Three hours since she sent him the text."

Cross had coaxed Brennan into handing over his phone again and he showed the captain.

Bouchard's lips twitched as he read it, and then he looked off again. "But there's been no contact from anyone claiming to have her."

"No, sir."

"And you don't think she ran off."

"I don't know. He says they have a healthy marriage. No big fights or anything."

A silence developed.

Bouchard said, "A baby crying . . ."

"Yeah. Maybe a baby or, I don't know. Could have been a lure. A fake cry, something to attract her."

Bouchard regarded Cross with his slate-gray eyes. "A fake cry?"

Cross shrugged. "A recording or something? Maybe not. Is the text enough to get the feds involved?"

Bouchard made a dismissive sound. "No. I don't know. A fake baby?" He seemed fixated.

"My daughter has one of these dolls, it cries, sounds almost real. Anyway, we checked with the hospitals — Hazleton, Lake Placid, Plattsburgh, Lake Haven — thinking maybe a baby was hurt, and Katie accompanied whoever it was to an emergency room. But nothing."

Like Brennan, Cross didn't think Katie Calumet was in the nearby woods, either. He thought it most likely she'd absconded with a friend for reasons unknown, but there was still that pinch in his gut that things were far worse. And he had a hunch there was something Brennan wasn't talking about. "Do you know about the Calumet family?"

"Never heard of them," Bouchard said.

"They're pretty loaded. Restaurants, hotels."

Bouchard let it sink in then turned around with his hands on his hips. He looked up Footbridge Lane, which stretched almost out of sight before intersecting with Red Ridge Road. "And you already called Stock County?"

"They'll help with the door-to-doors, yes, sir. Deputy King lives around here, too. He knows a lot of the people. I just figured it always helps to have a friendly face. He's with another deputy, and three troopers, and they're covering those couple houses up there, the Community Outreach Center over there, and Red Ridge. K-9 units just arrived and are in the woods."

Bouchard's gaze traveled to the rattle in the dirt. "No one has seen anything so far?"

Cross nodded up the lane. "Doreen Flaherty lives in that light-green house, see it? She's an early riser and says she saw a woman jog past at about six. She said, 'Black running skirt, peach-colored sport top.' Brennan was asleep when Katie left so he doesn't know what she had on, but he thinks it sounds right. He's going to get us a photo of Katie and we'll make copies, show it to Flaherty, show it around to everybody else. Sir, I really think we have to get the press conference going—"

Bouchard held up a hand. "I heard you. I understand."

"And we need to at least apprise the FBI of the situation, so if and when there's a call for ransom, or anything like that, we can hit the ground running."

Bouchard looked grim but thoughtful. "And Gates — she agrees with you?"

"Yes." Cross glanced at his watch. It was after nine. He felt impatient, a tension mounting.

"Alright," Bouchard said. "We'll do it right over there in the Community Outreach parking lot. I'll issue the flash lookout and get the social media alerts going. I'm going to act as incident commander and I'll expect your plan as soon as possible."

"Thank you, sir."

* * *

Brit Silas, a seasoned crime scene technician, began photo-documenting the scene as soon as she arrived. She appeared unhappy, waving people back from the shoulder, even though it had been cordoned off. Scott Fleming, the tire and foot track analyst, was on his way.

After a quick meeting with Silas, Cross gathered the deputies and troopers who'd returned from the door-to-doors.

"We've got one eye-witness report of a red pickup truck driving down Footbridge Lane at approximately midnight last night," said a female trooper.

"Three witnesses say they saw a woman jogging early this morning," said Deputy Peter King. "One says he recognized Katie from around town."

"No one from Community Outreach saw anything?" Cross asked.

King shook his head. "The first person there opened up at seven forty."

"That's it?"

They all looked forlorn.

"That's it," King said.

"Okay. Keep going. Widen out."

Cross thanked the deputies and troopers, then turned his attention to David Brennan.

Brennan looked shell-shocked, eyes glassy and ringed red. He had his phone back, thumb on the screen as he walked in a slow circle.

Cross approached him as the K-9 unit emerged from the woods, the cops blank-faced, dogs panting in the heat.

"Well, we've checked that off our list," Cross said about the area search. "Any word back from Katie's parents yet? Her father or her mother?"

"Stepmother."

"Stepmother, got it. Heard back?"

"No. I would have told you."

Cross was of average height, but Brennan looked over Cross's head as his eyes darted around, taking in all the activity.

"David?" He caught the man's gaze at last. "How about her mother?"

"Her mother died when Katie was sixteen."

"Okay. And Gloria is her only sibling."

"Right."

"What I really need from you, David, what would be really helpful is if you could head back to your house now — I'll have Trooper Farrington take you — and get a photo of Katie. A good photo, clear, of her face. Do you have something like that?"

"I got stuff right on my phone."

"Sure. Or, you know, professional would be best. If you got it." Mostly Cross wanted to give Brennan something to keep busy. "And I need a list," he said. "All of Katie's extended relatives, all of her friends, and their phone numbers.

Whatever you can find. We're going to have a look around your house. Not because of suspicion; we just need to look at everything. Maybe Katie got a recent piece of mail. Maybe she left a note—"

Brennan suddenly threw up his hands. "She's not missing! Someone took her!" His outburst drew attention.

Cross led him away from things, toward the woods on the other side of the blacktop lane.

"Someone tricked her," Brennan said, softer this time.

"Okay. It's possible. And maybe someone that knew Katie would respond a certain way?"

"What do you mean?"

"I don't know. You said she was the type to—"

"Just about any woman is going to respond to a crying baby. Probably most men, too." He paced around and ran his hands over his hair.

Cross thought he had a point. "Okay, but — I know this is personal — anything that might be . . . Did Katie ever lose a baby, anything like that?"

"No. But we've been trying." Brennan's voice was low.

"You've been trying? To have a child?"

"Not long. Nobody knows."

Cross absorbed this. "Not her sister or anything? No one in her family? Yours?"

Brennan sighed. "My family is . . . my parents are both passed. I have a brother who lives in Seoul. Otherwise, I mean, everyone who knows us knows we don't have any children. Or . . . I don't know what they think." He added, "I'm forty-four, Katie's thirty-three, so there's some pressure; some expectation."

Cross caught something, just the sense that Brennan wasn't completely on board with having a child. Or maybe it was resentment. Pressure from whom? The sister or stepmother, probably.

He placed a hand gently on Brennan's back and pushed him toward Farrington, who was waiting to take him home.

"We're going to have a press conference in an hour," Cross said. "You think you're up for it?"

"Yeah. I think so."

"Good. Think about what you want to say. Keep it personal, direct, honest. Just what type of person Katie is. We'll handle the details. Go home with Trooper Farrington now, get me that list of Katie's contacts. Someone is going to come by and have a look at her laptop, too. Okay?"

"Alright . . ."

Farrington led Brennan away by the arm. A vehicle came slowly down Footbridge Lane and Scott Fleming got out. He glanced over at the trooper loading Brennan into the back of a cruiser. Then Fleming ducked under the crime scene tape and approached Cross.

"Morning," Fleming said.

"Morning."

They joined Brit Silas and made a plan. There was only time for visible and plastic track analysis before the press conference. Latents and samples would take much longer.

"Right there," Fleming said, pointing. Cross saw the bit of dirt and mud on the blacktop leading away from the soft shoulder. Fleming had a large case with him. He opened it up and went to work.

Cross and Silas stared down at the baby's rattle.

"Why's it there?" Silas asked.

Cross had been wondering the same thing since the beginning. It supported the theory that a real baby was involved, in distress, and Katie had gone off with someone in an emergency situation. Or Katie had seen the rattle and *thought* she'd heard a baby, then something else happened.

It also could have been a sign of kidnappers, being either sloppy or clever. Sloppy, and they were amateurs. Clever, and they wanted the cops to find it — it was some red herring. But in either of those scenarios, it was a calling card. *This is an abduction.*

CHAPTER SEVEN

The rough terrain bounced her around. Katie drew a trembling breath and attempted to settle her nerves. She'd waited as long as she could withstand, and at last tore off the shroud.

Things stayed almost as dark. She was moving, no doubt about that, but there was hardly any light to see by. The carpet, the soft rattle of cabinetry, the mouse-shit smell . . .

Her pupils dilated. It was a camper, the kind that attached to the back of a pickup truck. Hard to tell if she was alone or not.

Carson could be with her. Maybe he was hiding in the narrow attic above the cab of the truck. She carefully rose to her knees and looked, able to discern nothing there but darkness.

The vehicle hit a bump, knocking her off-balance. She hit the ground hard on her shoulder, her hands still bound, and her head clunked against a cabinet.

She lay still, waiting for Carson to say something if he was hiding.

Nothing.

On her knees again, she shuffled toward the rear door. Locked. The door had a window, blacked out. All the windows were dark — maybe a tarp or canvas covered the camper.

She turned to the cabinet and found all the compartments locked down, too. Everything was buttoned up, in travel-mode. She kept searching, hoping for something to use as a weapon.

They'd left her alone back here. Thrown her inside and locked the door.

Her fingertips brushed an unfamiliar shape and she drew back. Squinting in the darkness at the object on the floor, she gingerly touched it again. Smooth surface, hard, then something like a tiny arm . . .

The doll that had been in the van was riding with her.

Katie felt a flash of revulsion. As her eyes continued to adjust, she could see how it lay on the floor, vibrating a little with the road, as if abandoned.

After a moment, she placed the doll in her lap.

It continued to be a rough ride, but she didn't know if they were off-road or this was just what it felt like to travel in a camper. She wondered what time it was. It was getting harder to keep track. Ten in the morning? Eleven? They kept driving and driving. She was miles from home.

Wherever they were going, they weren't crossing into Canada — customs would have a look inside a camper, she was sure. They could've crossed a bridge into Vermont, but she didn't think so.

She thought they were headed south, maybe westerly, toward the center of the state. Maybe the lower Adirondacks.

Kidnapped. Kidnapped for ransom.

It was wild to think about, but it was the only explanation. Her captors had to be people who knew her family. They'd known her name, after all.

She could still feel Carson's hand groping her breasts, hear his voice in her ear.

I know what you're thinking. I can read minds.

What else had he said? He'd used some peculiar phrases.

We'll all get along just like peas and carrots.

Peas and carrots? She thought it was a line from *Forrest Gump*. Maybe there was another source, but she didn't know it.

A kidnapper who quoted from the movies, acted like a deranged teenager. She held on to the baby doll and stroked its bald, plastic head.

Oh, tell it on the mountain, Carson had also said. She could hear the song in her head — he'd been humming it.

David was a music nut. In addition to his moderate success as a piano player, David jokingly called himself a "melomaniac" and had a huge library of tunes. He'd know what song it was.

She felt a pang of sympathy for her husband — he had to be going through agony right now.

Or, did he even know she'd been taken? What was happening back home? David wasn't the paranoid type, but he was protective. He was trusting, a kind man, but he had an edge. Surely he'd called the police and would be looking for her. Would he have any way of knowing she'd been taken? David would be anxious, even angry.

Thank God she'd sent him that text! It was almost prescient. She'd been joking, but nervous, too.

How could you be so stupid??

Katie closed her eyes and shook her head. *Stupid, stupid, stupid.* If she hadn't gone over to the minivan, drawn like a moth to the flame . . .

She should've heeded her conscience and called the police as soon as she'd heard the baby's cries. But who did that? It was only in hindsight people thought they should've summoned help sooner. In the heat of the moment, other instincts were in charge.

And it hadn't even been a real baby.

She lifted the doll from her lap and tried to see its face. Just faint glints of light in its eyes, a dull shine off its head.

Stupid.

She set the doll aside. It wasn't going to do any good to beat herself up. She needed to think. They knew who she was; they were going to demand a ransom. It was the only thing that made sense.

Unless they just wanted her for . . . other reasons. Carson had felt her up. She had sensed the aggression emanating from him in the van, could smell it in his sweat. Maybe he'd acted childish in some ways, munching his popcorn, but he'd been aroused seeing her in the shroud, her hands tied up.

She tried to drag her thoughts away from Carson and his rapist's vibe.

Oh, tell it on the mountain . . .

The verse came to her. It wasn't "oh tell it," it was "go tell it."

Go tell it on the mountain . . . that Jesus Christ is born.

A gospel song. A Christmas carol. Peter, Paul and Mary had done a version. She doubted Carson was a fan. Who else? Maybe James Taylor, or Paul Simon. One of those. Probably Frank Sinatra — Frank covered everything.

She could imagine Carson listening along to Frank Sinatra. Carson had that Five Boroughs accent, dropped his Gs. He was a city guy. Her parents lived in Manhattan — her father, Jean-Baptiste, and her stepmother, Sybil. Gloria lived in Brooklyn, where she ran her own restaurant, unaffiliated with their father's chain. They were all New York people.

Her father was French; his parents had emigrated from Nice. Sybil was Greek on her father's side, Italian on her mother's: the product of a frowned-upon marriage. Sybil was always bringing it up — that her own parents had fled to the States because of their love.

Kidnapped for ransom.

Katie's thoughts scattered when the truck slowed down. She tensed and grabbed the doll, as if it could provide her protection, then set it back.

She flipped onto her back and scootched close to the door.

When Carson appeared, she would kick him in the balls.

CHAPTER EIGHT

His phone rang while he stood in front of Katie Calumet's large house. "Cross here."

"A white minivan." Deputy King sounded a bit breathless. "Margie Dieffenbach lives across from the post office, just two doors down from the—"

"From the Community Outreach Center. Okay. She saw a white minivan?"

"That's right. Six eighteen, she said."

"She was that exact?"

"You don't know Margie. She walks her dog every morning at six. Takes twenty minutes. She'd returned, out on her front lawn, the dog doing its business. Says she saw a white minivan go by, she looked at her watch, wondering who was, you know, that time of day, going fast — and we've had those two meth busts on Everett Road in the past year. People see anything different, they think about it."

"She say the minivan looked like—"

"Just plain. Oh — dark windows. Didn't get a make or tags."

"Okay. Thank you, Peter." Cross hung up, flipped through his contacts for Scott Fleming's number, and dialed.

"Yeah?"

"Dr. Fleming. Can you say if the visible tracks could be from a minivan?"

"Was just going to call you. This is a sixteen-inch tire tread. I'm going to need to confirm it but right now I'm considering this a Yokohama Avid S33. It's a worn-out tire; all these original equipment tires have the same problem — they don't offer very good traction and they wear out quick."

"So could you say they were from a minivan?"

Fleming hesitated. "Yes, I could say that. Given the make of tire and the wear, the cupping . . . I would say 2008 to 2009 Dodge Grand Caravan or Chrysler Town & Country."

"And are the tracks from this morning?"

He hesitated. "Rained in Plattsburgh last night — did it rain down here?"

Cross tried to remember if the grass had been wet when he'd left home, either from dew or an overnight rain. He started into the house to ask someone for a weather report when Fleming decided. "Yeah. These are from this morning. I'm ninety-five percent."

"And how sure are you on the make of the tire and the probable make of the vehicle?"

"Uhm, eighty percent on the tires. I'm spraying for latents now, and we'll take a cast from the dirt . . ."

They didn't have time to wait for a cast — it was going on eleven o'clock. If Katie had driven by Margie Dieffenbach's house at six eighteen, that meant they were nearly five hours behind.

"How likely is the make of the vehicle?"

"2008 was the popular year for the Caravan and the Town & Country."

"I need your best guess, Dr. Fleming."

"Probably the Caravan. I'm going to say seventy percent on that one."

It was good enough for Cross. "Thank you."

He called Bouchard next and relayed the information from Fleming. Bouchard would update the BOLO — short for "Be on the Lookout" — which went to all police and was disseminated to the public.

"We need to get a bird in the air," Cross said.

Bouchard grunted. "Yeah. Okay."

"We've lost too much time . . ." Cross glanced at the house and saw David Brennan in the window, watching. Cross raised his hand to Brennan then turned away. "Five hours, sir."

"Well, where would they go?"

"We need to look at the border."

"You think they went into Canada?"

"It's a possibility."

"That's a lot to cover, Justin . . ."

"I know."

He hung up as the first news van showed up in the driveway.

David Brennan and Katie Calumet lived on Cobble Ridge, so named for a rugged section of timberline along Wolf Mountain. Their house was in the woods with no visible neighbors, the driveway steep. The press van struggled to climb the hill, tires spinning in the dirt. Cross headed down, slipping a bit because of his hard-soled shoes.

The press van pulled over and came to rest. They were looking to camp there, no doubt.

Cross signaled that they shouldn't be there with a wave of his arms. "Press conference is going to be in an hour at the Community Outreach building. This is private property."

The reporter, an auburn-haired woman in her late twenties, thrust a microphone in his face. "Is it true Katie Calumet was abducted from Footbridge Park early this morning?"

Cross eyed the cameraman, who staggered in the loose footing as he tried to frame a shot.

"One hour," Cross repeated. "At the Community Out—"

"Do you think this has anything to do with Katie Calumet's family fortune? Has there been a demand for ransom? Is the FBI getting involved?"

"I'll speak to you then." Cross turned and started hiking back up to the house.

The reporter shouted more questions but Cross ignored her as he climbed.

Brennan stepped out the front door and looked down the hill at the press van. "Missing white woman syndrome," Brennan said when Cross was close.

"What?"

"That's what they call the extensive coverage when a missing person's case involves a white, upper-class woman. Or girl."

Cross was a bit winded from the climb. He stood beside Brennan and watched the reporter direct the harried cameraman to set up a shot of her with the house in the background.

"Well, maybe that's good for us, right?"

Brennan just stared down the hill.

"Come on." Cross led the man inside.

* * *

Brennan had pictures laid out on the dining room table. "I couldn't decide which one was best," he said. He bit at his fingernail as he looked them over.

Cross selected the one that seemed strongest. He took a picture of it with his cell phone, sent it to Bouchard and Gates. So far the police had been working with Katie's Facebook profile pic, but this one was better, clearer. Katie had brown hair and dark eyebrows, with stunning aqua-blue eyes. She reminded him of a young Brooke Shields, a boyhood crush.

"I took that last year in the city," Brennan said. "Printed it out, framed it, and hung it in my studio." He pointed at another photo where Katie looked a bit younger. "That one was taken not far from here. We were helping out after Hurricane Irene — that was the first year we were together."

Cross looked over the rest of the photos and asked, "How did you meet?"

"She came to one of my shows, actually, in New York. It's not really a crazy story or anything. I played The Continental with my band and saw this girl after the show, started talking to her. I stopped touring pretty much right after, left the band."

"How come?"

Brennan shrugged. "I still love music, I still work at it. But I didn't want to be on the road. And part of it, you know, was about meeting women. But then I met Katie."

He grinned, and Cross thought it was the first time he saw something other than pain on David Brennan's haggard face.

They moved through the house and Brennan quickly showed Cross around. A computer forensics tech named Kim Yom searched through Katie's laptop in the living room. Brennan had given consent to the police to check Katie's email account. He even knew her password.

The house was spacious and rustic without being showy. Most of the downstairs was open-plan, high-ceilinged. Furniture was well-appointed but in keeping with an understated, Adirondack sensibility, Cross supposed. The few extravagances included a suspended accent lamp made of amber mica.

Upstairs was a master bedroom and en-suite bathroom, a guest room, another bath, plus one room that was mostly empty but for some boxes in the corner.

"We've been planning to turn this into a nursery," Brennan said in the doorway. His sadness had returned, his shoulders slumped.

"When did Katie last speak to her family? Do you know?"

They descended back to the main floor and entered the kitchen.

"Uhm, maybe a couple weeks ago. Glo had a birthday. She turned twenty-eight."

"And they still haven't called back?"

"Gloria did — sorry — meant to tell you. Jean and Sybil, their parents, have been traveling. Their flight returns this afternoon; they're flying into JFK."

"What did you say to Gloria?"

"I told her what happened. She's freaking out."

Cross leaned on the large kitchen island, topped with granite, fitted with its own sink, and looked across at Brennan. "What did she think?"

"What *would* she think? Katie wouldn't run off. If there was some emergency, we would've heard from her by now."

Cross nodded, then asked, "Do you know anyone who owns a white minivan? Maybe a Dodge Grand Caravan or a Chrysler Town & Country?"

Brennan thought for a moment then shook his head. "Can't think of anyone." His eyes widened with realization. "That's the vehicle? That's who took her?"

"We don't know."

Brennan came around the kitchen island and towered over Cross, getting agitated again. "But you're looking for it, right? Jesus, they could be anywhere by now. What are we doing? Why are we standing here in my kitchen talking about how I met Katie?"

Cross held the man's eye.

"Sorry." Brennan walked away and out the back door off the kitchen.

Cross followed and found Brennan taking a pack of cigarettes down from a hiding place beneath the back-porch roof. He stuck a cigarette in his mouth then patted at his pockets.

Cross had a lighter and handed it over.

"Thanks." Brennan blew out the smoke and relaxed. Behind the home, the land continued sloping upward, thick with birch and pine trees. "My mind is just going, going. I can't think straight. If I think about Katie, alone, with someone doing something to her . . . I'm just going to go fucking crazy."

"I understand."

"Because I have to think someone has taken her for money. I can't think of anything else. I have to think they want money and they're going to keep her safe. She's their only insurance. 'Proof of life,' or whatever they call it."

Cross looked into the woods with Brennan and thought about it. The scenarios were endless, the possibilities vast. Forgetting Canada, that left west to Rochester; south toward Albany, New York City, and beyond; east to Vermont, New Hampshire, who knew how far. Or why.

Maybe it was extortion, and Brennan was right. But only around 100 cases a year in the US were stereotypical abduction. Compared with the 65,000 persons considered missing and unsafe, it was a tiny fraction. Kidnapping for money was rare.

"I know I asked you before, but think again. Who would take Katie? Who would know that her family has money and might pay?"

Brennan faced Cross, exhaled more smoke, and said, "Who knows they have money? Plenty of people. And anyone would assume a family like that would pay a ransom." His eyes seemed to harden. "But who would be actually crazy and sick enough — maybe desperate enough — to try it? I can only think of a few people."

"Let's talk about those people," Cross said.

CHAPTER NINE

The door opened. Katie squinted against the blinding light and kicked out as hard as she could. She struck something solid and heard Carson yell. She kicked again and he snagged her ankle and yanked.

A moment later she was free-falling. Her breath exploded when she hit the ground. It felt like an enormous weight on her chest and she struggled for intake while she floundered in the dirt.

"Hey! Goddammit . . ." Leno wasn't far away.

Carson kicked her in the thigh. "You fucking *bitch* . . ."

There was a scuffle — two pairs of legs together, men grunting and fighting.

Then they settled and she was being lifted up, first to a seated position, where she finally sucked in a ragged breath. Her eyes watered and stung. There was a cloud of dust around her. She was hauled to her feet, and she started running.

"Fuck!"

They were in the woods, in a clearing, no one and nothing else around except for two wheel ruts through the forest where they must have driven in. Katie sprinted that way, holding her tied wrists against her stomach. She heard the footfalls behind her, closing in.

She was a good runner, a strong runner. But she was limping, her thigh throbbing with pain, her vision sheeting with tears.

Carson caught up and tackled her. At the last second she tried to brace for the impact but her hands were useless. When she hit, her face grated into the rocks and dirt. Then everything was still.

Nothing, for a moment, just Carson breathing on top of her.

He rolled off.

"Oh, just like that," he said. "Leave you just like that . . ."

She couldn't move. She thought a finger was broken from when she landed. Her face was hot, too hot against the dirt, something needling her skin.

Katie forced her hands in front of her, pushed herself up a bit, started to wriggle away.

Carson took her by the ankles and dragged her back. Then he was on top of her again, whispering in her ear. "You want it." He groped her like before, only this time he grabbed her backside. "Just admit it."

"Alright," Leno said. "Knock it off."

Carson remained, his face right beside hers, his weight crushing her into the ground. His expelled air churned up the dust, stinging in her eyes. "This is your last warning. Okay? You know what I mean, Katie-pie? Last warning. You fuckin kick me again, you run again, and I am going to hurt you." He paused, and added, "For a long time, too."

Then he was off her, and she could breathe again.

Katie rolled over, coughing and gagging, and forced herself to sit up.

She risked a glance at the two men.

They stood by the truck and camper. Leno watched her, his face now hidden behind a hunter's balaclava mask, just like Carson's. But she knew it was Leno, and Carson was the other one — Carson was a bit bigger than Leno, and she thought maybe younger, too. One of his long sleeves was hitched up toward the elbow and she saw tattoos. Hard to be sure. Who were they?

Leno spread his arms, speaking to Carson. "Hey — hey, what the fuck — am I regretting this?"

"No."

"You want to fuckin — ah, you need a minute? Need to go fuckin jerk off?"

"No . . ."

"Then settle."

Carson swore and paced in tight, angry circles, darting looks at her. Like an animal in a cage.

She attempted to stand up, which was difficult with her hands bound. A random memory surfaced — a conversation with David, something they'd read online about being able to get to your feet without using your arms or hands for support. If you could, it meant you'd live at least another ten years. If you couldn't, you had problems.

She struggled, got her knees beneath her.

Her whole body was shaking.

Do not cry. Do NOT cry.

Katie rose to her feet.

Leno came near, looking her over. "Goddammit," he said again. He turned to Carson and shouted, "Her face is all fucked up."

Carson threw up his hands. "I didn't tell her to do that!"

Leno grabbed Katie by the arm.

Don't pull away. Don't scream.

But she screamed. As loud as she could, she shouted for help.

He pulled her into a tight hug, clamped a hand over her mouth.

Carson came running, eyes burning with intensity, but Leno put out his hand, keeping him back.

Leno said to her, "Stop it. Or I'll let him at you."

Katie nodded. Leno let go. Then he hastily dusted her off. Carson was staring at her, she could feel it, but she kept her head turned.

"Get the first-aid kit from the glove box," Leno said.

"Are you for fuckin real? We have to—"

"Do it!"

Carson cursed and kicked at the ground. As Leno kept cleaning her off, Katie looked around.

The world shimmered behind fresh tears. She blinked them away and drew a shuddering breath.

Think.

The clearing wasn't very big, maybe thirty feet across, and surrounded by evergreen trees. She heard running water in the distance. Some birds were singing. The sky above was overcast, an ugly gray pate. A mosquito whined close to her ear.

Carson stalked over with a plastic first-aid case and threw it on the ground. He was still behaving like a surly child. He gave her a fierce look — *brown eyes, they're brown* — and acted like he was going to talk nasty again. But he returned to the pickup and started getting more stuff out.

He tossed a large, army-green duffel to the ground, and a pack, the kind for backcountry hiking.

Leno was all thumbs. He swabbed her face like he was cleaning the windshield of a car. She gritted her teeth and took it, her facial cuts stinging like wasps. Then he slapped on a couple bandages and stepped back to admire his work.

Finally, Leno pulled a cell phone from his pocket and took a picture.

"Throw me the rope," he called to Carson.

Carson pulled a blue mountain-climbing rope from the cab of the truck and chucked it over.

Leno put the phone away.

Basic phone, not a smartphone. Maybe a prepaid type.

Leno tied the rope around her waist. He paused to inspect the cuts and bruises on her wrists from the plastic tie.

"Hurts?"

Katie said nothing.

Leno dipped back into the first-aid kit and did some more antiseptic swabbing, this time at her wrists. He put all the used swabs back into the kit then tested the rope. He played it out, walking away from her, unfurling its full length. There was about twenty feet.

Katie watched Carson heft the pack onto his shoulders and maneuver himself to situate it right. He kept pawing at his face. The day was warm, extremely muggy. Katie imagined Carson was sweating a bit inside the mask.

"Get the other thing," Leno said.

"Stop fuckin ordering me."

Leno turned his head slightly. "Just get the other thing. For Chrissakes."

Carson muttered something and leaned inside the camper. "There it is," he said.

He walked over to Katie and held up the shroud.

"No . . ."

This time she was sure Carson was grinning beneath the mask. Then everything went black again.

CHAPTER TEN

"Ladies and gentlemen of the press, thank you all for coming," Bouchard said to the small crowd gathered in the Community Outreach parking lot. "This is an unusual situation. Katie Calumet — a member of your proud, tight-knit community — has gone missing."

Cross stood near Bouchard, Brennan beside him. Brennan was holding his prepared statement.

A few men from the volunteer fire department had erected a temporary dais using plywood and bricks so that the people talking could be seen by the cameras. Plattsburgh College had provided the podium and easel on which Katie's enlarged picture faced the crowd. Three affiliate stations had turned out, and at least a half-dozen newspapers.

"State Police Investigator Justin Cross will share the details of this case with you now."

Bouchard stepped back. Cross gave Brennan an encouraging pat on the back and then stepped up to the podium, which bristled with microphones.

"Thank you, Captain Bouchard. The particulars in this case have us gravely concerned for Katie's safety, and we're urging anyone who has seen her, or has any information, to come forward immediately."

He gestured to the road behind them, the park beyond. "Katie was last seen at approximately ten after six this morning, jogging down Footbridge Lane, on her way back home from her morning run. She was wearing a black running skirt and a peach-colored sleeveless athletic shirt, gray sneakers on her feet with iridescent orange laces."

He held a hand in the air, palm down. "She is five foot six, a hundred and twenty-five pounds, brown hair, blue eyes. At six fourteen this morning, she sends her husband a text message. In it, she tells her husband that she hears the sound of a baby crying and is going to investigate. That is the last he hears from her.

"At six eighteen — so, four minutes later — a member of the community observes a white minivan driving west on Red Ridge Road. And our forensics expert, Dr. Fleming, has determined that tire tracks leading away from the park are consistent with a minivan, which is most likely a white Dodge Grand Caravan. If anyone has seen a white Dodge minivan, we'd like to hear from you. I'll take any brief questions and then Katie's husband, David Brennan, has a statement."

The reporters started asking questions at once and Cross pointed to one.

"Stacy Keats, Channel Three. Investigator Cross, I understand there was a baby's rattle found at the scene, by the park? Can you explain that?"

"We can't explain that. We're analyzing fingerprints lifted from the rattle and testing it for DNA. It's consistent with Katie's last text that a baby was crying. That's all we know." He pointed to another reporter.

"Jeff Porter, *Adirondack Daily Enterprise*. Sir, has there been any contact from the abductors? A ransom note?"

Cross thought for a moment and said, "We haven't, at this time, determined that Katie was abducted for ransom. Certainly we're considering it, but there are other possible explanations for her disappearance we need to consider. No, we have not been contacted by anyone claiming to have her."

A third reporter: "What about the baby? Have there been inquiries into who the child is? Are you concerned for its safety?"

Cross shifted on his feet and cleared his throat. "We're doing everything we can to determine the particulars here . . ."

"What about Katie's family? Where are they?"

"We've been in touch with the family and they're on their way to assist us . . ."

"Is Katie wealthy? The Calumet family owns restaurants and hotels — don't you think this is most likely a kidnapping for money?"

Cross felt a bit battered, growing frustrated. "Most reported kidnappings are either the result of underage girls running away with adult boyfriends, or custody battles gone bad. The logistics of grabbing and holding someone, then successfully collecting the ransom, all without getting caught, are very difficult. A person would have much better chances of becoming a banker or CEO and just stealing the money legally."

There was a ripple of laughter and some stunned faces. Cross couldn't believe he'd just said it. He needed to get off the stage. "At this time, I'd like to ask David Brennan to share his prepared statement."

Another reporter blurted out a question before he stepped away — the woman from Brennan's house.

"Investigator Cross, if you don't think this is a kidnapping, there's a lot of attention here on someone missing for six hours. Is this because of Katie Calumet's financial standing and the fact that she's white?"

Cross began to speak, stopped. Started again. "We're giving Katie the same attention we would give any member of this community."

"You don't feel it's disproportionate from the response shown to women of different socioeconomic classes or ethnicities? And also, doesn't Katie Calumet split her time between here and New York City?"

Unreal. The reporter was trying to scandalize the situation.

"If anything, it's the media who reacts disproportionately. Thank you."

The crowd murmured as Cross turned to Brennan and introduced him. Cross shook Brennan's hand as he stepped onto the dais. Brennan leaned in and whispered, "Told you," and then took the podium.

"Hello, good afternoon." He pointed at the picture. "That's Katie, that's my wife. Right now, it doesn't matter why she was taken, or even who took her. It only matters that she's out there. It only matters that she gets home, safe. The police have given you the information — a white Dodge minivan. They've given you her physical description, now I'll give you her personal description."

Brennan gripped the podium, swept the crowd with his gaze, then stared into the picture again.

"Katie is kind, loving, and selfless. I know everyone says that when something happens, but it's true. She's the most giving person I know. And she's tough. Katie has been through a lot in her life. She's going to get through this, too. But she needs your help."

Brennan glanced at Cross, who nodded encouragingly. Katie's husband was far better in front of the cameras than he was.

Brennan finished by saying, "I want to thank all of you. I want to thank the state police and the sheriff's department, the crime scene technicians, the fire department, and all of the volunteers. I want to thank the community of Hazleton for coming together and being supportive, telling the police what they can. We have made Hazleton our full-time home for the past year, and this place means the world to us. Please, everyone watching this or reading this, please keep your eye out. Help us get Katie back home. Thank you."

Brennan stepped off and Captain Bouchard took his place as the reporters volleyed fresh questions. Bouchard brought the conference to an end as Cross walked off the dais with Brennan.

The police vehicles behind the dais served as a press barricade and the two men gathered there for a moment.

Brennan's eyes were welling up — he'd kept it together for the press but looked like he was succumbing to the emotion.

Cross said, "You know, I said that about kidnapping . . ."

Brennan shook his head. "No, I get it. I understand."

"What we talked about at your house, I'm giving that every consideration."

Brennan nodded now, and a tear fell. He turned and walked away, this big man weighed down by the circumstances like a millstone around his neck. At this point, there wasn't much else Brennan could do. Cross thought it was up to him now. Time to get to work.

* * *

The call came in to the substation twenty minutes after the press conference. Trooper Farrington handed Cross the phone.

"Cross here."

"Detective Cross, Trooper Alan Rowe. We found a 2008 white Dodge Grand Caravan off Route 8, couple miles west of Bakers Mills."

Cross swept his desk clear and brought out a fresh pad of paper. Trooper Rowe relayed the plate number and Cross asked, "How did you find it?"

"Regular patrol; we got the BOLO two hours ago, so . . ."

"Great." Cross tore the sheet of paper from the pad and got up from his desk so fast he banged it with his leg and knocked over a jar of pencils.

Farrington was hovering close and Cross handed him the note, saying, "Gates." Farrington nodded and hustled away.

"Thank you, Trooper," Cross said into the phone. "And you're securing the area."

"You want us to?"

"Rope it off — no one touches the vehicle inside or out. Okay? I'm going to get a crime scene team there to go through it as soon as I can establish if it's the right vehicle. Bakers Mills, that's on the way to Speculator?"

"Affirmative. About ten miles from 87, Brant Lake region. Also, sir, there's something on the ground beside the vehicle. Piece of paper."

Cross froze. He went through the options in his head and made a decision. "Got a pair of gloves, Trooper Rowe?"

"I do."

"Put them on."

"Alright — vehicle."

The connection was bad. "Say again, Trooper?"

"Hold on — them."

It sounded like he was saying he was going to get his gloves. Cross stared across the room at Farrington, on the phone at another desk. Farrington was talking and nodding. He glanced at Cross and covered the mouthpiece. "Gates is checking with DMV."

They waited for a tense minute and then Trooper Rowe came back over the line. "Okay. I've got my gloves on. Heading — the vehicle."

Cross fidgeted with his fingers, picking at the residue of nail polish still there.

Farrington called over. "Gates says the minivan was possibly stolen this morning."

"From where?"

"Ogdensburg. An older man and his wife; the Tremblays."

Cross nodded and listened as Trooper Rowe neared the van. He could hear the trooper breathing, the phone making static. "Okay," Rowe said, "I'm picking up the paper. Looks like, ah . . . looks like a — pt."

"Say again?"

"A receipt. A store receipt. From Kinney Drugs."

"Address?"

"This — from the Kinney drug store in Hazleton. Repeat, Hazleton."

Cross felt his skin crawl with adrenaline. "Thank you, Trooper. Sit tight, hold the scene, we're on our way."

He made a quick call to Gates, reporting the situation. "I'll get into her bank records," Gates said. "You get the receipt."

Cross grabbed his bag and hurried toward the door, Farrington following him out.

CHAPTER ELEVEN

Shock.

You're in shock.

In the darkness, it was the only thing that made sense. Walking was awkward and painful — her leg was sore from being kicked. Her face stung from the cuts. There was sand in her hair, grit in her eyes. Her head still throbbed from the punch — when had that happened? Time was doing funny things, making no sense.

She could smell her breath inside the shroud. Slightly sour, with traces of the coffee she'd sneaked in before going for her run. Sometimes a little caffeine helped get that runner's kick, even if the experts frowned on it.

Katie's foot slipped and her ankle bent. She cried out in pain and stopped walking. Carson tugged on the rope around her waist and then she felt it go slack, heard his feet as he came toward her.

"Shut up," he said. "Get moving."

She did as she was told. After Carson had slipped the shroud over her head, she'd heard him speak quietly to Leno but hadn't understood their words. But she'd understood it well enough when the truck started up and Leno drove away.

Leno had left her alone with Carson.

Then Carson had started walking, towing her along behind him like a pack mule.

"I twisted my ankle." Her words sounded strange to her own ears. Like someone else was talking.

You're in shock . . .

"I don't give a shit about your ankle."

Carson walked away and the rope tautened. Katie felt a jerk and stumbled a few steps.

"I said *come on*," Carson griped. He was twenty feet away, give or take. The length of the rope.

They'd been walking like this for a few minutes. How far were they going? How did he expect her to navigate the woods with a bag over her head? It was ludicrous. She put one foot in front of the other. One of her fingers felt fat and swollen — maybe not a break, but a definite sprain.

It was slow-going, agonizing, and every few seconds Carson yanked on the rope, forcing her to move faster. She continued to stumble.

"I can't see my footsteps!"

She kept going, bracing herself for his return. For his fists or his hot breath in her ear or his hands groping her.

I'm going to kill you, she thought.

It just came to her, as unadorned as any other thought, like, *You're in shock*, or, *I can't see.*

I can't see.

I'm going to kill you.

But he didn't come back to her; instead, she heard Carson laugh.

"Come on," he said in an odd voice. "Buck up, little lady." Like he was attempting to impersonate John Wayne.

They kept moving, but Carson's pace just wasn't sustainable. Katie fell again, and got up. Then again — she banged her shin against a rock and felt the skin tear — and then a third time, and a sharp stone stabbed her kneecap with a brilliant bolt of pain.

She dropped to her butt and held her knee and grunted and moaned.

She could sense Carson looming over her.

"Jesus," he tutted. "You are a fucking disgrace."

"I can't . . . see!"

Katie felt a kind of fury she hadn't known since she was a much younger woman. Leaving the school where her father had stuck her after her mother died — those had been the angry times. These days the most she flipped out was when her husband left the toilet seat up for the thousandth time. She felt like she could wrap her hands around Carson's neck and squeeze. She could take him by his testicles and pull them until the skin broke.

She didn't know Carson's face. It was a strange thing, sitting there, holding her throbbing knee, to realize that even though she had no idea what he looked like, there was a face she pictured.

Maybe it was his voice. People made up faces for others based on the way they sounded, she thought, though it was probably never right.

You're in shock, Katie.

—Yeah? So what?

"I can't see," she repeated. "I don't know how far we're going, but there's no way I'm going anywhere like this. I'm going to go slow; you're going to keep yanking the rope. Then I'll fall again. What if I hit my head on a rock?"

She stopped talking, wishing she could retract the question.

"Oh, this isn't that bad." Carson was condescending. "These woods are wide open. You're just making it all up in your mind. Get up. Get walking." He paused. She heard him breathing hard. "I told you what would happen if you gave me any more shit."

"I don't care!" Katie pulsed with frustration, rage.

Of course you care. You don't want that. You never want that. That would be the end of everything, and you know it. You would never be the same.

Think.

He said 'open woods.' You're not on a trail. There is no one around. How do you get out of this?

She waited for him to make his move.

"Get up," he said, but it was half-hearted.

"No. You can drag me."

"You want me to drag you? I will. I'll drag you right up these fucking rocks." He fell silent, as if thinking about it.

When he spoke again his voice was different, like he was facing away from her. "We're just at the beginning. We can't keep doing this."

For a moment, he sounded almost human. She felt herself calming. "How far are we going?"

"A ways."

"Just let me go, Carson. I haven't seen your face."

He said nothing. He was quiet for so long she thought he was contemplating it.

Katie felt hope seeping in. It doused the anger and softened her. Part of her mind protested the hope, warned against it, but she couldn't help it. Carson was nuts. Maybe he was crazy enough to listen to her. Maybe he didn't want to be here. Leno had put him up to all of it, she imagined, and Carson didn't really like Leno. He wanted out.

"Alright," he said.

She waited, her heart rate speeding up. *Alright?*

Suddenly he tore the shroud from her head. The light filled her vision, everything a green blur.

After a moment she was able to focus. The sun was shining in the forest; the trees gave off an almost iridescent color. The woods, like Carson said, were open. There was no maintained path, but he was following the semblance of a stream, runnels of rainwater threading the dirt and rocks.

The ground sloped up in a gradual incline. But further ahead she could see where the land was steeper, the trees thicker.

She looked up at Carson, right beside her, standing there in his balaclava mask.

She quickly turned away, heart slamming in her ribs again. Seeing him alone, no Leno around to keep him leashed, was a kind of confirmation. This was really happening. She was being forced into the woods, alone with an angry, dangerous man.

She stared down the slope at the direction they'd come, and then squeezed her eyes shut.

Stop it. Focus on—

He tapped her on the shoulder.

She turned and saw his outstretched hand. "Come on, Katie. Let's go."

She got herself standing without accepting his help. Kept her eyes downcast.

Carson chuckled again. "Hey, listen, give yourself a round of applause, right? Now you can see, right? No bag over your head. I have to keep mine, though — hot and sweaty and making me fuckin . . . making me resent you. That's the word. Making me want you to pay. Good negotiating, Katie. Oh wait — you can't applaud yourself, can you? Hold on."

Carson set down the duffel he had tucked under one arm and clapped for her, slowly. Each slap of his hands sent a shock wave through her. The clapping reverberated off the maple trees.

"Well done," he said in a bad British accent, muffled by the mask. "Well done, Katie. Good show."

She didn't move. He was right there beside her, and all she could do was stare at the ground.

"Please," she said.

As soon as the word left her lips she felt a sinking despair. Not just because of his threats and innuendos, but because at some point, without realizing it, she'd decided not to give up her power. It was about more than disallowing her abductors their satisfaction. It was knowing — somehow, deep down — that she wouldn't make it through this if she relinquished that power. Maybe it was for her physical protection, but mostly it was for her mental protection.

"Please," he echoed. "Yeah. Please. Please, oh please. I know. I hear you, Katie. Come on, let's go."

He started up the shallow stream.

She felt like she was going to cry. This was just what she'd been trying so hard to avoid. After all Carson had done to her. After all she'd been through, after forgiving herself for falling for the crying-baby trick, and now here she was, whimpering, asking for mercy.

Carson tugged the rope. "Come on, Katie. You can see now. No excuses."

She did as she was told. After a few minutes of walking, the despair and self-loathing faded away. The stream was cold, her sneakers soaked through. A kind of numbness filled her.

The birds were tweeting in the forest. The sun blinked through the canopy overhead. Here and there a squirrel darted across the path and charged up a tree.

They parted from the stream. The terrain grew steep, and she had to use her hands to climb over some of the larger boulders. She started to think about where they were, but apathy washed it away. What did it matter? Did knowing her position help her at all? She'd been naive. Thinking if she could keep track of their travel in the van, it would help. Thinking that by dropping some stupid receipt from her pocket, the police — or maybe her husband — would miraculously pick it up, know where she was, and rush to her aid.

Because that was what she'd thought, if she was honest. That somehow David, who was a musician, a former chef, and occasional carpenter, was also some kind of a super-human. That he would be able to find her because she left her little clues behind. That she needed to stay proactive, assist in her own rescue by staying vigilantly aware of where she was and what was happening.

It had been stupid and pointless. She was being led into the woods — who knew where, or who cared? — by a sicko calling himself Carson. No one following her trail now, not in here, not in all this wilderness . . .

"Come on, Katie," he called. "Come on, Katie, Katie Katie Katie . . . What's that bug called? A katydid? 'Katie did, Katie didn't, yes she did, no she didn't . . .'"

Think.

Carson had to know where they were. Didn't he?

They weren't using a well-trod hiking trail, they were off the map. How did he know where he was going? Compass? This was wild forest. Carson didn't strike her as some experienced outdoor guide. He seemed like city trash, or some horrible suburban mutation. At any rate, probably an ex-convict.

He had to be using something.

Like a GPS.

That was the only explanation. He wasn't just leading her blindly somewhere — he knew where he was going, a place to keep her while Leno, presumably, negotiated a ransom.

If Carson was using a GPS, maybe she could get it from him. Then escape him, find her way out.

Have to get free of the rope first. It was knotted around her waist, cinched tight, but she might be able to shimmy out of it if her hands were free.

Something.

She had to do something, or she was going to die.

She could sense it. Could see it in Carson's dark eyes.

He was insane.

CHAPTER TWELVE

It took Cross an hour to get to the Dodge Caravan. The troopers had barricaded the dirt area off Route 8 outside of Bakers Mills. Nothing around but woods, and across the road, a river, low in the late summer.

Cross approached the barricade and slipped under the tape. He stopped short when he noticed the multiple tire tracks crisscrossing the dirt. There would be little chance of getting anything useable. It was a rest stop and dozens of cars pulled on and off every day.

Trooper Rowe approached and introduced himself. Cross said he wanted to have a look at the vehicle.

Rowe hesitated but didn't question it. "Right this way."

They were careful, walking single-file, preserving the scene. But a tally was running in Cross's head — how much time was wasted protecting evidence? Katie Calumet was potentially drifting further away and falling into greater danger. Every second counted.

"You found the receipt here?"

"Yep," said Rowe. "It would have blown away, maybe, but got stuck right here under the tire."

The minivan looked generic. No noticeable dings or scratches. The Tremblays were a retired couple and had told

Detective Gates they kept a minivan because of their growing passel of grandchildren. Cross peered in through the windows and saw a child's car seat in the very back.

Rowe showed Cross the receipt, which he'd stuck in a plastic baggie. Cross gave it a quick look — crinkled, dated two months ago, and as Rowe had said, traceable to the Kinney drug store in Hazleton. The bank had already confirmed Katie's debit card had made the purchases the receipt listed.

This was their van.

"Forensics coming?" Rowe raised his considerable eyebrows.

"Dr. Britney Silas and her crime scene crew. They're right behind us. We're going to turn the scene over to her. So, you're on patrol, you get the BOLO this morning — how long until you spotted the vehicle?"

"Ten minutes. I was actually coming back to the house; my shift ended at eleven."

"Well, I appreciate you hanging around, staying with the scene."

"I can handle the overtime. What's the story on the reg? It's a hot car?"

"Yup. Boosted from an older couple from Ogdensburg. I'm waiting on more details. Right now we know they woke up and their car was gone. So, maybe sometime late last night, early this morning."

The trooper scowled. "They hadn't called in the theft yet? I've been on since last night, I didn't get anything over the MDT."

"No — there was some confusion about a relative of theirs they thought might've taken it. Mr. Tremblay has some health issues, and the wife has early onset dementia. Like I said, awaiting more info there."

They talked a bit more about the details of Katie Calumet's abduction but Cross continued to feel like time was slipping away. He wanted to get into that minivan and felt a wave of relief when Brit Silas arrived.

With her usual commanding presence, Silas whipped everyone into shape. Not a toe was to touch the cordoned-off area, now a crime scene. The photographer started clicking shots, while Silas and Cross suited up to have a better look inside the van.

It was hotter inside the vehicle and smelled like fermented fruit. They lingered over the child seat in the back.

Cross looked over the rear bench seat. "The Tremblays have six grandkids. There are impressions right there in the cushion — see that? Another child seat was strapped in. Maybe we'll find it tossed somewhere, prints on it."

"Little bits of food everywhere." Silas sighed. The two of them stood hunched over, shoulders touching. "What are those, peanuts? And popcorn there. And some sticky stuff right there, like spit. And that — it looks like blood but it could be grape juice."

"They left one child seat," Cross continued. "Why? This creepy baby trick they pull . . . However they do it, I don't know, maybe a doll in the seat. Using a real baby, that's too unpredictable. This way they can control it. The van windows are tinted. Maybe, you know, you hear the fake cries, you give it a look, and you think there's a kid in here, sweltering in the heat."

"This van is a total mess," Silas said. "It's going to take a long time to process, get samples."

"How long?"

She gave him a look in the tight space. "All day. Longer. I mean, what — I need elimination prints from six grandkids and their two grandparents? Parents, too? Hairs, clothing fibers, liquids . . ." She shook her head woefully. "This is a nightmare."

Cross had never heard Silas quite so pessimistic.

He squeezed toward the front and looked at the steering wheel. "We gotta prioritize. Steering wheel, shifter, console." He popped open the glove compartment, fished around for a second. Just vehicle information and what looked like some scripts for pills. He read one: head-meds for dementia. He put it back.

The minivan was getting stiflingly hot. He didn't envy Silas or her crew the task ahead.

Cross got out and walked carefully around the vehicle, pulling off his latex gloves. Why had the abductors left it? Were they now on foot? More likely they'd ditched the van for another ride. In the process, Katie had been smart enough — and courageous enough — to pull the receipt from her pocket and drop it. But he doubted they'd spent the time to clean the minivan; it was a mess. Maybe they didn't care?

The rest area had its share of trash. A faded can of Bud Light near the bushes, an empty bag of Doritos stirring in the breeze.

He looked up the road, winding on alongside the river. He didn't think there would be any more breadcrumbs like the rattle or the receipt. This was it. These people had Katie now and it was anyone's guess where they were headed.

He returned to Rowe and got the lay of the land. As Cross suspected, no one lived near enough the rest area to have seen anything.

Cross traversed the road and stood at the guardrail, looking down at the burbling river, more rocks than water. Too low for anyone out boating. Maybe an angler, though, a fly-fisherman — but no one was in sight. He didn't even know if it was a fishing river or not.

He drew a deep breath, let it out slow.

The gentle breeze tousled his hair. It was a warm day, everything still green, but with the faintest presage of autumn in the air.

Katie Calumet was in the wind, as they say.

CHAPTER THIRTEEN

She didn't think she could keep up the pace much longer. Carson had removed her shroud and walked up ahead, keeping his back to her, but she was aching all over. Her knee still smarted from the rock — every step felt like someone driving a nail into her patella. Her muscles cramped. She hadn't had a thing to drink since dawn. Coffee. She was surprised — and relieved — she hadn't had to pee yet, but now she was parched.

"I need something to drink."

"I give you a drink, then you'll have to urinate."

He'd already been thinking about it, apparently.

"Well, if I pass out, then you'll have to drag me along."

"You pass out, I'll shove a stick up your ass. Be back on your feet."

His comments were chilling, but she was growing inured to his more casual threats.

He led them through the woods, still no discernible trail in sight. She kept slipping because her running sneakers were wet and didn't have the traction for such terrain. And her tied hands affected her balance. Her wrists were a mess, purple and sore.

"If you cut the ties, I can go faster. Don't you have a . . . something? A deadline? We're probably supposed to be somewhere by a certain time, right?"

Carson was a lot of things, but he wasn't stupid. He only chuckled at her. Most of the time he had his head bowed, looking at something. It *had* to be a GPS device.

She needed to get close to him. She wanted that GPS. Then she would run, and he would never catch her.

An occasional hiker, she'd eschewed GPS in the past. But she could figure it out. Shit, her phone had GPS. She used it all the time.

She thought GPS devices not only showed you where you were, but could broadcast your position for others to find you, same as a cell phone. Carson had most definitely switched that function off. When she got a hold of it, though, she'd turn the tracking back on. Maybe there was even a distress signal, an SOS button. Either way, she'd use it to get herself the hell out of the woods.

Yeah, she could figure it out. She had to.

Katie looked at the sky through the trees. The clouds had dissipated into a thin gauze; the sun had passed its zenith and was lowering. She put the time at about two o'clock.

The longest she'd ever hiked without stopping was close to five hours. This could end up surpassing it. The best she could deduce, they were somewhere deep in the center of the Adirondack Park. The walk in had started as a gradual incline, then steepened. Now they walked parallel to the slope of the mountain.

"How far are we going?"

"You're being a nag." He jerked the rope and she stumbled but managed to keep her footing.

Carson suddenly stopped. Cocked his head, listening.

She heard it, too — somewhere down the slope, the soft burble of voices. Then laughter, from a child. A trail was nearby. An official trail with late-summer hikers. She knew it.

Katie stared through the trees, desperate for a glimpse of someone.

Scream. Scream now.

Before she could even pull a lungful of air, Carson had raced toward her. He drove her to the ground and clamped his hand over her mouth.

His weight was so pulverizing she couldn't breathe. His masked face loomed above her, turned to the side. "Shh. Don't make a fucking sound."

She clawed at him. She needed him off her.

People!

They'd heard hikers. People in the woods. Someone to summon help. It would all be over if she could just get free of him, just cry out . . .

It felt like her ribs were cracking. She drove her knee into his midsection and he grunted and rolled over, but kept hold of her.

On top of him now, her mouth uncovered, Katie screamed, a blood-curdling sound she hadn't known she was capable of. Carson slipped an arm around her, covered her mouth again, pinned her against him. He swung a leg over and tightened around her even more, like a boa constrictor — the more she struggled, the tighter he coiled. She thought about biting his hand, and did.

He yanked away and then hit her on the back of the head. The world flashed white, as if flooded with light. This time Carson flipped her over, got on top of her, and shoved her face into the ground, her mouth filling with dirt, her vision with black.

His hand was on the back of her head, pressing down like a garbage compactor. Her smashed nose felt like it could break. She struggled and drummed the ground with her feet and tried to get up.

She had no air. Her mouth and nose were buried in the dirt.

Carson was suffocating her.

She imagined how he looked above her, grinding her down, eyes wild, teeth gnashed. This was how she was going to die.

Her mother's face flashed in her memory — sad, kind eyes, long dark hair, a light smile curling the edges of her lips.

Katie bucked one last time, giving it everything she had.

Immobile. Helpless.

A strange peace slipped over her.

Carson let go. He rolled away, the absence of his weight making her feel insubstantial, like there was nothing to her. She raised her face from the earth, drew a shredded breath into her crushed lungs. She coughed and gagged and gulped in more air, half-expecting Carson to cover her mouth again, jump back on her, and plow her into the ground.

"They're gone," he said.

She dropped her head back to the dirt, face to the side.

Gone.

She listened, hearing only the sounds of the forest — the birds, leaves hissing in the breeze.

Gone. It was over.

Katie pushed herself up and onto her knees. Touched her nose with her bound hands and saw blood on her fingertips. Her hair was tangled with pine needles and small twigs. She turned to the side and retched brown spittle.

Then she looked up at Carson, standing nearby, looking down the slope.

"That was fucking close!" he said in an excited whisper. He even bounced a little.

He shook his head as if incredulous, walked to the bags he'd dropped, and picked up something from the ground.

The GPS was about the size of an old transistor radio, bright orange. He poked at it and scowled, staring at the screen.

"Not supposed to be there," he muttered. He scratched at his face through the mask. "This fuckin thing . . ."

If they'd come close to a hiking trail, it meant that they weren't too far from civilization — she'd even heard a child laughing. People didn't go on massive hikes with kids, only easier hikes: day hikes.

Katie spat out more dirt and pine needles. "Samatter? You lost?"

Carson kept focused on the GPS. "Shh."

"Fuck you," said Katie. Then she leaned onto her side and gagged again. More clogged dirt and blood-laced saliva poured out. She spat, and kept spitting, then sat back. "How about that water now, okay? To chase down the dirt."

Carson finally looked at her.

"Yeah — yeah, okay," he said. "Sure. Drink all you want." He fished a water bottle out of the bag and headed toward her, holding it outstretched. "And when you have to urinate, you go in your little skirt. Let it run down your legs. Maybe I'll lick it up aft—"

Carson's leg shot out from under him on the loose, slanted ground. He landed on his elbow, eyes wide in shock and pain. The water bottle and GPS went tumbling.

Katie scrambled for the GPS.

Carson looked around, saw her, headed her off. He scooped up the device before she could get to it, and then he tripped again, went down hard.

Katie laughed. Couldn't help it. She tasted the blood running from her nose into her mouth but she threw her head back and laughed some more.

Carson grabbed the water bottle next and threw it at her, but she managed to duck out of the way. She caught it before it could roll down the hill.

A sports bottle, the kind with a pop-top. She opened it and guzzled the water. Best thing to happen in her entire life, even if it felt like razors slicing her throat. Swallowing dirt, screaming for help — if she was a singer, her career would be over.

You're getting punchy. Losing it.

Go easy — there will be another chance.

Carson looked over the GPS, perhaps to see if it had been damaged, then clipped it to his belt. He stared at her. Even from a distance, she could see the malevolence in his eyes, like he wanted to tear her in half.

Finally he hefted the large backpack onto his shoulders. He was dressed in camo pants with cargo pockets, and a black T-shirt. The boots on his feet looked like top-of-the-line hiking gear, but none of it had saved him from landing on his ass.

Twice.

She felt another laugh bubble up and spat some bloody water before she could swallow it.

Carson glared at her some more and gave the rope a hard tug. "Get on your feet, bitch."

She pulled back on the rope and hoisted herself up. "Urinate," she said.

"What? Shut up, anyway." He looked down the hill, in the direction of the voices.

"Who says 'urinate'? 'I have to go *urinate*. You're going to urinate and I'm going to lick it up.' Who says that?"

"I said shut the fuck up."

"Yeah, yeah. Shut the fuck up. I know. Maybe you're an ex-con? Some of those tats look homemade. What did you do time for? Rape? You fucking asshole."

Carson started back toward her, though mindful of his footing.

"Oh boy," Katie said. Her voice was nasal, nose congested with blood and soil. "Here he comes. Here he comes to threaten me again. Big fuckin man."

He stopped short of her, and she sensed the emotions working through him. Her body tensed for the attack, but her mind was clear.

"You think you know me," Carson said calmly. "You think this is going to work, this little act. You think because you've been through a little bit of shit, now you're tough, now you've got nothing to lose. Trust me, Katie, you've got a lot more to lose. And I'm the perfect guy to take it from you."

His eyes were level and direct. She understood now that Carson wasn't crazy — he was something else. And she grew still, holding his inhuman gaze.

"We're not lost," he said. "There was a trail — didn't show up on the map. But we're on course, making good time.

There will be no more trails, no more people where we're going. This is not gonna end on your terms. Okay? You're not in control, Katie."

He turned and walked off. She stood until the rope tautened, then she was forced to follow.

CHAPTER FOURTEEN

Gates called Cross on his cell.

"We tried pinging her phone," Gates said. "Nothing. Inactive. But the phone company records show the last ping was at six twenty-two this morning. It hit off the tower between Hazleton and I-87."

"This is all clear evidence of interstate travel," Cross said. "Minivan confirmed stolen, eye witnesses, and tire tracks place it in Hazleton this morning; here it is five exits south near Bakers Mills, just a few miles from 87 . . ."

"Well, it's off the interstate now. I'm just saying, maybe they jumped on 87 and jumped off, but the feds don't get involved just because of a technicality that they were on the interstate for a few miles."

"Then what does it?" His voice went up an octave and he closed his eyes, rubbed a hand over his face.

"I've contacted them," Gates said on the phone. "They're monitoring. They're waiting to see what develops."

Cross opened his eyes and stared through the window of his car at the minivan. The area was crawling with techs. Traffic on Route 8 was slow, people rubbernecking the scene, state troopers urging them through.

"We're all waiting, now," Cross mumbled.

After a pause, Gates said, "You doing alright with this?"

He scraped at the lingering nail polish on his hand. "I'm supposed to get the girls back tomorrow. Once a month in the summer I get them mid-week."

"Right, right . . . have you talked to Marty?"

Cross's wife was born Marie Tabitha Rourke, and at some point in her youth it had been shortened to Marty and the nickname stuck. Tomorrow marked the third month of their separation.

"I haven't, no. She's working pretty long hours."

"Where do the girls go?"

"Marty found a good day care, and her mother pitches in."

Gates was silent. Cross knew she'd had her own issues with her job getting in the way of her family life. Only for her, Cross felt, people were a lot more judgmental. She asked, "We're supposed to be hearing from Katie Calumet's parents any minute now, right?"

Cross checked the time, just past three in the afternoon. "Yeah, I would suspect."

"And the sister, Gloria?"

"Yeah, Gloria Calumet. I spoke to her about an hour ago. Very distressed, very worried. She's driving up to the house — Katie and David's house."

"Okay. Well, we've got the hotline going and we're monitoring Facebook. Lots of people showing concern and support for Katie, no real leads. Her social media is pretty toned down anyway."

"David told me Katie 'wasn't much for posterity.'"

"Yeah I see that; her posts are few and far between." Gates seemed to be thinking. "You've spoken to David quite a bit — said he mentioned some names . . ."

"He talked about a former restaurant partner named Henry Fellows. Jean Calumet bought him out a while back. Fellows went on a downward spiral — he made some bad investments in the housing market and lost big after the crash. Fellows called Calumet a few times, at random, seemingly;

he'd be drunk, blaming his misfortune on Calumet. Calling him a predator."

"Sounds promising — what else you got?"

Cross sat up a little straighter, stopped scraping at his nails. "David also mentioned a lawyer who was fired by Calumet. He also mentioned a spurned chef from the Dobbs Ferry restaurant; name is Eric Dubois."

"Go on . . ."

"Dubois is interesting. But — also — what kind of struck me was the way Brennan talked about Jean Calumet, and his wife, Sybil. I mean, all these stories, presumably they come through Katie, you know, secondhand information — I didn't get the feeling that David Brennan and Jean Calumet are particularly close. Nor is anyone close with Katie's stepmother, Sybil."

Gates was quiet, mulling it over or perhaps waiting for more, but Cross didn't know what it all added up to yet. After a few more moments of silence, he said, "Sorry about the press conference today. I don't know what I was thinking."

Gates either didn't hear the apology or ignored it. "So what do you want to do?"

Cross watched the techs working. He glimpsed Brit Silas, walking away from the van, coming toward him.

"Can I call you back, Dana?"

"You bet."

Cross ended the call and rolled down the window.

Silas got right to the point: "We're going to need food, a place to take bathroom breaks."

Cross nodded. "Do you have water?"

"Yeah, some. But this is . . ."

"I know. I'll make it happen."

Silas lingered by the truck for a moment, then surprised him by patting his hand. "It's going to be alright, Justin. We'll get 'em."

She turned and walked away.

* * *

Cross headed north, back to Hazleton. With each mile he felt heavier, like he was letting Katie down. He reminded himself that Brit Silas was an ace crime scene technician and could potentially identify Katie's abductor, or abductors, thanks to the minivan. It was a major boon to the case.

Abductor or abductors? His gut said multiple persons involved. A driver and a heavy — someone to keep hold of her. But the idea lingered that they weren't concerned with the van. Maybe they'd taken pains to remove traces of themselves but otherwise left the van for police to fuss over, maybe even to slow the police down.

How smart were these people? Fly-by-night criminals looking for a payday? Or practiced professionals with a carefully thought-out plan? Was there anyone else, behind the scenes, like Fellows?

Why switch vehicles, if in fact they did? Because they figured someone would have spotted it?

And so they changed to what type of new vehicle? Something fast? Something rugged?

* * *

David Brennan had shut his driveway gate and the press vans were parked on the edge of the road. Two reporters were talking with a state trooper who saw Cross coming and opened the gate back up. The reporters ran over to the truck and jabbed microphones at Cross.

"Investigator Cross, what's the story on the stolen minivan?"

"Any word from Katie's captors?"

"Is it true Katie left behind a note of some kind?"

"Please respect the family," he said, "give them their space, and let law enforcement do its job. There will be another press conference soon. Thank you."

He drove through and up the drive. Cars everywhere. Katie's house was both part of an investigation and ground zero for running the operation.

The main living area consisted of three plush couches and two thick wooden end tables, all arranged in a horseshoe shape, open to a clerestory window. The window viewed the low sun burning through the forest. No one was sitting down.

Bouchard stood with Farrington and several other troopers. David Brennan was talking quietly with them.

Gloria Calumet was nearby, her back to Cross. She watched two CSTs dressed in white jumpsuits carry forensic equipment up the stairs. The investigation was getting samples of Katie's DNA but also scouring the house for a note from Katie, possible evidence of a planned departure, any signs of foul play. The main room had been cleared.

Gloria turned around as Cross neared. She surprised him with how attractive she was, momentarily distracting him when she offered her hand. "Nice to meet you," she told him.

"You too."

Maybe because he was in the man's home again, Cross started to think of Katie's husband more by his first name. David also shook Cross's hand. "Good to see you again."

"My parents are flying in," Gloria said, unprompted. "I booked them a room at the Hazleton Inn."

"They didn't want to just stay here?" Cross asked.

Gloria glanced at David, who gave Cross a look, as if to say, *See?*

Gloria said, "Sybil has certain needs," and left it at that.

"Okay. Well, I'd like to talk to them as soon as they arrive. Do you think that's possible?"

Gloria and David exchanged another look. "I'm sure you can stop by once they're checked in," Gloria said. "Just letting you know that my father is liable to say that they have had a very long day of flying and more could be accomplished after a night's rest."

"I need to ask — how does Katie get along with your parents?"

"Fine," Gloria said straight away. "Our father has always been there for us."

She looked uncomfortable, surrounded by strangers under terrible circumstances. Cross got the impression that Gloria didn't approve of her parents' behavior, but was their apologist. David just kept his thoughts quiet.

Cross decided more could be discussed with her and David in private. For now, he needed to get everyone on the same page. He'd already spoken with both Bouchard and Gates about whether to exclude Katie's husband or sister from certain things: They'd agreed to use discretion where prudent but otherwise keep them clued in.

"Okay." He clapped his hands together. "Forensics is still working on the abduction site and the abandoned minivan. We're getting elimination prints from the Tremblay family. We hope to identify latents found on the steering wheel and door of the minivan and match them to our abductors. There was no blood found — not Katie's, or anyone else's, at either scene. DNA is possible, but processing unfortunately takes some time."

"But you're sure Katie was in the minivan?" David asked. "Because of the receipt?"

"Yes. Together with the eye witness from Red Ridge Road, and the tire tracks, and Katie's text to you, we're fairly certain Katie was abducted at six fifteen this morning and the vehicle she was taken in was found alongside Route 8 outside Bakers Mills."

"So where do you think she is now?"

Cross hesitated. He glanced at Bouchard, who made a subtle nod. "My hope is that we get prints, we match with someone in our system, and get an idea who might be involved."

"You don't have any idea where she is." David's eyes were shining.

"We're confident we know where she was a few hours ago."

"And you've contacted the FBI?"

Bouchard answered, doing his usual tap-dancing about FBI prerequisites while David and Gloria visibly despaired.

Cross had a map he unfolded on the large coffee table.

"Listen — what's going to help us now is to exhaust all possibilities. Partly we can narrow that down based on the travel so far and the location of the minivan. Meaning, we're sure they're not headed into Canada. The minivan was discovered west of Bakers Mills. Route 8 comes to a T-junction not far from there, and it heads north while Route 30 goes south . . ."

"And then I-90, eventually." David leaned down for a better look.

"Yes, at Amsterdam. It's possible they got off I-87, took the county routes, and then got back on an interstate, being I-90. It's a slower way to go — the side roads are windy, bumpy, lower speed limit — but maybe they just wanted to be off the main roads." Cross marked Bakers Mills with his finger. "It's possible that they switched vehicles at this spot."

David stared at the map. "But also possible they took her into this area, somewhere. You're searching all around there?"

"Absolutely. Going door to door in Bakers Mills, we've got K-9 and bloodhound units in the woods all around the rest area, and a search and rescue team has set up an incident command nearby. They'll be combing through the woods there."

Cross stood upright and regarded Katie's sister and husband. "But they could've moved on. We have to accept that as a possibility, that they switched vehicles and kept going."

"Why?" Gloria engaged Cross with direct blue eyes.

"Why would they keep going?"

"Why any of it?" She was trembling. David reached her and put an arm around her shoulders.

Cross considered it. "Well, that's the big question."

"We're assuming they want money," Gloria said.

"We're not assuming anything. What we know is that your sister is missing; we know the facts that the evidence has borne out. The rest is guesswork. Where they are, and who they are. The 'why' will show itself eventually."

Cross glanced at Bouchard, and Bouchard cleared his throat and spoke for a while, just platitudes again, while Cross excused himself to get a glass of water.

He walked into the kitchen, open to the other rooms, so he could still see Gloria. As Bouchard spoke to her, she looked at Cross.

He filled a glass from the tap, drank, and leaned against the sink. His phone buzzed in his pocket — a call he had to take.

* * *

"You're a celebrity," Marty said after Cross slipped out the back door. "Did the girls do that to you?"

"What do you mean?"

"Your nails. There's pictures of your hand all over the internet — you've gone viral. One caption is 'Cross-dressing Cross.' You haven't seen any of it?"

"Oh, you're kidding me . . ."

"I didn't think I'd be the first person to point it out, sorry. Anyway, I was calling to say, you know, I realize this is a huge deal. I can keep the girls this week."

It was always bittersweet to get relief from parenting. Cross missed his daughters terribly when they weren't with him. But he had no choice. "Thank you, Marty. Is your mom going to help?"

"She's going to spend a couple nights. She's the one who pointed out the pictures of you."

"Oh, great . . ."

"What did you say at the press conference? Something about bankers and CEOs?" There was humor in Marty's voice. It struck Cross that this was the longest conversation they'd had for weeks.

He smiled a little. "Yeah, I don't know what I was thinking . . ."

"This is a big deal. Katie Calumet has been in local politics, her family is incredibly wealthy, and she's pretty. You're going to have round-the-clock coverage of this, all the news channels, papers, and bloggers."

He felt his smile weaken. "I know."

"Alright, I'll let you get back to it." She paused and added, "Be careful, Justin."

He ended the call then opened the browser on his phone and Googled "Cross-dressing Cross."

The first hit was a blog he'd never heard of. The headlining picture was a close-up of his hand grabbing the podium at the press conference earlier that day, showing residual paint on his fingernails. He skimmed another article entitled, "Cross Down-plays Possibility of Kidnapping for Money."

The article went on to accuse Cross of "burning the candle at both ends," alluding to a marital separation and several sightings of Cross out "on the prowl" at a local bar. It finished by posing the question of whether he was the right cop for this high-profile case.

Feeling nauseous, Cross found the picture had been tweeted a bit, some users as far away as California, and in some cases the hand close-up was paired with Cross's professional headshot.

Other articles focused on Katie Calumet, which was better, and the local news stuck to the facts. He'd been called for quotes several times throughout the day and saw he was accurately reported. At least there was that.

David stepped out of the house, not realizing Cross was there. "Oh, sorry. You want privacy?"

"No, I'm all done." Cross put the phone away.

David pulled a cigarette from his hiding spot. He lit it and asked, "You don't think this is about money?"

"I don't know whether it's about money or not."

"Did you give any thought to what we talked about earlier?"

"Of course. I spoke to the senior investigator. She made a call to a New York City detective and they're looking into Henry Fellows and the chef, Eric Dubois."

"And Lee Beck, the lawyer."

"Yes."

David nodded, blew smoke. "Good." He stared into the woods, appearing lost in thought. "God, I hope she's alright. This waiting is agony."

"I know."

David faced him. "What do you think? I mean, what do you, personally, really think?"

"I didn't mean to dismiss the possibility of ransom. I think it's very possible. Even probable, now that we have more info. Someone kidnapping Katie for other reasons? If they just saw her and grabbed her — no. This looks more premeditated than that. Stolen minivan, then a vehicle switch — they have a plan. I think we'll hear from someone tonight. At the latest, tomorrow morning."

"Fuck. It's nerve-wracking . . ." David suddenly dropped his head and sobbed.

Cross had been wondering if the big man was going to break down at some point. He moved closer and put a hand on his shoulder.

David wiped away the tears and stamped out his cigarette. He waved at the lingering smoke, as if dispelling his emotion.

"Katie is . . ." He tried to finish but emotion overtook him again.

Cross waited.

"You know? She's . . . she's all I got," David finished.

He went back inside. After a moment, Cross followed.

CHAPTER FIFTEEN

When Katie broke the long silence, her voice sounded alien in the dimming woods.

"Wherever we're going, we'd better get there soon."

Carson didn't respond. Katie thought he was winded. He was in decent shape — wasn't fat, anyway — but he didn't seem accustomed to this type of workout. Not that she was some CrossFit guru, but she had been running for two years now, doing yoga almost every morning. Her aches and pains were from Carson's assaults, not the hike.

Her finger continued to throb, her cuts were stinging, and she was bruised from head to toe, but she felt strangely good, alert.

That's what shock is.

The air was getting cooler. The lowering sun flashed amid the trees, which she thought were red spruce. Mostly they walked in shade, through an understory of striped maple and witch hobble. She'd seen some sugar maples further back, just before their brush with the hikers, but that had been a while ago. The forest had become wilder, and twice she'd had to wait while Carson struggled through the tightly packed evergreens. He'd rerouted them each time, muttering curses when the branches snagged the bags on his back. The rope was frequently getting twisted up, too.

They'd crossed another stream, just a trickle of water. It was likely more robust in the spring as the snowpack melted, but they'd been able to get over it by stepping on rocks.

She knew a few things about the Adirondacks from the nature hikes she helped coordinate for the Visitor's Interpretive Center at Paul Smith's College. Mountain living conditions were harsher than the valleys and flats. That meant stands of red spruce and balsam fir — the trees she was recognizing — placed them at least 2,500 feet in elevation. If she remembered her timberline forest facts, then at about 4,000 feet, the red spruce lost vigor and weakened, leaving the balsam fir to dominate. If they reached that elevation, they were in the High Peaks, an area she was somewhat familiar with.

"You're awfully quiet," she said to Carson. Her nasal passages were clotted with blood, making her sound sick.

That he hadn't spoken in so long was unnerving. She wanted to be able to predict his actions. But the wild and impulsive would-be rapist had changed over to this silent, determined person.

"Are you busy reading my thoughts about trees?"

Still nothing. The sight of him was fading with the eventide. She'd finished her bottle of water some time before and finally had to pee. She considered doing as he said and just letting it run down her leg. But no, it wouldn't come to that.

"I need to stop and use the bathroom."

"We're almost there."

At least she'd gotten him to say something.

She could detect the glow of the GPS as he hunched over it, pushing tree branches aside. The rope got snared again, jerking him to a halt. Carson freed it up and kept going.

"Why don't you just cut it? Where am I going to go?"

No response. She felt partly stupid trying to talk to him. She almost wanted to goad him, bring back the aggressive Carson. This subdued, unknowable version of him made her increasingly worried.

"I really have to go . . ."

"It's right here," Carson said.

Katie saw nothing. Then Carson pushed through some more trees and effectively disappeared.

The rope kept drawing her along until she passed the tree line and stepped into a clearing.

There was a log cabin sitting on a gently sloping field.

The sun was almost gone; all that remained was a pinkish blush of alpenglow. Seeing the log cabin set back in the high grass filled her with conflicting emotions. It was a sign of civilization; it was a place to rest, maybe eat — she was starving — but it also represented a kind of finality: She had to spend the night in there with Carson.

She saw an outhouse in the gloaming, twenty yards from the cabin, at the edge of the tree line.

Carson led her across the clearing. He stopped by the front door and took off his backpack and the duffel and slammed them both down on the uneven porch.

"God*damn*." He was breathing heavily again and he bent forward, hands on his knees, looking around. "Home sweet home."

Katie kept her distance. The rope was slack, hidden in the grass. "Are we going to eat?"

He patted the air with his hand, annoyed. "Yeah, yeah, we're going to eat. I'm fuckin hungry too, you know."

She said nothing else, her mind busy retracing their steps.

It had been an incredibly long hike, but she'd mentally pinned some of the landmarks — a cluster of sizeable boulders, two enormous oaks that had long since fallen and formed an X, a switchback where they'd zig-zagged up a steep section. And for a good portion of the middle of the hike they'd been walking perpendicular to the slope of a mountain.

She also thought she had a sense of the general direction they'd traveled — west. The sun had almost always been in front of them, and slightly to her left.

But then they'd humped it north too, up the face of the mountain, and the deciduous trees had transitioned to pines, then the red spruce and balsam fir. Here and there they'd descended south, once or twice seemed to double-back east, and Carson had done a lot of stopping and looking at the GPS and circumnavigating those impregnable thickets. After another long slog with the sun dropping ahead of them, they'd reached the clearing. It had taken six hours, she guessed. Seven at the most.

Carson snapped the rope, forcing her back to the moment. "I said come here."

She walked through the wet grass and he pulled out a pair of pliers from the backpack. "Give me your hands."

He used the pliers, which had sharp edges, to clip the plastic tie. Katie spent a moment basking in the wonderfulness that was having her hands free. Then she thought about the GPS.

"Feel better?" he asked. "Done complaining?"

"Yes, thank you."

Carson gave her a long look, his eyes glinting in the failing light. "Don't give me that passive bullshit. That agreeable, pliable bullshit."

"Okay."

She could see his eyebrows draw together in the holes of his mask. "Oh, see. There you go. That's it right there."

"What do you want me to do?"

He made a disgusted sound and turned to the front door, which was unlocked. Her hands were free but she was still tethered by the rope. He had gathered up most of its length and pulled the remainder taut and she followed him into the cabin.

It was dark within, redolent of must and neglect.

Carson flicked on a small flashlight he carried and shined it around. A cast iron wood stove dominated the single room, its stove pipe penetrating the roof. About half a face cord of wood was stacked beside it.

In one corner was a wash basin, a small propane range, and a wood block for preparing food. *The kitchen*, Katie thought. In another, the dining room — three straight-backed chairs, dirty and festooned with cobwebs.

The last corner of the cabin had a twin mattress on a box spring.

The bedroom.

It made her sick to look at. The despair seemed to suck at her heart.

"Well, it ain't the Waldorf Astoria." Carson tied Katie to the wood block in the kitchen area and stepped out, presumably to gather up the bags.

She dragged her thoughts away from the bed. What kind of cabin was this? Did it belong to Carson or Leno? Maybe someone they knew? Was it on private or state land?

A light breeze rustled the outdoors, like the dying exhalation of the day. She reached behind and felt the knot of the climbing rope around her waist. Started to work at it.

She listened for Carson, heard the splatter of his urine in the grass. He moaned with satisfaction.

She picked at the knot some more, scanning for a weapon. There was a first-aid kit in the kitchen area on top of a free-standing cabinet. Maybe in the cabinet there was a knife.

Behind the wood pile, she glimpsed the handle of a hatchet. Even better.

Carson stepped back into the cabin and dropped the bags. "Food," he mumbled. "Yeah, food."

He rummaged through the duffel then dragged it toward the kitchen. He started taking out items and setting them on the wood block. Katie saw bologna, processed cheese, a squished loaf of bread, a jar of mustard. Carson kept going until he'd emptied the bag of all its food contents, then looked over the spread, puffing his chest with obvious pleasure. More cold cuts, another loaf of bread, a half-dozen cans of soup, ramen noodles, spaghetti sauce — bachelor food. No water.

"What are we going to drink? You threw away the water bottle."

Carson flicked a look at her. He'd set his flashlight down on the range, and the light caught the side of his face.

Instead of yelling at her, he reached into the duffel again. He pulled out two six-packs of beer and set them on the floor.

Then he said, "Oh, yeah, and let's see if it's here . . ."

He went to the cabinet and showed her what was inside. He took the bottle of Jameson, knocked the first-aid kit to the floor with a bang, and slammed it down. "Haha!"

"I meant—"

"I *know* what you meant," he said, like she was spoiling the fun. "There's a pump out back. Jesus. A well. Don't fuckin worry about water, okay?"

"You carried a twelve-pack of beer fifteen miles?"

Fifteen miles was a guess. Six hours of hiking and she estimated they'd averaged two, maybe three miles an hour. She looked for a reaction, but Carson didn't satisfy her.

Katie was trembling, and she tried to hide it. She felt afraid — more afraid than she'd ever been in her life — but she knew she was also wet, and it was damp in the cabin, and she'd had nothing to eat all day, and only one bottle of water. She had no appetite but she needed to eat and drink. She would feel better, too, if she was allowed to apply some of the first aid to her many cuts and scrapes, maybe splint her finger, which felt like it had turned to hot stone.

She kept looking at the windows — the light almost completely gone, just this dark, dark blue in the glass.

It's too late to run now.

—I'll use the flashlight. Just need to eat first, get some water.

It's absolutely nuts to think you can find your way back, even with the GPS.

—I don't need to find my way back, exactly. Just out.

You're talking about running in the dark, in the woods, flashlight or no, with this maniac chasing you.

—I have to try.

You're at least a dozen miles into the middle of nowhere. Don't be crazy.

Her mind grew still as Carson unscrewed the top from the Jameson, pushed up his mask partway, and took a long drink.

Katie averted her eyes from his exposed chin, surveyed the food again. "How long are we staying? Is this enough to eat?"

Carson calmly screwed the top back on the bottle and set it down ever so gently. "God, it's like we're fuckin married. 'Where's the water? When do we eat? How long are we staying?' What did I tell you, Katie? You're not going to control this. Fifteen miles? What — you think I'm impressed you did a little math in your head? You're way fucking off, by the way. Just like you're way off thinking about how we came in, or where we are."

"Whose cabin is this? You knew the Jameson was there."

He stared, dumbfounded, then threw his head back and laughed. "You. You are something, right? Is that what they tell you? 'Katie, you're so full of spirit. Katie, you're just so strong. Oh Katie, Katie . . .'" He made smooching sounds inside his mask.

Finished with his antics, Carson clucked his tongue, scoffing at her, and walked away.

There was something wrong with him. More than the obvious. He was like an actor, some kind of perverse performer. Humming religious tunes, quoting movies, delivering grim monologues, or wallowing in periods of depressive silence.

By the bare bed was a small table and an oil lamp. He found a book of matches and fiddled with them. The first few didn't strike, but then the fire bloomed and he lit the lamp. The soft light spread through the room and created deep shadows.

Katie was still standing just inside the door, close to the kitchen area. She'd been able to pick a loop in the knot free. If she couldn't get the rest undone, the rope had some give to it and she thought she could slide it over her hips and down her legs. She didn't need twenty feet of rope trailing behind her as she ran through the dark forest.

This is nuts! Don't do this.

"So can I make myself a sandwich?"

Carson unclipped the GPS from his belt and tossed it onto the mattress. "Uh-huh. You think I'm going to make you something? Come to think of it, make me one, too. Extra bologna, extra mustard."

She got moving. She went about her business like she was in her own kitchen, setting out the condiments, arranging the ingredients. She opened the cabinet on the floor.

The smell was awful. She pulled out some plates, peppered with mouse shit, then saw a dead rodent in the corner, just a tuft of fur and a tiny skeleton.

"We might want to wash these."

Carson stomped across the floor. He grabbed up the basin and started for the door, then stopped in the doorway and glared at her.

But he didn't say anything. He left.

Katie set the plates aside.

Sudden tremors wracked her and she gripped herself in a hug. Hot tears welled and she took deep, shuddering breaths. The tears fell and she hastily wiped them away.

Don't let your mind go there. Don't let it.

—How can I not? I'm in the middle of nowhere with a violent psychotic. No one knows where I am.

Someone does. Leno does.

She busied herself preparing the food, using the excess plastic from the bread bag to lay out the slices. A quick search for cutlery revealed it in the drawer of the cabinet, also littered with mouse poop. She wiped the blade of a butter knife on her shirt, uncaring about mouse shit or dirty plates. She'd just wanted a moment free of Carson.

There were noises out back, squeaking sounds, what she assumed was Carson working the manual water pump.

She hadn't really looked at the walls when she'd first come into the room. One was decorated with an ancient pair of snowshoes. Another had something hanging that looked medieval; she thought it was an animal snare. It made sense — a place like this in the middle of nowhere was used for hunting, maybe trapping animals. There might be a rifle or shotgun somewhere. She glanced above the door and saw an empty gun rack.

Carson returned and heaved the filled basin onto the counter beside the range, water sloshing.

He strode back to the door and retrieved a large urn, also full of water.

"See, your royal highness? Plenty of water to wash and drink."

Then he found the beer and popped open a can. He slurped it down and then watched what she was doing. "How's the food coming? Jesus, come on, I'm so hungry."

"It's ready. I need to use the outhouse."

She figured there was no other way than to just come right out with it. She waited to see if he would remind her of his threats.

He flapped his hand at her, as if disinterested, wandering toward the food. "Fine. Knock yourself out."

He was letting her go.

She slowly turned, walked to the door. She stepped out into the darkness. Saw the stars overhead. A trace of violet sunset just above the trees.

Run.

CHAPTER SIXTEEN

Given Jean-Baptiste Calumet's net worth — and rumors that he was a driven, relentless entrepreneur — Cross expected a brawny, quick-tempered man, maybe a cigar stuck in the corner of his mouth. But Calumet was of average height, thin, with a quiet voice and kind of gentle way about him.

His wife, Sybil, also bucked the stereotype of the icy stepmother. She was athletic, an attractive woman in her late fifties, also with a reserved manner. There was, however, something Cross found cunning in her eyes, as if predetermining potential threats. Then again, her stepdaughter had been abducted. Wary was the general mood.

They ordered a late meal at the Hazleton Inn, the kitchen closing, just one other occupied table in the candlelit dining room.

Cross had given them some time to eat, but no one had much of an appetite. Gloria's food was untouched, Jean's and Sybil's meals lightly gone over. Only David had cleaned his plate.

"I'll need to ask each of you to provide fingerprints — we call them elimination prints — and submit to a DNA swab. It's non-invasive, just a quick swipe of your cheek. Is that alright?"

No one objected.

"Do you have children, Mr. Cross?" Sybil took a drink of her red wine.

"I do." Cross had opted for ice water. "Two girls."

"What are their names? How old?"

"Patricia and Ramona. Six and two."

"Good ages," Sybil said. "That four-year difference — that's the same as Katie and Gloria."

Sybil glanced at Gloria with a smile.

"We're five years," said Gloria.

Sybil's smile faded.

Gloria looked into a corner and grew somber. She had withdrawn since Jean and Sybil had arrived — or maybe, once again, it was just the shock of their terrible situation, and everyone was off.

It was hard to get a read on people in dire circumstances.

On the other hand, maybe it was in such circumstances that true character was revealed. Like meeting over dinner to discuss their missing daughter — it had been the Calumets' idea, not Cross's.

He stirred his chilled water with the straw and said about his daughters, "They're good girls."

"I'm sure they are. And their mother? What does she do?"

"She was a teacher for a while, college level, business courses. Now she works as a hospital administrator."

"Very nice," Sybil said.

The unspoken subject matter was looming large.

"I would also like to fix each of your phones with a recording app," Cross said. "We've done this with David's phone, but we don't know who may get a call, or when. It could be from Katie, and there could be vital information we need to save. Or it could be from her abductors. Does anyone have an objection to this?"

Again, no one did.

Then Gloria asked, "Abductors? Plural?"

"It's an assumption. There's likely more than one vehicle involved. Someone needs to drive, someone needs to keep her — keep Katie safe. It's in their interest."

"Assuming they want money," Sybil said. "With respect, there's a lot of assuming going on . . ."

"That's fair. You're right, we don't know yet." Cross cleared his throat and said, "We also would like to collect the data from your phones. Your call log, your texts. Anything on there could help us."

They exchanged looks; nobody moved. Then Gloria tossed her phone onto the table. "You can take mine. Anything you need."

"Thank you," Cross said without picking it up. "Just hold on to it for the tech when she comes. Her name is Kim Yom." He looked to the parents and raised his eyebrows.

"I'm sorry, I can't," Jean Calumet said. "I have confidential dealings with partners and investors. But I am willing to parse anything relating to Katie and turn it over."

Cross looked to Sybil, her mouth a grim line.

"Nothing on my phone will help you," she said.

Cross let it be for now. He'd talk to Gates and see if they would decide to press the issue.

"Well, thank you everyone. I know this is . . . this is a very hard time. I appreciate your cooperation." He started to rise and added, "I hope you're able to get some rest tonight."

Jean walked Cross to the door. "Mr. Cross, I know this can't be easy for you either. You have daughters of your own."

It was a nice thing to say, but odd.

"It's my job, Mr. Calumet. I promise you we're doing everything we can."

Calumet patted Cross on the back, nodding. "I know, I know. Much of it is out of our hands now. But I'm sure we'll get Katie back safe. Whatever they want, we'll give it to them, and we'll get Katie back. Good night."

Cross stepped onto the porch of the inn and Jean Calumet closed the door.

It felt like Calumet had just walked him to the door of his own house, not the restaurant of an inn where he'd booked a room.

Cross took a breath of the night air then walked to his car. The stars were turning on above.

And then it hit him: Calumet expected a ransom note or phone call soon. He was resigned to do whatever was demanded. Perhaps his demeanor, strange to Cross, suggested that he was dealing with it as a business expense.

The cost of being rich, perhaps.

Cross fired up the car and flicked on the headlights. It just didn't make sense, though. Kidnappings were rare. One didn't expect a child kidnapped for ransom as the normal course of being rich. There were plenty of rich people in the country; very few of them ever had kidnapped daughters. This wasn't Venezuela in the 1980s.

Maybe Jean Calumet had known this was coming.

Cross lit a cigarette. Seeing David smoke had tempted him.

The dark road slithered out of the blackness, the car headlights bleaching the evergreen trees.

* * *

The phone vibrated beside his head. It was 2:56 a.m.

His mouth felt like cotton. One double Scotch had become three. Luckily, exhaustion had claimed him before three could become four, and he'd passed out on the couch.

"Cross here."

"We just wrapped up for the night." Brit Silas sounded as alert as if it were 2:56 in the afternoon. "We went over the whole thing with pads and lint rollers. Then dusted everywhere. I had Joe Minnie do the front seats first and we sent those prints to the BCI hours ago. Justin, we got one match so far. From a partial."

Cross sat up on the couch so fast the empty Scotch glass tumbled to the floor with a bang. "You got a match . . ."

"Like you recommended, we did the steering wheel first. Nothing there but Mr. Tremblay and one of his children,

Jeremy Tremblay. So, unless we're thinking the Tremblays are behind this, our bad guys were wearing gloves."

"The Tremblays are not behind this."

She was quiet a moment. "I know. It was a joke. You know — middle-of-the-night humor."

"That's stellar material. So where did you find the partial?"

"In the back, one of the rotating seats. On the armrest. Maybe the gloves came off for a moment, as it were. Justin, he's in the system. Name is Troy Vickers, and he's been through Rikers and Anderton, got a sheet like the Dead Sea Scrolls."

It was unusual for Brit Silas to act this clever. She was really excited.

Troy Vickers.

Cross stood up and stripped out of his old clothes. "Give me the highlights of the sheet."

"Most recent, he assaulted and raped a college student attending Forrester University, here in New York State. He did three years at Anderton Correctional."

Her words were practically ringing in Cross's ears.

"Any grand theft auto? Where's he from?"

"No grand theft. But burglary, drug charges, two D-Dubs, other assaults preceding the rape charge. He's originally from Sherman Oaks, New Jersey."

"Sherman Oaks . . . that's the suburbs." Marty was from Jersey.

"That's what I got. I'm going to catch a few hours' sleep."

"Alright. Helluva job, Silas. Thanks so much."

"You bet. Go back to bed."

"Oh, I'm wide awake now."

He went to the bathroom, moved his bowels, showered, and shaved. He made himself breakfast and was at the substation before the sun rose.

If the abductors were going to contact police to demand ransom, by now they knew who to call. He'd been on the news, all over the internet — *Cross-dressing Cross*. He stared at the phone on his desk, willing it to ring, daring it to.

"Come on . . ."

In the meantime, he logged on to the system and read about Troy Vickers.

Before his days as a rapist in New York, Troy Vickers got a DUI in California, then an aggravated unlicensed driving six months later in the same state. California suspended his license and he moved back east where he collected more charges for attempted unarmed robbery of a drug store in Brooklyn. The fresh offenses landed him at Rikers, where he languished for a year.

He was a failed actor. His parents were upper middle class, from the New Jersey suburbs. He'd been in a toothpaste commercial at age eight.

But the acting life didn't seem to work out for Troy Vickers.

The next thing on his sheet was the rape of the Forrester University student, which landed him at Anderton Correctional for the three-year bit.

Cross sent Vickers' picture to all law enforcement in another BOLO and scanned through his list of aliases and known accomplices.

Vickers went by "Vicky" and "The Vic."

As nicknames went, Cross thought, they were particularly distasteful. Vicky was a feminine name and a "vic" was cop-talk for victim. It was like Vickers advertised his sick tendencies. Or others had pinned it to him.

He had no KAs, or, known accomplices. His work was solitary — drinking and driving, robbing drug stores for prescription pills, raping women.

Even criminals had ethics, and most didn't like rapists. More than likely, Vickers had endured further punishment in jail as an outcast among outcasts. Maybe he'd been segregated for his own safety.

Cross wanted more information on his time inside. Despite his poor standing among other inmates, it was possible Vickers had bragged to one of them about a kidnapping plan. At the very least, someone at Anderton was bound to know something about him. Cross was no penologist but suspected that most inmates relished bragging about their crimes and schemes.

He picked up the phone and got the secretary for Assistant Warden Carl Brill.

Brill agreed to send over basic prison records on Troy Vickers, but the information excluded visitation and phone records, which required a court order since they included third-party information.

On the phone with the secretary, Cross devoured the information as it showed up in his inbox: All inmates were given a type of IQ test as part of their mandatory mental-function evaluations. Vickers scored high. It didn't make him a smart criminal necessarily — he'd left his fingerprints in the minivan after all — but it meant something. Cross wasn't quite sure what yet.

Vickers had had four different cellmates during his stay; he'd been moved twice, and once during his stay a cellmate was released and another moved in.

"Who's there now?" Cross asked.

"Of those four . . ." she said, and paused, "Dauber, Hernandez, and McSweeney are still here."

"Who left?"

"Mark Johnson. Six months ago."

"Can you send me all their info?"

"Just the basics; same as Vickers."

"Fine. State prisoners can't access the internet, is that correct?"

"It depends. For Vickers, no."

"What about cell phone?"

"Again, no. Use of personal cell phones has to be approved by the inmate's counselor, and Vickers' counselor did not approve. And before you ask — yes, a counselor would have to be compelled by the court to discuss inmate matters."

"How can I see any mail correspondence?"

"You'd need judicial review."

The walls were stacking up, but Cross had expected them. He had plans to contact Judge King. "Okay. In the meantime, I'd like to set up visits with all three of the inmates still there."

She was silent a moment. "Of course, Investigator Cross. That, we can do."

CHAPTER SEVENTEEN

Katie lay in darkness, but the heat was growing in the cabin. She knew it was morning.

She hadn't run.

In the end, she'd ventured as far as the outhouse then collapsed into body-wracking tremors. She was injured, it was dark, she was deep within miles of wilderness.

After she'd returned to the cabin, Carson had waited until she forced down a bologna sandwich. Then he put the shroud on her and tied her to the bed, using the climbing rope.

He'd eaten, then drunk half the beer — she'd counted the times he'd popped a can open. He'd had three more shots of the whiskey, too, give or take an ounce, bragging about these (*down the hatch!*) as he imbibed. The drinks had made him chatty, and he'd babbled for a bit about all the places he'd been in the country. California. Colorado. New Mexico. The desert.

She didn't like that he was telling her these things. Knowing about him alarmed her, like he didn't plan to keep her alive.

And then she'd seen his face.

Just a glimpse — the shroud had hitched up as she rubbed her head into the mattress, itching at the needles and probably bugs in her hair. She saw him standing in the center of the cabin, lit by the oil lamp, his back to her. He'd turned and she'd seen half of his face. She'd quickly looked away, but he strode toward her, yanked the shroud down past her chin.

But he didn't say anything about it.

At some point she thought he'd unrolled a foam pad from the duffel, lain down on it, and gone to sleep.

With Carson snoring, she'd lain awake. What if he did something in the middle of the night? It panicked her that she'd seen him, and that he knew she had. Now maybe those sickening sexual comments he'd made, the way he'd groped her — twice — were going to turn into a full-blown assault. Because now he had nothing to lose.

All night, lying in darkness, listening to him breathe.

Just waiting for it to come.

She'd tried to distract herself, thinking how he had about half his beer left. And probably more than half the liquor, but not by much. And there was plenty of food, still, like he planned to be here for a couple of days. Was that just a precaution? Or did they expect a ransom negotiation to take at least that long?

What if she was wrong, though, and this wasn't about money?

But Leno had taken her picture. It had to be to show people she was alive.

Would law enforcement deal with the kidnappers on their terms? She'd seen the same kidnapping movies as anybody else, and doubted their accuracy. The only thing she knew was that law enforcement — probably FBI at some point — would want to catch the bad guys.

Her father was a different story.

Katie loved her father, but she knew him better than most. There wasn't a problem he couldn't solve with money. He'd come from money, had always had it, which might have lessened his appreciation for it. He'd give up his entire fortune if he thought it would get Katie back.

Sybil understood her husband's financial impulsivity and had convinced him to grant her power of attorney. Married for just three years, she now signed everything Jean signed and had a grip on the purse strings. Unlike Jean, Sybil hadn't come from money. Her family had learned to preserve what little they had through protectionism.

All night long, thoughts swirling, always coming back to her fear that Carson was going to do something any moment. Even the way he'd tied her up made dozing difficult. The ropes wrapping her wrists and ankles were tied to the bed corners so that she was splayed out cruciform.

Now the heat continued to spread in the cabin, and she could even feel the sun warming her skin.

She guessed it was around eight when Carson first stirred, mumbling something in his sleep.

More time passed. Nine in the morning? Later? She felt more terrified than she'd felt all night. That was worry and conjecture — this was certainty. He was going to be awake soon. The time was coming when he'd have to deal with her being able to identify him.

He was getting up. He sniffed, scratched around at something on the floor. She heard the zipper on the duffel bag, then nothing, just breathing.

"Good," he said about something. "Okay, good."

Then Carson got to his feet, the floorboards creaking.

He came closer.

He was standing beside the bed. She knew he was right there. Looking down at her.

"I didn't see you," she said. Her voice sounded so small, so timid; she hated it. She cleared her throat, mustered some gumption, but it was so tough, she felt so vulnerable. "I didn't see anything, okay? It was an accident. The thing — the mask on my head, it just lifted up. A little bit. I just — I saw the back of you, Carson. And then I looked away. I just want you to—"

"Shut up." His voice was gravel.

He sniffed again, grunted. He sounded hungover.

"I gotta piss," he said. "Then we're gonna talk, Katie. We're going to figure this thing out."

"I didn't see anything."

"Yeah you did."

"Let me go." Just whispers. The breathy pleas of a desperate woman.

"I'll be back."

She heard him moving away.

"You don't even want to be doing this," she said. "This isn't your thing. This . . . this isn't—"

The creaking footfalls stopped. "Oh no?" He was by the door. "This isn't my thing? You're right, Katie. Maybe when I come back I can show you my thing. Okay? Jesus — I gotta piss, alright? You're starting in like a goddamn . . . Just fucking hang tight."

He opened the door and left the cabin.

Katie didn't move. She started to cry. She didn't want to cry and fought against it.

She pulled at the ropes and strained with her legs.

His voice floated back: "Don't go anywhere." Then laughter, high-pitched, followed by more talking to himself, which faded as he moved further away.

She bucked and thrashed, the fear throttling her windpipe. She couldn't even scream.

Maybe when I come back I can show you my thing.

She stopped fighting, letting herself go limp, letting the tears come, no longer caring. Like Carson no longer cared — she could hear it in his voice. She was right about him, she'd known it all along — he might be a part of this kidnapping, but he was hired muscle, or something. It didn't matter to him whether this scheme came off or not. He'd just been waiting for his chance.

And now it had arrived. She'd seen him, he knew it, it was over.

Everything became quiet, just the blood singing in her ears.

Over.

Katie lay on her back in darkness, realizing that, during her struggle, the rope binding her wrists had loosened.

Or, rather, her wrists were bleeding; she could feel the wetness.

The blood was a lubricant.

She twisted her hands, rotated her wrists back and forth, and the ropes slid over her skin. The excruciating pain took her breath away.

But it was something. She might be able to just—

If she could get her hands free, even one, she could undo the other, then extricate her ankles—

You got it. Keep working. Almost there.

Several times she stopped.

She listened for Carson.

At one point, she thought she heard him laugh again. Or yell something.

Then, nothing.

Katie worked at the bindings, back and forth, twisting and pulling, her intensity growing. She stopped again, held an exhalation, then listened again.

Silence.

At least two minutes had passed. Maybe three.

Calm down. Think.

The tension was what was keeping the rope around her wrists. The blood definitely lubricated the ropes but if she was pulling, the loop tightened. She had to relax at the same time she tried to slip her wrist out and—

She got it.

One hand was free.

Fresh adrenaline poured through her. She could just reach her left wrist. Picked at the rope there — it too was just looped around, no knot — and got that hand out.

She tore off the shroud and squinted in the glaring light, dust motes dancing in the buttery sunrays streaming through the dirty cabin windows. The air was fresh and wonderful. Amazing.

She tried to sit up. The tautness of the ligature around her splayed ankles made it impossible. She had to contort her body, reach down and grip one of her legs, pull herself to a seated position.

What the hell kind of rigging was this? He'd used one single rope to tie her wrists, okay. But he'd used a carabiner at her feet, connecting two separate ropes. Trying to pull back the lever with her fingertips was maddening. More white-hot pain exploded from her sprained finger, radiating up her entire arm. Her hands shook and the carabiner kept slipping. She was able to get the lever back, but the rope tension made it hard to unhook. She kept working, perspiring, the cabin getting hotter as the sun rose.

It was such a painstaking process she had to stop and rest — her muscles were cramping from the angles and the exertion. Finally, she cried out and snapped the rope loose. Her legs were free. Just needed to slough the ropes around her ankles.

Five minutes. Had to be. *Where is he?*

Hope flooded her. Pure and bright and energizing as the sunlight. Something had happened. Maybe someone was here.

She kicked off the remaining ropes around her ankles. There was nothing left tying her to the bed and she got to her feet.

Or, maybe it was a game. Maybe it wasn't enough for him to have her on the bed, tied up. He wanted her to get free, wanted to chase her . . .

The world swam. She bent forward and breathed. Dropped to one knee, grabbing the bed for support, overcome with emotion. Her thoughts came in a torrent of debate:

Run!

—Take what you need first. Water. Something.

Go now, just run, just go!

—He'll come after you. He'll catch you.

She took several deep breaths, her teeth chattering.

She had to work quickly. Carson might be back any second. She'd already gone over this — all she needed was water and the GPS. Maybe a flashlight. She'd never let him catch her.

She stood up and crossed to the kitchen, ignoring the way her legs felt dead, her fingertips tingling, heart beating too fast. The liquor was on the wood block. She dumped it on the floor and set the empty bottle beside the pitcher, then poured the water in.

The water slopped everywhere, and by the time the pitcher was empty, only half the liquor bottle had been filled. There was more water in the wash tub. It was dirty, but she didn't care. She submerged the bottle and filled it.

Time to go.

She started toward the door when she glanced at the woodpile.

The hatchet cleaved a piece of upright wood.

Get it.

Her arms trembled and the sweat poured down as she struggled to wrench it free. It came loose at last, throwing her off-balance. She fell back and then immediately stilled. Listening.

Nothing.

Then, maybe a faint voice.

Chilled by the sound, she picked up the hatchet, searched for the GPS. There was so much shit on the floor. Carson had made a complete mess: His bedroll, a blanket, the duffel bag on its side, half the contents burped out — socks, a moth-eaten wool hat, a toothbrush, a rain jacket, a wristwatch in the mess. No bright-orange GPS.

Hurrying, she checked the cabinet. She looked under the bedroll. Nothing.

Forget it. Just get away.

She grabbed the flashlight off the range and slipped her hand through the tethered loop. With the bottle in her grip, she ran out the front door.

The clearing shocked her. It had been twilight when they'd arrived and she'd been under duress. It didn't look the way she'd pictured it — it was beautiful. The woods were close on one side, but the other side of the clearing was open to stunning views of a mountain range. It looked like the land dropped off dramatically; she could look above the tops of trees.

Obviously she and Carson hadn't arrived from that direction. They'd come through the forest right until they'd stepped into the high grass.

He was nowhere to be seen. Probably he had wandered off into the woods to take a dump; he'd been gone way too long for just a piss. She thought of her vow to kill him. She had the hatchet. She could come upon him squatting in the woods and drive the hatchet into his skull the way it had cleaved the wood.

Get going!

She started toward the tree line. Halfway there, she heard the noise again — definitely a human voice.

It sounded like a cry for help.

CHAPTER EIGHTEEN

By 10 a.m. Cross was at David Brennan's house in Hazleton. The driveway was snarled with news vans that had somehow gotten past the gate. They were trespassing, loitering reporters already primped and talking into the cameras. "Behind me is the home of Katie Calumet, abducted yesterday while on her morning jog . . ."

Inside the house was commotion. The Calumets were drinking coffee and eating breakfast in the living room. David was in the kitchen, leaning against the massive island, wearing an apron and looking like he hadn't slept all night. It appeared he'd just made the morning meal.

In addition to the forensic techs scurrying about, state troopers and sheriff's deputies populated the room.

Cross spied Sheriff Oesch sitting next to Jean Calumet on a couch, speaking quietly.

Dana Gates was alone near the stairs to the second floor.

Cross went to her. "This is nuts."

"I know." She dabbed her eye with a handkerchief, something she had to do because of a job-related incident, the same incident which had scarred her face.

"What's the sheriff's department doing here?"

"I don't know, but, from what I heard, Calumet supported Oesch when he ran for sheriff two years ago."

"He ran *unopposed* . . ."

She shrugged, stuck the folded handkerchief in the pocket of her suit coat. "Still needed money for the buttons and fliers, I guess."

"So Calumet supports the sheriff because his daughter lives in the county?"

"That would be the guess. But Calumet has money seeded here and there. He's donated big to the SPCA . . ."

"Katie is on the board . . ."

". . . and to the Waldorf School, Riverside. In case Katie ever has a kid, I guess. We need to get all non-essential persons out of here. Just you and me, the family."

Cross watched as Gloria stood with her plate and walked it to the kitchen. It looked like she'd found an appetite at last. She huddled with David by the sink, together washing dishes.

Cross turned back to Gates, who gave him a look: It was his job to clear everyone out.

He took a breath, walked to the middle of the large room, and clapped his hands. "Good morning, everyone."

The talk ended and heads turned.

"Everyone here is doing a great job. As you all know, Katie is our concern, finding her and getting her home as safely and efficiently as we can. To that end, I'm asking that only Katie's family and the CSTs remain in the house this morning. We want to . . ."

Jean Calumet was reaching for his phone.

". . . keep things as simple as possible."

Calumet's face turned red as he struggled to get it from his pocket and looked at the incoming call or text.

"What . . ." Cross said, starting over. "Wait . . ."

The phone trembled in Calumet's grip. His eyes seemed to twitch, the tears welling up. Sybil leaned close and got an eyeful of what was there. She put a hand over her mouth. Then she let out a sob and turned away.

Cross held out his hand. "Please! Let me see."

Everyone was crowding in behind Cross. The temperature in the room seemed to rise by a few degrees.

There was a crash as David dropped dishes in the sink, hurrying over.

Jean Calumet rotated the phone so Cross could see the image.

Katie had cuts and scrapes on her face, a swelling, split lip, frazzled hair. She was wearing the peach-colored top, smeared with dirt. Her wrists were tied, hanging at her waist.

The picture cut off at her upper thighs. Behind her, though fuzzily indistinct, were woods. Cross took it all in, every detail, and reached for the phone.

Before he could take it from Calumet, the picture disappeared. The phone vibrated. An incoming call appeared on the screen.

Calumet stood up and put the phone to his ear. "Hello?"

David lunged, but Cross caught him, held him back.

Calumet stared out the windows at the bright morning. "Yes. I'm Jean Calumet. Don't hurt her."

Cross's heart started pounding.

David made another grab for the phone. "Give it to me," he said through clenched teeth. "Jean, *give me the phone*. Let me talk to them."

It was all Cross could do to restrain him. Gates appeared and moved in front of David, her hands on his chest.

Calumet stepped away. "I understand." His tone was flat, his eyes dully shining. He listened then spoke a final time. "Okay. Yes. It will be done."

Then it was over.

Calumet put the phone back in his pocket.

Cross let go of David, who'd given up the struggle. "What happened? Did you just agree to pay a ransom?"

"I did." Calumet stared into space.

"How much?"

They were surrounded by everyone in the room. Sybil was still sitting on the couch, looking shocked. Gloria hovered close, her lower lip trembling.

"Ten million."

The reaction in the room was electric, breaking the spell that gripped them. Ten million was a lot of money. It had all just happened so fast.

Cross kept his hand out. "Please hand me your phone."

Calumet did.

Cross looked at the picture again. Where was she? He looked for a sign but all he could see was Katie, the damage in her eyes.

He'd forgotten about David, who suddenly snatched the phone away.

David stared at the image of his wife. He mumbled something incoherent. People were keeping their distance because Katie's husband simmered, about to boil over. No one moved.

Then the big man seemed to age as his anger dissolved into visible despair. His gaze slowly traveled to Cross, then he held out the phone.

Cross grabbed it and stepped away, searching for the call recorder app installed by Kim Yom. His mind raced in several directions and his stomach knotted.

David wandered to the couch and sank into it. Beside him, Jean Calumet was rubbing a finger over his lips, dazed. The rest of them stood around like onlookers at the scene of a brutal accident.

"Everybody out." It was blunt, but Cross stared them down and people got moving.

Sheriff Oesch rallied his deputies. The troopers filed toward the door.

"No one says a word," Cross said. "Not to a single member of the press, not to a wife or a friend, got it?"

Cross stopped Farrington from leaving. He wanted one state trooper on hand and Farrington had been there from the beginning.

Just like that, no consultation with Cross or Gates, Calumet had agreed to pay a ransom. It was Calumet's daughter and he'd already said he'd do whatever it took, but Cross had familiarized him with the procedure, and this was not the way things should go.

"How did they get your number?" Cross glared at Calumet, who still looked shell-shocked.

Sybil answered, her tone curt. "We don't know, Mr. Cross. But who did you expect them to call?"

"Maybe the info hotline we provided at the press conference. Maybe the New York State police. Maybe me."

"It's our daughter. Of course they would call us."

* * *

With everyone gone but the family and the core law enforcement, Cross and Gates shut themselves in the dining room, closing the door on Jean Calumet, who stood in the center of the living room like a statue, and Sybil, who'd come over icy cool now that the episode had passed.

Kim Yom, the phone and computer specialist, had set up her work station on the large, elegant table that dominated the room.

The app recorded all incoming calls on Calumet's phone to a Google Voice account. Calumet had agreed with the stipulation he be allowed to immediately delete any recordings not related to his daughter's kidnapping.

Yom accessed and replayed the phone call.

From the computer speakers: "*Hello?*"

"Is this Katie's father?"

"Yes. I'm Jean Calumet. Don't hurt her."

"Alright, Katie's father. I want you to listen very close, and you can have her back. Do you understand?"

"I understand."

"I'm going to call you back in one hour with two different account numbers. You're going to wire $5 million to one account, $5 million to

another. Once they've both gone through, I'll give you coordinates where you can then locate Katie. Are we clear?"

"Okay. Yes. It will be done."

The caller hung up. He'd been even and smooth, not a trace of nerves. Definitely a male, thirties or forties by the sound of his voice. A slight accent — maybe Jersey or Brooklyn?

Cross picked up Calumet's phone and dialed *57. He followed the prompts for tracing the call and listened.

"The last call to your telephone cannot be traced so no charge will be added to your bill. If the problem continues, call CenturyLink for further assistance."

Cross spoke to Yom. "Could they modify the phone so that call trace doesn't work?"

"Well, easier to just buy a prepaid. For around thirty bucks, you can obtain an anonymous dial tone. It's called an MVNO. No name required. No I.D. check, no billing information, no questions asked. You just walk into Walmart and walk out with a working phone line that's virtually impossible to trace."

"*Virtually* impossible," Gates said.

Kim Yom started to say more, but Captain Bouchard arrived. He pushed his way through into the dining room, eyes wide. "They called?"

Cross held up the phone. "We need the feds. We need a skiptracer. Yeah, they called."

"The FBI is right behind me," Bouchard said. "I got them. They're coming in."

* * *

FBI Agent Radu Sair gathered the family in the living room.

"So, we've had first contact." Sair glanced at his watch. "We have fifteen minutes until he calls back. When he does, we're going to track him."

Jean Calumet spoke up. "I'll have to keep him on the line?"

"No. If the trace works, it's nearly instantaneous."

Cross thought about Kim Yom saying how it was improbable to trace a prepaid phone.

"You're confident it's going to work this time?" Cross asked. "What's different?"

Sair gave him an impatient look then called over his shoulder, "Agent Paulson?"

Paulson emerged from the dining room, intent on the phone he was holding. He was the FBI skiptracer and had arrived minutes before with an impressive array of tech gear. He looked up, realized he was being asked to speak. "Ah, okay. So we're using NPA/NXX data. I can at least determine the carrier."

Gates said, "Subpoenas will take weeks."

Paulson shook his head. "Your Dr. Yom is most certainly right — they'd be using a burner. Burners lease service from different cell carriers. Through NPA/NXX, we'll know the brand. If it comes up as Verizon, Cingular, or T-Mobile, it's a Tracfone. If it comes up Sprint or Nextel, it's Boost Mobile."

"So we'll get the brand?" Cross looked between the agents. "Then what? We go to every Walmart nationwide and look at the record of prepaid purchases, then watch their surveillance video?"

Sair was impassive. "It goes quicker than you'd think."

"What about a stingray?"

The agents traded looks. Sair stepped closer to Cross and lowered his voice. "Yes, we'll be using cell tower simulators, too. We'll be collecting cellular info in a general search. But the stingray has a limited range. We've got four ready to start trawling, but in no way does that cover the territory we need to cover."

Cross had a tough time swallowing it. This was the FBI's plan? They could fly a spy plane over the entire region equipped with a stingray. He knew the technology was controversial and might drag Fourth Amendment concerns into the mix, but that hadn't stopped the feds before.

He held his tongue for now. Jean and Sybil Calumet were watching and listening closely; Gloria looked more dubious by the second, David downright anxious and depressed. He hadn't moved from the couch since the call came in.

Sair resumed his general address. "Okay, so, again — best-case scenario, the trace works and we get the number, the subscriber, the whole turkey. Second-best scenario, we learn the carrier, but if through NPA/NXX data we learn the carrier is servicing a burner phone, then we go after purchases. Only one in thirty cell phones are prepaids. If the phone was a recent purchase — even a couple months — we have the capability to parse that data very quickly."

"How will you know who to look for?" Jean Calumet asked.

Sair turned to Cross and raised his eyebrows. His expression invited Cross to share his information with the family.

"We've potentially identified one of the men involved," Cross admitted. "His fingerprint was found in the minivan. It's a partial print, and with partials it's possible to mismatch. So I've been working to verify his identity in other ways."

David roused from his stupor. "Who is it?"

Captain Bouchard cut Cross off. "We can't discuss that at this time."

Sair stuck his finger in the air. "People, it is very, *very* important that we get one thing straight: When the abductor calls back, we give him *absolutely no indication* that we have any idea about a suspect, that we are performing a trace, that we suspect a burner, absolutely nothing."

"I'm not stupid, Agent Sair," Jean Calumet said. "So if we look at retail store video, what if it's not this man who purchased the — you call it a burner?"

"We have an exhaustive list of known associates," Sair said.

Cross had pulled Vickers' rap sheet, and Vickers had no known associates. Unless the feds knew something he didn't, it was a bald-faced lie.

"Now," Sair said, "the next thing: As soon as we have the account numbers, Agent Paulson will run a trace on those accounts. This isn't easy — there are many privacy entanglements and firewalls. With luck, we'll at least get the bank."

Calumet interjected again. "Can't you submit a court order? I have the contact information of three judges in my phone. We'd get the owner of the bank accounts much sooner than the owner of the phone, wouldn't we?"

"Unless the abductors are foolish — and I hope they are — the accounts will be offshore. Probably Swiss. Look, this is not about any one smoking gun, people. This is about all these things working together. What phone are they using? We get that. What bank are they using? We get *that.* Who is one of the men involved? We already *got* that. All of this together, and we take down the bad guys."

Sair dropped his hands to his side. Cross thought there was a bit of theater to the agent's spiel, but he was grateful for Sair and Paulson nevertheless.

"Once this call happens in . . . six minutes," Sair said, "we're going to take off like a rocket."

Calumet said, "What if we just pay, get Katie's location, and go get her?"

"We're going to," Sair said. "That's exactly what we're going to do. Katie is our number one priority. Getting the bad guys is secondary. We won't do anything to jeopardize her safety."

CHAPTER NINETEEN

She listened, grasping the hatchet, standing halfway between the cabin and the edge of woods, and heard the cry again.

"Help me . . . !"

It was another trick. Like the fake baby crying in the minivan, meant to lure her. Carson was some kind of perverted performer, playing a sick game.

Or, maybe it was someone else. The cabin's owner. What if he or she had had a confrontation with Carson?

It could be anything, anyone. Even if it sounded like Carson, the environment might be distorting acoustics.

Katie started away toward the woods. She was getting out of here.

"Katie! Help!"

She froze. There was no more question — he was calling her name. It had to be Carson. And he sounded hurt. If this was more of his cat-and-mouse routine, he was convincing.

She'd seen an animal snare in the cabin. Maybe he'd stepped into one. Maybe his fucking leg had jagged metal teeth in it right now, he was bleeding out, and she could watch him die.

Playing a game, not playing a game — she didn't know. But he was definitely far enough away that she could redouble her search for the GPS. It might still be in the cabin somewhere and she'd been too panicked to find it before.

She made her decision and sprint-skipped back into the cabin, hobbling on her bad leg.

But his voice drifted over again, her name, followed by a pathetic wail.

Maybe he has it. Something happened to him; he's hurt.

Go get it.

She considered it. Had he clipped the GPS to his belt at some point?

She could have a look. Just a look. It really could mean the difference between success and failure, life and death. For starters, she could determine where the hell she was. That alone would be a huge psychological relief. And, earlier, she'd been confident she could make it out on her own, thinking that being lost in the woods was better than anything else, but now she was in pain, even more exhausted, emotionally wrecked, and barely able to use both hands.

She stopped, scanned the clearing, the trees, listening intently. Waited.

Carson's voice, weaker: "Katie, pleaaase."

She moved toward it, where the land dropped away and overlooked the treetops. The closer she got, the sheerer the drop revealed.

She lowered to her knees on the jaunty precipice, crawled to the edge, and looked down.

Carson was on the rocks below, his body mangled. Blood spatter surrounded him in a way that reminded her of a raspberry smoothie dropped from a high angle.

A few feet away from where he'd fallen: the bright-orange GPS.

The whole thing made her stomach roll, and needles of heat pricked her neck and ears. It wasn't the gore. It was just the sight of him, triggering a fresh wave of revulsion. For him, for herself, for all of it. A desire to turn back time. To have left last night instead of succumbing to fear and so-called better judgment.

Where had the judgment gotten her? Almost killed.

On the other hand, if she'd run, he would have surely chased her. She'd stayed, and look what happened.

He saw her.

"Katie! Help me!"

His voice was hoarse from all the yelling he'd already done.

She tried to shake off the mix of emotions roiling through her and get her bearings. She already knew they had done a good deal of climbing, but this was a substantially high elevation.

The mountain was part of a chain curving toward the sun, so, the south. The summits and ridges were unfamiliar to her. The High Peaks were busy with hikers all summer long, loaded with trails, surrounded by villages, but these were not the High Peaks. As she scanned for any signs of life — a winding road in the distance, a farmer's field — there was nothing to see but the timberline forest undulating into the distance, the crescent shape of the massif bent toward the southern sky. She didn't recognize any of it.

"Katieeeeee . . . !"

Carson reached up at her from the craggy boulders below.

She wanted that GPS. It looked intact — those things were encased in rubber, built to survive all sorts of trauma.

He could suffer and die, for all she cared. And from the looks of his legs and one of his arms, it wouldn't take long. Maybe he would bleed out, or maybe the animals would come for him in the night. Once he was dead, she'd take it.

She moved away from the edge and Carson shrieked.

Back at the cabin, she gathered up all the mountain-climbing rope and carabiners. One of the items from the duffel was a belt that mountain climbers use for rappelling. Now it made some sense why Carson had this gear — it was more than just ropes to tie her up. He'd planned an exit that would involve some steep descents.

A drunken mountain climber. What a joke.

Feeling confident, angry, and strangely bemused, she measured out the rope, feeding it through her hands. There was the twenty-foot length used to pull her along, and there was another shank about triple that. She'd been bouldering a few times; even if ropes weren't used for bouldering, she had some basic chops when it came to footholds and handholds. But did she want to risk a fall with the poor shape she was in? And though the GPS had appeared intact, it could've been invisibly damaged, not functional, not worth it.

She set the gear down and turned to the food items. She made herself a sandwich and chewed it up while staring at the hatchet she'd set aside. He was still yelling out there, just a faint sound, like a mewling animal in a trap.

There was no telling how long it would take him to die. An hour. A day. Maybe waiting it out was not the best option.

Her stomach clenched, threatening to bring up the food she'd swallowed. She sucked in a deep breath through her nostrils and willed it to stay down.

Maybe there was another way to Carson. A longer way down, a more gradual descent. She hadn't really given it a thorough scout. She could go now and see, bring the hatchet with her. If it proved too difficult, or rappelling was the only way down, she'd abandon the effort.

She grabbed the urn and a small towel from Carson's things. She left the cabin again and went to the well.

Working the pump handle, she filled the urn. Her wrists were still bleeding and there was more blood running from a cut on her leg. Katie bit back the tears and endured the pain while she cleaned herself. The water was frigid.

Finished, she returned to the cabin. The first-aid kit was scrappy but there were a couple of alcohol swabs and a roll of gauze. She wrapped her wrists, grabbed the hatchet, then went back to the ledge and peered over.

"Katie! Oh God, thank God. Katie . . . ahh! Katie, I broke my legs. My legs are fucking broken . . ."

She investigated the area around the cliff. Moving up the ridge a ways, toward the peak of the mountain, she discovered a narrow switchback trail that hooked around toward the drop. It might take a while, and there could be hidden dangers, but she wouldn't know unless she gave it a shot.

"Katie!? Where you goin'?"

You're wasting time. Get out of here. You've got no one to chase you now — go!

—I could be in the woods for days. Even a week.

Everything she'd seen so far confirmed how deep she was within the Adirondack Park. While she couldn't name the surrounding mountains, she was sure she was isolated by miles of rugged terrain.

The most robust mountain climbing she'd ever taken, years before meeting David, was Dix Mountain. It had entailed hiking in, camping, and summiting the following afternoon. Two full days, and that was as a spry twenty-five-year-old equipped with all modern hiking amenities on a well-worn trail.

Six million acres in the park, she reminded herself, half of which was state-run wilderness preserve. The numbers meant little until you were out there in person, then the scope of it was truly overwhelming. People went missing almost every day in the summer. It might as well have been Alaska.

I'm getting the GPS.

"My legs are fucking broke!" Carson's voice reverberated through the trees, a lonely, broken sound.

She loved it.

Katie headed up the ridge then started down through a thick carpet of berry shrubs. She could no longer see the cabin now.

Whose cabin was it?

If it was a decommissioned ranger station, there would have been signs. Some documentation, something. In case a person just like her found themselves stranded and lucked upon it. The cabin had to be a privately owned place.

She knew of a few people who owned vast tracts of wilderness, even whole mountains.

Hefting the hatchet, she continued to descend, thinking about her hike up Dix. Thinking about her life before David.

When she met him he'd been coming to the end of a career that'd never quite gotten off the ground. In a dimly lit bar, the profile of him curled over the piano, she'd seen it in the roll of his shoulders, heard it in the notes he played — he'd been at the end of something, and so had she; both of them ready for a change, and she'd chosen him. Picked him out — picked him up, as it were — and the rest was history.

She wished she could talk to him.

The thing she missed about him the most surprised her. She no longer expected his rescue. She didn't need him to beat the shit out of Carson.

She missed talking with him.

It was one of the best parts of their relationship — they communicated. They helped each other out. There was a difference between that and trying to fix the other person's problems. Support was not about taking over. She missed his support.

Katie ignored the tears that fell as she curved back toward the drop, and Carson.

This was going to work.

CHAPTER TWENTY

Agent Paulson was holding the phone when it rang. He handed it to Calumet.

"Hello?"

Cross could hear the tinny voice on the other end but not make out the words. The voice fell silent and Calumet looked at his wife. After a moment he said, "Okay."

Calumet knelt beside the coffee table. He took the pen and paper and wrote down the account numbers as the kidnapper relayed them, repeating them back to the kidnapper in groups of three. Calumet didn't need to do this, but it probably helped him cope.

Finished, he stood up, glanced at Agent Sair, and said into the phone, "I need proof of life. The picture isn't enough. I need to know that Katie is still okay."

The voice on the phone grew louder, like the kidnapper was upset. Calumet started pacing around the room.

Cross looked at David, tried to read the man's expression. There was a lot going on in David's mind, Cross thought, and Katie's husband felt helpless. But there was something else. Cross wanted to dig deeper on it when the time was right. Those subtle tensions between David and Katie's parents.

"Okay," Calumet said. "But please, listen. This money is in my name, and my wife's name. To authorize this amount we have to go to the bank, in person. We both have to sign a—"

The voice emanating from Calumet's phone crackled with anger.

"I understand . . ." Calumet made gestures in the air. "I understand, but—"

"What does he want?" Sybil asked.

Calumet fell silent, clenching his jaw. He stared off into the distance, then his gaze wandered to Cross.

"Please," Calumet said. "Please don't hurt her. Don't hurt my baby girl . . ."

He seemed to wait for a response, then hung up the phone.

Paulson took the phone from Calumet and hustled it to the dining room, like it was a ticking bomb. The agent plugged it into his system.

Sybil rose and went to her husband. "They want more, don't they?"

"Twenty million. Ten in each account."

The room was dead quiet.

"I said I'd pay it." Calumet kept looking at Cross. "How could I say no?"

Sybil drew near him, but Cross thought she looked stiff. "We can't. We don't have it."

Calumet glared at her, his composure deteriorating. Cross had wondered when the cool, soft-spoken man was going to break down. This was it.

"Of course we have it. This is Katie."

"Okay," Sybil said, licking her lips. "We have it, but it's not liquid. We have almost no equitable securities."

"Then we'll liquidize all deposits, stocks, and shares. I don't care about any hits on the open market."

Katie's parents stood in the center of the room, staring into each other's eyes. Then Sybil looked around at the people watching. "Will you excuse us, please?"

Paulson called out from the other room. "We got it! It's under Verizon." He stepped into the doorway, visibly excited. "That means Tracfone."

"Let's go to work." Sair followed Paulson back into the dining room.

The attention off them, the Calumets slipped away upstairs.

Cross was bewildered. The whole thing was messier than he'd expected. He joined the feds and Kim Yom in the dining room along with Bouchard, Gates, and David. Everyone stood; no one sat down at the expensive table. They listened as Yom played back the recorded conversation.

The kidnapper relayed the two account numbers. Calumet asked for the proof of life.

"*Oh big talk*," the voice said. "*You got the feds there now, I bet. Huh? You want to get your daughter killed!? I deal with you. Only with you, Daddy. For the inconvenience, now it's 20 million.*"

Calumet agreed then explained how it was going to take some time.

"*You got twenty-four hours*," the kidnapper said with mounting hostility. "*Do you hear me? I don't care if you have to move heaven and earth.*"

"I understand . . . I understand, but—"

"This is very simple. I know you've got the money. You move those numbers. That's all it is, numbers. You have them moved from A to B. They show up in B within twenty-four hours or my guy will fucking kill her."

Agent Sair leaned over Paulson, who was in front of a large screen showing voice analysis in a spiky graph. "It's a bluff."

"*Please*," Calumet said on the recording. "*Please don't hurt her. Don't hurt my baby girl . . .*"

The call ended.

"It's a bluff," Sair repeated, straightening. "He's going to risk $20 million over some arbitrary time constraint? He'll go longer. They always go longer. They just want to keep the pressure on."

"You've done this a lot?" Cross asked.

Sair gave him a side glance. "A couple times." He pointed to the voice graph, a jagged line with jaunty peaks. "Look at his stress. Look at when he says, 'That's all it is, numbers.' He's not confident. He knows it might take longer." Sair touched Paulson — who had moved to a different but connected computer — on the shoulder. "Where are we on the bank numbers?"

"Hold on, almost done."

Agent Paulson finished tapping the keys. Each account number was broken into four groups of digits and beneath each group was a blank field. The other cops watched a beach ball icon twirl on the screen.

Then the first field began sorting through a series of possible alphanumeric characters, so fast that the characters seemed to blur together. The first field locked in a series of characters, then the second, third, and fourth. Same for the other account number; now each account number had an accompanying code.

"What's that?" Cross asked.

"Nation codes. That just told us the bank is in Switzerland."

"That's good," Sair said.

"How is that good?" Cross glanced at his supervisors, hoping he wasn't out of line. But Bouchard and Gates seemed just as interested.

"You hear about the Swiss Federal Banking Commission not divulging any accountholder information," Sair said, "but there is international mutual assistance in criminal matters. Kidnapping is just as much a crime in Switzerland as it is in the US. They'll cooperate. If you'll excuse me, I need to make a call."

Sair didn't move. After a moment it was clear he expected the rest of them to leave.

Cross led them out, including Yom. Only Paulson remained in the dining room with Sair, who put a phone to his ear and shut the door.

"What's that all about?" Dana Gates asked when they were back by the couches.

"I don't know," Bouchard said.

"He's calling his supervisor to say it's real," Cross said. They all gave him a look. "I was reading about this last night before I went to bed."

Well, three Scotches and I passed out, but close enough.

"There's been a lot of virtual kidnapping. People call you up, armed with info they've got on your kid from social media, and demand you send them money. Get the police involved, they say they'll kill them."

"She's *gone*," David said. "We have witnesses, you found the minivan . . ."

"I know. They're just being thorough. This is good for us. His supervisor might reinforce us with more help."

David didn't seem so optimistic. "How long will it take to get the information on the Swiss accounts? So, what, they find out it's this Vickers guy, they freeze the accounts, any assets, he doesn't get the money? That doesn't help Katie."

"They'll let the money transfer happen. They'll freeze the accounts afterwards."

"There are people you can hire," David said. "People just waiting in Switzerland to work with a criminal who wants to set up an account. It won't be in the abductors' names. It'll be some third party."

Katie's husband sounded like he'd been doing some research of his own. Cross wished he could be more comforting.

He also wanted to get back to Anderton Correctional. He needed to check in with Brit Silas, too, and find out what else was recovered from the minivan.

"It's all a timing thing," Cross said weakly.

"Yeah, well, while they try to get it right, Katie is out there." David went out the back door, presumably to have a cigarette.

Gates wanted to check in with Silas and the minivan. She stepped out the front, dialing her cellular.

Bouchard put a hand on Cross's shoulder. "So far so good."

"Is it? This is nuts. I've never worked with the feds before."

Bouchard glanced at the closed dining room door. "You'll get used to it."

CHAPTER TWENTY-ONE

"Katie, thank God."

Carson coughed and spat up blood.

One of his legs was twisted so bad there was a bulge in the leg of his pants where there shouldn't have been, soaked red. Probably the bone had broken through the skin. The other leg was folded at a wrong angle, too. Carson looked a bit like a marionette dropped by the puppet master.

He reached a clawed hand toward her. His dark eyes were shining with emotions she'd never expected to see. He was completely helpless, and he knew it.

"Katie. Oh, Katie, I'm so fucked."

She moved toward him with the hatchet.

The GPS was on the other side of Carson. The way the rocks and boulders were arranged, she needed to step beside Carson to get to the GPS.

"Don't move."

She crawled around him, holding the hatchet up, ready to hack at him.

Her wounds ached as she stretched for the GPS, out of reach. She had to let go of the hatchet and use her good hand if she wanted to get it. At last she got a finger on the device, inched it closer, grabbed it. The moment of truth.

The cracked screen displayed schizophrenic digital numbers like hieroglyphics.

"Is it working?" Carson was trying to see. He shivered as he looked around, wide-eyed, blood trickling from the corner of his mouth. He'd landed on his back, the legs beneath him in that terribly *wrong* way, one arm torn to shreds, the other flailing around, clutching for the device. "I sort of. Landed on it." He was breathing irregularly, his speech clipped. "Let me see it. I can. Fix it."

"It's broken." Katie took a cleansing breath, let it out slow. "Where are we?"

Carson laid his head back against a rock, looked up at the sky. "It was. A cheap one. I'm gonna. Die."

"Where are we?"

She was stretched out behind his head, the two of them draped over the rocks like awkward sunbathers, she thought. Like perverse lovers.

Carson just stared into the sky. It was a postcard of a day, little white puffy clouds, deep-blue firmament.

"I'm twenty. Eight," he said.

"I don't care how old you are, Carson. Tell me where we are."

"My name is Troy."

"I'm going to leave. Tell me where we are, or I'm just going to walk away. You'll die right here, alone."

He tried to look down at himself. His head was shaking badly, as if he'd lost all physical control.

He moaned, a wretched sound. "Oh no. No, no, no . . ."

"Tell me where we are."

"We're in the woods, bitch! I don't know. I didn't write. Anything down. I was relying on the. Fucking GPS."

"You were going to leave a different way than we came in. You brought climbing ropes. You were going to come down this way?" She looked beyond the immediate area. The land continued to pitch downward, terribly steep.

"Yeah. Leno said. It would be shorter."

"Where is Leno?"

"Making the calls."

"Where? From here, in the woods? Or, what — a town?"

He didn't respond.

She raised her voice. "What's nearest to here?"

Carson didn't reply.

"Do you have a compass?"

"No."

"You brought me out into the middle of the woods and didn't take a compass? What if your cheap GPS broke, like it did? You didn't think this through, Carson."

"Troy . . ."

"How did you fall down here? Huh?"

She laughed, feeling cruel, unable to stop it, not wanting to anyway. "You idiot, Carson."

She looked up at the sky and laughed some more. She couldn't stop. She had to force herself to get a grip.

When it passed, she looked at Carson, expecting him to be dead.

He wasn't. He was crying.

She got up from the rocks, moved toward the trail. She clipped the broken GPS to her waist. No compass, but she was fairly sure the rocky drop where Carson had fallen faced south. She would go out the way they came — even if it was longer, it was obviously safer. And there had been a wristwatch among Carson's things. Every break in the trees, when she had some sun, she would make a sundial in the dirt to provide a rough bearing. It was something, at least.

"Wait . . ."

She stopped.

She turned.

"Please don't. Go."

"Goodbye, Carson."

He was sobbing. "Don't let me die here."

He started to get up. It was painful just to watch, but he managed to get one leg working and flip himself over using his good arm. He gnashed his teeth and groaned.

The other leg was useless, twisted in that way which was nauseating to look at. Blood all around him. Leaking from somewhere she couldn't see. His flaccid penis half out of his pants, dangling like a broken finger.

He forced himself up, balancing on one knee, and gave her a determined look.

He was only hastening his death.

"I have to go," she said. "I'm burning daylight."

"Just help me. Up. To the cabin."

"No way. You'll never make it."

"You'll never make. It either."

She stopped again. Keeping her back turned, she said, "Yes I will."

But his words pierced to the core. She needed more time. It was already too late to leave. The sun would set — these days it was getting dark by seven thirty — and she'd still be in the woods. Despite all her internal pep talks, it was a major concern.

Carson shouted and fell over.

He was done, lying face down on the rocks now, his body going through spasms. He coughed and gagged up more blood. He had multiple breaks and fractures, internal as well as external bleeding, probably a concussion.

She moved closer to him.

What are you doing?

"Tell me where we are. Maybe you do that, Carson, and you won't wind up in hell."

Carson's lips scraped against the rock. He was trying to talk. She crawled back onto the rocks and leaned down to hear.

"Jones. West. Canada."

She felt a shiver. "Canada? We didn't cross any border." West Canada made no sense. Did he mean British Columbia? That was on the other side of the continent. "What's Jones? Who is it? Is that Leno's real name?"

"I go through. Black to get out."

"Black?"

"Forest."

It was exasperating. He wasn't making any sense. "This is a black forest? What does that mean?"

"Black river . . ."

"How do I get out? We came near a trail on the way in. There's got to be more. Or a ranger station. I think DEC sets up posts in case of lost hikers."

A thought suddenly occurred to her and she couldn't believe she hadn't considered it before: She needed to build a signal fire. The smoke could potentially be seen for miles. Especially if they were looking for her, if they had a general idea of where she might be.

For God's sake, there was a wood stove in the cabin. Firewood piled right beside it. The wood had grayed and grown cobwebs but it would burn.

She scrambled off the rocks again and jogged up the trail. If Carson was calling after her, he'd finally lost his voice and she couldn't hear.

She didn't look back.

* * *

There were no matches. Not near the wood stove, not in the kitchen, nowhere in the cabin. Not a single ever-loving match.

Carson had lit the oil lamp. They had to be here. Unless he had those, too. She looked through all of his things again, scattered over the plank floor.

While she searched, she kept checking the wristwatch, second-guessing herself.

This is pitiful. You should be on your way.

It was almost one in the afternoon. It had taken six hours to hike in, give or take. She was pushing it now. Every minute she dallied at the cabin increased her chances of running into darkness before she could escape the woods, if she was still going to do that.

You should have left hours ago.

—A fire is better. When you're lost, they tell you to stay put anyway.

David still smoked. He tried to conceal it but of course she knew he snuck them. There was probably a lighter stashed out on the back porch near wherever he hid the cigarettes.

She searched every odd place in the cabin, any conceivable hiding spot. She checked for loose floorboards. She went out to the porch and dragged her fingers under the lip of the roof. Mouse shit and more cobwebs but no matches.

It flashed through her mind that she could try friction, or a makeshift flint using rocks, but that would take a while and ensure she was staying here another night, not a savory prospect. What if she wound up unable to get a fire going after spending all this time? Then she would've just wasted a day, no matter what the experts supposedly said about staying put. She had to make a decision: commit to a fire, or hike out right now?

CHAPTER TWENTY-TWO

Katie's husband hadn't just stepped out for a cigarette. Cross found him in a smaller building on the property, digging out hiking gear. There was a growing pile which included Nalgene water bottles, boots, binoculars, a compass, a sleeping bag. He emerged from the building with another armload and spied Cross.

"I'm not just sitting around anymore. I can't do it. She's out there."

"David—"

"I'll join the search in Bakers Mills. You saw the picture. She's in the woods."

"Listen, we were hoping for a geotag on the photo they sent; no luck. But there was a timestamp. Very likely that shot was taken *after* the stop in Bakers Mills."

David stood, chest heaving from exertion, and dropped the supplies at his feet.

Cross said, "You know, is this . . . ? I think you need to consider what you're doing, ask yourself what's best for Katie . . ."

David just stared.

Cross started to speak again when David punched the door beside him, cracking it.

"Ah! Goddammit! I can't just *sit* here!"

Cross held up his hands. "Please. Give me just five minutes. Five minutes, can you do that?"

David regarded Cross with haunted eyes. Then he turned and disappeared into the dark building.

Cross trotted back into the main house.

Jean and Sybil Calumet were clearly fighting upstairs, their tense voices audible. Gloria was alone in the kitchen, talking on the phone, pacing, looking upset.

The place had spun deeper into chaos.

Cross looked through the front windows. More news vans had arrived, growing the media village at the foot of the hill. The troopers had their hands full keeping the eager reporters behind the police tape.

"They want another statement," Gates said, drifting close.

"What do the feds say about press statements?"

"Same as we thought: The abductors aren't supposed to know anything. But I don't think they were guessing about the FBI being here. They knew."

Cross looked at the dining room door. "Bouchard brought the agents in his own car, right?"

She nodded.

"Okay. So they're monitoring the news. That could mean they're in a town or something. Or one of them is. Or they've got internet, at least."

Gates led him to the next room, a study turned partly into a music studio. On the way they passed the staircase and heard the Calumets still arguing.

She pulled the door to the study closed. "Or someone here is talking to them."

"I don't think so."

She raised her eyebrows. "Can you be sure?"

"No. But think of the sloppy mistakes the kidnappers have made. The baby rattle left behind — turns out it belonged to one of the Tremblay's grandkids. It just fell out of the minivan, probably when they were trapping Katie in there. And the partial print. And sending a photo by phone. This is bush-league stuff."

"They're smart enough to have set up a Swiss bank account, maybe even knowing the moves the feds would make. At least anticipating they'd get involved."

Cross fell silent, wondering how what he was about to ask next would go over. He looked at Gates levelly. "Listen, Brennan wants to go off and find her."

"Oh boy . . ."

"He gave us some names, right? Where did we get?"

Gates sat down in an elegant wing back chair and took out a small spiral-bound notebook from her pocket. She wet her finger and flipped through.

"I found Henry Fellows, the ex-partner. He lives in White Plains; he runs a small business there. The ex-chef, Eric Dubois, is working at the Olive Garden in Manhattan. Kind of a step down." She glanced up. "You seemed to think the Dubois thing had some legs."

Cross leaned against a massive electronic keyboard. The thing was so big you could stick a mast in the center and sail away to Bora Bora with it. "Maybe. Chefs are temperamental." He smiled but she remained serious. He listened.

"Lee Beck has got a pretty good thing going as an estate lawyer, putting together wills, that sort of thing. Maybe there's resentment there from one of these people, or maybe Brennan is grasping at straws. His wife has been kidnapped; he's desperate."

"That's what I'm saying. So, look, you know what I want to do. I want to get back to Anderton Correctional and talk to Vickers' former cellmates while we're still waiting on the court order. The AW set me up time for us to interview them. If there's any connection to one of these people, maybe it tumbles out."

"Good."

"And I want to take David Brennan with me."

She blinked. "You want to take him to *Anderton* with you?"

"For the interviews. He may recognize a name, make a connection I don't. He'll feel like he's doing something; maybe it will calm him down so we don't have someone else go missing. And he'll be with me — I can keep an eye on him."

Cross looked at the closed door to the study, thinking how stiff and tight-lipped David and Gloria were around the Calumets. "Plus, whatever this family has going on — we separate them, maybe we'll learn more."

"Justin, we don't want him to know every detail of what and how we're investigating. His deposition describes him waking up, seeing his wife's text. She's the only one who could corroborate where he was in the twenty-four hours prior to that — and she's been abducted."

"Besides one disorderly conduct fifteen years ago, and some speeding tickets, he's never been arrested. We've got nothing, no reason to suspect him. If he's acting, Dana, he's a master. The guy is a wreck."

"He could be a wreck for any number of reasons. He could have been forced into something that—"

Cross was shaking his head. "I think he's legit."

"My point is, we don't know anything."

"You're right. We don't. But let me take him. He's not going to do anything with me there. Otherwise, he's going to run off after his wife."

"You know we can't let him do that. If it comes to that, we'll have to arrest him."

"Exactly. And then what? He'll be in our custody anyway."

She thought about it, shaking her head and staring at the floor. "Okay. I'll clear it with BCI." She started for the door and stopped. "But this is on you, okay? And you can tell Brennan that the troopers are all on the lookout in Bakers Mills and searchers covering miles of woods. We're not just twiddling our thumbs."

"I told him. But they're not there. They switched vehicles. I'm more sure of it all the time."

"Then where the hell did they go? Okay, you've got Katie Calumet, someone fairly recognizable — certainly now that she's all over the news. Where do you take her?"

"Someplace remote."

"Well," she said, glancing out the window, "this is the Adirondacks. We've got millions of acres of 'remote.'"

CHAPTER TWENTY-THREE

Carson hadn't moved from the rocks, where he lay on his stomach, head twisted to the side.

His breathing seemed less labored and he was babbling. As Katie approached, she thought he was in some kind of euphoria. A stage just preceding death, perhaps.

"We used to drive into the Bronx when we were just kids and we'd score dime bags on Fordham Road. My parents put me in a religious school for acting and we'd sing Jesus songs."

When she was within a few feet, his wild eyes focused on her.

"What kind of parents do that to a kid?"

He began to sob again. He mashed his face into the rock and cried, the words mostly unintelligible. More about his family. About the first girl he'd raped. Blood spurted from his nose.

Katie felt cold inside. She still hated Carson. He'd done terrible things to her. To other people.

"It's alright, Troy."

He looked up at the sound of his name, his eyes wet and shot through with a filigree of burst capillaries. He was just about the most pathetic thing she'd ever seen, his body shattered, the life draining out of him. His blood was drying, staining the rocks black. Except for what still seeped from his nose and dribbled from his mouth.

Katie turned her head at the sound of a crow cawing from the branches of a large evergreen.

"I'm sorry," he moaned. "Katie, I'm sooorrreeee."

It was becoming unbearable. Compassion or no.

"Kill me," he said. His eyes went wider, darting around, and he tried to lift himself up with his one good arm. "Katie. Take that hatchet and kill me."

She considered it. She'd already psyched herself up and thought she just might. But now, this close to him, imagining herself driving the sharp, heavy wedge into Troy's skull — it just wasn't in her.

Instead, she lay the blanket she'd brought down from the cabin over him.

He moaned as she did, resting his head again, resigned, realizing his death would be more painful and slow than a mercy killing. He mumbled and apologized some more, but his voice was failing, his train of thought off the rails.

Troy talked about his parents like he'd regressed to childhood. His tone took on a petulant quality, and then he growled with anger as he disparaged his father. "Fucking asshole never loved anyone but himself."

Katie listened, her hand lightly touching Carson's back, and she looked up at the sky.

"Who hired you, Troy?"

"He hit me. I never listened and so he just fuckin hit me. My mother watched. She was weak. He was the boss. She was too . . ." His words trailed off into something unintelligible.

"Troy? Who hired you? Was it a man named Henry Fellows?"

She couldn't understand his response. He seemed to have lost the power of speech at last. She repositioned so she was on her knees and leaned her head down.

His breath was sour. "Leno."

"What's Leno's real name?"

The light was fading from his eyes. He could no longer focus on her but stared into some middle distance.

"Where am I?" she asked. "You said 'black.' Black what?"

His body jerked, as if with intense hiccups, and he stilled. He drew another breath, then another. His lips moved, but no words came out.

Then he was dead.

Carson — Troy — was no longer there. Just his body, broken and befouled, lying on the rocks.

She started going through his pockets. She held her breath, avoiding the stench. Her hand became wet with his urine and blood.

She diverted her mind, wondering where he'd gone, where his soul, if he had such a thing, had traveled.

She didn't necessarily believe in hell. But she hadn't ruled out some other trajectory for the energy that once animated a person.

It had to go somewhere.

Her hand closed on the book of matches in one of his cargo pockets. Her heart pounding with relief, she pulled it out. Generic, white covering. Twenty matches left inside, give or take.

She stowed them in her zip pocket and climbed away. Before leaving Carson once and for all, she took a final look back.

The profundity of feelings conjured memories of her mother. Sounds, mostly, that Monica Calumet had made — singing, laughter. The way she'd smelled. The way she'd looked in the casket, when Katie was sixteen. It hadn't looked like her mother there, laid out in the satin lining, the white lace of the dress high around her neck. It had looked like someone had made a statue and placed it there, and her real mother was somewhere else.

Katie began the climb back to the clearing. She gathered some fir boughs along the way that had been shaken loose by recent storms — anything wet she could put in the wood stove to create thicker plumes of smoke.

Back in the cabin, she started the fire by shredding the six-pack carrier and applying kindling. Once it was going, she made herself another meal, forced it down. She added the wood from the pile nearby. She then used the outhouse (a wretched place, listing to one side, the boards rotting) and got ready for the next step.

Gathering rocks from the high grass and around the perimeter was tough with her bad hand and sprained finger, but she selected those at least as big as a volleyball and arranged them in the center of the clearing. She spent a good deal of time tamping down the grass so that the rocks would be visible from above.

As she worked, she imagined what people might think, watching her. Maybe it was the way Carson thought. Like life was really a movie, and the audience was judging every moment.

She should have left already!

—No, no, this is smart. When you're lost in the woods it's better to stay where you are.

Bullshit. Run, girl, run!

She wasn't running, though. At least, not yet. Her body still ached everywhere, and she'd only just stopped bleeding. Her wrists were actually the worst — possibly getting infected, the gauze coming loose by the time she'd finished with the rocks — her arms sore and sprained finger throbbing despite being ginger about it.

She'd tried to put away the experience with Carson. The molestations, the brutal assaults, watching him die. Tried to push it all off a mental edge, the way Carson had gone off the edge.

It left a void.

The void sucked in a darkness, inky-black like the shroud, where things lurked unseen.

Drawing closer.

Causing her to think terrible thoughts. Like she was never going to make it out of this.

Like she should just end it herself.

Even if she did make it out, she'd never be the same. She'd want to see around every corner. She'd shrink from human touch. Maybe even her husband's.

The cabin was too hot with the wood stove cranked, so she lay down in the grass near the letters she'd spelled out.

SOS

CHAPTER TWENTY-FOUR

David Brennan stared out the car window in a daze. Cross switched on the wipers as a light rain began to fall.

They drove north along the interstate toward Anderton Correctional.

It hadn't taken much convincing to get David along. He seemed ready to do whatever it took to get Katie back.

Cross asked, "What's going on with your family?"

David sighed, said nothing for a moment. Then, "Jean made some bad investments. He's hurting. Sybil started to take over. She fired their financial manager, hired a new firm."

"Who's the former manager?"

"A guy named Perry Swan. But no suspicion there. He and Jean still play tennis; they're friends."

"You sure?"

"Yeah, I'm sure. In fact, I'm surprised Perry hasn't shown up yet. He and Sybil aren't the best of pals, but he loves those two. Katie and Gloria, I mean."

"How about Gloria? Tell me about her."

David batted at his pockets. "Mind if I smoke?"

"Go ahead. I'll take one, too."

They lit up and David went on. "Gloria's got that younger sibling thing. You know, a bit enabled, a bit babied. Her father gave her a lot of money to get her business going in Brooklyn. She's got a restaurant there of her own, and a whole foods store."

"How does she do?"

"She does alright. She's had a little scandal, though."

"Tell me about it."

"It's been resolved, I think. She had a couple health code violations."

"Bad? Like, forcing her to shut down?" Cross was reminded of Gloria pacing around on the phone, looking distraught.

"No, I mean, she's in the clear. I don't know, exactly."

"Is she married?"

"She was close, then she called it off. I think Gloria's scared of commitment. Maybe it . . . I don't know. But so she . . . How do I put it? She's always a bit *embarrassed* around her parents. Does that make sense? Alone, maybe she feels accomplished. But being with them, they're a reminder of how she's gotten help."

"It makes sense." Cross flicked ash out the open window and felt drops of rain sneaking in. "How about you and Katie's parents?"

"Yeah, so, you know. We're good. They were skeptical of me at first — her father was; Sybil wasn't on the scene yet — because of how much older I am. I don't see them much. This is the first time we've been together since last Christmas. I mean, all of us. Katie went down earlier this year and spent a week. They have a place in Dobbs Ferry, near the restaurant, right on the water. And they have a huge apartment in Manhattan. But I think they've listed the apartment."

"Because of the financial troubles, you mean? They're looking to sell."

"Yeah. That apartment is worth something astronomical."

"Penthouse on the Upper East Side, I can imagine. But you think they're hurting now, enough so that 20 million might be an unreachable goal?"

Just hearing and saying these numbers aloud, Cross felt surreal. He'd made 72,000 the previous year, after taxes. Marty did a bit better, and for a time they'd been comfortable.

He repeated the question, "You think the ransom is too high for them?"

"Yeah."

"So maybe this is someone who doesn't know the financial situation of the Calumets all that intimately?"

"Well, no one does, really. This is all family business. To anyone else, you know, people take it at face value. It looks like Jean and Sybil are loaded, doing just fine. Even I don't know the half of it, just this little bit Katie has shared with me in confidence."

At the mention of his wife's name, David became morose. He took a long drag, finishing the smoke, and pitched the butt out the window. He seemed to regret it instantly and said, "Shit, shouldn't have done that. Katie would kill me."

"For smoking?"

"For littering."

Cross flicked his own butt out the window. "We're in it together."

* * *

They arrived at Anderton Correctional, the huge wall foreboding, and went through the tedious process of gaining entry. After they'd turned out their pockets and endured the metal detector, Carl Brill, the AW, met with them and led them to the visitation area, peppering Cross with questions about the case. Cross kept his answers short.

Brill had procured them a private room. Cross and David sat to one side of a scratched-up table. After waiting a few minutes in uncomfortable silence, Cross second-guessing the decision to bring David, he heard the rattle of chains.

The door opened and two corrections officers brought the inmate named Alex Hernandez into the room and sat him down.

Cross had a small tape recorder he switched on. "Is this alright?"

Hernandez eyed the device and shrugged. He slouched in the chair. Tattoos covered his body, right up to his jawline. There was a teardrop inked beneath his eye. He was short, solidly built. After glancing at Cross and David, his eyes wandered the bare room.

"So, Mr. Hernandez. Thanks for meeting with me—"

Cross was interrupted when the door opened. Brill entered the room, dragged a chair to the corner, and sat down.

Cross resumed. "It's my understanding you spent time here with Troy Vickers, as a cellmate. Is that correct?"

Hernandez stared at Cross for a long time. Cross held the man's eye.

"Answer the question," Brill barked from the corner.

"This is gonna help me, right?" Hernandez asked. He looked from the AW to Cross. "Reduce my shit?"

"I'm gonna look into it," Cross said. "That's all I can promise."

Hernandez looked disappointed, but said, "Yeah, yeah. He was my celly."

"For how long? What were the dates — you remember?"

"Nah, man. I don't remember no dates."

Brill spoke up. "June eighteenth to April tenth — almost a year."

"Okay," Cross said, feeling a thrill. "So that's a fair amount of time . . ."

Hernandez bounced his knee. He looked at David. "So someone snatched your old lady, huh? I seen you on the news, bro. The Vic took her? Ah man; condolences and shit. Must be bustin' you up, right?"

Cross held out his hand. He didn't want David to engage Hernandez.

"Did Vickers ever talk about anything like that? About kidnapping someone for ransom?"

"Yeah. Yeah, we talked. Shit, we shared a lot. We read poetry, we measured each other's dicks, we got to know each other. What does that mean, 'look into it'? I'm gonna get something for this, or not?"

Brill snapped at Hernandez, "Inmate one-oh-one-four-six-nine, knock it off. Just answer the investigator's questions. You understand what he's asking."

Hernandez gave Brill a menacing side look. "Yeah, I know what they're asking. And he knows what *I'm* asking."

Brill opened his mouth but Cross had an answer. "Mr. Hernandez, if this ever goes to trial, it will be me who refers you to the DA to testify. And if that time comes, you and your lawyer can negotiate for a reduction in your sentence. But without me, without this moment right now, and your cooperation, that chance will never come."

Hernandez stared off, unfocused, letting it sink in. Then his eyes cleared. "Yeah man, yeah. I'll tell you everything I know. He liked the canned peaches at jug-up, I can start with that."

Cross sat back, waited.

"He, ah, he talked about shit."

Cross tilted his head.

"Women," Hernandez said. "And, ah . . . he ah, he was gonna do something."

"Like what?"

Hernandez looked like he was thinking, coming up with something to say.

Cross exchanged looks with Brill, who leaned forward in his seat. "Inmate, you told me that you and Vickers—"

"Well maybe I ain't saying shit until I get something. Okay? And that's fuckin that. No pay, no play."

It was going in circles. Brill shook his head and looked at Cross again. "Investigator Cross, I'm sorry. I think Mr. Hernandez has the wrong idea about this."

"Okay, Mr. Hernandez, last chance. You—"

"Hey man, Vickers was in seg for nine months, okay? I don't remember dates, but I remember that. I had my own cell for practically a year."

"Is that true?" Cross asked Brill.

"Gen pop can be a hostile place," said Brill, reddening, "and Vickers was convicted for rape. He had some issues, and we separated him for his health."

"So Mr. Hernandez here didn't really spend much time with him after all . . ."

"That's not true! I got to know him real good. You don't hear what I'm sayin'?"

The tension in the room was ratcheting up, and Cross's heart was beating harder than usual. Like not having a lot of money, he also didn't spend much time in maximum security prisons. But the truth was Hernandez had barely been a month in the same cell as Troy Vickers. He was just playing a card, trying to get something for nothing, and Brill had neglected to mention solitary confinement before now.

"Thank you for your time, sir," Cross said, then nodded at Brill. "That's all."

"Naw man, naw . . ." Hernandez became more agitated. "Come on, man! I'm gonna testify or what? You *said* I was gonna get my chance, cop. I'm cooperating, motherfucker!"

Brill jumped up and knocked on the door. The corrections officers reentered to remove Hernandez, still yelling, spit flying from his lips.

The door closed. Brill wore the guilt on his wide face. "Sorry about that."

"Yeah," Cross said. "No problem."

He glanced at David, who seemed calm but kept staring at the door.

A few minutes later the staff brought in the next inmate and Brill took up his position in the corner. Hopefully this one would be better.

Louis Dauber was thin, effeminate, traces of eye shadow beneath his jittery globes.

"Vickers and Dauber were cellmates for four months until Vickers' release," Brill said, then added: "Together the whole time."

They went through the same song and dance about the possibility of a reduced sentence, but Dauber seemed less concerned about quid pro quo than Hernandez had. Cross asked, "Did Vickers mention anything about any crimes he had committed, or planned to commit after his release?"

Dauber shifted position and crossed his legs, chains banging together. "This is about that abduction, right? That's some cold shit. I been abducted. I been abducted by the State of New York."

"Quiet with that," Brill grumbled.

"Well? So what? It's true. It's true, *sir*. I am a kidnap victim. I get raped in here, and they put me in with a rapist, how's that?"

"Enough!" Brill said, rising. He eyeballed the recorder on the table, then he looked at Cross.

Cross dipped his head and held out a hand again. He wasn't interested in investigating the penal system.

"Please keep your comments focused on the matter at hand," Cross said to Dauber, and Brill slowly sat back down, temporarily mollified.

"I *am* talking about the matter *at hand*," Dauber said.

"At any time did Vickers talk about kidnapping, or mention a woman by name he was planning to kidnap?"

"Man, we don't talk about that shit."

David interjected before Cross could stop him. "Yeah you do. And when you're not talking about your past crimes, you're thinking about the future. Ways you're going to make it on the outside."

Dauber looked at David like he was seeing something familiar. "What do you know?"

Cross decided to let it play out.

"I know enough." David was firm but in control. "Give me some of Vickers' ideas. What was he going to do when he got out?"

Dauber uncrossed his legs and slumped back in his seat. He picked at his fingernails, bitten beyond the nubs. "Man, that's all he ever talked about. His boy. Johnny M."

Cross jumped back in. "Johnny M.?"

"Uh-huh. Johnny M. Talked about that guy like he was bottled Jesus."

"Like what? What did he say?"

Dauber scowled, looked at Cross like he didn't get it. "I dunno, man. It's not the specifics."

"The specifics are exactly what it is. What did he say about Johnny M.?"

"You don't get it. Let me tell you — okay? Everybody needs protection. Either you're the biggest and baddest — and there's only a few of those — or you need protection. You need a gang, you need a protector. Like me, you know, I'm someone's bitch. Alright? I ain't gonna hide it. What am I gonna do? I'm gonna take it up the ass or I'm gonna take it in the—"

"Inmate," Brill said. "Curb that."

"It's true. No one wants to hear it. But Vickers, he had someone."

"Johnny M."

Dauber nodded and kept picking at his fingers. "Yup."

"But on the outside, you mean. Someone to help him get set up, or whatever, once he got out."

"Right."

"Can you tell me anything about Johnny M.? How they met? What he was into?"

Dauber said nothing more. He had to hunch over to bite at a hangnail.

"Answer," Brill ordered.

Dauber flicked a look at the AW. "I already did. Vickers never talked about abduction, just Johnny M. That's all I know."

It went on for another ten minutes, with Dauber repeating the refrain, *That's all I know*. David seemed satisfied by it, once more lost in thought.

The staff hauled in McSweeney next, a large man who mumbled when he spoke. He'd only shared a cell with Vickers for a week. They didn't talk about much of anything. McSweeney had never heard Vickers refer to anyone called Johnny M.

"Oh . . . well," he amended toward the end of the interview, "he did say he had a visitor one day. But it was a lady."

* * *

Cross was waiting for the guard to wave him through the security portal when his phone buzzed. Gates informed him that the court order was signed and a trooper was almost to the prison with it.

"That's good timing."

"I spoke to Jean Calumet," Gates explained.

"So he's not all hat and no cattle, I take it."

"What?"

"He used his influence with the judge. He wasn't bluffing."

"Oh. Correct." She paused. "When you get back we're going to have a talk about your use of cowboy humor, Justin."

* * *

Ten minutes later, the trooper had passed the court order to a correctional officer who brought it to Cross in a sealed envelope. Cross had the staff escort David to the waiting room and Brill conceded to access of the visitation list.

They had to relocate to another part of the prison and walked together through a cell block filled with the echoing chatter of a hundred inmates.

Brill seemed uneasy. "The mouths on these guys. That's one of the worst parts of it. I started this job twelve years ago — I was a good Catholic man. The stuff you hear in this place. It's just nasty." He shook his head, contrite. "You do me a favor? Maybe those interview recordings . . . you know? Nobody needs to hear that. We can destroy those, okay?"

"Sorry, I can't do that." Cross knew Brill was more worried about liability than he was with the sacrality of the prison. Men talking about being raped, men going into segregation — which was largely being phased out of penal institutions — wasn't for public consumption.

"Well," Brill said, getting a tone. "What if I have a problem with that?"

"I'm sorry if you do. I guess you'll have to speak to your warden. Our court order, from a state judge, covers everything we're doing here."

They stopped at the doors to the visitation area and a corrections officer buzzed them open. Cross went through and the AW stayed behind, glowering through the reinforced glass at Cross. Then Brill turned on his heel and strode away, tearing into the envelope.

The secretary from the phone the previous day greeted Cross and took him into another room.

"Any nice nail colors today?"

"Ha ha."

Christ, when were people gonna let it go?

The secretary printed out Vickers' list of visitors. It was very short, consisting of two names. One was Elaine Vickers. Good chance it was his mother or sister — Troy Vickers was unmarried.

The other name caught his eye. Janice Montgomery.

Johnny M, Janice Montgomery.

Cross bet there was a connection.

CHAPTER TWENTY-FIVE

She woke up with a start to a rustling in the forest. The light was waning. Her heart pounding, she sat up then saw a doe and her two fawns grazing along the edge of the woods.

I fell asleep. I can't believe I fell asleep.

After the long, fitful night, then climbing down to Carson twice, exhausted from spelling out her SOS in heavy rocks, she'd passed out in the grass.

Katie got to her feet.

The doe heard her, twitched its ears, stuck its white tail in the air, and leapt away, the nimble fawns bounding after.

The wristwatch hung from a rope she'd tied around her waist. It was going on five in the evening. She'd been out about three hours.

The hatchet!

It was in the grass where she'd slept. She picked it up.

A tendril of smoke rose from the chimney. She went inside to find the wood was cinder and the wet stuff long gone. She jammed some fresh boughs in the stove. The needles glowed red and snapped in the heat.

She took the urn to the well and refilled it. Then tossed a bit of the water on the fire, enjoying the hiss it made, grateful for the billows of smoke.

What had she been thinking before she'd succumbed to fatigue?

It was distant now, the blackness somewhat retreated.

She didn't even want to remember, exactly.

She went into the clearing, frustrated how the high grass was already springing back up, partly concealing her hard work.

Futility, that's what she'd been feeling. Profound loneliness.

She sat in the grass and hung her head. Thought of David — pictured him as if he were beside her, his hair drawn back in a ponytail, his big grin and bright eyes. Odd how she was feeling closer to him with each passing hour.

Though music was his passion, David had supported himself as a chef. After they'd dated for just over a year, he'd gone to work for her father in one of the restaurants. David had always said how he admired Jean's work ethic; a successful career built from nothing. But not long after they'd started working together, David walked away from it. They transplanted to his family home in Hazleton, and, living more cheaply, he could again focus on music. No gigging, just studio work.

He'd never really talked about his falling out with Jean, much as she'd tried to get him to open up about it. She figured a husband and father-in-law's relationship was tricky.

Her relationship with Sybil was tricky, too.

Katie told herself it was an old cliché — the young girl disliking the wicked stepmother. Sybil wasn't wicked, but the women kept their distance.

More now that Jean had mysteriously given Sybil so much clout in his business affairs. Husbands and wives split the spoils, that was the rule, and Katie knew her father was an equitable man — it wasn't that. Sybil deserved equity, but Katie and Glo worried over what it might be about.

If he was covering up an illness, they wanted to know, wanted to help. Maybe he was reluctant to be truthful because they'd lost their mother.

She and Gloria had done some poking around, got nowhere, and eventually, over the previous Christmas, confronted him about it. Just her and Glo, cornering him in the Upper East Side home.

He'd told them he was fine. Said that he wanted "another pair of eyes on things."

Katie sat in the clearing and thought it all through, as she had many times before, coming back to the same place: If it was a lie, and he was truly unwell, Sybil being able to sign things and know the family finances was a good thing — the family business could carry on if something were to happen. But if it was true, and he'd only given her the keys to his kingdom because he thought he needed help — Katie wondered about that, too.

He'd never done that with her mother.

She continued to turn it over in her mind as she rose and headed toward the outhouse. On her way, she heard another noise from the woods.

She turned, expecting to see the deer again.

This time a man was there, in the trees, watching her.

Katie suddenly couldn't move. Her legs weren't responding.

She broke the spell at last and ran for the cabin. She slammed the front door closed and walked backward, gripping the hatchet, until her legs bumped the bed.

Stupid, she thought, suddenly feeling like the idiot in the horror movie who runs deeper into the house when they should be hightailing it out the front door: *You just trapped yourself.*

But running hadn't been an option. The bag she'd packed — Carson's bag — with the liquor bottle of water, climbing rope, and flashlight — was in the cabin. Sprinting into the woods, directionless and afraid, would've been the wrong move.

The doubt bubbled up.

Had she even seen anyone?

Katie moved cautiously toward the window, peered out through the dusty pane of glass. The woods were thick with balsam fir, the roll of another peak visible in the distance. But no human beings anywhere.

She returned to the bed and sat down, her heart skipping beats. She stuck her head between her legs and took several deep breaths.

Leno.

It could be Carson's partner, back in the woods with them because something had happened.

But the figure had looked like an entirely different person than the one who'd dabbed at her wounds and taken a picture of her the previous day. Even with the balaclava mask, she would've seen the wild gray beard and shaggy hair. His clothes looked different, too, layered and tattered.

Maybe an associate of theirs, then.

A third man; someone sent to check up on her.

There may have even been a rifle in his grip.

He wouldn't be a searcher, not alone, not this far into the wilderness, with no planes or helicopters in sight since she'd been watching the sky.

The cabin was beastly hot, the wood stove still cranking. It had to be 100 degrees in the unvented space. She couldn't stay here long in the stifling heat. She wondered if she could even keep on staying at the cabin at all with someone else in the area.

Maybe whoever it was had been drawn by the smoke. Maybe he could help her.

She watched the wood stove, saw the licks of fire through the seams of the cast iron door. She thought about getting such a heavy thing out this deep into the woods. Must've taken four or five men. Maybe he was one of them and this was his place.

Or, he was mentally deranged. He might be desperate, hungry, who knew.

Had she even just seen anyone?

She tried to recall the moment with clarity: She'd been thinking about her family. Sitting in the grass, feeling beaten, missing her husband, just awakened after sheer exhaustion had forced her into a dead sleep. It could have been a dream, something left over from sleep.

The cabin was so hot, her hands sweating, the hatchet slipping in her grip.

She made a sudden decision, took up the backpack, and ran out the front door. Scanning the woods, she cut through the clearing, heart pounding in her chest. This was it. She was going to get the hell out of these woods, even if the daylight was fading.

More movement — in the corner of her eye.

Katie cried out involuntarily and halted in her tracks. The motion had been to her right, something low to the ground, just at the edge of the clearing. She dared to look fully in that direction and she saw it, loping along, then slipping out of sight.

A dog?

Her hands trembled, sweat cooling on her skin, pulse pounding in her temples.

She'd had occasional heart palpitations since her teenage years. They came on particularly during periods of stress, but recently they had worsened. David had worn her down about seeing a doctor, who'd diagnosed it as tachycardia.

It felt like her heart was fluttering in her throat. Katie clutched her chest and stared off where the dog — if it *was* a dog — had disappeared.

"Hello?"

The tremble in her voice only intensified her alarm.

She looked at the cabin, twenty yards away, front door gaping open. Too hot in there, but not safe out here, either — there was possibly a man, maybe his dog, circling the grounds.

Or, not a dog — something else.

Her heart was out of control. She dropped to her knees and lowered her head again.

Calm down. Calm down . . .

There was another noise; the snap of a twig. She stood and broke into a shambling run toward the cabin, gripping the hatchet with two hands, gritting her teeth against the fear.

She stopped on the porch and waited, feeling the intense heat emanate from the open door. She needed to ventilate the damn place.

With a rush of inspiration, not caring whether it was smart in the long term or not, Katie ran into the cabin, shut the door. Then she smashed the windows with the hatchet.

The act was terrifically satisfying, and the sound of the breaking glass imbued her with a sense of power. Maybe whoever or whatever was out there would be scared off.

She felt the air breezing through, and the cabin instantly started to cool. Not by much — it was still over ninety degrees — but enough that she felt encouraged. Now she needed to lie down. Her heart kept slamming. Her vision was spotting, like she wasn't getting enough oxygen.

She dropped onto the bed, willing herself calm, and took long, slow breaths. She pictured herself together with David, as they'd been last Christmas in the city, bundled up in the cold, walking the streets, hailing a cab, and laughing as they rode uptown amid the twinkling lights.

She imagined herself on her morning runs, the mist hanging suspended in the air, the drowsy prattling of the Ausable River as she ran alongside its banks.

Gradually, as she relaxed, her heart slotted back into a regular rhythm.

But she didn't dare get up yet. She'd closed the door when she'd come in — no lock on it, but it barricaded against any animals, at least.

You're losing your mind. You're still in shock. You're imagining things.

When she felt strong enough she rose from the bed, checked through the window again. Still no sign of anyone.

She wasn't in the habit of hallucinating, but she'd never been abducted and dragged to the middle of the mountain wilderness before, either. Whether someone was really out there or not, one thing was clear — she couldn't escape the woods in a blind panic. She needed the benefit of full daylight, she needed her wits about her, and she needed her heart to beat steadily.

Leaving under any other circumstances was a bad idea.

She stayed in the cabin, keeping track of time. She'd let ten minutes pass, then see. She moved near the door. It was hinged so that it swung into the cabin. If anyone barged in, they were going to get a hatchet in their chest. *How's that for a horror movie?* She wielded the hatchet like a baseball bat and flexed her legs, bouncing a little.

A sense of absurdity washed over her: The idea that anyone out here was working with her captors seemed more unlikely as time passed. Carson was dead. By now they would've discovered his body and taken action. Anyone else, unless they were completely deranged, could possibly help her.

It might be some kind of mountain man. She'd read about Adirondack hermits, men who cast off society to live in rugged isolation.

Feeling a bit more confident, the new idea taking shape, she opened the door. "Hello?"

Her voice echoed in the woods, a lonely sound.

She left the backpack on the porch and moved cautiously into the clearing, looking everywhere. Her heart rate was up again, but the beats were holding steady.

She stopped then continued a few steps, stopped again, listening intently. She moved toward the cliff where Carson had fallen.

Carefully nearing the edge, keeping low and spreading out her weight, Katie looked down and her breath caught in her throat.

The animals down below were picking at Carson's corpse.

Coyotes, five or six of them, taking their meal. Two of them right on top of Carson, the others nipping at each other. One circled the body then darted in for a bite.

Jesus. Oh Jesus.

She backed away, mindful of her footing, trying to be quiet. She hurried back to the cabin as fast as she could without making too much noise.

Coyotes.

Not a dog.

Wild animals.

* * *

Katie let the fire die down, just one log at a time to keep it smoldering, then used what water was left in the urn to wash herself, cleaning the dried blood from her body. She cleaned more blood from the cabin floor with the remaining water in the wash tub. After all the scrubbing, she felt stultified and lay down on the mattress. The daylight was waning.

They'd been picking his body apart.

Carson had fallen to his death, and now the animals were eating him.

How had it happened? She'd assumed he'd wanted to relieve himself. It would be just like Carson to decide to step to the edge of the drop, proud to eject a urine stream over the treetops. Then, still a bit drunk from the night before, he'd lost his balance.

But what if that wasn't the right story? What if someone pushed him? If the man she saw was some hermit who had abandoned society and all its trappings, why investigate a cabin showing signs of life? Because he was territorial? Because he was insane?

Smashing the windows felt like a terrible mistake. The cabin was raised off the ground by piles of rocks, footers that helped to elevate the windows, but could a coyote jump through?

She watched out the windows as darkness gathered, jumping at every noise. She needed to calm down. The animals had just fed. Coming across a body on the rocks was one thing; leaping into a log cabin with a living human inside was something else, wasn't it? Unless they were desperate, they'd leave her alone.

She hoped.

CHAPTER TWENTY-SIX

Cross pulled up to the Montgomerys' address on Oak Street. Two state troopers were already at the scene, waiting for him.

"Anyone home?"

"Doesn't look like it," one of the troopers said.

Cross thought the place was typical for Lake Haven, a town triple the size of Hazleton and thirty miles away. The house straddled the line of ramshackle and historic, likely built in the 1950s as a "cure cottage" for sufferers of tuberculosis. Its prominent feature was a huge, rambling porch with multi-paned windows.

The inside looked dark, the place unlived in. No car in the driveway.

The adjoining garage was empty, but for some antique-looking yard equipment.

The troopers joined him in the front yard. He sent one around back and asked the other to stay out front, keep an eye on things. Cross climbed onto the weather-beaten porch and knocked on the front door.

He waited, peering in through the windows. In proximity, there were still only minimal signs of life. A table sat in the center of the living room, covered in tools, as if some remodeling was going on.

According to BCI, Johnny and Janice Montgomery had bought the place just two years before, though it was unclear if they'd used it as a residence or an income property. It was big enough that it could be both, too. BCI was working on more information.

Cross and the trooper watched a compact SUV roll slowly past, the old woman behind the wheel rubbernecking the scene.

When she was gone, Cross knocked on the door again.

They'd been married for five years. Her maiden name was Connolly, and she was born in New York City. Both of them had lengthy rap sheets, though mostly small-time stuff, including a few marijuana possession charges.

Jonathan Montgomery had also been born in New York then moved with his mother to Pennsylvania at age five. He'd been in a juvenile detention center in Pennsylvania but those records were sealed. As a young man, he'd caught his first offense back in New York City selling fake watches. He'd held a series of odd jobs on his résumé prior to moving upstate — high school janitor, convenience store worker, auto mechanic — but had no employment history since he'd relocated.

Janice Connolly had been a nurse in Brooklyn and her record showed a recent charge of theft while employed by the hospital — prescription drugs. It hadn't been proven, but she'd been fired anyway. Her employment record showed a string of waitressing jobs after that; then she, too, seemed to disappear.

Cross thought they sounded like quite a pair. But his enthusiasm ebbed the longer he waited on the porch. If he wanted to go inside, he'd need a search warrant. There was plenty of probable cause at this point; he just needed the official paper like before. It was in the works, but for now he stepped off the porch, shaking his head at the trooper on the front lawn.

The trooper was looking at something down the street, something Cross couldn't see from his angle. He jogged over for a better view.

A pickup truck idled at the intersection a few houses down.

As soon as Cross stepped into the street, the pickup took off with a squeal of tires.

"Go!" Cross yelled at the trooper. He ran to his car, pointing toward the intersection. "Blue Dodge on Spring Street!"

Cross jumped behind the wheel, engine still running, and hit the gas. He screeched around the corner onto the next street.

The pickup rounded a bend in the road up ahead. Cross checked the rearview mirror and saw one of the troopers catching up.

After rounding the bend, there was another intersection. Cross saw the brake lights flare as the pickup dropped down a steep hill.

Holy shit, he thought, he could be on the heels of one of the kidnappers.

The streets were narrow with no shoulders, packed with houses, families. He had to be careful. He tapped the brakes and descended the hill.

The next intersection was a main road leading in and out of Lake Haven. The way it curved, no truck was in sight either direction. Would the driver head out of town or deeper into it?

Cross spun the wheel in a hasty decision and roared toward town.

He grabbed the radio. "Did you see the driver?"

"A little," the trooper said.

"Man or woman?"

"Man."

Cross bulleted through a green light and the trooper behind him flipped on the emergency lights and siren. He listened as the troopers called in the chase to dispatch.

The road dipped, bisecting two business plazas — grocery on the left, banking on the right — and Cross spotted the truck ascending the hill on the other side. At the top of the hill was another streetlight, turned red. The pickup truck shrieked to a halt behind a line of cars. Then it started to go around them.

The truck picked up speed and tore through the intersection. A car coming the other direction swerved to avoid it and blared their horn. On the radio, the dispatcher polled the call to all active deputies and troopers.

There was a one-way street at the bottom of the hill and Cross took it. It was the wrong direction, but mercifully the street was empty. He saw the trooper zip past in his mirrors, headed up the hill after the pickup anyway.

Cross pulled onto the next street, now driving parallel with the other. But he had to slow way down — this was the main strip; people were everywhere. It was late in the afternoon, work was getting out, and tourists abounded.

He turned into a parking lot and weaved his way out the back side, onto another one-way street, until he rejoined with the initial road. It hadn't worked, and the gap between Cross and the pickup had widened.

"Dammit."

The truck was far ahead, having turned onto the road alongside Lake Flower, leaving cars helter-skelter in its wake and pedestrians scrambling. One of the troopers appeared, cruising along in closer pursuit.

Cross slowed for the next intersection and had a moment to think — there was no Dodge Dakota registered to either of the Montgomerys. They had one car, according to the DMV, and it was a Ford F150.

He fell in behind both troopers. The lake slipped past on the right; the lowering sun flickered amid the motels along the shore.

The Dakota led the chase out the other end of town. On the radio, the troopers were calling for a road block.

"Who the fuck is this?" Cross yelled. He was nervous, excited, terrified it would end badly and someone would get hurt. He eased off the gas.

The Dakota swerved around a slower-moving vehicle and the troopers followed. Then the road opened up, the speed limit turned to forty-five, and the Dakota really got going fast.

Cross stomped the gas pedal again, determined to see it through. They were doing sixty, then seventy, eighty.

They flew past SCI Cold Brook. Past a gas station, a restaurant in the middle of nowhere, a golf course, then nothing but a long corridor of tall pines. Doing eighty-five, now ninety.

"Jeeeesus . . ."

The Dakota suddenly swerved. The driver had been trying to overtake another slower vehicle and nearly collided with a car coming the opposite direction. The edge of the tires caught and the truck flipped — once, twice, again — chewing up the soft shoulder. A broken side mirror flew through the air, a window shattered, the metal crunched.

Cross slowed way down and gaped at the spectacular wreck as the Dakota finally came to a rest. The troopers in pursuit slammed on their brakes. More police vehicles arrived from the other direction, lights flashing red and blue through the tire smoke and road dust.

Cross pulled off the road, jumped from his car, and ran toward the truck.

On its side, smashed to hell, the truck engine was pinging. Something dripped. A trooper caught Cross by the arm and held him back. The other trooper was on his radio, calling it in. Everyone on the road had stopped. One motorist left their vehicle and ran over.

"Hey — whoa!" Cross yelled.

"I'm an EMT," the civilian said. But she changed course and approached Cross and the trooper on the road shoulder.

They heard the screech of tires as another motorist hit the brakes. They'd been coming up on the scene too fast, hadn't been paying attention. The car skidded into an angle half on the road and half off, and came to rest.

More sirens in the background as an ambulance made its way.

Closer to the EMT, Cross thought he recognized her. She'd been at other emergency scenes where he'd been involved. He thought her name was Darby.

Most vehicles didn't automatically explode after they crashed like in the movies. Still, caution was prudent. Cross nodded to Darby and they jogged to the Dakota. They saw the man inside through the windshield, bloody and unconscious. Cross scrambled up the vehicle and tried to open the passenger door, which was now like an overhead hatch.

The door stuck.

Cross called through the broken window, "Hey! Hey, can you hear me?"

No response from the driver. Darby climbed up next to Cross. The vehicle groaned and wobbled beneath them, like it might roll over onto the roof.

"Careful," Cross said. "Let's go. Let's get down."

"We need to get him out."

"We need help."

The rest of the police found spots to pull over. Fire police — men from civilian vehicles in bright yellow jackets — put out cones and directed traffic. A few bystanders were out of their cars and stared as the ambulance arrived, siren wailing.

Cross faded into the background as the responders debated what do with the precarious vehicle. The troopers, paramedics, and fire police swarmed it, then tipped it back onto its wheels.

The Dakota slammed down on the ground, upright again but mangled and shattered, the doors crimped shut.

A trooper knocked remaining glass from the passenger window and clambered into the cab. Another climbed up beside him. Cross watched as they hauled the man out.

Darby had wandered close, now standing beside Cross.

She asked, "Who is that?"

"I don't know."

The guy was big, over six feet, and solidly built. It took five responders to lower him onto the stretcher and fit it into the back of the ambulance.

Cross drew near and gave him a closer look. He was mid-forties with graying dark hair, unshaven, blood running from his scalp. Cross wanted to question the guy right now, but he was totally out cold.

Cross nodded to the paramedic standing by. The paramedic hopped in the back of the ambulance and closed the doors, and the ambulance tore away, back toward Lake Haven.

The hospital there was a relatively limited facility when it came to major trauma, Cross thought.

"Probably airlift him to Burlington or Albany," Darby said, picking up on his thoughts as she wandered closer.

"Thank you for your help."

"That was something . . ." She frowned and looked Cross over. "You alright?"

"Yeah. Nothing happened to me."

"Okay, good. Ah man."

Cross tried to focus. "Darby, if you could provide a statement, your contact info, to one of those officers over there, that would be great."

"Of course."

As soon as she was gone, Cross bent forward and grabbed his knees. The world swam for a moment so he closed his eyes and took a deep breath through his nose.

"Holy shit," he whispered.

* * *

The Dakota was registered to Jeffrey A. Gebhart, a carpenter who owned and operated his own small business. Gebhart had a nearly clean record; the only things spotting it were a few minor traffic infractions. He'd been audited once by the IRS.

"So why the hell did he run?" Cross asked the empty room.

Cross was in an office at the state trooper headquarters in Cold Brook, less than a mile from where Gebhart had flipped the truck. Gebhart was now being flown to Albany, as Darby had predicted. He was in critical condition, hanging on to life by a thread.

Gates arrived and Cross filled her in on the events leading up to the chase. "Montgomery might be into flipping properties," Cross told her. "Gebhart works for him as a carpenter, that's my guess."

"So what's he afraid of?"

"He knows something. He's in on this in some way. Otherwise — born and raised in Lake Haven. He's a carpenter, unmarried, just a typical Adirondack boy. Been in business for himself for years. But he was a backcountry caretaker for two summers in his twenties, so . . ."

"For DEC?"

"Yeah. Plus he's got his guide's license," Cross said. "From his Facebook profile, he's got a lot of family who are hunters."

Cross showed Gates pictures of Gebhart and other men posing with game they'd shot — deer, grouse, turkeys, pheasants. In one picture several men were gathered around a rustic cabin with a mountainous backdrop.

Gates leaned over Cross, who could smell her shampoo. Cross was in awe of the senior investigator. She'd had that harrowing case years before involving murders at Plattsburgh College. Her injury was from a window shattering in her face while chasing down a suspect. As a result, she had the leaking eye. Rumors were that the case almost ended her marriage. Yet after a period spent convalescing, reconnecting with her husband and daughters, she'd carried on as an investigator.

And people still talked behind her back, said she was a neglectful mother.

"I'll keep Internal Affairs back for as long as I can, but they're going to need to talk to you, Justin."

"I know."

"They're going to want to know everything . . . how this thing got so—"

"Gebhart ran," Cross said. "Saw cops outside Montgomery's home, and he bolted. He's got no warrants, nothing." He pointed to the picture of the cabin on the screen. "I think the kidnappers brought Katie into the woods."

Gates stepped away and sat down beside Cross. She looked like she was letting the full weight of it settle. "Well, we need to talk to Gebhart's family. And post someone at the hospital."

"What about getting another warrant from Judge King, this time to search any of Gebhart's hunting cabins, or his family's?"

"I want to bring Cobleskill into this."

"Absolutely, let's bring in the DA. Vickers clearly knows Montgomery — Janice Montgomery visited Vickers in jail. My theory is Montgomery knows Gebhart. And Gebhart has backcountry experience, plus a family full of hunters . . ."

"What's Gebhart's status now?" Gates asked.

"Critical condition. Flying into Albany Medical."

Both of them sat back, thinking.

"Someone hires Montgomery to kidnap Katie," Cross said. "Montgomery taps Vickers as his number two. Montgomery has the plan — he gets information from his buddy, Gebhart. Someplace remote to take Katie while they await payment. The hirer — he sets up the accounts. He's the mastermind. Montgomery and Vickers do the heavy lifting. That's what I got, Dana. That's what feels right. I think Katie is out there somewhere, in the park. And I think it's Johnny Montgomery who's been calling from the Tracfone. Just need to confirm it."

Gates stood up, gathered her things, including a photograph of Montgomery from his driver's license.

Cross, still sitting, watched her. "Where you going?"

"We gotta take this to the feds. Plug Montgomery into their cell phone trace, Gebhart too. See if either of them bought a prepaid phone recently and got caught on camera."

"Yeah. Supposed to be they're already doing that with their vast list of accomplices for Vickers." Cross rolled his eyes. "There were none."

"I know. I think Sair was just trying to placate the family."

"Well, we got the real deal now. So what do you want me doing?"

"You've got a friend at DEC, right?"

"Yeah. Laura Broderick. Just bumped into her yesterday morning."

"Pick her brain. Find out what you can about decommissioned ranger stations and privately owned hunting cabins. Let's see what we can learn while we confer with Cobleskill about how tight we can squeeze around Gebhart's family and friends."

CHAPTER TWENTY-SEVEN

Stay put.

That was the conventional directive for someone who became lost in the woods, and she kept coming back to it. Unless you knew what you were doing, were able to gain higher elevation for perspective, knew your windward from your leeward, it was best to remain stationary and wait for rescue.

But I'm not lost, Katie thought, lying on the mattress. Troy had said something about 'black,' which jogged a memory of looking at a map not long ago — was there a Black Mountain? She closed her eyes, tried to bring up the image.

Not Black Mountain . . .

Black River Wild Forest.

She opened her eyes. Was that it? Was that a place? Or was she inventing it based on the dribbling thoughts of a dying man? He'd said Jones, too, and mentioned Canada. Just his synapses firing off at random, pieces of his past, who knew.

Maybe it didn't matter. She was *somewhere*. And if she stayed here, either the stranger might return, or the coyotes might invade.

It was dark now; no way was she getting out of the woods. But come morning, it was time.

She never could keep still, anyway.

The flashlight was sitting on the range, throwing an oval of light on the wall. She crossed the room and shut it off. The wood stove flickered around the edges of its door, but the cabin was mostly dark.

She needed the toilet. For the past hour she'd tried to pretend otherwise, but it was either do it in the cabin or go to the outhouse. She hadn't seen or heard anyone — man or animal — since shutting herself in here.

Katie took a breath. Flicked the flashlight back on.

She stepped outside, where a crescent moon spread a cool pale light over the forest. Low, dark clouds surrounded the nearest peak like a cowl. She hurried to the outhouse and closed herself inside, heart pounding.

Listening intently to her surroundings, she waited, breathing shallow.

Finally she relaxed enough, did her business, and was about to get off the crooked toilet when she stopped.

She'd set the flashlight down beside her, enough to illuminate the small space, and her underwear.

She picked the light up, shone it more directly.

There was blood on her underwear. Not much, just a few small spots.

"Ah God . . ."

For years, her cycle more or less followed the moon and she tended to ovulate at or just before the full moon; menses came with the new moon. But she tended to clock things by the calendar rather than lunar phases. And she was very regular.

She counted up the days; her period wasn't due for at least two more.

Maybe it had come early.

But it didn't feel that way.

It felt like something else.

They'd been trying to get pregnant for a little while — at least, they'd stopped trying *not* to get pregnant. Glo called it "pulling the goalie."

And now there was blood. Not much, just this little bit.

And your breasts are sore.

—Hardly. Everything is sore, so what.

First trimester spotting is common.

—Oh stop — it's not "spotting" . . .

But it was. Katie was pretty sure most spotting happened about a week after fertilization, during implantation. She'd be right about there — the timing was right.

She'd wandered into David's music studio just a couple weeks ago and started pestering him. Flirting with him. Kissing him. He'd been powerless against her.

They'd had sex on the ground beside the electronic keyboard.

She knew.

No . . .

Katie pulled up her underpants and running skirt and left the outhouse, ran back to the cabin. She paced the room, feeling helpless, thinking she ought to lie back down but wanting to cry.

Or scream.

The wind gusted through the ragged windows in an oscillating whistle.

Pregnant.

In truth, she'd had intuition about it already. Even before everything had happened. Before the minivan. It had been on her mind to use the early pregnancy test she'd bought at Kinney Drugs. Just a feeling, pushed to the back of her mind once abduction and scavenging animals and potentially hallucinated mountain men had hijacked her thoughts.

A baby.

It was what she wanted. It was what David wanted, too, even though he had his concerns. He tried to hide them but she knew he worried about being a father. His own father had been a great musician but a lousy parent. He didn't have much family, and was a bit of a loner.

But they wanted a child. The time had come and . . .

And now here she was.

In the middle of nowhere, lost, barely holding on.

No, not lost — Black River Wild Forest.

You're somewhere. And you can get out.

She had to now — she had to hold on, she had to get out. She had to do whatever it took.

CHAPTER TWENTY-EIGHT

Cross met with Laura Broderick at The Knotty Pine, a bar on the outskirts of Hazleton. The sun was down, the place lively inside. Cross wanted a beer, but not while on duty, and not in public — even if this felt like the longest, wildest day in cop history.

"They're now called interior outposts," Laura said, sipping a Genesee Cream Ale. "You know, in the state master plan, they're still referred to as ranger cabins because back in the 1950s, that's what you called them."

"Is there a map of them all? In the master plan?"

"Not in the master plan, that's just a shit ton of words. I mean, you're going to find this map and that map, but not one single map, I don't think. There's only four active cabins right now."

"How many not in use?"

"Well, tough to say. In the 1970s, to bring certain regions up to par with what the Land Use Master Plan had defined as 'wilderness areas,' most outposts were burned down. Cedar Lakes, Shattuck Clearing, Duck Hole. But there's plenty out there that were just left to rot. You want to tell me what this is all about?"

"You know a guy named Jeff Gebhart?"

Laura studied the ceiling a moment. "Yeah, maybe. A while ago. Not a ranger, not a sworn officer; a caretaker. He had Mount Colden, I think, couple summers."

"That's him. Listen, I'm going to need you to consult with us, work with us. But keep it quiet. Can you do that?"

She set her beer aside and wiped her mouth with a cocktail napkin. "Course I can. You mean now?"

"Yeah. You can finish your beer. First just a few more of my own questions. How plausible do you think it would be for someone to hide out in one of these decommissioned outposts?"

"No, like I said, not so many left standing. And the ones that are sit right near the trails. So if someone wants to hide, that's not the way. Maybe in the dead of winter, but not now. But your hunting camps aren't gonna have well-defined trails. Owners generally want them to stay hidden. Only family or close buddies know. So, yeah, perfectly plausible hideouts. We've even got some we call 'outlaw cabins.'"

"How many?"

"Outlaw cabins?"

"Yeah, or hunting cabins."

"No telling. Hundreds. Way more abandoned hunting camps on state land than outposts, that's for sure. Way more. When the state acquires land, they keep the cabins. They might burn some of those, too, if they can be found, but a lot are just lost."

"How far back do you think some of these places are? I mean, how deep in the Park?"

Laura looked into the corner a moment. Her hand seemed to find its way back to the beer. "Well, Colden is an interior outpost, and that's seven miles out." She met his gaze. "You're going to have hunting cabins that are ten, fifteen miles into the middle of nowhere. Which is a hell of a long way from anywhere if you're not an expert. And even then . . ."

Laura took a swig of her beer.

Cross didn't move for a moment, letting it all sink in. Then he patted Laura on the arm and said, "Let's go talk to the FBI."

* * *

Agent Sair had been joined by more federal agents. Agent Paulson was gone, working from an undisclosed location as he searched hours of footage from local retailers, using facial recognition software in the hopes of identifying Montgomery or Vickers — and now Jeff Gebhart, too — buying a prepaid phone. Supposedly Paulson was also going through the stingray data with another agent.

Two agents brought Laura into the dining room for a briefing while Sair took Cross out the front door.

Even at night, reporters were camped down the slope of the property, getting their sound bites. Some websites were streaming live coverage, mostly just showing the house.

"We've got a problem," Sair said. "The Calumets aren't able to pay the 20 million."

Cross had figured. "Where's David? I haven't seen him."

"He left with Jean Calumet an hour ago. We have an agent following them. They went to the room at the inn." Sair lit a cigarillo. "We've looked into the Calumets. Their cash on hand, their assets. Unless they liquidate, yeah, they don't have it. We also looked at Henry Fellows. Fellows is being investigated for tax fraud."

"Yes, Gates was looking into that."

"I know. Gates is being debriefed now, at a safe location. We've got our own people with eyes on Fellows in White Plains. The others are dead ends."

"You mean Eric Dubois, the chef, and Lee Beck, the lawyer."

"Yeah, dead ends." Sair flicked ash and seemed to want to leave it at that.

"What about proof of life? It's been a long time since that photo."

"We assume it."

Cross let that sink in and looked down at the lights of the news crews. "Our techs lifted Katie's prints from the house here and matched them to prints found on the sliding door of the minivan. It puts her in the minivan, but that's it."

"You don't think she's alive?"

"I think if she's with this Vickers guy, it's a question. He's not a good guy. Don't we have to force the issue? Get them to send a picture or video before any payment disbursal?"

Sair squinted against the smoke from his cigarillo as he looked at Cross. "You think it matters? Jean Calumet right now is pulling out of his holdings and investments, freeing up whatever cash he can."

"How do you know that?"

Sair raised an eyebrow. "The same way we had Katie's prints before your forensics pulled them from the house. We're the FBI."

Cross was a bit shocked at the arrogance, but he'd already suspected the feds would look deep into Jean Calumet, and it wasn't unheard of that the FBI could have fingerprints of someone without a rap sheet.

"I still think we ought to push harder for proof," Cross said. "We can use a photograph as a lead, help us determine the location, see what shape Katie's in, learn things from that, too."

"Cross, take some time for yourself. You look dead on your feet. Go get a couple hours' rest." He clapped a hand on Cross's shoulder. "Tomorrow is going to be a big day."

* * *

Cross drove home, just five minutes away, and fixed himself a sandwich, ate it standing in the kitchen. He jumped in the shower. He was sore from the chase, his leg bruised, shoulder tender. He wondered about Katie Calumet out there in the deep woods, and what shape she was in, as he let the hot water beat down.

His phone rang while he was still in his towel.

"How you doing?" Marty asked.

Cross hadn't expected to hear from her, and not at almost eleven at night. He grabbed a beer from the fridge and sat on the couch. "Think I've been up for twenty hours. Feels like Coast Guard days. How are the girls? Everything okay?"

"Everything's fine. They're good. They're asking about your case."

"They've heard?"

"Of course. And they know you're on it. Petrie asked me, 'Mommy, is Daddy going to find that missing lady?'"

"Tell them I'm working on it."

"You think she's alive?"

"I don't know."

"Where do you think she is?"

"She might be in some old hunting camp. Somewhere near Bakers Mills, or maybe . . . I dunno. A lot of mountains in there — Panther, Crane, Pillsbury . . ." He rose from the couch and went to the closet, holding up his towel with one hand.

"It's crazy. Just crazy. Well, the girls were asking about you, I wanted to tell you."

"Thank you." He dug through the junk in the closet. "How's the new job?"

"It's good. It's real good. We meet every morning for a fifteen-minute staff meeting, and I like that. The people are good."

"That's great, Marty."

He found a couple of Adirondack Park brochures and a topo map. He pulled everything out and went to the dining room table, cleared it off with a swipe of his hand.

"What was that?" Marty asked.

"Nothing. Just moving some stuff around."

His towel fell away. He glanced at the windows, suddenly paranoid a reporter would be out there. It was the last thing he needed — "Crazy Cop Works Missing Woman Case in the Nude."

He didn't see anyone peeping in, but he shuffled off to get dressed.

"How's the house?" Marty asked.

"Uhm, the house is good."

The house had been a contentious part of their separation. It was the first home the girls had ever known, and Cross had been reluctant to uproot them. But Plattsburgh was forty minutes away. After six months, Marty didn't want the commute any longer. And Cross didn't want to move.

The girls would go to a different school in two weeks when the year started. It had all been settled on amicably enough, though Cross felt like he'd gone through it in a daze.

He pulled on some pants and quickly returned to the map.

"Okay," Marty said, sounding distant. "I'll let you get back to work."

He spread out the topo map and traced a finger down to Bakers Mills. Crane Mountain was close to Bakers Mills. But the Crane Loop Trail attracted a lot of hikers, and it was peak season.

He followed Route 8 west to Speculator, which was close, and then looked at the surrounding area.

Plenty of mountains, plenty of wilderness. Less touristy.

"Alright, Marty, good to talk to you."

He hung up and set the phone aside, then looked at it. He realized he'd just been abrupt. Kind of an asshole.

Why can't we move? Marty hadn't understood.

Petrie is in first grade next year. She's already done kindergarten, made friends . . .

Don't use the girls. You don't want to move because you don't want to support my job.

He remembered the argument clearly, despite everything which had followed their ultimate loggerheads moment feeling hazy the way it did. He picked up the phone to call her back.

But what would that do? It had been months. Marty had settled in. Petrie was starting school. Ramona was doing a mixture of day care and hanging out with Marty's mother. They'd stopped arguing and were getting along, able to talk. Everything was falling into place.

Except, he missed them terribly.

He'd been drinking himself to sleep most nights.

When the weekend was over and the girls went back to their mother's, he felt lost and broken.

He set the phone down again and returned his attention to the map.

"Snowy Mountain," he said, touching it with his fingertip. It was one of the tallest mountains in the Southern Adirondacks. He flipped through one of the brochures and found information on Snowy — a 7.8-mile hike, considered *Difficult*. That meant maybe fewer tourists, but it would still have worn trails. Would Katie's kidnappers take her somewhere that was used by the public, even a little?

Kane Mountain — distinct from "Crane" Mountain — had a restored fire tower which offered "spectacular views" according to the brochure. Cross wanted people in that fire tower, and any other towers, on the lookout. For what, though? Maybe smoke from a cabin. Something. They needed to be doing aerial searches. Why was the FBI being so obstinate?

He looked at Cellar Mountain. Not as high in elevation as Snowy, but it wasn't in the brochure. No hiking trails, no fire towers with spectacular views. Part of the Blue Ridge Wilderness. Southwest of that, West Canada Mountain, part of another wilderness area, well off the beaten path.

Cross left the map and rummaged through a kitchen drawer full of bric-a-brac until he found some Scotch tape. He fixed the topo map to the wall then went searching for thumbtacks.

By midnight he had marked several places. They had a map like this at headquarters, showing the route the minivan was thought to have taken before winding up near Bakers Mills. Cross highlighted that route on his own map then drew lines to the thumbtack points on five different mountains, places that seemed remote enough, places that would likely have abandoned hunting camps.

Then he sat down and drummed up a list of his own demands — things he was going to make sure happened the next day, not take no for an answer.

The beer he'd started earlier in the evening sat half-drunk on the table beside the maps, and Cross went to bed.

CHAPTER TWENTY-NINE

Gates called while Cross was headed out the door, six hours later.

She sounded weary.

"We've had to detain David Brennan."

Cross opened the car and dropped into the driver's seat. "What happened?"

"He tried to leave again. To sneak out last night, go find Katie."

"Ah Jesus. Well I mean, maybe we just . . . I don't know."

"He was starting to get physical with one of the troopers at the gate. Listen, we'll talk more about it in a bit. Right now I need you to follow up on the Gebhart lead. His brother is Abel Gebhart. I'll give you the address."

Cross followed the instructions and drove the thirty miles to Abel Gebhart's home.

It was a small house on the outskirts of Vermontville, lots of land, mountain views. Cross put the vehicle in park and got out. He was on his way to the front door when it opened.

"Can I help you?"

"You Abel Gebhart?"

The big man, burly-bearded, stepped away from the house. He was dressed in jeans and a flannel shirt, despite the heat. Steel-toed work boots. "Yeah?"

Cross pulled his badge. Slowly. "Investigator Cross."

Abel narrowed his eyes. "Cross-dressing Cross?"

Cross stopped walking, keeping a few yards' distance. His heart sank. *Crap*.

Abel took a step forward. He pointed his finger. "You ran Jeff off the fucking road."

The hostility emanating from the man, the foul language — Cross felt his stomach turn pulpy and his palms start to sweat as the adrenaline kicked in. "Well, your brother ran from the police, Mr. Gebhart. Obviously that's piqued our curiosity."

"And so you come here, trespassing on my property, expecting me to what — talk shit about my little brother?"

Cross saw a child's face in one of the grimy upstairs windows behind Abel. A little boy looked out at them.

"Not at all." Cross put his badge away. "I came to talk to you about hunting."

"About hunting," Abel mocked. "Where you from?"

"I was born and raised around here."

"Uh-huh. Why don't you get in your car and turn around."

"I'm investigating the kidnapping of Katie Calumet."

Abel was already headed back inside. He flapped a hand in the air. "Yeah, yeah. Well I've got nothing for you."

"You or your family own any hunting cabins?"

Abel stopped, keeping his back to Cross. Then he slowly turned. He started across the gravel driveway, rapidly closing the gap.

At the same time, Cross heard a vehicle come rumbling up from behind. A pickup truck, two more men inside.

"You got a warrant to be on my property?" Abel stopped, his face inches from Cross's. He was half a foot taller, thirty pounds heavier.

"I'm in your driveway, which is accessible and visible from a public highway, conducting an open investigation. I can come back with a warrant and we'll search everything you own, if we have to."

Abel just stood glowering, trying to intimidate Cross. The doors to the pickup opened and the other men got out. Cross heard them moving up behind him.

His phone buzzed in his pocket. He ignored it and took a deep breath.

"I can also have state troopers show up at your house, arrest you, and you spend forty-eight hours in a holding cell. Maybe we end up charging you, you go to jail. Or . . . we can just talk."

"There's nothing to talk about. I don't know my brother's business."

The two other men flanked Cross. They were holding coffees and egg sandwiches. "Good morning," Cross said. He returned his attention to Abel, still staring him down. "Let me ask again: Does your family own any hunting cabins?"

"That's nobody's business but ours." Abel's eyes glinted in the thin morning light, but he was losing his edge.

"It's my business."

Abel spat to the side. "Well you better get that warrant, then. Come back and arrest me or whatever else you said."

"Okay, have a good day." Cross walked back to the car, his pulse racing. He opened the door.

Abel called over. "Only I won't be here. Got to go down to Albany, see my brother. He's in a coma because of you."

"Well he shouldn't have run."

Cross sank into the vehicle, cranked the ignition, and tore out of the driveway. He watched the three men in his rearview mirror, standing side by side.

* * *

"You really want to go forward with this theory that Katie is out in the middle of the woods?" Sair paced the living room at Katie's house. Cross sat with Gates on the couch.

"Yes, we do," Gates said. "And Captain Bouchard is behind it. DEC is ready to jump in."

"But this area you're talking about, this region in the Southern Adirondacks — which mountains did you say again?"

Cross spoke up. "Snowy Mountain, Kane, West Canada Mountain, maybe one or two others. None of them that far from Bakers Mills. We could use your resources, but we'll do it without them."

Sair cocked an eyebrow. "We don't take over investigations, Cross. We help, we advise. *My* advice is that if you're going to do this search, it needs to be toned way down because they're probably watching, could be expecting something like this. No helicopters, for one thing. I'll speak to the DEC commissioner. Who is their press operations?"

"I believe no one right now. The position is vacant."

"Vacant? So who's handling press releases? Who the hell is the department spokesperson?"

"Probably someone from general counsel. I don't know, Agent Sair."

Sair gave Cross and Gates a look like he disapproved of the whole thing.

Cross said, "We have a BCI Investigator in Albany with Jeff Gebhart, the carpenter who ran and crashed his truck."

"How's that looking?"

Gates answered. "Hasn't woken up yet. We're ready to question him. Cross just came from his brother's house. They did everything but run him off with shotguns."

"Where are we at with the payment?" Cross asked. "What has Calumet come up with?"

Agent Sair took a breath and glanced around. He spoke in a low voice. "Calumet has some issues."

"What?"

"That information is privileged."

"Then let us sign an NDA or read an affidavit or something."

Gates reached over and touched Cross's hand. She'd obviously already been through this with the feds.

Sair set his jaw and put his hands on his hips. "We'll consider it."

"But he definitely can't pay? What can he come up with?"

"Twelve million was the number I was given."

"So, what do we do?"

Sair glanced at his watch. "It's nine o'clock now. We're keeping the Calumets secluded at this point; we've appropriated the inn. The kidnapper said twenty-four hours, so that's at one o'clock. When he calls, Calumet will offer the twelve. Hopefully they take it. If not, I don't know. Like I said, I don't think they're unwilling to wait another twenty-four hours. That's a bluff."

Sair sat down across from the investigators and lowered his voice even further. "What I *will* say is that Calumet might have it, but there's a $5 million withdrawal last summer, and we don't know where it went."

Frank Paulson came out of the dining room, interrupting before Cross could ask more questions. Paulson was followed by two other feds. They gathered with Sair and headed for the dining room. Sair beckoned Cross and Gates to join them.

Paulson was already fiddling with the computers when the investigators entered the room.

"We got him," Paulson said. He tapped the screen.

Cross moved closer. "Montgomery? Or Gebhart?"

"Jonathan R. Montgomery," Paulson announced. "At a Target in Plattsburgh on August the sixth, buying a burner. A Tracfone."

"Boom," said Agent Sair. He cut Cross a look. "Told you we didn't need a stingray."

There was a knock on the dining room door. Sair opened and Captain Bouchard entered with Laura Broderick behind him, followed by three new faces. The house was filling up with people again.

Things became hectic. The newcomers were Elena Cobleskill, the district attorney, another forest ranger named Joe Pike, and the deputy commissioner of the DEC, Helen Teague. With Montgomery's identity confirmed, the focus shifted to capturing him before delivering payment.

"We've got the MVNO number of the phone," Paulson explained. "We plug it into the system and the phone will start pinging. We can get Montgomery's location almost right away."

Cross picked his way through the small crowd and got beside Cobleskill, the DA. "We don't need a warrant?"

She shook her head. "The US Court of Appeals has ruled that law enforcement agencies don't need a probable-cause warrant to track prepaid cell phone locations. If we have the number, we're good to go right now."

Agent Paulson and Kim Yom were already working the system, and Cross saw a map come up on the main screen. It was similar to the topo map at his house, but with an overlaying grid.

Sair stood in a corner of the room with Bouchard, preparing the deployment of state police. Laura Broderick looked at Cross. Further efforts to find Katie appeared to be on hold. The FBI was about to pounce on Montgomery.

CHAPTER THIRTY

Katie heard a noise outside the cabin and sat up on the mattress. She picked up the hatchet and moved to the windows. It was morning; she'd finally fallen into a deep rest and slept late, until almost 9 a.m.

She peered out through the broken glass at the tree line surrounding the clearing.

The man was back: the grizzled figure she had questioned hallucinating.

He was no figment of her imagination. He was standing amid the trees, looking at the cabin, holding a rifle with one hand, real as the constant throbbing pains in her body.

He stepped into the clearing and gazed upward, like he was watching the smoke rise from the stack.

Katie did her best to keep out of view, but he had to know someone was in the cabin. It was just a matter of time before he opened the front door.

They were miles away from anywhere, deep in the wilderness. He was definitely not a searcher — he was carrying a weapon, not a radio or a GPS. She didn't think he was Leno anymore, not the way he looked or the way he was acting, but she considered again that he could be an associate. Some mountain-man contact they had in place in case things went awry. Maybe, she thought with a trace of shocked giddiness, his code name was Jimmy Fallon. The new guy.

After standing there checking the cabin over, the broken windows, he looked at the ground. He seemed to grow interested in something and moved off in the direction of the rocky cliff.

Katie huddled by the adjacent window so she could visually follow his path. He slipped out of sight, but she was fairly certain he was tracking Carson's trail to the edge of the clearing, to where Carson had fallen.

She stayed where she was a moment, calming her heart rate. Then she left the window and quietly opened the front door.

Holding the hatchet in both hands, she edged to the front of the porch and watched him. If he'd heard her come out, he made no move to show it but kept on toward the cliff, until he was mostly hidden by the trees before the drop.

The cabin was no longer safe. Coyotes and strange men had interfered with that.

And she could be carrying a tiny life.

She ran inside, grabbed the backpack where she'd stashed the liquor bottle of water, the climbing rope, and a few other supplies, then left again. She cut across the clearing, sparing a glance the way Fallon had gone, but he was entirely out of sight.

She reached the woods. There was a semblance of a trail, just some of the brush trampled when she and Carson had arrived two days before. She was finally ready to get out of here. She'd tried for the GPS, found it broken, couldn't fix it, but she'd since rested and gathered more supplies. And she'd seen Carson die with her own eyes, so she could be certain he couldn't chase her.

But then there was this new player. Someone totally unknown. She wasn't sure what gave her greater pause — that he might come after her, or that he'd seemed generally disinterested in her.

Why hadn't he ventured inside? He'd roamed about like someone in his own backyard, or at least familiar with the woods. Maybe even someone who knew where they were located. If he was truly a hermit, he'd know the lay of the land. He could escort her out, or at least tell her the way.

"Dammit," Katie muttered.

Every time she tried to set off, something seemed to keep her in the woods.

She moved up the slope of the mountain, keeping the cabin in sight through the trees. The woods were thick, with plenty of robust balsam firs to hide among, and she found her spot.

She could see the north side of the cabin and the front porch. She waited for what felt like an eternity until Fallon reappeared on the far side of the clearing.

He walked with a slight limp, picking his way along like someone not in any hurry. For a little while he continued to search the clearing. He found the rocks she'd used for her signal then moved on from them. He was like a dog, in a way, nosing out the interesting smells, the signs in the grass.

She'd left the door to the cabin wide open, and at last Fallon looked there and moved toward it. He disappeared inside and she heard him walking around on the plank floors, glimpsed him through a broken window.

She waited, growing uncomfortable as she squatted among the fir trees. He took an unnerving amount of time in the cabin. What the hell was he doing in there? Making a sandwich? She supposed he was just taking everything in, evaluating.

Finally he reemerged; there was something in his hands. He walked a ways into the clearing and sat down with whatever it was, examining it.

If he was with Carson and Leno, why wasn't he radioing someone? For that matter, if he was working with them, he seemed to know the woods — why not send her in with someone like him instead of Carson? Fallon didn't seem to care that someone had obviously been inside the cabin, with the door shut, smoke billowing, and now they were gone.

He wasn't part of it, and she couldn't keep hiding here forever; she was getting stiffer by the second, her abused muscles still sore from all the recent exertion.

But even if he wasn't with them, even he looked old and a bit hobbled, he had that rifle. He might try to hurt her. She didn't know anything about him, how long he'd been out in the wilderness, or why.

It was safer to wait, damn the soreness.

Just a little longer. A few more minutes. Then, keeping her distance — and the hatchet in her hands — ready to run, she would try to talk to him.

CHAPTER THIRTY-ONE

The convoy of law enforcement vehicles barreled along the freeway, lights flashing but sirens silent. Cross and Gates followed in his car, pushing it to ninety.

The feds had gotten a fix on Montgomery.

"Malone?" Cross asked. "Malone is over 100 miles north of Bakers Mills."

"I know. But it's right near the Canadian border — crossings at Trout River, Fort Covington, Cornwall . . ."

It was nine in the morning. The kidnappers were due to call the Calumets that afternoon. Cross thought it was insane, but the feds acted confident.

The convoy slowed as they rolled into the outskirts of town, alongside a wide river that had once provided water power for saw mills. Those days were gone and now there was a college, several County Seat buildings, shopping centers. They came to a stop at a gas station and convenience store with tractor-trailers in the parking lot.

The dozen vehicles — state trooper cruisers, black SUVS, and Cross's sedan — pulled in and surrounded the store, blocking the entrance and exit.

Troopers pulled rifles and took aim over the hoods of their cruisers. A helicopter thundered overhead.

Sair was holding a satellite-assisted tracking device. Cross knew it was so precise that it told the feds that the phone was inside the store. The rest of Sair's team, dressed in Kevlar flak jackets, flooded in.

Cross pulled his weapon — only the second time in eight years being a cop he'd ever taken it out from the holster. He and Gates were also dressed in bullet-proof vests. They jogged toward the entrance.

He heard shouts from inside and their radios crackled with tactical communications. Gates stuck out her arm, stopping him.

Sair entered after the team, now gripping his handgun. More shouts, and Cross heard Sair yelling, "Come out of the bathroom!"

Gates withdrew her arm and they cautiously proceeded forward. The store was in disarray, customers cowering among the few tables, the clerk peering over the counter. It was the type of place that sold pizza and cold subs in addition to the two aisles of junk food. Cross saw a pimply-faced cook in the back, looking excited by the whole thing. FBI agents had knocked over a rack of sunglasses, and someone's bag of groceries had exploded on the floor, splashing milk.

More than half the team was searching the store, but a group of three had converged on a door in the far corner, next to a vending machine. Their weapons zeroed in.

Sair yelled again, "Montgomery, we know you're in there — this is the FBI, come out with your hands up!"

The lead SWAT member looked at Sair, who gave a nod. An agent kicked open the door, shouting, "Get down! Down on the ground!"

Sair ran forward and Cross and Gates followed.

They crowded outside the bathroom door, looking in at the sixty-year-old man crouched on the floor beside the toilet, terrified, his hands trembling over his head.

The tension lasted another few seconds as the reality sank in.

The agents lowered their weapons. Sair holstered his gun, and the investigators did the same.

"Ah shit," Cross said under his breath.

The agents helped the man out. His fear soon turned into indignation and he started yelling at everyone about police brutality. When he shoved past one of the team, he was tackled to the ground and handcuffed.

"Whoa, whoa!" Cross said, getting closer.

Sair ignored Cross and loomed over the man. "Where is Jonathan Montgomery?"

"Who? What?"

Sair persisted a moment longer. "Where is Katie Calumet?"

But the older man clearly had no idea who they were talking about. Either that or he was giving them a performance, but Cross doubted it.

An FBI agent called out, "There it is; got it."

Cross moved in tighter, bumping against Sair as they both squeezed into the doorway. The tiny bathroom was overrun with law enforcement, barely elbow room. One agent had taken a towel from the dispenser and used it to pick up a device out of the trash beside the toilet. He held it up for everyone to see — a prepaid Tracfone.

"Everyone," Sair barked. "Fan out. Let's go."

The trio of agents collected themselves and left the bathroom. The rest of the team, having turned the store upside down, spread to the outside, still on high alert.

The search continued on the store premises, but Cross didn't think Montgomery was anywhere around. He looked at Sair and thought the agent's expression suggested he was coming around to the same conclusion — Montgomery had baited them.

The man from the bathroom was yanked to his feet and brought outside. Customers gaped as the procession passed. One teenager took a picture with her cell phone.

Agents whisked the man away into the back of a tinted SUV before Cross or Gates had a moment to question him. "Hold on," Sair said to the investigators, and got into the vehicle.

Cross didn't want to wait around for the excuses and backpedaling. This was an obvious screw-up. And of major proportions.

"Cross," Gates said beside him. "You go. I'm staying."

Cross didn't argue. He jumped into the car and hit the horn. One of the troopers moved their cruiser out of the way and Cross nailed the gas, bouncing out of the parking lot.

He glanced in the mirror before tearing off down the road and glimpsed Gates walking toward the SUV. Sair got out to greet her, his posture sagging.

Cross raced back to Hazleton.

CHAPTER THIRTY-TWO

The hermit started back toward the woods and Katie got ready with the hatchet. He disappeared into the trees. He was very quiet for an old man with a limp, but she heard a twig snap and jumped. He was close. By the time she was ready to run from her hiding spot he was right on top of her.

Katie stood and raised the hatchet, her heart beating in her throat.

"That dead feller down there," the man said. "He yer husband?"

His words were such an accented mumble she could barely understand him.

It took her a second to find her voice. "No. He's not my husband."

"Took'r pretty bad fall."

This close to the man, just a couple yards, Katie got a much better look. He had wiry eyebrows, eyes set with deep wrinkles, gnarly gray beard. Despite his limp he looked healthy enough, though there was a distinct smell coming off him. Earthy, homeless. His gaze was milky, like cataracts forming.

"He's dead," she said about Carson.

"Yah." The hermit looked off in the direction of the cliff. He kept his rifle casually at his side.

Katie lowered the hatchet but kept a good grip on it. She decided to confide in him. "He kidnapped me. The man down there took me up here, blindfolded, two days ago. Do you know where this is? You must know. Do you live around here?"

She stopped herself, wanting to give him time to absorb it, to answer. The hermit, *Fallon*, she thought with no further trace of giddiness, kept staring off toward the cabin and the cliff beyond.

He didn't answer her and she wondered if he'd heard her or was ignoring her. She spoke up, repeating that she'd been kidnapped, and she was lost. "Is this Black River Forest?"

That got his attention and he turned his face back toward her. "Yah. Black River."

She felt relief but pressed on. "What mountain is this? What's the nearest town? Can you help me get down off the mountain and back to town?"

He seemed to avoid her gaze, and it made her uneasy. Maybe he wasn't outright threatening, but he was strange and unpredictable. She kept her tight grip on the hatchet. If he came toward her, she would be ready.

"Yah, that's gonta be Atwell or Hoffmeister, dependin' on which way ya come out."

She wasn't familiar with the places he spoke of, but it was miles ahead of feeling utterly in the dark. "And what mountain is this?"

He looked around, as if seeing his surroundings for the first time. "Don't know the name. Mebbe Jones."

She tried to think. Carson had said Jones. She'd thought he'd meant a person, like Leno or another contact. A place they were supposed to meet, even if it had made little sense.

Jones. West. Canada.

Carson could have been talking about a mountain.

Her hike of Dix had been almost a decade ago. There were hundreds of mountains in the Adirondacks. But surely only a few in Black River Wild Forest, one of many distinct regions of the park. "So you think it's Jones?" She struggled to remember more names, anything she'd seen over the years. "What about Panther? Panther Mountain?"

He pulled something out of his pocket and held it out to her. "This yours?"

Katie stared at the object then took a step forward. It looked technical, like a radio or something.

He continued to hold it out to her, still not meeting her eyes, oddly unemotional. It occurred to her that he might've spent years in the woods without human contact. Social skills could atrophy.

At last she tucked the hatchet up under her arm and took what he was holding, turned it over in her hands. It wasn't a radio — she thought it was a satellite phone.

"Oh my God . . ."

She poked at the buttons. She'd never used a sat phone before. It looked like one of the first cell phones she'd ever owned — a Nokia — though it had the brand *iridium* written above the blank screen. It was one solid piece, encased in a rubberized red shell.

She found the power button and pressed. She waited a moment then let out an excited breath when the screen came to life.

"It works! It has power."

She started pacing around without thinking about it, staring at the screen. After a fancy little intro of graphics ("iridium everywhere . . ."), a menu display showed her several options.

INSERT SIM CARD
ADD TO SIM CARD BALANCE
DIRECT INTERNET 3
ADVANCED

There was nothing that read, simply, CALL, and her hopes immediately started to sink.

She talked herself out of the dread and selected the ADVANCED option. Another screen listed more options, none of which made any sense — VCOMPORT was written in green, then things like INSTALL USB DRIVERS, FILES FS and LANGUAGE — nothing that seemed simple.

Maybe simple was what it took.

She dialed 911 and pressed the single green button on the keypad. The phone chirped three times and a battery icon flashed on the screen — just one percent life remaining. A moment later, the screen went black.

"No . . ."

Katie looked up from the phone and saw that Fallon had moved off, back toward the cabin. She hurried to catch up with him, slapping the branches away. She stopped along the way to further investigate the phone.

"Oh okay," she said, hopeful again. There was a red button right on top of the phone next to the antenna. She pressed it and looked at the screen. To her delight, a small icon that looked like a beacon started to flash.

The red button had to be an SOS. Maybe it was using backup battery. Still, she wanted to find the docking station for the phone, if there was one. An extra battery, something she had missed going through Carson's bags.

"Hey!" She caught up to Fallon. "Where did you find this?"

He had reached the clearing and was back to snooping around in that odd way he had.

Fallon faced the cabin. "In 'ere."

"Will you show me?" She felt more energetic than she had in hours.

He stopped what he was doing and headed into the cabin without another word. She couldn't believe when he showed her — Carson's duffel bag had a small, zipped pocket she'd ignored. Her focus had been on the GPS; she hadn't considered a satellite phone. She riffled through the contents of the bag again, this renewed hope revving her up.

But there were no batteries. There was a plug-in adapter, which was useless — the cabin didn't have power.

She found a brochure for the phone, of all things, unfolded it, and devoured everything printed on the glossy pages.

Unfortunately it was more of an advertisement than it was a manual. A rugged-looking guy on the cover held the phone to his ear as he gazed over a massif of mountains in the distance. The phone had "unparalleled reach" and was "feature-rich."

She found where it mentioned the SOS button — she'd been right. She looked at the screen again and saw the comforting icon for her broadcasted signal.

How did it work? Emergency services everywhere were dialed into the satellites these things used? Maybe someone right now sitting in a 911 operations center was seeing a blip broadcasting somewhere in Black Forest?

Katie read the fine print on the last page, feeling her heart sink deeper: "The programmable, GPS-enabled SOS button with a Satellite Emergency Notification Device (SEND) is ready to alert your programmed contact of your location and help to create a two-way connection to assist in the response."

In other words, the SOS worked for anyone else who had a phone linked to this one.

Someone like Leno.

She might've just alerted Carson's accomplice.

She kept reading, the fear sliding over her.

Fallon was back outside, doing whatever the hell strange mountain hermits did, but he was once again looking like her only way out of here.

According to the brochure, the SOS indeed operated off an internal battery with a two-year life. However, that GPS-enabled SOS with emergency services was supported by something called GEOS Travel Safety Limited, at "no additional charge."

There was an asterisk after "no additional charge" and she read one of the very last sentences of the brochure, feeling nauseous.

In order for the phone SOS to work with emergency services, like 911, it said, "Registration with GEOS is required."

She resumed clawing around in the bag even though she was sure she'd already dumped everything out. The brochure had gotten stuck in the fabric, but nothing else had. The contents were in a pile in the middle of the room and she went through them all again, item by item.

The heat in the cabin was starting to get to her. The sweat ran down and she fought against the undertow of despair.

A busted GPS. A sat phone with no battery to call anyone, and very likely no registration with any GEOS whatever. Just another useless gadget, frustrating her.

And the sinking idea that she might've just notified Leno — or anyone else monitoring the phone from the Carson-and-Leno gang.

She picked it up to press the red button again, to kill the beacon, but hesitated, thinking there was still a slim chance that the phone could've been registered. Maybe it was stolen. Maybe whomever it had been stolen from had an active account.

But there'd been a damn brochure. Like Carson and Leno had just bought it. These phones could be expensive, hundreds of dollars, some of them more than a grand, but maybe for these assholes it was just a start-up expense. Tax deduction, right, guys? For your entrepreneurship as intrepid kidnappers.

She almost threw the phone across the room, but she tapped the red button instead, and the icon disappeared from the screen.

As she got to her feet and prepared to head back outside and try to have a better conversation with the socially-challenged Fallon, another thought struck her: Even if the SOS hadn't just alerted someone working with Carson, there could have been a check-in time. If so, Carson was dead and hadn't checked in with anyone for more than twenty-four hours now. The phone, for a few minutes a sign of good fortune, was now a terrible harbinger.

The phone meant someone could be coming.

Katie didn't waste any more time. She found Fallon by the cliff edge of the clearing. She approached with caution, keeping a safe distance from the hermit, bringing herself to the edge.

There were no coyotes below. There wasn't much of Carson left, either. Just an unrecognizable effigy of bones and shredded flesh inside cargo pants and a bloody T-shirt.

Fallon squatted a few yards upslope from her, looking down. Then he rose and headed toward the berry bushes, like he was going to make his way down there.

"Wait . . . Excuse me, sir. Can you wait a second? Please . . ."

He halted, keeping his back to her.

She quickly caught up to him. "Thank you . . . Listen, I really need to get out of here. I need to get back home." Katie couldn't help the tremble in her voice. "Do you understand? Can you help me get back to Atwell, or Hoffmeister?"

Nothing, not a word or movement, just a few blinks of those cloudy eyes. Then Fallon said, "Yah." But he stayed where he was, his forehead wrinkled in a frown, his lips working like he was chewing.

"Oh . . . thank you. And please, listen, I'd be happy to . . ." she sputtered, feeling the gratitude well up, the slight sting of tears on the verge, "whatever you need . . ."

Fallon turned his head just slightly and looked at her out of the corner of his eye.

"You're bleedin'," he said.

She felt something now she hadn't noticed before, a light tickle on her cheek. She touched her face and saw blood on her fingertips. A branch or something had cut her while she was in the woods. It wasn't much blood, just a small tear.

He turned away again, looking like he wanted to go down to where Carson was. Why, she didn't know. But she got the sense Fallon was anxious about something.

"You're worried about the coyotes?"

He didn't answer.

"I'll go clean up. I'll make sure there's no blood. You think they'll come back?"

Nothing.

"Okay, listen, I'll wash. You do whatever you have to do. Please don't leave me, though. Will you promise me? Sir?"

He cut another look at her, grinding his lips together. He was still scary, his lack of communication was unnerving, but Katie was growing more assured that Fallon wasn't going to try to hurt her.

"What's your name?" she asked.

Every answer began with a pause. "Hoot."

"Hoot? It's nice to meet you. I'm Katie."

She stuck her hand out; he looked and then took it. His brief, gentle grip was cool and coarse as sandpaper.

She repeated, "I'll just go clean up, and I'll wait for you. Okay?"

"Yah."

"But, Hoot. There could be someone else coming. What you found is a satellite phone. It could've been a way for them to keep in contact with each other. Someone might be on their way." She watched him closely. "I'm sorry."

He stood there for a few more seconds then made a small grunt and moved off to the trail which wound down to the rocks below.

CHAPTER THIRTY-THREE

Agent Frank Paulson looked embarrassed when Cross came into the dining room. He was younger than Cross, maybe just thirty, and perhaps not accustomed to making mistakes. He was explaining those mistakes to Captain Bouchard.

"It was a burner," Paulson said. "We should've figured it would be switched. But usually when they're switched, the old burner is destroyed . . ."

Bouchard turned to Cross. "What happened?"

Gates had called him ten minutes after leaving Malone. Cross relayed the story to Bouchard: "A truck driver on his way to the border found the phone in his rig. Someone, probably Montgomery, tossed it in there, and when the driver found it he threw it away at the next gas station."

"But he wasn't at the gas station. How in the hell did we find *him*?"

"When he gets to the border, he thinks maybe he ought to tell someone about finding a random burner in his truck, and CSBA call it in."

"When did it get stashed in his truck?" Bouchard asked. "Where?"

"Could be anywhere. Unfortunately this guy is hauling FedEx. He's made about twenty stops today, originating in New York City. And he doesn't lock his doors."

"Jesus . . ." Bouchard rubbed his jaw then asked, "We're certain he's not working with these guys?"

"We're certain. He's clean. His log is good. Gates is checking for anything, though, just in case."

"Shit." Bouchard glanced at his watch and said what everyone was thinking. "Montgomery is expected to call again in thirty minutes. I guess at least we'll have another number to work with."

"Yeah, and then they dump that phone, too . . ."

Paulson spoke up. His skin had turned a shade of red. "So far we haven't found anything — besides the phone — in or around the convenience store that points to Montgomery. But the store is shut down until further notice, we're scouring the town, checking motels, restaurants, the public washrooms at the beach, anywhere and everything. Plus, CBSA turned the guy's truck inside-out."

"Great," Cross said with a touch of sarcasm he couldn't help.

* * *

Cross and Bouchard left for the inn, ten minutes away.

The place was empty except for law enforcement and the Calumet family. The feds had turned the restaurant into a command station. A new skiptracer manned the controls, doing what Paulson had — and there were more screens, hard drives, and mysterious black boxes than Cross had ever seen in one place. One looked like something from a *Star Trek* episode — the size of a shiny bread box with several colored lights and toggle switches. A stingray.

David Brennan was sitting in handcuffs. He was in the corner where dining rooms chairs had been stacked out of the way. He looked a bit like an animal in a cage of bristling chair legs. A state trooper hovered near, but Gloria was right beside David, her arm around his shoulders.

Jean and Sybil Calumet were center stage. They wore fashionable athletic clothes. A hip New York couple, Cross thought, though Jean looked aged and slightly hostile.

"Have we worked out the finances?" Cross asked. There was no reason to treat the subject delicately. Either the money was ready or it wasn't.

Geoffrey Wick was the new FBI agent in charge, tall, deeply tanned, with platinum-white hair. "We have," said Wick.

Jean Calumet's cell phone sat on a table, hooked into various devices and a speaker phone, all resembling some kind of technological life-support system.

The phone rang and Gloria jumped.

Calumet reached out and hit the answer button. "Hello?"

Nothing for a moment, just breathing. Then, through the speakers: "You fucked up."

"We've got the money," Calumet said evenly. "Almost the whole way. We're able to pay 17 million. That's all we can do. Anything else and you'd have to wait a while."

Cross felt mixed emotions. He'd never been involved in something like this, and just hearing the kidnapper's voice in real time was surreal. Calumet had a kind of poise he hadn't shown before now, as if he'd been backed into a corner and didn't like it — he'd gotten meaner in the past twenty-four hours. Maybe it was a version of Jean Calumet others were familiar with, people like the disgruntled ex-chef Eric Dubois, or former business partner Henry Fellows.

"That's not what I mean," the kidnapper said. "I said I only wanted to deal with you . . ."

"You *are* dealing with me. Of course my family is here. Of course the police are here. I have no control over that."

"Shut your fucking *mouth*!" The voice, already louder than anyone there in person, rattled the speakers.

The kidnapper spoke again, calmer. "Whatever happened, I'm holding you responsible."

"I don't know what—"

"I said *shut up*. Now listen up. My account shows *nothing*. No deposit. Not a cent."

Calumet opened his mouth to explain, but Cross caught his gaze.

Cross shook his head and Calumet pursed his lips.

"So here's what I'm going to do," the kidnapper said. "You have six hours. Six hours from right now to transfer the money. Now, before you start babbling about how it takes time for the deposits to show up — I know that. I'm not stupid. The numbers route the money in such a way you can't cancel the transaction once it's sent, so don't even bother. Or go ahead, knock yourself out. I'm sure the FBI has told you they'll be able to get the money back. I'm sure everyone's very fuckin smart over there. Huh? Right, Jean? Six hours, or I'm going to split her from her crotch to her fucking throat."

It sounded like the kidnapper was about to end the call, and Cross spoke up. "We know who you are."

Cross could feel all of the eyes in the room suddenly on him, but he ignored them.

"Who the fuck is this?"

"Investigator Cross. We know who you are, John."

The kidnapper went silent. Cross thought he could hear the faintest of noises in the background, like running water, maybe a river, or falls.

"Jonathan Robert Montgomery. Did time in a juvie facility in Pennsylvania. You met your wife, Janice, in Brooklyn. You own a house in Lake Haven."

More silence, just that burble in the background. Then, slowly, "Investigator . . . Justin . . . Cross."

Cross felt like an electric shock went through him. Had he just made a terrible mistake? He risked a look at Wick, and the agent was clearly displeased.

"Mr. Cross," the kidnapper repeated. "Going to crack his first really big case, is that right? Look around you. Take a good look at Jean-Baptiste Calumet. Look at his wife. Look at his daughter. I'm sure they're all right there. Take a look at

Katie's husband. You want to do some investigating? There you fucking go. Six hours, Cross."

The line went dead.

"Something happened," Cross said.

Everyone was talking. Bouchard was pissed. Wick was livid. Sybil gave Cross a look that could cut glass. Only David seemed to regard Cross without enmity, though something else lurked in his gaze . . .

Cross shouted above the voices, repeating, "People! Something's going on out there. You could hear it in his voice — Montgomery said, 'Whatever happened, I'm holding you responsible.' Something has gone wrong."

"Of course it did," Jean Calumet said. "He's talking about this . . . this *bait* phone." He rose from the couch, his hands fisted. His face blushed with anger and he turned on the others in the room. "All of you have put Katie's life at risk. I would have just paid. Gotten her back."

Cross shook his head. "Something else. Are you listening to me?" At this point he couldn't help it. The emotions had gotten control of the room, himself included. He glared back at Calumet. "And what are you talking about, you 'would have paid'?"

"Cross!" Bouchard reprimanded.

"You didn't have the money anyway," Cross finished.

Bouchard neared, and Cross was sure his captain was about to grab him and drag him out of the restaurant when the agent at the controls spoke up. "We got this one! Different signal strength — more powerful."

Wick strode over. "Bought at the same location?"

"No. Montgomery only bought the one prepaid at the Target in Plattsburgh. The one we traced to Malone. This one is another species of phone. Hang on . . . We got the identifying numbers on the hardware, just need a few minutes to double-check everything . . ."

Cross was sick of chasing phones.

"Are you crazy?" Jean Calumet bellowed. For a small, sometimes diminutive man, his presence had swollen, his voice filling the room. He grabbed his phone and unplugged it from the wires, shaking with rage.

"Hey!" Wick yelled, grabbing for the phone. "Hey, hey, don't do that! The trace is still running!"

Calumet gripped the phone and glared at Wick, daring the agent to take the phone back.

Sybil rose beside him, calmly, brushing lint from her yoga pants. She looked at the police like they were insignificant then took her husband by the arm.

"We're done here," Sybil said. "This is a family matter." She faced Wick. "You can speak to our lawyers about anything else."

She took Calumet by the hand and made as if to leave.

Cross stopped them. "Listen. I'm with you. You're right — we went after a bait phone. Our priority needs to be Katie. And I'm telling you I think something happened out there, wherever she is. We have to work together now . . ."

Jean Calumet took a threatening step forward. "This is *my* daughter, *my* life. You have no right to hijack my life and put Katie in danger like this. These people would've let her go. I know it. I'm going to pay, and that's it."

"This guy," Cross reasoned, "you heard him — okay? He's rattled. Who is Montgomery to you, Jean? Do you know Johnny Montgomery? Troy Vickers?"

Calumet lowered his voice to a menacing whisper. "I don't know any of these people. But he wants to deal with me, and me alone. He said so from the beginning. We're leaving."

"Sit down, Jean." It was David. "Or I'm going to start talking."

Calumet was stunned. The air was so thick with tension it felt heavy, like gravity was stronger here. Nobody moved.

Cross faced David. Before he could speak, Calumet shouted across the room, "Look at you — you think anyone wants to listen to you?" He pointed at David, presumably indicating his handcuffs as he snarled, "Are you . . . Is this helping anything? This is what you do? Katie is out there and this is what you've got, David? You don't . . . Nothing you could say would change anything anyway. You're worthless."

Cross continued to stare at David, thinking, *What do you know? What haven't you told me?*

David addressed the group. "If my father-in-law is right about one thing, we need to pay these people and get Katie back. That's the only move." His gaze zeroed in on Calumet. "But you need to sit down, shut up, and do what you're told."

Jean Calumet was fuming but stayed in the restaurant, even as his wife Sybil pulled on his arm. Finally, she gave up.

Bouchard spoke in Cross's ear. "Kitchen. Right . . . *now*."

* * *

They stood among the stainless steel features of the inn's large kitchen.

Bouchard paced. "Jesus Christ. Do they *know* the kidnappers, or what?"

"I don't know. But I think Brennan is right. Even Calumet is right. We just need to pay. No more traces. And we need to widen the search."

Bouchard pointed at the wall. "I've got 300 people out there, searching Bakers Mills and the outlying area. We're talking about Bakers Mills, to Speculator, further west to Old Forge, then south, east, north — what? Search an area of six, maybe seven thousand square miles? We've had DEC keeping an eye out for smoke for the past twenty-four hours. But fires are allowed everywhere outside the High Peaks. There are fires all over the place. We're out of moves."

Bouchard stopped pacing and gazed levelly at Cross. "And what are you talking about? 'Something is wrong,' you keep saying. Look — maybe Katie's abductors didn't expect that truck driver to find the phone as quick as he did, and throw it away somewhere close enough for us to find it that fast. That's what went wrong — whatever you heard in his voice. First you think they're 'out there,' and now you think something happened — we don't have evidence for any of it."

Cross was silent.

"What about Gebhart?" Bouchard asked.

"Still comatose. There's a chance he might not even wake up. What's David Brennan doing here? Gates said he got physical with a trooper. Why is he—?"

"The feds don't like all the press at the house and are keeping the Calumets sequestered. I wanted everyone in one place, so I had Brennan brought over."

Bouchard leaned heavily against the large stove. He scrubbed a hand over his face.

"You called the kidnapper by name." Bouchard looked older than usual, tired. "That was a unilateral decision you made, and it could have terrible consequences."

"Cap—"

Bouchard lifted his hands and drew a deep breath. "Agent Sair was explicit — we should give the kidnappers no indication of what we know, or think we know."

When Bouchard met eyes with Cross, he seemed saddened. "I'm going to let you go here, Cross. I want to defer to the FBI completely. We have strong evidence of foreign commerce now that we know the bank is in Switzerland, and that puts it fully in federal jurisdiction."

"Captain Bouchard . . ." Cross said, straightening his spine.

They stood facing each other, and Cross's phone buzzed in his pocket. He took the call.

"Gates?"

"Call came into the hotline a few minutes ago," she said. "A family on the Northville-Placid Trail heard someone scream yesterday."

Cross caught a breath and held it. Then he relayed the information to Bouchard and put the phone on speaker so they could both hear. "Dana, I'm here with Bouchard. Why are they just calling in now?"

"Just got back home. That's a long hike. They hadn't seen any of the news. And they weren't sure — they thought the noise they'd heard might've been an animal. Then they saw the report about the minivan."

Cross locked eyes with Bouchard. "That's the right region. I mean it's another forty-five minutes west of Bakers Mills, right? But Speculator is close — could be the route they took."

The captain was rubbing his chin, thinking. Then he looked at Cross. "Could have been anything. Could have been anyone."

Cross waited, holding Bouchard's eye.

"Go," the captain said.

"Dana, I'm on my way."

CHAPTER THIRTY-FOUR

Katie watched Hoot investigate Carson's body on the rocks below. She heard the oscillating pitch of a plane passing overhead and looked up. It was a commercial jet, at least 20,000 feet up, pulling a perfect white streak.

Were there any aircraft searching for her now? Or anyone on foot? Did anyone have even the slightest clue where she was? And now she was leaving. If a low-flying plane saw her SOS, she wouldn't be here.

When Hoot finally came back up the ridge, she was exhausted from searching the cabin yet again. But no mirror, not even a shiny belt buckle for signaling planes. She had the hatchet, though, and thought the blade could potentially reflect light.

The wristwatch attached to her rope belt read two fifteen. Precious hours slipping away.

She fell in step with him as he wordlessly crossed the clearing, barely seeming aware of her.

"Are we ready to leave? Everything good?"

She braced for his response — *Ah-nope, we'll wait for tomorrow* — but was pleasantly shocked when Hoot said, "Yah. Get yer stuff."

"I've got everything. Just one thing I need to do."

She hurried back to the cabin. Hoot kept on moving toward the woods, like it made no difference. If she wanted Hoot to get her out, it was going to be on his schedule, apparently, and she needed to hustle.

She set the sat phone down on the gas range and pressed the SOS button. While she'd waited for Hoot she'd written a note on the inside of a piece of box board from Carson's snacks using a piece of charred wood from the fire. It read, simply, *Katie Calumet.*

She didn't know where she was going, on what route Hoot was going to take them out of the mountains. Even if she had, she wouldn't want to leave the information to fall into the wrong hands. Just her name, just an indication that she was alive, and if there was a chance any emergency services were monitoring, it would lead them here.

She found Hoot already into the woods and caught up to him.

She'd bathed again, even washed out her running skirt and top, redressing herself in wet clothes. Maybe not the best idea as they were still damp and she could feel her skin chafing, but if the lingering scent of blood meant coyotes on their tail, she could live with a damned rash. It was the rest of her aches and pains that made the going rough.

Hoot moved fast. He seemed to know right where he was going, even though Katie didn't register any sort of trail. She glanced back through the trees and caught sight of the cabin.

She drew a shuddering breath and felt the sting of tears.

Fuck you, cabin.

Maybe, if she got out of this, she'd come back one day and see it burned to the ground.

For now, she was once again plunging headlong into the unknown.

The thought occurred to her repeatedly — if she made it out of this — *when* she made it out of this — she would never look at the mountains in the same way again.

Following Hoot, it became even clearer to her that she'd made the right decision. It was wrong to think the woods were a trifle compared to other extremes in nature.

They were not.

Ten minutes after they'd left the clearing, Katie was utterly lost. She'd gotten her bearings back there, able to orient herself to basic directions. She had planned to use a sun dial along the way, which, by scratching a clock in the dirt with noon as due north, was how to create a compass. Even then it had only been a guess which way she would travel. She'd settled on east, but, of course, she'd never left.

Hoot made his way confidently along, but even he stopped several times, seeming to ponder his next move. The stout balsam firs were accompanied by taller trees, blocking much of the afternoon sun. The ground was often rock, crusted with black and yellow lichen, or the short berry shrubs. But then it changed, the ground was softer, and they descended in elevation.

Hoot stopped again. "Someone's followin'."

Katie caught up with him and halted. "You're sure?" She spoke in a whisper.

"Yah."

She saw nothing but green, barely even a trace of their own passing. There were sounds, like pine cones falling, birds, and squirrels. How Hoot discerned human noise in the soundscape, she had no idea.

But then she heard it. A puffing sound, like someone hurrying along, short of breath. Faint, but there, beneath the rustling of the breeze.

She held the hatchet tightly as something cold flashed through her. She glanced at the rifle Hoot was holding.

"What do we do?"

He didn't answer. How very like Hoot not to answer.

If it was Leno following them, he'd be livid, desperate. His prime asset had escaped custody and his partner was dead.

Hoot got going again, changing direction.

They moved perpendicular to the slope for a while, then ascended, back to where the ground was mostly rock. Gaining elevation was terribly discouraging. She wanted to be going down, not up. She wanted out of these woods, endless and disorienting and misleadingly benign as they were.

She'd never paid much attention before but now recalled the statistic about how hikers went missing nearly every weekend in the Adirondacks. It was surprising people didn't talk about it more. They lived in the mountains or visited for pleasure, and once a week someone slipped into oblivion and hardly anyone noticed.

Hoot was going even stronger now. He seemed to have an unlimited reserve of energy. He made almost no sound but stopped frequently to look and listen.

"Where are we going?"

"Goan go up there ta chapel. Can see all around from there."

"The chapel?"

"Yah."

"Is he still following?"

"Yah."

Hoot kept moving. In a few minutes they started down again, and Katie realized they'd crested a summit and were descending the other side. In the valley was a small cabin.

There were still no trails to speak of, not even something worn down by Hoot, let alone hikers.

How was Leno following them? If it *was* Leno, anyway. The short time she'd been around the man, he hadn't struck her as a particularly outdoorsy person. He'd sounded like a thug, barking at Carson to knock it off and shut up, driving the hell out of the minivan like someone more accustomed to city traffic than wilderness navigation.

But she really had no idea about him. He could be an accomplished woodsman; he could be Daniel fucking Boone for all she knew.

She focused on her footing. They were rapidly descending into the valley between peaks, the ground a scree of rocks, as if from a landslide.

At last they reached the log cabin. Ensconced in evergreens, it was even smaller than the other.

A rank smell emanated from inside that Katie identified as dead animal.

Hoot opened the front door and the stink worsened. She glimpsed the interior and saw animal skins hanging. Hoot was tanning hides. They looked like coyote, and one smaller fox.

She stayed outside as Hoot rattled around, perhaps getting more bullets for the rifle. He slung a pack over his shoulder that looked like one a soldier would own, dark green, with a crude peace sign stenciled on the flap. Her own pack was getting heavy, despite its few contents.

He shut the door and hustled away, and Katie followed, glancing around the property at Hoot's things — sawhorses, a pile of hand-hewn lumber, even a homemade wheelbarrow fitted with two bicycle tires.

Behind the cabin was a small clearing and a section of garden, surrounded by a high netting. Hoot was living off the land, hunting for meat and hides, growing vegetables, building his little world. Who knew how long it had been since he'd set foot in hers.

He led them up a trail. Katie was fatiguing — they'd been going nonstop for the past hour at least. She was scared and getting frustrated not knowing where Hoot was leading her. She wanted him to tell her the way out.

She wondered if he even knew. How long had he been out here? When had he last ventured into civilization? A few months ago? A few years?

The terrain grew steep, and she slipped on the mossy ground. She had to crawl in places, almost like rock climbing, clutching small outcroppings like handholds, hoisting herself up.

Hoot scrambled apace, widening the distance between them. She gritted her teeth and moved faster but tried to stay nimble, not slip and fall.

They finally reached a bare spot on the mountainside near the summit. Bare rocks like huge platelets, weeds sprouting from the sutures. She took a handful of tough bramble and yanked herself to her feet.

Nestled into the trees at the top of the rock face was a lean-to, a log cabin like the others but with an open face. There was nothing in it except for a blanket and a small statuette of the Virgin Mary in the corner.

She realized this was what Hoot called the chapel. And once she'd dropped her bags and heaved a few breaths so she wouldn't pass out, she gazed back over the landscape and understood.

The view was spectacular, a rolling range of mountains cupping a deep cirque inclusive of several small ponds and a larger lake. More importantly, it overlooked Hoot's cabin in the valley below, with good sightlines on the approach.

But, she thought, whatever she could see, someone there could see her, too.

Hoot grasped her hand, making her jump. He led her into the trees alongside the lean-to, where they hunkered down. Now they had the view but were hidden.

Before she could speak, the man following them reached Hoot's cabin.

He came in slow, crouched down, and he could've been holding a weapon. He was far away, but she thought she recognized the dark hair, the way he moved.

Then as he drew a bit closer, she could see the boots and pants — he'd been wearing them when he'd taken the cell pic of her.

She was sure it was Leno.

CHAPTER THIRTY-FIVE

Cross turned off Route 30 and onto Jessup River Road, the sedan kicking up dust. He was just northwest of Speculator; the pot-holed road was enclosed with trees, but then a break revealed a range of mountains stretching off into the distance.

Katie. Hang on.

He glanced back at the road.

"Shit!"

Cross slammed on the brakes and skidded to a stop behind a tangle of parked cars and trucks. An angry sheriff's deputy in a brown uniform came running up, waving his arms.

Cross flashed his badge as he got out. "Sorry."

The Hamilton County deputy eyed the badge. "Your people are back there."

He pointed to where Dana Gates and several others huddled around a civilian near a trailhead sign. Laura Broderick was among the group.

Cross dove back into the sedan, grabbed his topo maps, and hurried over.

Gates saw him and made introductions. "Investigator Cross — Todd Sloan. Mr. Sloan is from Philadelphia. He comes up here every summer to take his family hiking."

Sloan was a fit, muscular man in his fifties. He had a firm grip and offered Cross a wan smile.

"Mr. Sloan just took us in to where he could approximate hearing the scream."

Laura Broderick had her own map spread out on the hood of a trooper vehicle. She showed Cross where Sloan had led them.

"Here is the Northville-Placid Trail. You can see where it connects to all these others. Sloan heard the scream here, he thinks. You still feel that's accurate, Mr. Sloan?"

"Yes."

"Okay." Laura placed her finger on a black dashed line on the topo map that twisted and turned but ran mostly north–south. To the west of it, there was nothing but green, indicating thick vegetation. Pure wilderness.

"This is about 300 square miles of nothing," she said, brushing it with her hand. "No hiking, no snowmobile trails, nothing. Just bushwhacking. Very few people venture in."

Cross walked away from the group and took out his cell phone. He turned the camera on and then swept it around the clearing.

There were too many vehicles in view. He moved beyond them, trying to get an image with only trees.

"Cross?"

He rotated around, looking at the screen. Gates and Laura caught up to him.

"What's the matter?" Gates asked.

"I don't know. This is a heavy-use trail? The Northville-Placid Trail? Right?"

"Yeah." Laura scanned the area as if trying to see what he did.

"They wouldn't take Katie into the woods from here," Cross said. "Too many people around. In the picture Montgomery sent, there's nothing but forest. And the trees are different."

He could tell Gates and Laura were giving each other looks.

Laura said, "This is the second-largest wilderness in the Preserve. A hundred and seventy thousand acres . . ."

"You wanted 'remote,'" Gates chimed in. "This is remote."

"What's the terrain like?"

Laura answered. "It ranges. Swamp flats, rolling hills, steep rugged mountains, some sheer cliffs. The topography rolls west to east and rises south to north. Most of the mountains are 2,000 to 3,000 feet in elevation. In here you got Panther Mountain, Jones, and West Canada. Up here Cellar Mountain. Down here, Fort Noble, Lewey. Lots of streams, lots of lakes, ponds, beaver flows, and wetlands."

Cross looked back at the road. The deputy was still there.

"I saw a couple turn-offs," Cross said. "I want to go check them out."

He looked at Gates.

"Yeah, let's go."

They headed back east on Jessup River Road, Gates riding shotgun, Laura in the back.

"This has got to be enough to do it," Cross said. "Move incident command from Bakers Mills to Speculator; expand the search."

"I think so," Gates agreed.

"We need to cut David Brennan loose."

"Justin, he's . . . Bouchard told me what happened at the inn. What's going on with this guy and Katie's family?"

"I don't know. But maybe he'll tell me. Maybe it tumbles out if we let him do what he wants — let him help. He's got a phone and we can tag him."

Gates thought about it. "Alright. I'll see what I can do."

"Any word on Gebhart?"

"They can't operate on him because of his brain swelling, something like that. Still comatose."

"Well his brother knew something. Gebhart gave Jonathan Montgomery the location of a cabin, and it's out there. Hey, here we go . . ."

Cross cranked the wheel and fishtailed onto a dirt road. He righted the course and noticed Gates grabbing on to the handle above the door. "Ride 'em cowboy," she said.

The dirt road was short, and they came to a stop — a grassy clearing. Cross leaned over the steering wheel and peered out the windshield. "Why's this here?"

"It's private," Laura said from the back seat. "You might've seen the posted signs if it wasn't for all the dust in the air."

Cross glanced at her reflection in the rearview mirror. She smiled, then they stepped out.

Laura walked toward the trees, gesturing. "This goes back to Otter Lake. This whole wilderness is surrounded by private land. Where we are, this is some of it — but then once you get in there it's all Adirondack Forest Preserve."

Cross turned to Laura. "You been in there?"

"Oh sure."

He waited, inviting her to share more.

"It's pretty down and dirty. Beautiful. Like I said, a little bit of everything. Peaks, valleys, swamp, you name it. Not for the faint of heart. People who dive in there really like to be off the beaten trail. We pull a few of them out every summer. No cell phone coverage."

"How do you find them?"

The forest ranger made a crooked smile. "We look."

Cross held up his phone and swung around in a circle. He stopped and centered the screen on Gates.

If she had been roughed up with her hands tied, she could've been Katie Calumet.

This was the place.

CHAPTER THIRTY-SIX

Katie crouched beside Hoot, close enough to see the wiry gray hairs sprouting from his ears. Hoot watched Leno like a hunter observing prey. He looked through the scope of the rifle, his burly beard twitching occasionally as he perpetually chewed at something, mashing his lips.

In the valley below, Leno finished checking out the cabin then looked up toward the lean-to. Katie tensed, though she was sure the foliage concealed her. Either Leno would move off, or he would start up the hillside. He'd tracked them this far, so Katie wasn't surprised when the kidnapper made his decision and began coming her way.

"What do we do?" she whispered.

Hoot took his eye from the scope but kept the rifle ready. There was a small knob he twisted upward then pulled back, revealing a breech.

"This has a built-in magazine," he said. "You gotta manually load each round."

She didn't know why he was telling her; he just seemed to do it automatically.

"Takes five rounds." He loaded in the first bullet with calloused yet nimble fingers. "Push it down'ta the magazine;

it fits with the follower plate. Doan try to fit an extra round inta the breech. Just fill it with the five."

"I don't . . . Okay. I see what you're doing."

"All five are in. Push the bolt forward far as you can; close it. Yah. Bolt-head strips a bullet from the magazine. Now she's ready to fire."

"Okay."

Katie swatted at the insects swarming her head. The bugs were bad — the way they seemed to get worse just before a storm, when everything hung thick and still.

"You grab it 'ere, like this. Don't touch the barrel. When you're ready, there's the safety. This is fire; this is safe. Slide it back'ta fire, like this. Then put your finger inside the trigger guard, right dere. Use the scope for long range. When you're ready'ta fire, take a big breath, let it out part way. Then hold and squeeze the trigger. Don't pull it; squeeze it."

"Alright."

"To shoot again, you'll hav'ta slide the bolt back, get another round in dere."

It was the most articulate Hoot had been since she'd met him. He was calm, exuding a cold focus.

She felt the sweat running down the sides of her face. Thunder rumbled in the distance. She tried to commit the rifle lesson to memory while she watched closely for Leno.

There was a faint rustle in the trees on the opposite side of the bald rocks, but Leno didn't appear. Then there was a crunch. The noise emanated from a different spot, like Leno was still moving through the woods, not showing himself.

"He goin' around behind us," Hoot whispered.

Katie's heart pounded. She clutched the hatchet and waited, breathless. Hoot crawled away, moving behind her.

"Wait," she called in an urgent whisper.

He turned to face her, still on his hands and knees.

"If something happens — how do I get out? How do I get to Atwell?" She'd been trying some variation of *Where am I?* and *How do I get out?* since they'd left the original cabin.

"Southwest. This is Twin Mountain. You need to go o'er the next peak, make camp by the lake. Go o'er Spruce the next day. That's a big 'un. Then there's the trail to Haskell Road. You might get out in two days, or could take ya three."

A flood of relief. At last she had some references, some direction. She thought she'd heard of Haskell Road before.

But maybe it was wishful thinking.

Hoot moved deeper into the trees before she could ask more questions. She didn't risk calling to him. Then he was gone, leaving her alone.

She waited, getting pins and needles in her legs from crouching. She thought she detected Hoot still moving, but farther away. The bramble was thick, and she couldn't see shit. She tried to get a better view of the far side of the peak, where the trees were stippled, the visibility better.

And then she saw Leno, moving through the tall pines, just for a second. He was at least a hundred yards away.

She waited a few more seconds, building up the nerve, then she bolted from the cover, sprinted across the open rock, and plunged into the stand of spruce on the other side, the downslope providing all sorts of momentum — too much momentum — and she fell.

She sprang back up, gnashing her teeth against the terror of harming her baby. Fresh pain grasped at her leg, like something had finally given — her quad muscle tearing — but she kept going, skip-running down into the valley.

Of all things, the tale of Peter Rabbit occurred to her. She remembered her mother reading it, and the part after Peter left Mr. McGregor's garden where he went "lippity lippity" along.

She scurried into the cabin clearing, darted past the sawhorses and wheelbarrow, and slipped in the front door.

It took a moment for her eyes to adjust to the gloom, but she saw a rifle hanging on the wall. It looked just like the gun Hoot was carrying.

As she reached for it, she heard a shot.

She froze, her hand inches from the weapon.

It could have been a bolt of lightning. The sky was really rumbling now, and the sound might have been the onset of a storm. The mugginess was cloying, the cabin rank. Flies buzzed in the dirty windows.

There was another crack from the hilltop, and the sound rolled away, echoing off the mountains.

It had to be gunfire.

Two shots, within seconds of each other.

She took off her backpack, grabbed the rifle and pulled it down.

There had to be bullets somewhere in the cabin; she'd heard Hoot collecting a few handfuls earlier. She started going through his things.

The cramped space was oddly tidy, all of his tools neatly arranged, hanging from wall pegs. She brushed against a dangling coyote hide as she reached for a burlap sack on a nail.

There was a box of ammunition inside.

Katie lowered to the dirty floor and opened the gun's breech the way Hoot had just shown her, by moving the bolt upward and sliding it back.

Her hands were steady as she loaded in the five shots and slid the bolt back with a click. She'd never held a rifle before, let alone fired one.

Someone was coming down the hillside — a snap of branches. They were moving at a good clip, careless about the noise they were making.

Her heart slammed against her ribs. Movement like that, it didn't sound like Hoot.

"Katie!"

The voice sent a spike through her heart. She panicked. Leno was out there, howling, coming for her, making a racket.

His figure slid past the window. She tried to breathe.

A few seconds went by. She struggled to stay composed, though her heart was beating so fast she thought it would give out.

Leno appeared in the window, smacking his palms against the glass, leering, his eyes wide.

"Katie Calumet!" He loomed there then jerked away, leaving a red print where his hand had been.

He was wounded. Or he was covered in Hoot's blood.

She couldn't think. Her hearing had gone — just the thrum of blood in her ears.

Then she saw it: Hoot had installed a deadbolt on the door. In a rush, coming into the cabin, she hadn't noticed.

She started to get up, stopped.

Leno wouldn't leave, not even if the door was locked. He'd smash the window, maybe shoot at the door; he'd force his way in however he could.

This was it.

Feeling numb, as if bathed in ice water, she aimed the gun at the door, tucking the back of the rifle up under her arm.

She gripped the stock and stuck her finger through the trigger loop.

The safety.

Leno was right outside, his footsteps coming to the door. Katie found the lever and clicked it back to the fire position, the way Hoot had done it.

Leno yanked the door open. "Alright now, Katie, you—"

Katie squeezed the trigger.

Leno hadn't expected it.

His mouth had formed an oval, his eyes widened with surprise.

Now he lay on his back, wheezing in the dirt, trying to roll over and get to his feet. He was wearing camo pants and a camo hoodie, like a hunter. Katie could see the dark blood spreading through the shirt.

She thought she'd shot him in the stomach.

The rifle trembled in her grip. She got a better hold of it, took a deep breath, and stepped toward Leno.

Leno managed to get over then up on his hands and knees.

Shoot him again.

She'd never fired a gun, never shot anyone, never even been in a fight. Once in the eighth grade, Mary Tamburlaine had pulled her hair, and Katie had slapped the girl on the arm, forcing her to let go. That was it. Now a man was crawling away from her, and she'd put a bullet in his body.

He was reaching for the handgun he'd dropped when he fell over. He was almost to it.

But he wasn't moving.

Katie got closer, aiming down the sight of the rifle at the back of his head, and moved in front of him. She was able to hook the heel of her foot over the handgun and drag it through the mud toward her. She got a hold of it and tucked it in the waistband of her skirt.

Then she ran.

As close an approximation to running as she could, anyway, hobbled by her many ailments, especially the pain in her leg. She went back into the woods toward the hillside and the chapel, justifying her actions as she snapped and cracked through the trees, tearing at the branches — she wasn't a murderer.

You're scared. And now you've left him alive. You don't know anything about guns. What caliber did you just shoot him with? Maybe it missed his abdominal artery, maybe it's just a "flesh wound."

Maybe so. But she had his handgun.

He could have another weapon. Or get into Hoot's things, find another rifle — Hoot had one with him on the hill. You just left the most dangerous man in your life alive when you could have ended it.

She scrambled up the hill and came to the section of rock, searching for Hoot.

He wasn't at the lean-to, and she pushed her way into the bramble flanking the cabin, to where she'd sat beside the hermit twenty minutes before.

She clawed her way to the other side of the thicket, to the more open area. Spotted Hoot twenty yards away, just his hand, sticking out of the bushes, and she ran over.

His eyes were open, but he wasn't moving or breathing. His neck was covered in blood. The bullet wound was high in his chest, likely his heart had been pierced.

Leno was a better shot than she was.

Katie lost tension in her legs and dropped to her knees, suddenly weak, short of breath. Her mouth filled with saliva and her stomach rolled.

She pulled herself away from Hoot and threw up. Everything came out of her.

Shaking all over, feeling cold and exhausted, she rolled over onto her back and stared up at the sky as the first drops of rain started to fall.

* * *

It became a downpour.

Lying face up, Katie let it soak her. She closed her eyes as the droplets pinged off her lids, opened her mouth and let it rain on her tongue. Then she sat up at last and looked around.

The world was a gray wash, the trees sagging in the deluge, water already coursing down the rocks in great streams.

No idea what to do next. The sun was going down somewhere behind the thick pate of dark clouds.

She glanced at Hoot and considered doing something with his body, but she was in no shape to drag him back down to the valley, and she had more pressing concerns.

Maybe Leno was just waiting for her to come back. Or maybe he was making his way up the hillside.

She didn't see anyone. The hush of rain drowned out any sounds.

She waited.

It occurred to her that Leno could have a sat phone, paired to the one she'd found in the cabin. She'd been afraid Carson's phone meant someone was coming — now she knew it was Leno. Carson could have easily been checking in with him when Katie wasn't watching.

Carson's sat phone hadn't been subscribed to the emergency service network, and probably Leno's wouldn't be either, but Leno might have been the one making ransom demands, and his phone — if he in fact had one — was likely to have battery power.

She shakily rose to her feet. She hobbled back to the thicket around the lean-to, sure that any noise she made was concealed by the storm.

If Leno had a phone, even if it had gotten wet, it was built to be rugged. More shock-proof than Carson's GPS, possibly.

She snuck up alongside the lean-to and risked a look into the open structure. No one there.

Her view overlooked the valley, but not with an angle on the front of Hoot's cabin. If Leno was still there, she couldn't see.

She needed to get closer.

In a minute.

Katie stayed in the chapel, keeping cover out of the rain. There was no need to rush down there. Leno was shot — let him bleed out. Even if the bullet wound hadn't been instantly fatal, it could still be a mortal wound, certainly not survivable without medical attention.

Her monitoring mind mused about having such thoughts. Three days ago she'd been focused on an upcoming presentation for the SPCA board, and obsessing over whether or not to spend the money on a new pair of running shoes (she hadn't).

Today she was in the middle of the mountains, miles from anywhere civilized, considering how long it would take for the man she'd just shot with a rifle to die.

What would she do if she was in his position? If he had made his way in, it was more than reasonable to think he knew the way out. In addition to the sat phone, he might've had a GPS, like Carson. Or maybe the sat phone itself had GPS. So he might be cutting his losses, desperate to survive his wound and making his exit through the woods right now.

But she'd seen his face. If he wasn't hurt too badly, he'd try to salvage the kidnapping, counting on the ransom money to keep him out of the law's reach.

Or, he might try to kill her. Just tie up the loose ends and then vanish.

The rain showed no sign of letting up, and she wasn't getting any drier sitting in the lean-to. She wouldn't be safe in the chapel tonight, despite Hoot's statuette of the Virgin Mary.

And her view was disappearing with the daylight.

Stay here, and risk another confrontation with Leno — on his terms.

Take control, confront her fear, maybe get a sat phone or a GPS out of it at last.

Katie tucked the rifle under her arm and moved down the rock face, careful this time not to take a tumble. She kept watch for Leno anywhere near the cabin until the forest obscured her view.

It was dark within the trees, everything a white noise of rain, gloomier by the second.

She said a small prayer that Leno was dead, and that he had a sat phone on his person somewhere, one with battery, one that worked.

Just this one thing, God.

I haven't asked for anything so far. I've been patient.

Now I'm asking.

Just this one thing.

Just this.

CHAPTER THIRTY-SEVEN

It was growing dark as Cross drove into the small town of Speculator. A light rain began to fall.

The main drag passed the fire station. Bouchard had gotten in touch with the local fire department and the three-bay firehouse was going to become the new incident command.

The press had already begun to gather, their contacts within the community doubtlessly tipping them off that the locus of the investigation had shifted. One intrepid reporter was braving the worsening weather, standing with his back to the fire station, face glowing in the camera light.

There was a diner further down the street. Cross needed a place to meet David and Gloria — David had been released by Bouchard after Gates made convincing statements. And Cross needed to go through the plan he was going to lay out for Burt Frost, the man heading up the massive search and rescue effort.

The small diner looked open, and Cross killed the engine. The rain was really coming now, pelting the car like stones. He ran inside holding an arm over his head.

He'd barely shaken off the water and taken a booth by the window when David called, minutes away.

"Order us whatever you're having," David said. "We haven't eaten all day."

That makes three of us, Cross thought.

* * *

An odor of greasy hamburgers filled the air. Country music played in the background, a child wailed at a table where parents looked red-faced and overwrought. The cook called from the kitchen that an order was up.

David and Gloria entered; David sat down across from Cross at the booth and Gloria excused herself to the bathroom to wash up.

David used a napkin to blot his wet face and ran a hand through his dark wet hair.

"Thank you. You know, for . . ."

Cross nodded.

"You probably have some questions."

Cross glanced out into the advancing darkness. Right now, Burt Frost was putting out the call to searchers to converge in Speculator at the firehouse as soon as the storm cleared. Volunteers would be preparing to leave their families to search for someone they'd never met.

"I'm only interested in what could help us get Katie back," Cross said.

"And so am I," David said. "If I wasn't completely focused on that, I'd be pretty upset that I was detained for trying to help my own wife." There was a vein protruding from his forehead.

"I know." Cross omitted any comments about David getting physical with a trooper, how he could be in worse trouble right now if Bouchard had decided to take him to the woodshed rather than let him go. "I've been putting myself in your shoes from the beginning," Cross said. "But I think there are things that . . . I need you to be straight with me now."

The waitress came, interrupting, poured coffee, and left.

David took a sip of the hot liquid and grew contemplative. "You know how in families, people try to help, everyone has their advice, or suggestion, and mostly you just want them to leave you to your business? This is that on a nightmare scale."

"What do you mean?"

"Too many cooks in the kitchen."

"Well you're going to have that, with something like this," Cross said. "But what would you do differently?"

"They should've just dealt with me," David said.

Cross wasn't sure who he meant — the police or the kidnappers.

The wind threw a spray of rain against the windows. The storm was getting worse and Cross could see trees bending in the dark.

"We have to find her," David said.

"I know. We're close."

David lowered his head. "Ah man, this thing is so fucked up."

Gloria returned and sat next to David. "That's better." She'd managed to partially dry her hair and Cross could smell the hand soap.

"Let's go through it," Cross said. "The three of us. Let's figure this thing out. Let's start with what's happening with Jean and Sybil. David, you said, 'I'll start talking.'"

David closed his eyes a moment. The way Gloria was watching her brother-in-law, Cross felt like she was as in the dark as Cross was. But both of them had secrets, Cross thought. It was in their body language; it was in everything they didn't say.

"Jean is not a bad guy." David opened his eyes. "He's just made some bad deals. Sybil is trying to protect him."

"What sort of bad deals?"

"I can't really say."

"You can't say or you don't know?"

"I don't really know any details."

Cross opened his mouth to pressure David, but Katie's husband put up his hands again. "Trust me, if I thought it would help find her, I'd make some up."

"Okay — you realize you were the one who gave me the names. We've been looking into Henry Fellows, Eric Dubois, Lee Beck . . ."

Gloria scowled, staring at David. "Fellows? What did you say about him?"

"Just that Jean and Henry had their differences. You know how Henry was — Katie said he was calling Jean for weeks. He was suicidal at one point."

Gloria was shaking her head. She stared into her coffee and said, quietly, "It's not Henry."

"How do you know?" David watched her intently.

She struggled to meet his gaze.

"Excuse me," he said, abrupt. "My turn to wash up."

David rose to his feet and Gloria slid out of his way. He walked away toward the bathrooms.

Cross felt like he was watching some absurd play, characters getting on and off the stage.

After a silence, Gloria said, "David worked for my father a few years ago."

"I didn't know that."

She nodded. "He helped with the final construction of the Dobbs Ferry restaurant. Mainly setting up the kitchen, but he even helped my father create the menu. David is a great cook. He was a chef for years while he played in his band."

Cross's mind was moving in several directions. He seized on one train of thought. "Gloria, did your father ever run into anything . . . buying his hotels, the restaurant he built from scratch — did he ever encounter any resistance?"

"Resistance?"

"Pushback. Anyone who, I don't know, thought they had claim to an area. Or demanded a no-bid contract, you know, that they were entitled to the construction work, things like that."

Her expression grew somber. "You mean organized crime."

"I guess, yeah."

"Not that I've ever heard of. I mean, it's not Atlantic City, you know? He built the restaurant in Dobbs Ferry after the previous one burned down. That site was dormant for a few years, he bought it, and then he built. I don't remember who he hired. Some company from Yonkers, I think. David did some finish work toward the end, on his own."

"Do you know how your parents were able to come up with the money? They seemed to be struggling, but they suddenly jumped from twelve million to seventeen . . ."

Cross trailed off as he watched Gloria's eyes tracking someone moving through the diner. A moment later, David sat back down.

"Listen," David said. "None of this matters. What matters is we need to be out there looking." It looked like he'd taken a moment to calm down; his hair was fixed, the vein in his forehead less prominent.

Cross said, "It matters if this thing — you don't have details, okay — but whatever it is, if this kidnapping grew out of it . . ."

"I don't think so."

"Then why bring it up?"

David pursed his lips, folded his arms, and stared back at Cross.

"Okay," Cross said, exasperated. "We'll let that be for now. Let's try to think like the kidnappers — whoever they are. What was their plan? Okay? We know — we strongly suspect — Johnny M. talks to Jeff Gebhart, finds out about the park, where the most remote locations are, abandoned cabins, that sort of thing. Right?"

David nodded agreement.

"Okay. So, Johnny enlists Troy Vickers to help with the heavy lifting. They boost a minivan in Ogdensburg. But — there's a second vehicle, and they switch to it a few miles west of Bakers Mills, leaving the minivan behind."

Their food arrived, another interruption. Maybe meeting over a meal was a bad idea. The waitress set out the steaming plates and asked if anyone needed anything else.

"Thanks, we're good," Cross said.

David and Gloria were watching him, waiting. No one touched their food yet, though Cross's stomach clenched with hunger. He tried to pick up the thread again.

"We don't know what the second vehicle is, but maybe it's something with off-road capabilities. A rugged SUV or a four-by-four truck, something. They get as far as they can into the interior, you know, in the vehicle, then take Katie into the woods, to one of these cabins, at this point on foot. But probably Johnny M. stays behind, makes the first call to Jean, demanding the ransom. He uses a prepaid Tracfone, but then he plants it on a tractor-trailer, so we chase it almost all the way to Canada."

David leaned in. "Didn't you speak to this guy's brother? Gebhart? Why aren't they telling us what cabins they have? Or know of?"

"They will. Or they're going to go to jail. But let's say Vickers is the one to go in with Katie. Okay? Montgomery stays out, makes the calls. He places a second call fifteen minutes later, doubling the ransom . . . What?"

David sat up straight, pulled in a long breath. "I came up with it."

"You put up the rest of the money?" Cross asked.

Katie's husband looked down at his steaming food. "It was money I had gotten from Jean for the work I did."

"I'm sorry — we're talking about $5 million. Right?"

David's eyes snapped up. "It was insurance."

"What do you mean? For what?"

"Sweeten me up. Keep me quiet."

"About what?" But Cross could already see they were back to the same place.

David said, "Look, I'm sorry — I'm not going to sit here and incriminate Jean. I can't do it. And I don't think it's related. But yeah, I took money. And then I used it, for this."

"You took money, hush money, but you don't know anything?"

David grabbed the table hard enough to rattle the cutlery. "I know enough to have been paid to stay out of it, and enough to know this—"

"No — you don't know enough to say one has nothing to do with the other. Okay? You don't."

David slowly sat back, at last defeated.

Gloria had paled. She stared into space. Suddenly her brow furrowed in anger and she leaned toward David. "You know what Wick said? That FBI agent? They want to look at my businesses. My store, my restaurant. Want to talk to all my employees." Her lip trembled and her eyes welled. "Does that have something to do with what you're talking about, David? Or *not* talking about?"

"No. Nothing. I don't know."

"Okay, let's all take a breath." Cross focused on David. "Don't you see how this has broken your family apart? Maybe someone who wanted to get back at your father-in-law? I don't know everything about kidnappings; only that they're rare, and they hardly ever work. Is it possible money wasn't the object? If you tell me what happened, maybe that's exactly what *does* help get Katie back."

David shook his head. "Our family was already broken apart," he said. "This is about money, and that's it."

David surveyed his food, picked up the cutlery, and started eating. Gloria stared out into the storm. Despite the tension at the table and whether or not it was impolite, Cross relished the salty diner food.

After a few minutes he wiped his mouth. He had a new tack. "David, you pointed me toward Henry Fellows, Eric Dubois, Lee Beck. People you thought might have the emotionality, the audacity, or be in the financial straits to attempt something like this. I'm wondering if we've missed someone."

He looked at Gloria, thinking that investigating her restaurant and stores — employees — wasn't such a bad idea. But she didn't look like she needed to hear that.

Jean Calumet had far more people working for him anyway. Someone who coveted his wealth. Who might've despised him — fueling their drive to take from him in such a violent and risky way.

"It's too late for secrets," Cross said. "We all want Katie back, safe and sound. David, when I say I don't care about the investigation into your father-in-law — I don't. Any more than I care about what you did to get that money. I ask only in the interest that it helps your wife. If we know who took her, then that's a hell of a lot better than spending days looking for her, maybe weeks — especially when she's out there in the wilderness in weather like this, possibly injured, who knows."

All three of them looked out the plate-glass window of the diner. Night had fully arrived. The lights from the restaurant lit the rain silver as it pummeled the cars in the parking lot.

David spoke up at last. "I know you're looking out for Katie's best interest, and I believe you. But whoever hired these guys — Montgomery, Vickers — they left the specifics up to them. That's my gut. Wherever Katie is, the only people who know are the ones who have her."

"Are we talking about organized crime? The thing you . . . The thing Jean Calumet got involved with, that you're supposed to stay quiet about?"

David vehemently shook his head. He started getting out money to pay. Cross thought he was through talking, but as he slapped down a couple twenty-dollar bills, David said, "It was about tax stuff. That's all I'm going to say. You're barking up the wrong tree."

Cross wondered if he meant fraud. But he decided not to press any further on it and accept David's answer for now.

Cross pushed the twenties back at David. "This is on me. Actually, it's your tax dollars already at work."

He offered David a smile, but Katie's husband was sullen.

The three of them left the diner, bracing against the wind and rain. Cross jumped into his car as David and Gloria piled into a Land Rover.

They drove a short ways down the street to the Leaf Blower Inn and pulled in. Cross watched as David got out and jogged to the office with the "no vacancy" sign lit in the window. The state police had already booked several rooms, and David was checking in. Cross would do the same, but he was fixed on Gloria, still seated behind the steering wheel.

He got out of his car and trotted over.

She rolled down the window and squinted against the rain ricocheting in.

"Your room is a double," he said. "Hope that's okay."

She shook her head. "I have to go back to Brooklyn."

He just stood there, getting soaked all over again. "Tonight?"

"I left everything," she explained. "I can't just stay away. Especially not if . . . you know, they're coming down to turn everything inside out. If I get going now I can be there early in the morning. Just need a couple days . . . Then I'll be back."

Cross reached through the open window and patted her shoulder. "Alright, well . . . drive safe. We'll do everything we can for Katie."

"I know you will." Her eyes were welling but she offered a smile then rolled up the window.

Cross watched her back away then turn and drive off into the night.

CHAPTER THIRTY-EIGHT

Leno was dying. He had crawled away from Hoot's cabin and was making his way into the woods on his hands and knees. Katie watched him try to get on his feet, and then fall. She stood behind him in the rain, holding the rifle.

"Who hired you?" She had to nearly shout above the storm.

He didn't answer. After falling, he lay there, face down. She wanted to search him for a sat phone, but he could be playing possum, trying to lull her into letting her guard down, so he could snatch the rifle from her. She wasn't taking any chances.

She'd stashed the handgun. One less gun, one less opportunity to get shot. But what about Hoot's rifle? Too many guns to think about, and she hated guns.

She looked around. Leno had left a trail through the mud on his way to the woods.

She edged closer, keeping her feet spread.

He was still.

Just pull the trigger.

She was in the same position as before she'd run away. Shooting Leno had been a reaction — a rush of adrenaline and instinct. Shooting a dying man as he crawled away was another story. Her body was shaking. She was cold and scared and it was dark. He was moving into the woods.

Lightning flashed, brightening everything to a surreal daylight for a flickering second. Thunder followed close — the storm was right on top of her. Katie continued to hold the rifle on him, willing Leno to just drop to the ground again, to be still, to be dead.

He tried to stand up, his back to her.

Then he fell again.

Pull the trigger.

She racked the bolt, sending a fresh round into the chamber.

Something else caught her eye. Close to the cabin, near where she'd shot Leno, a backpack and the other rifle — Hoot's rifle. Leno must've dropped the items when he opened the front door.

She walked backward, keeping her eye on Leno. When she reached the items, she knelt and checked the pack over. It bore the peace sign stencil. It was Hoot's.

Katie heard a noise and glanced up.

Leno was gone.

"Ah *fuck*."

She stood, swept the area with the rifle. The storm had turned the air cold, and she was shattered from everything; the past hours of running and hiding, going up and down the mountain, being on constant alert.

She dared to venture into the woods a little, looking for Leno, or signs of him, but it was pitch-dark, just a white noise of rain in the forest.

He'd clearly been in rough shape. Hopefully he'd just crawled off to die alone.

But she would have to wait until morning, or at least until the storm had passed, before searching for him and finding out for sure. For now, she needed rest; she needed food and water and to be dry.

She needed warmth. For days she'd been languishing in the heat; now the temperature was plummeting and she was drenched.

The handgun was on the ground where she'd stashed it. She ferried it into the cabin, went back for the pack and the other rifle, brought them inside.

Hoot's cabin was in good repair — even with the torrential downpour, the place was bone-dry. His wood stove wasn't as robust as the one from the previous cabin, but it would certainly heat the small space efficiently. A dismal-looking cot in the corner constituted the sleeping quarters.

She used the lock on the door this time, sliding it home with a satisfying *snick*, then groped around until she found matches and kindling among Hoot's well-organized things, got a fire going.

Her thoughts went to the hermit, lying up there near the chapel, his body exposed to the elements.

She couldn't do anything for him now. She had to focus on surviving.

With the door secured and the fire snapping, she stripped out of her wet clothes. She had to constantly reassure herself that Leno was in a shape too grievous to come back and attempt to harm her, and she had all the weapons. She hoped.

She hung her wet clothes from the rafters and wrapped herself in the blanket on Hoot's cot in the corner.

The blanket stunk of mildew and old sweat, but it was dry, and warm, and she sat cross-legged in front of the fire, the hides swinging gently around her in the wafting heat, their ropes creaking.

* * *

The coyotes howled during the night.

Katie lay awake listening, pointing the rifle at the door, waiting for either Leno or the animals to show up on the other side.

She and David had heard coyotes before from their own property — they sounded like crazed teenagers. *Yipping and hollering*, David had said. He'd been in a pair of overalls that day, splattered with paint and sawdust while he worked on the house. She was partial to him when he was that way, his brow furrowed in concentration, smelling of cut wood.

She liked the musician-David, too — she'd fallen in love with the guy in jeans and a sport jacket playing tortured blues on the piano — but it was the more bucolic, handyman-version of him that had won her over for the long term.

Musicians were great, but men who could cook, fix up the house, and do their own laundry — those were the keepers.

He would've made a good father too.

—He still can. This isn't over yet.

But her whole body seemed to deflate in a post-adrenaline crash, sheer exhaustion and despair creeping in, and Katie let out an inadvertent moan.

She'd been in a state of high alert for hours, climbing and running and falling and shooting guns. It couldn't be good for her body.

Couldn't be good for the baby inside her.

Normally, a woman would know, she thought. But there'd been so much rain, everything soaking wet, blood from her cuts and scrapes running down her legs, so many other pains and traumas . . .

Lying in the darkness of Hoot's cabin, the live coyotes still yipping outside, their dead cousins hanging from the ceiling, thinking about the potential loss of her pregnancy filled her with a thick sorrow.

Thinking about what could have been, and what might now never be.

CHAPTER THIRTY-NINE

The Leaf Blower Inn parking lot was chock full of vehicles — a few troopers but mostly volunteers working the search. Cross kept a spare bag in the back of his car with extra clothes in it for just such an occasion. He had the bag and was headed into his room, planning to shower and reboot himself before heading over to the fire station, when his phone buzzed.

"Petrie wants to talk to you." Marty sounded tired.

"Is everything okay?" Cross keyed into the room and tossed his bag on the bed.

"She's been asking about you since I got home. She keeps talking about some dream she had."

Cross began to understand, and his heart eased back into cruising speed. Patricia had a vivid imagination, and often scary dreams. "Put her on."

"Hi Daddy," Petrie said a moment later. Her voice was unbearably small and cute.

"Hi Petey. How you doin'?" Cross sat down on the bed.

"Good. Daddy, where are you?"

"I'm in a place called Speculator. You remember the playground? Where we played rocket ship on the swing set that time?"

Cross had a sister who lived in Syracuse, and when they went to visit her they sometimes took a route through Speculator. But they hadn't done it since he and Marty separated.

"Yeah I remember and there was the mud from my juice."

It took him a moment but he got it. "That's right. You spilled your juice cup in the sand and it turned the sand into mud. Wow, Petrie. You've got such a good memory."

"Yeah. Daddy, where are you?"

"I told you, honey. Speculator."

"Oh. Speckle-ator." She sounded like she was getting sleepy. "Daddy?"

"What?"

"I had a dream."

"Yeah? Mommy said. What was it?"

"My bed."

"The dream was about your bed?"

"Someone came into the room and was circling my bed and they wanted to sell it and keep it for themselves."

It wasn't unlike Petrie, or any six-year-old, to tell a story with contradictory statements. But his smile faded as he considered what it might have to do with his separation from her mother.

Or maybe that was overanalyzing.

"Yeah, but it was just thoughts in your head, right? Nothing that can hurt you."

"Yeah. Love you, Daddy."

"Love you too," he said, but Petrie had already handed the phone back to Marty.

Marty cleared her throat. She sounded like she was maybe getting sick. "How's it going down there?"

"Wasn't the worst dream she's had."

"No. Not that . . . No."

"Uhm, we're expanding the search."

"Good." Marty sighed. "I hope you find her. It rained pretty hard tonight."

"Here too." Cross looked out the motel window at the wet and shining asphalt. The storm had just abated, but tree limbs were down, and the lights in the room had flickered before he went out to the car for his things.

He wanted to tell her about David Brennan. How Katie's husband had come up with $5 million, the paper trail for which could put him in jail, the way things were shaping up. He wondered what she'd think of that.

He said, "Alright, Marty, I got to go."

"Take care of yourself, Justin."

He skipped a shower. After rinsing his pits and brushing his teeth in the bathroom, he put on a fresh shirt. He picked up his weapon, checked through it, gathered his badge and wallet.

There was a knock on the door.

David had changed clothes, too. Dressed in cargo pants and a skin-tight athletic top, he looked like a member of an insertion team about to be dropped into a Columbian jungle. A determined glint shone in his eyes. "I'm going over there with you, alright?"

"Yeah. That's why you're here."

They left for the fire station.

* * *

The fire chief had moved the fire trucks outside and set up long tables in a horseshoe shape, folding chairs beyond them, arranged classroom-style. The space was set up for organizing the search, bringing the volunteers up to speed when they arrived. First Cross needed to formulate the plan with Burt Frost, a short, burly man with sparkling eyes and a deep voice.

"What have we got for maps of all interior outposts?" Frost asked, scanning what Laura Broderick set out on the tables.

"Unfortunately we don't have one single map that shows them all," she said. "We have several, and that's what I'm trying to piece together here. And I've got Mindy Atkins on the phones, talking to everyone who ever sold their land to the state. If they had a cabin, we're going to take this topo map here, and we're going to mark it down. Hopefully by morning we will have a lot of them. But I doubt we're ever going to get all of them."

The door banged open. Captain Bouchard and Trooper Farrington brought Abel Gebhart into the fire station. Gebhart looked furious. He locked eyes with Cross as the police referred him to the maps.

"Show them what you showed me," Bouchard barked.

Gebhart reluctantly had a look. "This is our family cabin right here," he said, pointing.

"That's Indian Lake," Cross said.

"Yeah. We have a fifty-acre piece of land. Cabin is dead center."

Cross looked at Laura Broderick. "That's north of Route 28. That's thirty, maybe forty miles from where Sloan heard the scream."

"Who's Sloan?" Bouchard asked. "That's the civilian? The hiker?"

"Yeah." Cross looked at Gebhart. "What else did your brother know about?" Cross circled an area with his finger called Blue Ridge Wilderness. "You go hunting in this area?"

Gebhart just glowered. "Maybe."

"What about down here?" Cross pointed to Black River Wild Forest, about twenty miles southwest.

Gebhart shrugged. "It's possible."

David, who'd remained standing quietly by, stepped forward. "Hey — my wife is out there. Okay? This isn't about your civil liberties, so just answer the question."

Gebhart squared up with David, getting red in the face. "The fuck you say to me?"

Cross moved closer. "Alright, gentlemen, let's—"

Gebhart cocked a fist back, hitting Cross in the nose with his elbow. Cross saw stars and stumbled back. David reached for him and missed.

Gebhart glanced at Cross then took a swing at David anyway, landed a punch on his neck. David stayed up, turned in to Gebhart, and shoved the man to the ground. Then David got on top of Gebhart, raised his fist to hit him.

"You fuckin . . ." David managed. His whole face shook with rage. But he didn't hit Gebhart, and the cops pulled him off.

Gebhart scrambled to his feet.

Trooper Farrington grabbed Gebhart from behind and put him in a hold. But Gebhart was going wild, trying to pull free, yelling obscenities, spit flying from his lips. Another trooper moved in to assist. The two wrestled Gebhart to the floor.

Cross shook off the pain stabbing through his nose and eyes. "Get him up!"

The troopers hauled Gebhart to his feet. Farrington was getting out his cuffs, but Cross took Gebhart by the arm. He yanked the man back toward the maps. "Show us. Now!"

Gebhart bared his teeth and stabbed a finger at the maps, then swept it in an arc. "This! Okay? We've been all over this whole area! Blue Ridge, Little Moose, all the way down to Black River, to Atwell. There are a shit ton of cabins back in there. Happy?" Gebhart jerked away from Cross.

Farrington got a hold of the man again, locked cuffs around his wrists, red-faced and huffing from the effort. Bouchard had a grip on David but didn't have him cuffed and let him go. He jammed a finger in David's chest. "Is that it from you? Am I going to have to bring you in? Think you can help your wife from jail?"

David glared at Abel Gebhart as he was led away. Gebhart took a parting shot from the door. "You'll be hearing from my lawyer. All of you." The door slammed shut and he was gone.

David walked over to some of the chairs and sat down. The fifty-odd people in the room were all staring.

Cross looked at the maps again.

Laura Broderick acted like none of it had happened. She continued as calmly as before. "These are the two interior outpost cabins for Snowy Mountain."

"DEC cabins."

"Correct."

"And they're both active?"

"No. One of them was decommissioned. The other one is still there; that's, ah, Doug Frechete who's caretaking there. We talked to him already; he hasn't seen anything."

A bright red drop landed on the map.

"You're bleeding," Laura said.

Cross looked at it a moment before realizing it had come from him. He wiped his nose with his thumb, wiped his thumb on his pants.

"These are too far north anyway," Cross said. "What about in here?"

"One decommissioned outpost here, Fort Noble. One here, Cedar Lakes. I think that one was let go in ninety-two."

Cross grabbed a marker from a pile nearby. He circled the two locations on the map. "What about right here in the center? West Canada Mountain Primitive Area?"

"No ranger cabins there."

"What's a 'primitive area,' exactly?" Cross asked.

"Primitive area means, among other things, forest that hasn't had a fire in a few hundred years so it's old growth — not that fresh, crisp green, but tangled and messy."

"How much of this land in here was acquired by the state?"

"Well, all of it."

"What I mean to say is — is Gebhart right? Private hunting cabins in here that were left when it was turned into the Preserve?"

"For sure."

"How many? He said 'shit ton.' Can you quantify that?"

Cross heard some chuckles. His silly joke managed to lighten the mood.

Laura scratched her jaw. "Tough to say. This part of the park is a bit better for growing marijuana. So you've got hunting cabins and you've got outlaw cabins. Between this primitive area and down through here in Black River Wild Forest, I'd say forty? Fifty? I really don't know."

Cross turned to Frost and Bouchard. "Well, this is our search area. Right here."

Frost clucked his tongue, looking it all over. "That's a bit to cover."

"I know. But we're putting two choppers in the air at first light. Right, Captain?"

Bouchard nodded. "And three planes. Look for smoke; look for any signs."

Frost spread his hands out over the map, avoiding the splotch of Cross's blood. "I think we do our bump lines like this," he said, and he made arrows with a marker. "Go the way the contours are rolling."

Cross looked at David, sitting a ways away. "David? Anything to add? Let's say Katie was taken to one of these sites. And something happened. What would she do? Would she stay put? Or try to walk out?"

David slowly rose. He gave Bouchard a quick glance and approached. He scrutinized the map, as if he could visualize his wife amid the elevation colors and grid lines.

"She'd stay put, unless she was scared by something."

"So we focus on hunting cabins," Cross said.

"It's conceivable she could find her way to a decommissioned ranger outpost," Bouchard said. "Maybe she could even walk out."

"Sure," Laura said. "But — when's the last time you went hiking? Like, off-trail, backcountry hiking? You've got cliffs, you've got tight stands to go around, you've got creeks and rivers to traverse, and for every obstacle you circumnavigate, even if you've got a compass, know your way around in the wilderness, I mean — it can get disorienting real quick. We search for a hiker a week, at least. I go out hunting, and I'm walking in what I think is a straight line, then I look at my compass — my heart does a flip; I'm turned 180 degrees around in the opposite direction. Point being, getting disoriented happens to even experienced woodsmen."

"What's her visibility like out there?" Cross asked. "I've been hiking a few times — you can see roads in the distance."

"It all depends," Laura said. "You've got summits with a view, and plenty of others where there is no view, no bare rock, trees all around. This area here is packed with vegetation. Like I said, real easy to get disoriented, real easy to get injured . . ."

Laura stopped herself. Cross thought everyone was suddenly especially aware of David Brennan.

He smiled thinly, then he left, probably to smoke a cigarette.

Bouchard caught the eyes of another trooper, jerked his head at the door. The trooper went out to watch David.

Then Bouchard drew near to Cross. The captain was looking at the knuckles of his right hand, grazed from the melee, presumably. Blood welled at the highest knuckle point, like a raspberry drupelet. "Let's talk a minute," he said to Cross. They walked to the coffee station. Cross poured a cup of coffee.

Bouchard took a napkin and dabbed the blood. "You think he's going to make it?"

"I think if we don't let him come with me in the bird, he's going to go completely nuclear."

Bouchard shook his head vehemently. "In the air with you? No way. Wick wants to talk to him, for one thing."

"Is that what he said?"

"That's the vibe I'm getting. All of them — the Calumets, David — they're being looked at."

"Well, until there's some indictment . . . I mean . . ."

"I'm not even sure why I'm letting *you* go up."

Cross looked at Bouchard over the rim of his coffee mug. "Yes you are."

Bouchard crumpled the napkin, stained red, and tossed it. "I was ready to reassign you not too long ago, Justin."

"But you didn't. Hikers came forward; I know where she is. She's in there, right on or around West Canada Mountain."

Bouchard lowered his voice and darted his eyes around, probably checking to make sure David Brennan hadn't wandered back into the firehouse. "What if she's dead up there?

Huh? You telling me you think it's a good idea to have that man with you inside a tiny helicopter, looking down at his wife sprawled out on the rocks, or something? Anyway, it breaks with so many protocols I wouldn't know where to begin."

Cross sipped his coffee.

Bouchard tried not to look at him as he fixed his own cup. He flexed his wounded hand, studied it. Then he cut a look at Cross. "Goddammit," he said. "Alright. One trip."

CHAPTER FORTY

The sunlight surprised her. Katie got up slowly from Hoot's cot, her muscles stiffer than ever. She stared at the bloody smear on the cabin window as she took the liquor bottle of water from her pack and drank the last few ounces. Time to replenish her supply.

Amazed that she'd ever been able to find sleep, she lifted her bruised arms above her head and gave herself a sniff. The smell could've knocked over an elephant — she'd never been this ripe in her life.

When I get out of this, I'm going to shower for a month.

The sumptuous thought was met with discouraging debate. *You're miles from anywhere and no one knows where you are. Leno is still out there. You have no food or water.*

She went through her running warm-up, just static stretches, rotating her hips then bending and touching her toes. Her lower back was tight — it had been since wrestling with Carson that first time — but it was livable.

Her right leg was a different story. She couldn't straighten it out to get the full length.

It didn't fare any better from a seated position. She couldn't even flatten her leg on the floor. Each time she tried, the pain shredded through her. The final attempt was so bad she became light-headed.

She didn't need a physical therapist to know she had a disabling injury — her leg was going to continue to be trouble and would surely get worse if she didn't take care of it.

She rose slowly to her feet, determined to quiet the doubts. She needed a compression bandage. And she needed to locate water. If some old mountain man had lasted out here for years without any modern amenities, she could too.

Twin Mountain to Spruce to a trail which led to Haskell Road. That was the route Hoot had indicated. Once she made it to the trail, she could just walk out.

Unless, of course, Leno anticipated her and made his way to the trail, too. He didn't have a gun, but he could still be lethal.

She had to plan for at least a two-day trip. Surely there would be places she'd have to double-back, go the long way around, and she had to accept the idea she'd likely lose her bearings at one time or another.

Maybe three days, then. Even Hoot had thought so. It seemed like a lot when it had only taken six hours to come in.

Of course, Carson had used GPS. And he'd dragged her like a pack mule, only letting up a couple of times.

Like when they'd heard the hikers.

When she'd screamed.

Katie looked through Hoot's things for something to wrap her thigh in as she considered it. Carson had brought them close to a trail by mistake. He'd had the advantage of GPS, but the trail hadn't shown up.

Did it make more sense to try to go back out the way she'd come in? Why did Hoot lay out an alternate route? Maybe she'd run into that same trail . . .

Of course, they were a ways from the original cabin on Jones Mountain, if that, in fact, had been where Carson had brought her. She'd followed Hoot for four hours to get to Twin Mountain. If she'd had her wits about her, she might've paid more attention to which way they'd gone from the first cabin to get to Hoot's. But Leno had been behind them, and she'd struggled just to keep Hoot's dogged pace.

Maybe Hoot knew of something he hadn't told her, such as a big lake, or rapids, a waterfall impeding the more direct route.

She riffled through a box of trinkets in the corner, and her hand closed around something smooth. She held it up and let it dangle. Katie was no military expert, but she thought she was looking at a Purple Heart. Hoot was old enough to have been in Vietnam. He'd survived war, survived living off the land for God knew how long, only to wind up killed in cold blood.

Because of her.

No, because of Leno.

—Either way, right now, Hoot's body is rotting up by the chapel.

She needed to at least bury him. He'd saved her life.

In his pack she'd found a green canteen with the initials "B.T." inked on one side, plus a compass and a pocket knife. She had both rifles and Leno's pistol so she was well-armed, but she needed something reflective, too, for signaling planes or even people she might encounter from a distance. She held the Purple Heart medal in her palm, moving it around in the light.

There was no way she could take the man's medal. She lay it back in the box. The glass surface of the compass was probably better anyway.

Unfortunately, Hoot didn't seem to own a single map, but there was a small cooking pot she crammed in her bag. She set the bag aside for now.

She found a wool scarf among Hoot's few clothing items and duct tape with his tools — barely anything left on the spool. She wrapped her leg with the scarf, cinching it tight to the point her vision blurred with tears. Holding the scarf end with her teeth, she wrapped it all in the remains of the duct tape.

Her wrist bandages were in tatters, and she pulled them off, leaving a small pile behind.

With the sun just rising and shining through the trees, she left Hoot's cabin, scanning for signs of Leno.

Leno's pistol wouldn't stay safe tucked into her running skirt and she didn't want to leave it in the cabin. She decided to bury the handgun and the second rifle; one was enough for her to keep, and she didn't know how to shoot the pistol anyway.

Hoot had fixed his roof with rubber gutters that channeled the rain down into barrels for collection. That was his fresh water source.

She filled her bottle and Hoot's canteen and drank, feeling better. The water had an earthy taste, slightly metallic.

She buried the pistol and Hoot's rifle beside one of the barrels.

Time to look for Leno.

The forest surrounding Hoot's cabin was thick with undergrowth, and the trees formed a canopy, everything dark and dripping. She thought she saw tracks in the mud where he'd fallen, and pushed her way into the woods, daring to go just so far. She breathed slow and tried to stay calm. Saw blood on a rock, then some more on a tangle of shrubs, but she was no tracker. Leno was gone, or he'd managed to get in somewhere hidden, where he'd finally expired. Either way, she was wasting time. She was going to have to live with not knowing.

Finally she headed up toward the chapel, the rifle strapped across her back, her heart steady. A solid stick she found along the way served as a crutch.

Want to lose that pesky extra weight, tone those muscles, even lower your resting pulse rate? Try our patented and proven "Kidnapped by Assholes and Dragged into the Woods" program!

She climbed up the rocky parts of the slope and pushed her way through the firs.

For three days and three nights, you'll be subjected to every torture imaginable. Molestation! Physical abuse! Gunplay! Wild animals! Hurry and join now while spots are still available.

Reaching the chapel first, she sat down in the lean-to to rest. The view was breathtaking, and she rested, taking it in.

She had to pee.

It had occurred to her earlier, just a flitting thought, that Hoot had no outhouse. Somewhere he must've dug a latrine.

She moved alongside the chapel, looking for a spot. Even in such circumstances, she thought, modesty prevailed.

A log nestled into the brush would do nicely. As she got closer and took her skirt down, she realized the brush wasn't really brush.

The leaves were unmistakable. The buds like green nuggets, threaded with a filigree of orange and red hairs.

"Hoot," she said. "You old dope-smoker."

The plants were all around her. Probably enough weed here to smoke up all of Hazleton. For weeks.

A war hero who'd learned a trick or two in Cambodia, no doubt.

Finished with her call of nature, she found some other leaves amid the marijuana plants and cleaned herself. She walked back around to the front of the chapel, drank some more water, and headed in the direction she'd last seen Hoot.

The view, the pot plants, even the need to pee had lightened her spirits — frequent peeing was a typical sign of pregnancy.

Maybe all was not lost.

But when she considered the ordeal ahead of her, the shape she was already in and might be in by the time she got out — if she ever did — her mood darkened again. Certainly women could endure all sorts of trials and still carry a baby to term, but there were no guarantees.

Katie approached the spot where Hoot had fallen.

She covered her mouth with her hand in an effort to keep from gagging up the water she'd just poured down her gullet.

Hoot was a little ways from where she'd left him. Part of him was, anyway — he'd been torn to bits by the coyotes and was barely recognizable as human.

She started toward him and stopped when she heard an animal's growl. There was a coyote behind her, boldly crossing the bare rock, its head low and teeth bared.

Something snapped in the woods near the body parts. Another coyote lurked there, almost blended in with the vegetation.

The fear jolted through her, and her stomach eddied.

"Hey! Get the fuck *out of here*!"

She swung the rifle around in front of her. It was already loaded, the safety off. She pointed the gun at the animal on the rock and fired before she'd even thought it through.

The kick of the gun was fierce, but she kept a grip on it.

She missed the coyote, which took off in a sprint. She swung the rifle on the other one and screamed again. "Ahh! Go, you fucker! Get away from him!"

The coyote jerked into a run, joining the other. Both moved deeper into the woods, their gray fur disappearing.

"Yeah! Huh? How do you like it, you fucking bastards?!"

Swearing like a sailor, her feet planted wide, she realized that the coyotes were just doing what they were designed by nature to do. She was on the board at the SPCA for God's sake. But she didn't feel bad. This was another world, where different rules applied.

Katie waited a full minute until she was sure the animals were gone.

She didn't have a shovel, but the earth was soft around where Hoot's remains were scattered.

She propped the rifle against a tree and started to dig. Shoveling with both hands plunged in, perspiring, breathing deep and fast, something came over her.

But she didn't have a word for it. There was a sensation she got on her runs, but nothing quite like this. Jogging was just a taste, a tiny sample of this.

This nameless thing. This sense of being *here*.

And yet, not here. Not her identity. Not the woman she thought she knew, the one she saw in the mirror as she applied her judicious amount of eyeliner in the mornings. Not the woman who preferred to grind her own coffee beans.

Not the daughter of Jean-Baptiste Calumet.

Not rich. Not motherless. None of those things.

Something else.

Shoot at coyotes! Dig your friend a grave! Completely lose your sense of identity!

All this could be yours . . .

Even her black humor faded as she worked, careful not to tire herself out even more, but managing to dig a shallow enough grave to drag the pieces of Hoot together and then cover them with earth.

Katie stood back, appraising her work. She wiped her runny nose with the back of a dirty hand, and picked up the rifle.

* * *

Tall pines took the shape of the wind, their branches like reaching arms, wagging at the distant peaks.

Burying Hoot had cost her some time, but she had the rising sun at her back and was moving due south. She'd picked up a few more items from the cabin before leaving for good — some clothes for the cold and rain.

There were at least five miles between her and civilization, maybe as many as fifteen. But she'd decided that the best way to go was the one Hoot had prescribed.

For a while she moved with confidence. Her heart beat hard but steady. Her leg felt okay as long as she kept mindful of it and didn't overextend. The crutch helped.

She continued to marvel at the beauty of the wilderness. The massiveness. Ridges where she could see well into the distance. But only the jets flying far overhead, leaving their white streaks, connected her to the world.

Still nothing low enough to be a search plane.

The land sloped down for a while as she made her way into the valley between Twin Mountain and Spruce. Then she was deep in the forest, and there were no more views. She checked the compass every few minutes and adjusted her direction if needed.

At eleven, she stopped and took a drink of water then decided it was a good time to eat. Hoot's stores had provided her some granola and dry oatmeal, but little else. She took a few handfuls of the grains and choked them down with water.

She didn't know what frightened her more — the prospect of getting lost, or giving up and turning around. Though, she had to believe that something like Hoot's cabin, small and remote as it was, would be on someone's map, somewhere. The Forest Preserve, or the DEC, emergency services, something. Was it a mistake to have left?

Second-guessing like this, she sat on a boulder and put the water into her bag. Then she did nothing.

Go.

She ignored the voice, just thinking.

Go! You're wasting time!

—I need to rest.

The minutes drained away. Her heart rate eased down a few notches and the sweat cooled on her skin.

She stared at an oak. She thought it was an oak, anyway. Craggy bark that formed an almost infinite variety of patterns. A soft wind shook the boughs, and rainwater pattered to the ground. It coursed down through the crevasses and fissures like hanging tinsel.

More sounds emerged. She hadn't heard them like this yet. Birds in the trees, first singing far off, then closer.

Something scurried. A squirrel shot halfway up the tree, stopped, then raced up the rest of the way.

Katie was motionless.

Breathing.

A different sound came from her left, rousing her emotions. It sounded like something bigger, cracking through the undergrowth. She tensed and readied the rifle.

Leno.

She slid off the boulder and crouched behind it. She waited, thinking that if he had been following her, it was better that he made himself known now.

A small black bear came trundling out of the bramble. It stopped and circled around, sniffing at something, then bounded back into the brush.

Katie didn't move. The cub would have a mother somewhere close by. The last thing she needed was to tangle with an angry mama bear.

The cub had been behind her. Katie made the decision to keep going. She hurried away from the boulder, limping briskly, dropped the crutch, and broke into a shambling run.

Her leg throbbed. She held her arm up to shield her face from the clawing branches. Her heart was pounding, her leg growing hot, pain shooting up into her midsection like arc-welding sparks.

When she thought she had put a good distance between herself and the bear sighting, she slowed. Caught her breath. Took out the compass.

Her thigh muscle was still sparking, and at the same time turning to a kind of hot stone.

In flight, she'd veered off course. She was headed north now instead of southwest, almost completely in the wrong direction. Carson's wristwatch was attached to the pack. Already going on noon. She estimated she'd made it about two miles away from Hoot's cabin. Two miles in four hours. Half a mile an hour. At this rate she'd still be in the woods come nightfall.

But there was no longer any consideration of turning back. She held the compass out like a divining rod and kept moving. She could barely put her weight on her leg.

After an awkward, painstaking climb over a scree of rocks and navigating a thicket of tightly packed, slender trees, the ground began to slope upward again.

It seemed ludicrous to be ascending in elevation when she was trying to get out of the woods, but it might be a good sign, too — this was Spruce Mountain. Just one more peak between her and salvation. Once she crested it, she might see the Haskell Road trail, maybe even the hamlet of Hoffmeister in the distance.

She could do this. She had to do this.

She hobbled to a ridge and continued to climb gingerly, minding her footing.

A bird — something big, like a hawk — took flight from a tall tree and screeched as it beat its long wings in the air.

CHAPTER FORTY-ONE

Cross and Brennan were in the air, flying over the park in a rescue helicopter. They banked over an expanse of green, but Cross saw the first hints of autumn colors amid the peaks. He tried to focus, but lingering dreams replayed in his thoughts.

He'd slept for five hours before rejoining the others and launching the chopper from the parking area near the firehouse. It was a spot close to the playground where he'd pushed Petrie on the swings — Ramona had still been too small.

Marty had frequented the dreams — she was lost, and when he found her, she didn't want to return home.

"How are your kids?"

The question beguiled Cross; it was so in line with his thoughts. They were speaking on radio headsets.

"What makes you ask?"

David looked out at the rumpled terrain. "I came by your room last night, heard you talking, left, and came back later. Everybody good?"

"They're good, yeah."

"Good."

Laura Broderick was up front with the pilot. The pilot pushed the stick forward and the helicopter swooped down, making Cross's stomach lurch. At least it wasn't one of those army-type choppers with the open sides. The rescue helicopter was a single-engine, six-passenger machine, part of the New York State Police aviation unit. In addition to the pilot there was a hoist operator, making five total persons aboard. There was room left for one more.

The helicopter bucked a bit, and the pilot said something about mountain updrafts. Once it had gotten into a stable hover, Laura pointed out the first cabin they'd located. Cross saw a roof caved in from a fallen tree, no signs of activity.

After circling the site for a minute, Laura instructed the pilot to move on.

As they gained some altitude and swept away from the cabin, Cross watched David. He was staring out the window, a placid expression on his face. His hands were tucked neatly between his knees. There was something penitent in the pose, Cross thought. At times, David was either wild with emotion or oddly subdued. But Cross couldn't begin to imagine the state he'd be in if it was Marty out there. If his nightmare were real.

Before they'd taken off in the helicopter, the dawn just tinting the sky, Cross had taken David aside, Bouchard's words ringing in his head. "I know this is hard, but I think you need to be prepared . . ."

"She's alive," David had said.

A few minutes later they arrived over the next cabin on Laura's map. This one was in even worse shape than the first, all but completely collapsed. They moved on to another, one that looked more promising, and hovered for a bit, Cross taking pictures with a telephoto lens. There was nothing that indicated anyone was there or had been there for a long time, but it was in good enough shape to be significant, and they marked it down.

It was going on noon. Cross ate a granola bar, though they had to go back and refuel the helicopter anyway. They made a pass over one final cabin.

David banged on the glass. "There! There!"

Cross saw it. Someone had spelled out an SOS with rocks.

"Take it down," Cross said.

There would be no landing on the mountain — no place for it. The aviation unit was trained for a crew member to come down from the hovering helicopter and send an injured person back up. The mission was to get a preliminary visual then send in a team.

David had gotten the wildness back. "Katie did that. I know she did. What else could it mean?"

Cross put a hand on the excited husband but kept quiet. Like Laura said, people went missing all the time. Anyone else could have done it . . .

But his arms rippled with gooseflesh. Katie was in the wilderness below.

"Send me down there," David said.

"No can do," Cross said. "I'm going."

He was already being buckled into the harness by the hoist operator. Aviation unit members trained each month for hoist rescues. Cross had five years with the Coast Guard. He had a high-powered radio, a gun, and, according to his estranged wife, a whole lot of stubbornness.

The door rolled back and the wind came blasting in, the air thundering.

Cross was instructed to sit, and his legs dangled over a fifty-yard drop. Then the time came to let gravity take over.

He pushed off and the hoist suspended him then gradually lowered him to the ground.

The second he touched down he unbuckled the harness — if an updraft pushed against the helicopter, he could be dragged along the ground like a doll. But the pilot kept it steady and the conditions were right. He waved an arm that the hoist was free and the operator recoiled the cable.

He checked his radio, and Laura responded, "We got our eyes on you." The helicopter ascended to a safe height and hovered.

Cross drew his piece and started toward the cabin. He stepped up onto the porch and pressed his back against the wall. He took a deep breath then stepped quickly through the open door.

The interior smelled like woodsmoke. There were signs of life everywhere — someone had dumped a duffel bag on the floor, contents helter-skelter. Empty beer cans were piled in a corner.

An undressed mattress had blood on it. A sat phone was on the floor. Beside it, on the back of a piece of box board, someone had written *Katie Calumet* in soot.

This was the place. All the concern that the hiker had heard something other than Katie's scream, or that Abel Gebhart sent them on a wild goose chase — gone. They'd done it.

No one was home, but Cross didn't like seeing the blood. He continued the sweep, radioing back to Laura as he did. "All clear in the cabin."

"Alright. Keep your eyes peeled. Over."

Cross left, keeping his weapon ready. He cautiously circled the building. He saw a well with a pump handle, and an outhouse in disrepair.

Still no signs anyone was around. Not a sound, not a rustle in the trees.

"Katie! Katie Calumet!" His voice echoed. He took out his improved topo map, courtesy of DEC. This was the Black River Wild Forest, in a section that protruded into the larger West Canada Lake Wilderness. The latter was an area of almost 250 square miles, 160,000 acres. 168 bodies of water, 11 lean-tos and likely several hunting cabins like this one.

Black River Wild Forest rolled southwest. Laura had said there were 9 lean-tos in the 120,000-acre region, more hunting cabins, too.

Laura's voice crackled over the radio. "So, you're on Jones Mountain," she reminded. "The summit is about another 500 feet up from you — 2,800 feet in total. Let's say you started in Old Forge; to take a trip and summit Jones would be a very long, twenty-mile hike. Fifteen if you came from Speculator."

"What's that peak there to my six?"

"That's West Canada Mountain. And you can't see it, but behind you over the Jones summit is Panther Mountain."

"Closest trails?"

"Ah, those would be 115 and 114 in Black River. About four miles from you."

"That's to the west of here?"

"Affirmative. The village of Atwell isn't far, either. Maybe six miles. But we're not thinking they came in that way."

"No. We're not."

"There's also an unmarked trail, about five miles away. It's the tail end of Haskell Road, just a couple wheel ruts, probably."

"Got it. I remember."

"And now — be careful — just to the south there from where you're standing are cliffs. Over."

"Alright. I'm going to check it out. Over, out."

A murder of crows interrupted the stillness. He couldn't see them, but they came from the direction Laura had indicated. Cross saw the cliffs and slowly approached the edge, crouching down, spreading out his weight.

He lowered to all fours and then to his stomach, inching along until he could peer down the drop.

"Oh shit . . ."

The crows surrounded a body on the rocks below. The pecked at it and tore flesh from bone.

Cross felt clammy, his throat dry, palms sweating.

Hard to tell who it was. Who it had been.

He thought back to the final call from Montgomery, the frustration in the kidnapper's voice. Something had happened, something unintended. Cross wondered if Vickers had gotten into some trouble, but it might've been Katie. She could have tried to run — in the dark, maybe, hands tied, who knew, and taken a fatal tumble into the abyss.

He backed carefully away from the crumbling ledge and gained his feet. He took up the radio.

"Ranger Broderick, meet me over on channel two," he said, aware that David was listening in on the main frequency. David's headset was only able to pick up what was said in the helicopter, or what came in on channel one.

"Go for Broderick on two," she said.

"We've got a body. No way to visually ascertain who, from this position. How long will it take to get a medical examiner up here? We'll need forensics on the cabin, too."

"My guess is about four, five hours. Over."

Cross sighed. It was a long time to wait to find out who it was. Maybe there was another way down so he could get a closer look. He relayed this to Laura, who advised him to be careful.

She added, "David is asking questions. What do you want me to tell him?"

"Tell him there are signs Katie was here. Leave it at that."

"Roger. We're headed back to refuel. Over and out."

Cross put away the radio. He heard the chopper fade into the distance and tried to pick out a safe descent to the rocks below.

* * *

As Cross made his way down to the body, his thoughts swung to Katie and David, and the health of their marriage. He doubted David had anything directly to do with his wife's disappearance, whether he was a party to tax fraud or not. David seemed genuinely devoted.

Cross wondered about his own devotion.

There was something subtle which happened in a marriage, he thought. He'd been married to Marty for eight years. In the beginning, he'd checked in with her on just about everything he did. From major things such as new car purchases to minor stuff such as meeting a buddy for a beer after work. She'd done the same, seeking his approval to spend a few extra hours with her own friends, inquiring about the best time to go for a jog, what he preferred for dinner.

But it wasn't the kind of permission that was always sought outright — that was what was subtle — sometimes it was non-verbal. It was just there, in the fabric of their lives.

Part of seeking and granting permission was to avoid the little fights and arguments that peppered a marriage. If you didn't get the permission, if you didn't sense the concession, a little black spot formed.

After a while, those black spots grew.

He grabbed a slender tree for balance, realizing his failure. He'd retreated from the whole crazy, complex scenario, withdrawn into his work, and atomized himself to the point that he'd refused to ask Marty's permission for anything, nor granted it when she needed it.

He'd rebelled.

In his mind, at the time, it all made sense. Screw the subtlety, fuck the game, he was going to do what he needed to do when he needed to do it.

And his marriage had wound up like that body on the rocks.

Cross yelled and waved his arms, scaring off the picking crows. They took to the surrounding conifers, where they cawed and capered at his intrusion.

The body was in catastrophic condition. It was face down, head turned to the side. The eyes had been pecked out. The muscles and tissue had been ravaged by something other than crows.

Cross was no wildlife expert, but he didn't think there were wolves in the Adirondacks. Bears wouldn't have done it, though.

A pack of coyotes, then.

But despite the poor condition of the cadaver, Cross was pretty sure it was a man. What little was left of the clothing didn't offer much, but one hand was still whole, shaped like a claw against the rock. A man's hand, not a woman's.

Cross grabbed the radio and sent word back to incident command. He'd already relayed his position to Burt Frost and explained the situation. Now he had visual confirmation.

He climbed closer to the body. The sun was just breaking over the cliff and the rocks sparkled with mica. The crows continued to jeer from the trees.

Two of the pants pockets were still intact, and Cross fished around for a wallet, turning his head to the side to breathe clean air. The smell coming from the body wasn't so good.

He didn't find anything and scrambled away, gasping for air.

He didn't need a wallet anyway; from the other side of the body, he got a closer look at the face. It was in rough shape, but Cross had stared at a mug shot of Troy Vickers long enough to believe this was him.

Cross perched on a rock, breathing hard, and looked down the steep slope, then glanced up at the clifftop, imagining a scenario in which Vickers lost his footing and tumbled. Another in which Katie Calumet pushed him. Where would she go?

Montgomery might've ventured to the cabin. That had been Cross's theory for a while now. Montgomery comes in, absconds with Katie to a second, backup location. Or Katie had already fled and was out there on her own.

There'd been blood on the bed, and the windows were smashed. Cross considered the terrible possibilities of what might have happened to Katie Calumet.

CHAPTER FORTY-TWO

Mom?

Katie came to a boggy area. She set down her foot, put some weight on it, and sank up to her knee. The ground was too mushy and the bog seemed to stretch on forever.

It was good news, on the one hand. Bogs occurred in lower elevations. The last nature walk organized by her Riverside School committee at the VIC had been a bog walk.

A bog was a small lake or pond that had gradually filled in with sphagnum moss, forming a mat five feet thick. Not suitable for walking — she'd have to go around.

That was the bad news, because she was already losing daylight.

She saw what was called the pitcher plant, a species that devoured insects and looked a bit like a child's pinwheel toy with the fans crumpled.

Mom? You there?

So far she'd stuck to her course as best as she could, only a handful of times doubling back to get around an unpassable area — rockslides or groves of white pine too tightly packed to slip through. But she had never really regained confidence after the black bear encounter.

As the sky dimmed, she was suddenly sure she was nowhere near the trail, that despite following the compass, she was no closer to civilization than when she'd started out eight hours before.

Mom? Talk to me, mom. Please.

The prospect of circumnavigating the bog was very unsatisfying. Katie looked at the compass for the tenth time since coming to the edge of the soft ground. She needed to keep heading toward that setting sun. And it would be no good to camp here for the night. The bugs were bad, and it smelled like rotten eggs: dead, decaying biomass in the thick and mushy underlying peat.

Stinky peat! the kids called it.

Katie slogged her way back a few steps then started the slow, tedious process of going round, practically dragging her bad leg behind her.

I'm sorry, mom.

I need you.

The doctors had said tongue-tying things like "takotsubo cardiomyopathy" and Katie had heard further terms like "apical ballooning syndrome" and "stress cardiomyopathy."

It all meant heart muscle failure brought on by severe stress and chronic depression.

Some people called it broken heart syndrome.

At first Katie had resisted such nonsense. But she'd done her research since then and knew that women's hearts were more affected by stress and depression than men's. Monica Calumet had also just gone through menopause, when heart failure becomes more common.

No one had seen it coming. On a Tuesday in the middle of summer, Monica had complained of chest pains. She'd been at home, doing nothing strenuous.

Once admitted to the hospital, she told the doctors she'd been getting dizzy and fatigued at times, every now and again with abdominal discomfort. But she was otherwise in good health.

They'd let her go.

Three days after being released from the hospital with an appointment to return for follow-up tests, she'd suffered a heart attack while walking in the city. Clutching her chest, she'd staggered out into the street to hail a cab. A delivery truck barreling along wasn't able to brake in time.

Katie kept moving around the bog, but she needed to make a wider circle — the ground kept sucking at her feet. Her running shoes were filled with squishy muck. The sweat was rolling, despite the late hour and lowering sun. The flies swarmed her head.

Mom! Help me — God! Do something!

A warm woman, so slight there seemed to be nothing to her. Monica Calumet was an ex-hippie from the sixties, a bohemian type who'd later had some religious conversion which had always been nebulous to Katie, her sister, and their father.

Mom! Monica!

No answer from beyond the grave. No sense of her mother's spirit watching over her as Katie struggled to get free of the fucking marsh trying to suck her down like something from a child's nightmare.

Monica hadn't died right away.

She'd been rushed to the hospital. Katie was at school, unaware. Her father had gone to be with his wife in her last hours. She was lucid, Katie had learned, but Jean never spoke of their last moments together, their last words.

They'd only let him see her for a few seconds before rushing into surgery to try and free the ribs crushing her lungs, to revive the heart which was in critical failure.

Ten years later, he'd married Sybil, a woman in just about every way the total opposite of Monica Calumet.

Katie pulled her foot out of the peat. Instead of extricating herself from the bog, she seemed to be getting deeper in it.

She needed firm ground. The light was dwindling. This was taking too long. That she'd ever thought she could walk out of the Adirondack wilderness on her own seemed utterly ridiculous now. Something dangerously naıve, the same stupid thing every other fool thought when they got turned around in the woods. When they wandered off the beaten path for a little sightseeing, then either spent days getting themselves out or called for help if they had service.

No service for Katie. Not a GPS that worked, or a sat phone with batteries.

I'm not getting any love from your god, Mom.

She laughed abruptly, aware that the sound coming out of her was a bit deranged, but she only laughed harder when she was overwhelmed by how typical this all seemed — she saw herself from above, this foolish woman angry at God when she was just frustrated with her own human limitations.

Angry with Sybil because she represented the loss of Monica.

Like something from a bad Lifetime channel movie.

The NeverEnding Story! That was the children's movie with the kid sinking in the swamp. The horse had been called Artax, or something — she couldn't recall the boy's name, though.

She slapped a mosquito biting the back of her neck. The flies and mosquitoes were working in concert to drive her insane. She wondered if they were able to communicate, if there was an interspecies form of data transmission.

You're not so unique, Mr. Mosquito. You're a dime a dozen. I kill you, and no one cares. You live in a swamp. You live in this dismal shithole among the Pickerelweed and Swamp Candles. You live . . .

She stopped when she saw the lilies; something jogged in her mind.

The foam boards she'd spent a few nights working on for the nature walk, the presentation to the children after they'd returned from their hike to review the plant life they'd seen.

The Yellow Pond Lily.

The bog at Paul Smith's College was Barnum Bog, called so because it had Barnum Creek flowing through it.

Certain plant species grew on the margins of the brook, and only because it *was* a brook, and freshwater.

Bogs and marshes weren't interchangeable terms. She'd been thinking of this surrounding muck, graying in the fading light, as both. But a marsh had water moving through it. And a marsh had Yellow Pond Lilies and Swamp Candles. Like this one.

It filled her with a kind of frisson, renewing her energy.

She hadn't seen the point in following a winding river before, which might only prolong her walk out, but now she wanted it . . .

She followed the lilies wherever she found them. They almost seemed to glow in the failing light.

The walking got easier — she was still knee-deep, but the thick peat was giving way to less viscous water. She even heard the sound of it flowing, a marvelous thing — water purling over the spongy vegetation. The moving water sounded almost like wind at first, then it babbled and splashed in proximity.

She was able to follow the creek out of the marsh, climb up onto a bank of dry land.

It was getting colder. A bracing chill to the air that tasted sweet in her mouth. The day had been clear, the heat had escaped, and it was going to be a cold night.

She had Carson's book of matches, plus a small box from Hoot's cabin, and she kept them all dry inside a plastic baggie from Carson's snack supply. Now she raced the darkness, searching for birch bark and kindling and wood.

A coyote yipped in the distance, and its voice was joined by a chorus of others.

CHAPTER FORTY-THREE

The powerful two-way radio crackled with static and a voice said, "Gates for Cross, over."

Her voice was a welcomed relief. Cross had only been on his own at the cabin for a few hours, but it had gotten lonely fast. He sat on the front porch and thumbed the button. "Go ahead, Gates."

"The cabin on Jones Mountain belonged to a man named Jack Holderied. He's been dead for twenty years. The state acquired the land before he passed."

"Copy that."

"Might be that Abel Gebhart knew about it, so did his brother Jeff, and Jeff told Jonathan Montgomery. But Abel Gebhart has lawyered up for now and isn't talking. And Jeff Gebhart is still in a coma."

"Got it."

A pause. "How you doing, Justin?"

"I'm fine."

"David is coming in on foot with Laura Broderick."

Cross sighed. "Roger that. What's his state of mind at this point?"

There was only a static reply. Cross got up and moved away from the cabin, trying to get a better radio signal, and caught the tail end of what Gates said. ". . . let him help."

"Please repeat, over."

"I said it's the only real choice, at this point, to let him help."

"Feds don't want him?"

"They seem to be waiting, like everyone else."

"I'm waiting, too. For the crew to get here and scrub the cabin. Place is in pretty good shape. There's a clearing, but not too wide, trees all around, a cliff on one side, pretty secluded. Over." He looked down at the rocks Katie had used to spell SOS.

Cross listened for anything else Gates might add but got only static.

"You there, Dana?"

He thought he heard Gates buried beneath the distortion saying, *Hang in there.*

"Over and out." Cross hung the radio from his belt.

The sun was starting down, would drop behind the next summit along the range in a couple of hours.

* * *

When the team finally emerged from the woods, led by Laura Broderick, the clearing was dark with shade.

The four CSTs looked exhausted from the hike in but worked quickly, setting up battery-powered lights, opening crates of tools — fingerprint dust, jars and vials, ultraviolet lights. Two of them went down to the body on the rocks; two stayed with the cabin.

Laura walked over to Cross.

"We've got 400 searchers in the woods right now," she said. "Tomorrow morning there will be almost 800. A hundred are headed right to this spot. Some will turn around, walk right back out, others will continue on the ridge there, some down the other side."

Cross just shook his head. It was a massive undertaking. He trusted Burt Frost knew what he was doing; the searchers were well-instructed and would keep tight bump lines — no one else would get lost.

"You think she's alive?" Laura asked.

"I think there's a good chance."

"And the blood in the cabin?"

"Probably hers, yeah. We'll find out. I'm sure she's, you know . . . she's been banged up."

"What about your man on the rocks there? What happened to him?"

"Don't know. Looks like he did a little boozing. Maybe he thought he could fly."

Laura looked toward the cliff. Then she patted the rucksack she was holding. "Brought you an extra sleeping bag."

"Thanks."

"I'll get a fire going."

Laura hustled off and started gathering kindling. Cross watched her, feeling suddenly like he was in some old-timey story about cowboys and mountain folk. Jeremiah Johnson. He'd planned to take his family camping when the girls had gotten a bit older. Those plans had been back-burnered during all the problems he had with Marty. Now the summer would soon be over.

There was always next year.

But thinking about it left a cold spot in his stomach. He moved away from the SOS rocks and joined Laura in culling wood for the fire.

CHAPTER FORTY-FOUR

The darkness pooled around her, beyond the throw of the firelight.

She remembered a discussion with David about how the fire shrank your pupils, made the night even darker. To see the stars you had to move away.

She hadn't remembered that camping trip with David until now.

And how they'd lost their bottle of wine due to her husband's tendency to leave caps only partly screwed on. Cheap jug wine they'd brought. David swore by it. Her husband was always playfully tearing down Katie's more "cultivated" ways.

Miss Manners, he would say. *Which fork do I use for the salad? Fork number three or fork number eight?*

She craved her husband. Wanted to talk with him, feel his arms, smell his breath after he'd snuck a cigarette on the back porch.

Davy (which he hated to be called), who left the caps of things half-screwed. Jugs of wine. Jars of pickles. Laundry detergent. You name it, he would extract product from the jar or bottle and then leave the cap hanging there, waiting for her to come along and spill whatever it was.

"Do you do that on purpose?" She'd usually laugh it off. Sometimes, if it caused a stain, she'd get aggravated.

She even had a theory that the habit, while a small psychological tic, hinted at a deeper truth — David was afraid of commitment.

That was psychobabble at best, but it was true her husband was first a musician, then a motorcycle enthusiast who joined one of those clubs for a year and raised hell around the country, then a cook, a chef, a carpenter, and back to a musician again.

"I've always been a musician," David would say. He'd get that look in his eyes like she could never comprehend the life of an artist. And maybe she couldn't. Katie was no good with a paintbrush or a piano. She needed a plan, an established order. She understood that there was intense training and precedent for a lot of the arts — but what did they say? It was the era of post-postmodernism and nobody knew what the hell they were doing anymore. Photographers, maybe, but that was about it.

David never had a plan. He would sit down at their giant Yamaha electronic piano and play by ear. Sometimes he'd just fiddle around on it; other times his playing would capture her — he'd get into a flow which drew her into the room like one of those cartoon characters floating toward the scent of pie on a windowsill.

Did you record that? she'd ask.

Nah.

Can you play it again?

Probably not.

It baffled her.

Couldn't commit to putting the lid firmly on a pickle jar. Couldn't commit to a song, couldn't bear to repeat anything.

Yet he was committed to her.

Katie watched the fire and felt warm in Hoot's old woolen pants and sweater. She pulled the anorak jacket over her, its waxen, musty smell powerful but strangely comforting.

She was going to survive this.

She had clothing, she could make a fire. She had water enough for two more days. If necessary, she'd boil water from a river to purify it — she had the small pot with her. Getting giardiasis and diarrhea was the last thing she — or her baby — needed.

But she turned her mind away from pregnancy.

The column of smoke drifted up from the fire. The darkness surrounded her but the fire illuminated the tree boughs above. The smoke threshed the boughs and rose into the night sky.

Why didn't anyone see these fires she was making? Weren't there people whose job it was to sit in fire towers all day and spot smoke?

What was David doing now? Was he out in the woods, calling her name? How many searchers were there? Did they consider her worth thousands of dollars of resources? Was her father footing any bills? How much had Leno and Carson demanded?

She heard the snap of a twig and sat upright, a chill rippling through her.

Leno, who'd crawled away from her into the forest. How badly had he been hurt? She thought she'd shot him right in the gut. She'd seen the wound. But what if she'd been wrong? What if the bullet had just passed through his love handle? What if he'd made a strong recovery? He could be out there right now, closing in on her.

She pulled the rifle close. She had three rounds left in the magazine. She'd done her best to plan for this; it just wasn't something she thought about — guns, ammunition. She should've purloined the whole box of ammo from Hoot's burlap sack in the cabin, or checked his pockets before burial, but she'd neglected to do so. She'd been too focused on getting out.

Still, despite the urgency and the exhaustion, she'd taken water, rain clothes, a compass, a flashlight, a wristwatch, matches.

You saw him dying. Leno was crawling away on his hands and knees. He slinked off into the woods and died. Maybe you couldn't find him, but he's probably face down in the dirt.

It had to be true. There was just too much woods out here for him to have followed her. She'd been all over the place, avoiding obstacles and backtracking. He was an imagined threat, when the real dangers were almost scarier. She could fall and break an ankle. The coyotes could come back — she hadn't heard them again since building the fire, but they could be on to her scent, tracking her, waiting for her to fall.

And she needed food. She had a few paltry items left in the bag — two of Carson's granola bars, a small bag of oatmeal from Hoot's cabin. She had no idea what the old mountain man survived on, but there'd been no freezer full of coyote meat, nor the power to keep it cold. She couldn't imagine eating coyote after that unbelievable stink. They were probably killed for their hides anyway. If larger animals like deer couldn't be properly stored, he probably relied on rabbits and grouse and other small game. Hoot probably had spent the majority of his time hunting and preparing food.

What a life. Subsistence living. Just doing what it took to keep alive.

That instinct, so powerful. The will to live. She felt it running through her, a kind of sanguine electricity.

The thought of the blood channeling through the network of arteries and veins and capillaries.

And the baby. Her heart pumping not just for one, but two.

The heart her mother had given her. Faulty. Destined to break.

Mom?

There was no answer. The wind picked up a bit, spinning the cinders into a cyclone churning up from the fire, a dance of uneasy spirits.

CHAPTER FORTY-FIVE

Just before nightfall, Cross stole a moment and got a bite to eat. He sat by the open fire, shoveling in something that resembled hummus but tasted like chicken. The tranquility of the twilit wilderness was broken by the rattle of a portable generator, and an eerie light shone in the broken cabin windows.

Laura Broderick was nearby, resting after her long hike in — four and a half hours for her, an experienced forest ranger. Granted, she'd been leading a group of less ruggedly-inclined CSTs and a civilian, David Brennan.

David found Cross by the fire. Cross hadn't seen Katie's husband come into the clearing with Laura, but knew the man was around. Cross had been waiting for this.

David looked tired but determined. "So, she was here?"

"That's what the forensics team is determining."

David stepped closer, his eyes glowing in the firelight. "Was . . . she . . . here?"

Cross let out a deep breath. "I'm pretty sure she was the one who spelled out the letters with the rocks."

"Was she in the cabin?"

"She was probably in the cabin, but we won't know until . . ."

Too late — Katie's husband was already headed for it.

Cross caught up. "It's part of the investigation, David; can't go in there."

"Let me look."

Cross grabbed him by the shoulder but the bigger man shook it off.

Cross shot a look at Laura, who scrambled to her feet. They might have to restrain Katie's husband. Again.

But David stopped on the porch, pushed the door open, and looked in.

The place was bathed in cool light, giving the logs a sick, bluish look. The windows were each shattered. Various items strewn across the floor. The mattress in the corner lay bare, except for the blood stains, turned black by the special lamps. Two busy technicians gave them sharp looks, like cult members who'd had their strange ceremony disrupted by outsiders.

Cross stood just behind David but didn't touch him again. He was close enough to smell the man's perspiration, hear a whistling in his labored breathing.

David grabbed the edges of the doorway. Then he lowered his head and turned away, stepping off the porch and moving back toward the fire.

He passed it and walked to where Katie had placed the rocks. Cross watched her husband as he looked over the site, knelt down, touched the stones.

Cross intended to say something about tampering with evidence, but what was the point? They were just stones and it was the middle of the fucking wilderness. Everyone knew Katie had been here, and, without needing an autopsy, that Troy Vickers was dead on the rocks below.

Katie's kidnapper had met with some tragedy — fate, maybe, playing a role — and she'd gotten away. It wasn't much more complicated than that. They just needed to find her.

This had to be the worst of it for Katie's husband. Not knowing anything was bad, but knowing she'd been here and gone, that she could be alive or dead, as close as a few hundred yards or lost miles away, had to be agonizing.

David rose and met eyes with Cross.

"We'll find her," Cross said.

David gave everything another look — the stones, the eerily lit cabin — and then his gaze wandered toward the hulking mountains, black against a dark blue sky.

"No," he said. "I don't think we will."

* * *

The next day, a group of searchers found a cabin in the valley of two peaks known collectively as Twin Mountain.

Word came back that there were clear signs of a struggle. More blood, multiple sets of footprints in the mud. A rifle shell lay near the cabin doorway. Bloody bandages were found inside.

A second forensics crew was deployed from Speculator. The site was four miles southeast from the first cabin, deeper into the West Canada Lake Wilderness. Cross made the trek with David and Laura Broderick and reached it in the late afternoon as a light rain fell.

A field test determined a blood-type match: It looked likely that Katie had been at both cabins.

Then, on the eastern summit, a body was discovered.

It was in worse shape than Vickers — impossible to tell at first whether it was a man or a woman. Someone had buried it, but it had been disinterred, most likely by coyotes. The corpse was ravaged.

David paced and pawed at his face and stared until ultimately it was determined to be male.

Spent cartridges were found nearby, more shells from a rifle, and at least one spent cartridge from a handgun. Microstamping could eventually identify from which gun the cartridge cases had been fired, but Cross already had his suspicions.

Two scenarios emerged once the preliminary medical examination had concluded: One, that the body was Johnny Montgomery. That someone, perhaps Katie, had managed to shoot and kill him. Skeptics, including Bouchard, keeping in contact by radio, didn't think it was very plausible.

The other scenario, advanced by Laura, was that the body was a man named Barry Turner, a hermit the locals in Speculator called "Hoot." An army-issued rucksack and a Purple Heart medal had been found in the cabin. No one there had seen Turner for more than three years, but someone, likely Montgomery, could have found his cabin and killed him, then buried the body.

Cross extended Laura's theory: Turner had been helping Katie, but Montgomery had found them.

It gelled with the idea that Vickers and Montgomery had been keeping in touch, Vickers had met with his tragic end, and Montgomery had entered the woods. Somehow, he'd been able to track Katie and Barry "Hoot" Turner to the mountain man's cabin, and conflict had ensued.

Just before dark, the forensics team found a pistol and a rifle buried behind the cabin, next to a rain barrel Turner must've used for his drinking water. Both guns were given to searchers to take back to the lab, and serial numbers could potentially reveal their owners. But inside, a homemade rifle rack had supports for two.

Cross liked to think Katie had escaped, and she'd armed herself with that second rifle.

The day had crackled with energy, the sense that the search was getting somewhere. Laura and the other forest rangers deliberated on the likeliest routes out of the woods from Turner's cabin, and the search parties reconfigured under Frost's direction.

"If she just went due south from here, in six miles she'd run into Route 8," Laura told Cross in private when they took a food break. Despite the long hours and days without modern amenities, Laura Broderick looked fresh and fit. Cross didn't feel as perky. Laura continued, "The problem with that, though, is straight-up bushwhacking for half a mile, and Big Rock lake."

"What about east? The way we came in?"

"Due east and she'd come across the Northville-Placid Trail in nine miles. Right, how we came. But that's if she'd be in any condition to recognize a trail. Easy to miss. If she got turned around, though, and headed north . . . she could be trekking for fifteen miles before seeing a trail or a road. She veers northwest, its twenty miles. Even with a compass, moving at two or three miles an hour . . . you see how it can go."

"Anything else?"

Laura looked away, but Cross knew she was analyzing maps in her mind; she'd committed the topography to memory. "Southwest. Over or around Spruce, then maybe to Haskell Road."

"Problems with that?"

"Well, Indian River could be a problem. Haskell Road runs on the west side of it. Indian River has rapids. Not too bad in the late summer, but still treacherous in places." Laura stuck out her hand like a blade. "If she cuts that line south-southwest, then she's into a pretty boggy area between Baldface and Bethune. Through that way and you've got Fayle Road, maybe Mountain Home Road. If she was with Turner, and he advised her, my guess is that's what he'd tell her to do, if he got a chance to tell her anything at all."

Laura dropped her hand and put both on her hips. "Any way you slice it, though, it's shitty going. Real tough. For anyone."

CHAPTER FORTY-SIX

Katie was ravenous.

Five days. Since they threw her down and closed the door on the minivan, she'd had a couple of sandwiches to eat, some dry oats, not much else. All while hiking and climbing and fighting and running.

Starving.

She aimed down the rifle sights as she imagined a hunter would. The rabbit sat low to the ground, eating something at the base of a large tree.

Katie pulled back on the bolt and a round entered the chamber.

The rabbit popped up onto its hind legs with the sound, but it didn't run.

Two hours, this had taken. Sitting still, like she had done before. Listening to the forest come alive. Waiting for something to wander into her midst.

She worried about more bears, coyotes; but she had to eat. She'd never been so hungry. The need for food had started to beat a drum in her head and she knew it wouldn't stop until she did something about it.

The idea that she might be extra-hungry because she was eating for two flitted through her thoughts even if she was trying not to think about it.

It was impossible not to think about it.

There were women who said they knew the moment they were pregnant. Katie had always thought hindsight was 20/20. Easy to say you "knew" conception had occurred that night on the dining room floor while you and the hubby went at it after two bottles of wine. But did you really know it at the time? Or did you just reverse-engineer your knowing?

As it turned out, the insight took a different form. It wasn't some kind of intellectual conviction, a mental thing — *I'm pregnant.*

She just *felt* different.

Yeah, well, you've been feeling all sorts of different lately. Hard to say about this.

—It's there. Period would've started by now. I'm peeing all the time, even while rationing water, my breasts are sore — I've changed. My body has been hijacked.

Katie watched the rabbit. She had one eye shut. The little burrs that made up the gunsight were aligned. Her stomach flexed as she considered the meal. She'd never skinned an animal in her life. Maybe she would just cook the fur. Didn't people have to pull out the buckshot from the flesh?

No buckshot here, kid. This is a rifle.

Could rifle bullets be too big for small game like this?

Only one way to find out.

She pulled the trigger.

The gun kicked against her shoulder and the barrel arced up. She'd managed to keep her eyes open, at least, and could see the tree bark explode above the rabbit, which took off like a rocket.

"Fuck."

Katie set the rifle down and lowered her head. She was on her stomach and rolled over, staring up at the trees. Her fingers found their way down to her midsection and she folded her hands over her belly.

She breathed. Closed her eyes. Breathed some more.

The rifle shot had been loud, and her ears were ringing. She waited patiently for it to pass.

The forest was still. Not so much as a chirp from the woodland creatures. She needed to start all over again.

She had two rounds left.

CHAPTER FORTY-SEVEN

Hundreds of people combed the woods on the third day of the search.

And then the fourth.

Two main groups performed relays with the initial cabin as one locus, Turner's cabin the other.

Helicopters could be heard thudding through the air day and night. Supplies were dropped — food, fresh clothing, batteries, more tags. At least 100 spots were marked by searchers — broken branches, cairns of rocks, anything resembling a footprint or scrape of blood on a tree. An empty bag of potato chips was found, looking like it had been manufactured a decade before.

Dogs were out — a state police bloodhound unit, barking through the forest.

Katie Calumet had been in the woods for seven days.

Cross received periodic updates from Gates. Occasionally they spoke by radio, when it was something general. Otherwise Cross was texting with her on a secure sat phone.

Frost had doled out dozens of the phones to law enforcement. In some distant, bean-counting part of his mind, Cross kept a rough tally of all the expenses this case was racking up.

The search equipment — flashlights, tags, ponchos, radios, sat phones, GPS trackers — rented gear, for the most part. The meals, the mileage for personal vehicle use, the fuel to keep the helicopters in the air; it went on and on.

A prison break in recent years that had a thousand cops chasing down a fugitive for twenty-three days ended up with a price tag north of $1 million. If the search for Katie Calumet went on much longer, it was going to wind up somewhere in the same vicinity.

God's country. Cross had never realized how big the park was. Standing on the bluff that was half of Twin Mountain, gazing out over the sweeping expanse of vegetation, the undulant folds of the earth itself — it was stunning. There wasn't a sign of civilization in sight for 360 degrees. At night, the profusion of stars was breathtaking.

On the bluff was a good place for a signal, and as Cross noted some of the deciduous trees had tips turning color as autumn continued to sneak in, he pulled out the sat phone and sent a text to Gates.

Any luck locating Montgomery's wife?

He waited for a return text, was surprised when the sat phone rang with an incoming call.

"I just got out of a debriefing with Agent Wick. It looks like Jean-Baptiste Calumet has cooked the books a bit with his taxes. Don't ask me how it all works, but the gist of it is: Calumet buys some prime, seaside real estate somewhere, builds a luxury hotel and resort, fills it with all sorts of expensive things, and then nobody ever stays in it."

"He's not laundering money or anything?"

"I don't know. The FBI isn't saying that. What I heard is overstatement of deductions, concealment and transfer of income, underreporting income — and he's got more than one set of financial ledgers. The IRS is working with the feds on it."

Cross scraped a hand over his stubbled jaw. Marty's brother, Jude, had worked IRS criminal investigations for years, and he'd once told Cross how car dealers, salespeople, and restaurant owners were among the types identified as most likely to commit income tax fraud.

"Eric Dubois is where it gets interesting," Gates said.

"Oh? Do tell." Cross glanced at David, sitting with some other searchers further away on the bluff.

"Dubois was the chef from Dobbs Ferry," Gates said.

"Right. He took over after Katie's husband, who helped get that restaurant going."

"Dubois was dating Gloria Calumet."

Cross didn't say anything for a few seconds. Then, as much to himself as to Gates, "Did they know? Katie and her husband?"

"I have no idea. Dubois says it was a brief fling, so maybe she never mentioned it. And you can't go asking anyone either, because this is coming out of a closed federal investigation."

Cross suddenly craved a drink. He realized he was on a sobriety streak. All this time in the woods and no one had brought any booze along. "Well, I could just make conversation," Cross said.

"Yes, you could do that . . ." Gates sounded conspiratorial. "Look, the feds and the IRS are looking at Calumet for the tax fraud — and he's outraged. You haven't seen a newspaper for a couple of days; he gave a statement to the press about inappropriate government action. He called it a witch hunt. His daughter is missing and the FBI is investigating him for what he claims is just wild conjecture and outright lies from people who'd like to see him fail. He's a successful businessman, an immigrant, etcetera. The feds barely seem interested in the kidnapping, or Vickers and Montgomery, because despite all this, there don't seem to be any connections between the kidnapping and Jean Calumet's financial issues."

"Really?"

"That's the vibe I'm getting. And it's pretty strong."

Cross scratched some more at the beard growing on his jaw, and turned his back on David and the others.

"Yeah, but we still have a case."

"I don't know, Justin . . ."

"I'm not talking about impeding, not even assisting, per se. Just keeping with our own case. We *do* still have a case. And it's finding Katie, but it's finding out who did this, too. Even if the feds don't seem to care."

"Justin, I . . ." Gates sound weary. "I can't go down to New York City right now. I'm . . ." She seemed to search for the right words. "I'm trying to put my marriage back together. My family. I've been away so much."

"My marriage has already come apart."

"You don't know that."

"I'll go down to the city. Find Eric Dubois and talk to him, talk to Gloria."

"You need a break. You need to see your own daughters . . ."

"I'll take a break. I'll see them. And I want to find Johnny Montgomery's wife, too."

Cross spared another look at the searchers sitting around on the bare rock, lunching under the sun. It startled him a little that David was watching.

Cross waved a hand, wondering if Katie's husband had any idea Gloria had dated Eric Dubois at one time.

He also suddenly felt torn — like leaving was giving up on Katie.

"There's one more thing," Gates said. "Jeff Gebhart is awake."

"You're kidding."

"He's still in critical condition, but he came to."

"What has he said?"

"Not much yet. He doesn't remember the crash. We asked about Montgomery, and he stopped talking completely. Won't say anything about a cabin."

"He's afraid."

"Maybe. Yeah, probably. That and his brother Abel went to see him. With the lawyer."

"Jesus."

"Yeah."

Gates fell silent and didn't speak for so long Cross thought the satellite call had been disrupted. Then she said, "Listen, this is unfamiliar territory. I'm not going to pull rank on you or tell you what to do, one way or the other. Maybe Bouchard will, but I won't. You decide, Justin."

It plagued him for the rest of the afternoon.

After lunch, the searchers rallied and started down from the bluff, descending the backside of Twin Mountain toward Spruce, the next peak in the chain. They moved through the woods in a phalanx, and Cross listened as Katie's name was called out over and over. It suddenly seemed tedious, like it was leading nowhere, and at last he made his decision.

Before he got a chance to call Gates back with his answer, the dogs started going crazy. One of the searchers cried out, excitement in their voice, and a touch of horror.

"I've got a body!" The searcher's voice echoed in the deep woods. "People, I've got another body here!"

CHAPTER FORTY-EIGHT

It was just about the most delicious thing she'd ever eaten in her life.

Either the same rabbit or one just like it had returned to the spot fifteen minutes later. This time she'd squeezed the trigger and forced herself to stay steady while the gun fired. Her targeting had been better, but she'd still missed.

With one round left, she'd waited another twenty minutes. Whatever was beneath that tree — clover, mushrooms, something — the rabbits wanted it.

Third time's the charm.

The rifle shot got the brown, furry creature in the head. Katie had leapt up, forgetting her injured leg in a moment of ecstasy. She'd been reminded of it a split second later as her thigh gave off a trumpet of blinding pain and she'd hit the ground.

Crawling to the rabbit, she'd pulled out Hoot's pocketknife. Just a little red thing, blade about two inches, but sharp. He'd obviously used something much bigger to skin those coyotes but she'd never found it. Never searched his person, though, either.

The rabbit's limp body had been soft and warm. She'd gripped it, and, crying, used the pocket knife to saw off its head.

Whether it was right or not, she didn't know. But none of the hanging skins in Hoot's cabin had featured heads.

She wouldn't look at the rabbit's tiny severed cranium, but dragged herself a ways away, then tried to peel the skin from the neck down like a banana. It was impossible until she used the knife, sawing as she pulled. But the thing was so small and floppy, it kept slipping in her grip. The knife would plunge in or glance off. Twice she cut herself. She blinked back more tears. She gritted her teeth. She screamed.

She left the carcass in the dirt and rose to her feet, yelling for help.

I'm not going to stop until someone hears me.

—You'll drive yourself crazy.

Shut up. She the fuck right up. I'm so fucking sick of you, I'm gonna fucking yell until someone HEARS ME.

Katie collapsed to the ground. Rolled over onto her side.

She was aware in some oblique way that the little glen she was situated in, the shade dapples and sun streaming down in bars of light alive with dancing insects — she was like some perverse Disney princess waiting for Prince Charming.

She went back to the rabbit. Getting the fur over the paws seemed impossible, and she gave up. She chopped those off, too.

Must've been where "lucky rabbit's feet" came from.

Getting a fire going was easier. She was becoming a professional pyro. In minutes she had a good blaze going. She hoped, as always, that someone spotted the smoke, but this time that hope was overshadowed by the joy of cooking.

A large stick, rammed right up the rear of the thing and out its neck. Two other sticks jammed in the ground, as Y-shaped as nature made them, and she hung the rabbit there to cook.

When the muscle was blackened, she picked it up by the spit. The meat was hot, barely cooked, but she bit into it.

It was gamey, sort of penny-flavored, in definite need of salt, but outstanding.

That had been two days ago.

Katie hobbled along on her crutch, her stomach gnawing at her again. The hunger beat its familiar drum. Her usual mental refrain — that she was lost, that she should have found the trail by now, that she was walking in circles — was going strong.

She blotted it out with a song.

"Go tell it on the mountain. Gooo tell it on the mountain. Gooo tell it on the mountain . . ." She turned her face to the sky and yelled the last verse. "That Jesus Christ is bornnnn!"

Her voice cracked on the last word. She'd screamed herself hoarse more than once so far.

The woods parted. She stopped at the edge of a small lake, checked her compass. The needle blurred in her vision. She felt drunk. Thirsty. Time to make another fire. Boil water.

She dropped her pack and pulled out the pot, set it aside. Went to work looking for birch bark and small sticks for kindling. Set it up and pulled out her matches.

She had two things of matches — a generic white book from Carson and a small box that said "Diamond" and looked like it had been manufactured in 1950. Those were Hoot's — just a few rattling around, so she went for Carson's, which she'd been using all along.

About six left.

She struck the first one, and the head crackled but the flame died.

She struck another one; this time there wasn't even a crackle, and the head stripped off.

The whole booklet felt softened. She felt around inside the pack. Damp in there. But she'd been keeping the matches inside a plastic baggie. Had she not sealed it up well enough the last time? Or forgotten to put the booklet back in the baggie?

She went through the rest of them.

No flame.

Took out the box of Diamond matches, slid it open. The few in there seemed dry, and the first one caught.

"Time for a trip to the hardware store," she said.

She fed the flame to the birch bark, which crackled and smoked, and the fire grew. The smell of burning birch never got old. It was comforting, and her giddy, punch-drunk feeling abated.

Katie grew somber. She sat and tried to fold her legs Indian-style.

It's bad to say "Indian-style." No one says that anymore.

When we were girls we would say "crisscross apple sauce."

—So fucking what.

So what.

The hunger was so great, her whole body felt it. Desiccated, she crawled to the edge of the lake with the pot, filled it up.

She looked back at the fire, realizing she'd forgotten to forage for any bigger pieces. The small twigs were turning gray, the fire dwindling.

She hobbled in a circle, grabbing everything she could find.

Maybe it was all a dream.

Maybe she'd been running this whole time. Loop Three, the big loop. A car coming round the bend by that big gray house with the red trim she admired. Nice cedar shakes for siding.

Watch out!

Boom. The car impacts her, throws her back.

How far had Monica flown through the air? Or had the truck run her over, pinned her beneath the wheels?

She'd never asked.

What had Monica said to Jean before she died?

God will take care of me.

Maybe that's what. Monica would say something like that.

God will take care of me now.

Katie fed the larger pieces of wood to the fire, making a teepee shape. The flames, almost snuffed out by her negligence, started to lick the wood. To taste it. Crawl up and devour—

Loop Three.

The kidnappers had been watching her. They had to have been. Studying her. She hadn't been random; they'd known her name. How else would they have known the way she ran, passing the Footbridge Park near the end?

Unless they'd had some other information about her.

She went back for the pot. When the wood burned a bit more, the teepee would collapse and there would be a nice bed of coals for the pot. In an hour or so she could be quenching her thirst. If she wanted it cold, she could wait for morning.

Katie limped back to the water's edge. She tore off Hoot's sweater, stripped the pants, pulled down her running skirt. She waded right in, feeling the cold, mucky bottom suck at her bare feet.

The water came up to her breasts.

Katie bent her knees and submerged.

CHAPTER FORTY-NINE

Cross watched as the rescue helicopter lowered the hoist with the human-sized basket.

When it touched down, he and the others strapped in Montgomery's body, then the airlift crew hauled it up.

Jonathan Montgomery had been shot through the side of his stomach. He'd apparently administered himself first aid and tried to staunch the bleeding — he'd managed to disinfect the wound and apply a compress but had bled out in the end.

Gut wounds were a terrible way to die, Cross thought.

As Montgomery's body reached the helicopter, Cross turned to David Brennan. "You should camp here for the night." He had to speak loudly over the thudding noise.

The helicopter hovered. The basket began to lower back to the bluff.

There was room for one more passenger, and Cross had radioed that he wanted to fly out.

David's long hair was blowing around his head. He clapped Cross on the shoulder. The man had a grip like a Viking. "Thank you for everything."

Cross didn't feel particularly proud.

"Don't give up." He didn't know what else to say.

"I'm not going to." David smiled. It looked to Cross like he'd lost several pounds, his cheekbones prominent, his hair sweaty as he tied it back.

Cross climbed into the basket. He watched David shrink away on the ground then stared up at the cargo winch, where the retracting chain disappeared into the chassis.

He was grabbed by the crew and yanked into the helicopter. With the basket stowed, the cargo winch swung out of the way and the helicopter banked in the air, causing his stomach to drop.

Montgomery was beside him, wrapped in an evidence bag.

Johnny M., at long last. Vickers had died; now his partner was dead. Cross recalled his press conference speech with a bittersweet tinge. Ill-advised though it may have been, he'd been right that a successful kidnap-and-ransom was hard to pull off.

But it wasn't over. Katie was still out there.

The helicopter turned east and flew away from the setting sun. Cross risked a look out the window at the expanse of wildlands below.

God's country.

* * *

It felt like he hadn't been home for ages. The place was drafty and Cross closed a few windows he'd left open. The weather had taken a sudden dip in temperature and he thought of Katie Calumet exposed to the elements.

He took a shower and watched the water turn brown as four days of being in the woods sluiced off him and swirled down the drain.

Despite what he'd said to David, he was suddenly overcome with the assurance that they weren't going to find her. He imagined Katie's husband out there for weeks, maybe months, eventually alone, walking himself down to his bones, calling out his wife's name.

Was there ever a point when a person gave up? What was that point like — how did it feel? Was it a numbness, was it a relief?

He shaved, standing with the towel wrapped around his waist, the bathroom steamy. He wiped away condensation from the mirror and stared into his own eyes.

The doorbell rang. Before he could finish cleaning up his face, he heard the door open and the telltale voices of his daughters.

They were babbling about the first-fallen leaves. Ramona only had a few words in her repertoire that Cross knew of, but "leaf" hadn't been one of them.

"Leaf!" she was shouting. "Leaf-eaf!"

He found them taking their shoes off in the entryway.

"Daddy!" Petrie ran to him and threw her arms around his legs. Ramona dropped the red leaf she was holding and charged for her father, too.

He hugged them both back and said, "I'm going to go get dressed, okay? I'll be right back."

He glanced at Marty, a bit self-consciously since he was mainly naked, but she just smiled and corralled the girls. "Let daddy finish up."

So bizarre that his wife was a guest in his home, a place that they had bought together. A house in which they'd shared a bed.

Cross grabbed some deodorant from the dresser and swiped it over his armpits. He pulled on jeans and a T-shirt. He ran fingers through his hair, stared at his reflection again. Was his own wife making him a bit nervous? Damn right she was.

It was getting dark out and he flipped on some lights as he returned to the girls. They'd come into the living room and Petrie had already taken to the corner where Cross had set up her "workshop" — she could spend an hour sitting and stringing together beads for necklaces and bracelets. Ramona had a coloring book on the floor and was busy slashing the face of Curious George with a red crayon.

Marty was organizing something in the girls' bags and Cross invited her to sit. She took the armchair next to Petrie's workshop and Cross sat down on the couch, Ramona near his feet.

The air felt charged, like he and Marty had things to talk about. But both of them knew it was impossible to really converse when the girls were around. So they settled into small talk, steered clear of Cross's case, and focused on the girls.

Ramona, dissatisfied with her rendering of Curious George as a psychopath, tore up her work and crumpled it into a ball. She found this amusing and decided to tear the next page in the coloring book, too, and Cross intervened.

They spent the next half hour trying on different jewelry from Petrie, dealing with Ramona's whims — first she wanted to tear the coloring book, then she wanted a horsey-ride on daddy's back, then she wanted to play with the Bitty Baby and feed it and put it to bed, and then she wanted a snack.

He and Marty fell into a natural rhythm in the kitchen, getting the girls their before-bed snacks (carrots and pretzels for Petrie, applesauce and pretzels for Ramona) then brushed their teeth. They did paper-rock-scissors to determine who would change Ramona's diaper (Cross lost) and then Marty lay down with both girls and read them a story.

Cross slipped out of the bedroom and went to the kitchen. He debated whether or not he should have a drink in front of Marty, decided the answer was to fix one for her, too.

She didn't like beer, but she'd have a whiskey and coke, he thought. Marty had never been a tomboy, per se, but she was never one to shrink from a real drink.

He brought both glasses back into the living room. Marty was still in with the girls so he decided to check his email on his phone.

No updates from the searchers. Montgomery's body was undergoing a full autopsy. External would be completed later that night, internal sometime the following day, or maybe the next.

The Tremblays were back home — they'd told troopers that they were sick of the press hounding them day and night and so had taken off for a couple days, shut off their phones. Cross could understand.

Jeff Gebhart had dramatically improved and was going home in the next day or so. DA Cobleskill was toying with charges such as conspiracy to commit kidnapping, but there were still too many holes to make it stick, and the prosecution was on hold.

Marty walked into the living room, stirring him out of his thoughts. He put his phone aside, several emails left unopened.

"I thought you'd have the news on," she said, taking the chair by Petrie's workshop again.

"I was just checking my messages."

"I've had it on all week," she said. "Never watched so much TV in my life."

"Yeah." Cross eyed the remote control sitting on the table beside the couch. It could wait a few minutes. "How's work?"

She pushed her shoes off and sat cross-legged in the chair. Cross thought she seemed very comfortable. She was wearing yoga pants, a hooded sweatshirt. She looked good, especially for a thirty-something mother of two who was working her ass off as a hospital administrator. "Work is okay," she said.

"What's wrong?"

"Oh nothing, nothing. You know, it's just politics. I'm getting used to it."

"Politics . . . You just mean . . ."

"I mean politics. You know? There are people making decisions for medical reasons; there are people making decisions for political reasons. Takes a lot of money to run a hospital." She acted like she wanted to say more but looked at the blank TV screen.

"Yeah, I can imagine," Cross said, really having no idea. He grabbed one of the drinks from the end table and walked it over to Marty. "Here."

She gave it a look, hesitated, then took the glass. "Thanks."

He sat back down with his own. For a second or two it felt like the wrong thing to do, like he'd made a mistake offering her a drink, then he took a sip. The carbonation soothed his throat and the whiskey warmed his stomach.

"Where's Dana?" Marty asked. "Still out there?"

"No, she never was. Been working other aspects of the case. But she's home now, taking some time with her family."

"That's good."

He opened his mouth, closed it again, took another sip of the oaky drink.

He wondered if all cops were doomed to troubled marriages. How did a person strike a balance between family and a job like this? Dana Gates seemed to be finding one. What was the key? Effective compartmentalization, a proper wall between work and home life?

But when a cop did that, when anyone did that — did the work suffer? Did the home life?

He thought of Gloria Calumet. She'd left the search and returned to Brooklyn to check in with her restaurant and store, her employees. Some would call that responsible — with 1,000 people searching for Katie, her presence wasn't going to make or break the search, and she had businesses to run, possibly an FBI investigation to deal with.

Others would find it reprehensible. They'd say she was callous, abandoning her family in their time of greatest need. Forget the business, screw the government.

He watched Marty. She kept staring at the dark TV, then she raised the glass to her lips. When she drank, he felt relieved. Maybe he was overthinking it, but somehow the act removed a barrier between them.

"You want me to turn it on?" He was already reaching for the remote.

"No, not unless you want to. Do you want to?"

He dropped the remote on the couch. He'd been in the woods for a long time. Despite showering, he could still smell the campfire smoke on his skin. She picked up on his thoughts, as Marty was prone to do. "What did you eat out there?" she asked.

"Ah, food kept coming out. We had a couple supply drops, and then there was sort of a bucket brigade. Hot dogs. Beans. Fruit. Lots of granola bars. I mean a *lot* of granola bars. I'll be pent up for days."

Marty screwed up her face. "What do you think she's eating?"

"We found some minimal groceries at the first cabin. Not much at the second. Honestly, I don't know."

"The second — that was the mountain man's cabin. Some pot-growing hermit or something?"

"Yeah. He hasn't been officially identified yet, but . . . yeah."

She scowled and shook her head, then took a longer pull from her whiskey and coke. "The whole thing is awful," she said quietly.

They let it settle. Cross switched topics. "How are the girls doing, how's your mother handling it?"

"Good. They're all good. The day care is excellent, my mom is filling in the gaps. It's working out."

He felt a familiar mix — glad his girls were in a stable situation, glad for Marty, too, but simultaneously disappointed it all seemed to be okay.

"Listen. Thanks for bringing the girls here tonight. It's really, ah . . . I know it's out of your way. I just . . . Seeing them here is . . ." He struggled to find the words.

"No, it worked out. I've got tomorrow off, school is still two weeks away for Patricia. They needed to see you."

The idea that Marty thought his daughters needed to see him filled Cross with emotion. He leaned forward, holding his drink, biting back the sudden, unexpected tears. "You know, I never thought I'd be a part of something like this."

When he looked up, Marty was gazing back, her own eyes brimming.

"I mean, this isn't the first abduction case I've had, but nothing like this."

She blinked at him, and her emotion dried up. She sat back and then turned her face away.

You idiot, he realized. *She thought you were talking about you and her. The separation.*

"I know," Marty said flatly, "I understand. This is a big one." She took a drink then added, "But it's not unusual for you to get swept away by your work."

She changed her position, planting her feet down, no longer in the comfy repose. "And that's why we've, you know . . . that's why we have this arrangement. It's best."

"It's best for whom?"

She just gave him a look then stood. "Justin, I'm not going to do this." She walked out of the room, put her glass in the sink; he heard her run the tap.

"Do what? Talk? We said we'd talk, too. You'd bring the girls for the night and we'd talk."

Stop it. What the fuck are you doing? Why are you arguing *with her?*

She returned to the chair and sat down. She had picked up her shoes along the way and started putting them on. "I'm coming back in the morning, right? You've got to go to the city, you said? To see about the sister or something?"

Things were falling apart. This wasn't how he wanted tonight to go.

"Marty, wait a second."

She stood in her shoes and stared at him. He knew that look — she'd wrapped herself in a kind of emotional insulation now.

He'd blown it.

He set aside his drink and looked down at his hands. They shook a little and he wrung them together, then found her gaze again.

"I'm sorry."

"For what? You don't have anything to be sorry for. I understand you have to go down to—"

"I'm sorry I cut you out of my life."

She blinked. "It's your work, you're a professional and need to use discretion, just like I do."

He took a cautious step toward her. In the corner of his eye he could see their reflection in the blank flat-screen TV. She on one edge, him along the other.

"That's not what I mean. I mean, I cut you out of this part of me that . . . I don't know what to call it. I just thought I had to be a man. Whatever that means. Do what I needed to do."

She was quiet. Her lower lip started to shiver. "You left me. Maybe not physically, but in every other way."

"I know. I know I did."

A silence developed. He found it hard to meet her eyes. When he did, he saw her looking levelly at him. She straightened her shoulders. "Justin, a couple only really has a couple different arguments, and they have them over and over again."

He got stuck on the idea that she'd just called them a "couple." Did she still think of them as together?

"Okay," he said. "What is this argument about?"

"For us it's always been about the work. We both have careers. This is about you wanting to have your career, and wanting me to stay home and raise the girls."

He opened his mouth to defend, but nothing came out. She had boiled it down. For some reason, though, he tried a pathetic, "That's not true."

"Sure it is."

"I *want* you to work. But—"

"But part-time, okay. Well, what about you? Why couldn't you cut back on your hours with the state police?"

"Because it doesn't work like that."

She was nodding. "Exactly. See? The same argument. And it doesn't work like that for me, either. You don't work part-time as a hospital administrator."

"Well, you didn't have to take the job." His voice rose an octave; he couldn't help it.

She clapped her hands together, once, and smirked. "There you have it."

"Well? Two people both working full-time, with two kids?"

She widened her eyes at him. "Are you kidding? People are doing it all over the country. Most people can't survive without two incomes."

"We could have."

"Maybe. Barely. With nothing left to put away, nothing for the girls — what if we wanted to put Petrie in piano classes, or one of them needs a tutor? Hand-to-mouth is not ideal." She shook her head and flapped a hand in the air as if finances weren't the point. "Justin, I know you're not one of these guys who thinks the woman's place is in the home. I married you. So, what is it?"

He began to respond but caught himself again. He didn't want to say what it was. He realized he didn't even know.

Maybe he was just an asshole and needed to change.

He wished he knew how.

Marty stared at him, and he felt like she was reading his mind.

"Look what happened to Dana," Marty said. "Dana Gates worked her ass off — multiple homicides at the college, and she worked day and night. People were gossiping — you told me yourself — how she barely spent enough time with her own girls. What a bad mother she was. If that had been you on that case — you think people would've talked about you behind your back about how you were neglecting your family? No. They would've commended you for your dedication."

She averted her eyes and moved toward the door. "I get an opportunity for a job, something I've been working toward for years, and it's this huge inconvenience. You don't want to move, you don't want to take fewer hours—"

"I told you it doesn't work like that, I can't just—"

"So, this is where we're at. Two separate households, two separate lives—"

"Double the expenses," he shot back. "It doesn't make any economic sense. We're back to each barely scraping by."

"Well?" Her hand was on the doorknob. "What do we do then, Justin? You tell me. Aside from me quitting the job I worked so hard to get, what do we do?"

He didn't have an answer for that, either.

Her eyes were welling again; she was close to letting her guard down and crying, and he knew she didn't want him to see it. She hastily mumbled something about being back by nine the next morning, opened the door, and left.

He didn't stop her.

He watched as she backed out of the driveway and drove off into the night, then went and fixed himself another drink.

The TV was waiting. He settled back on the couch and turned it on, trying to steer his mind away from his personal life and back to the case. It was impossible. That wall he'd tried to build between work and family life was crumbling.

The eleven o'clock news came on, and the top story was Katie Calumet. It was enough to pull him out of the doldrums and focus.

There she was in the picture he'd chosen from her house with David.

"Katie Calumet remains missing tonight as searchers prepare for their fifth day in the West Canada Wilderness, an area in the southwest Adirondacks."

The image switched to a helicopter shot over the wilderness. *"But as the investigation continues, complications arise. Law enforcement and searchers have been scouring what's known as a 'primitive area,' and the rugged terrain takes a toll. Several injuries and at least one case of dehydration have been reported."*

The news anchor appeared, talking into the camera. "*We turn now to Dr. Peter Harmon, a wilderness survival expert. Harmon says that every day a hiker is in the woods, chances are slimmer that—*"

Cross sat up and clicked off the TV. He walked into the kitchen, feeling the effects of the drink. After several sober days, he was buzzed off just two weak whiskey and cokes. And he didn't want to hear an expert predict Katie Calumet's low chances of making it out alive. He ran the tap and rinsed the glass, then gulped some water.

He snapped off the lights and went to the bedroom, climbing into bed.

He couldn't sleep.

Taking his blanket with him, Cross crept into the girls' room. Another thing he'd gotten used to was sleeping on the hard ground.

He covered up with the blanket and listened to the sounds of his daughters' breathing.

CHAPTER FIFTY

Katie heard the helicopter and shrieked. She waved her arms; she fanned her dwindling fire, watching the smoke roll up through the evergreen boughs, dissipating ineffectually in the pinkish dawn light. She held up the compass, flicked its face toward the sky, but the sun wasn't even above the horizon yet.

Then she grabbed the pot, threw the remaining water on the flames. The fire hissed, bellows of steam rising into the trees. The sound of the helicopter sank away, and with the fire gone, the cold rushed in.

"Goddammit." She slumped to her knees and dropped her chin to her chest. "God . . . dammit."

It had been four days since leaving Hoot's cabin. She was tired; she was unbelievably hungry. She'd never known this kind of doubt and isolation. The hunger made it hard to think. Her last meal — a frog she'd chased around the edge of a small pond for an hour before catching it and cooking it whole — was long gone.

The ground was wet. The night had gotten cool, and morning dew glistened on the leaves. She no longer thought she was between Spruce Mountain and the trail Hoot had told her she would find. Way too much time had passed. Even at her slow pace, she had to come to grips with the fact she was off course, and had been for a while.

The helicopters had awoken her — the first one, 6 a.m., coming from the south, then this one from the west a half hour later — and knowing they were out there helped keep the fear at bay. But if they hadn't seen her by now, or her campfire smoke, would they ever? She didn't know whether helicopters meant searchers on the ground, too. For all she knew, Leno had made it out of the woods and was still negotiating with the police, acting like Katie remained hostage.

She *was* a hostage, anyway. Whether or not Carson or Leno had her tied up didn't matter; the woods had her now. And they didn't seem to want to let her go.

She'd gotten somewhat used to the plaguing sense of being lost. At first it was unsettling, even panic-inducing. A person normally spent all of their waking time well-oriented. They didn't walk around thinking about north and south, but knew their route to work, to the grocery store. Anywhere else, they increasingly relied on GPS.

It was an endless nagging in her mind that if she'd acted more swiftly when she'd been Carson's captive — if she'd snuck the GPS from him while he'd slept off the drinking that first night — she could have hidden it from him, made up a story. Something.

Or, that she'd missed something with the sat phone she'd recovered. She was too non-technical, and somebody better with those sorts of gadgets would've figured it out.

And consuming her, night and day, the guilt playing on an endless loop in her mind: the theory that she had inadvertently alerted Leno when she'd activated the SOS feature on the phone, and that blunder had directly led to Hoot's murder. She was horrified that she'd gotten someone killed.

She rolled back onto her butt and listened as a second helicopter faded into the distance. She looked at the wristwatch looped through the belt of Hoot's pants. Six forty-two in the morning. Normally she'd be taking a run about now. The last one hadn't gone so well.

Her wrists would likely bear scars from the plastic ties she'd endured, the ropes binding her to the bed. Her hands were filthy, dirt caked under her nails. She'd never been one to keep long nails, or paint them, but a few of them had broken anyway. There was a runnel of dried blood between her fingers that wound down the back of her hand.

She lifted her shirt. Her skin was covered in scrapes and bruises. The bruise on her right side looked like a colorful Rorschach inkblot.

She'd peed in the woods so many times it was starting to hurt — likely she'd gotten a UTI after wiping herself with leaves for the first couple days. But she was getting less and less water now, going infrequently.

The matches were gone. No more boiling water anyway. If she wanted a drink it would be straight out of a river or pond, but she hadn't seen one in a while.

Weight loss, infection, incessant, maddening hunger, the edges of dehydration — but the worst was probably her torn quad.

Her leg had swollen to almost twice its size from her hip to her knee. The skin was hot to the touch. She could only walk on it for ten, fifteen minutes at a time, then she needed almost as much rest.

No, that's not the worst.

—Okay, maybe not.

You probably lost the baby.

—I don't know that.

Even well-fed mothers getting plenty of bed rest and not potentially lost for all time have miscarriages. Give it up.

You're a wreck.

Your body is inhospitable.

It happened days ago and you know it.

It's over.

She turned her mind away. Had to.

One thing was true: She hadn't had a good poop since the outhouse at the first cabin. Just once, a piercing in her stomach causing her to run through the woods, hunched over, clutching the rifle against her churning stomach, until she'd found a suitable log to hang her ass over.

If only her husband could see her now.

If only she could laugh with Gloria about everything. Her hair, for one thing — greasy and tangled like a madwoman. She'd pulled at least five beetles out of it since starting out of the woods — and one good-sized spider.

Maybe I'll start eating the bugs, Glo.

It wasn't a half-bad idea. Some survivalists swore by eating insects, said they had protein.

But you had to eat a lot, she figured.

Maybe they even soothed the stomach, good for digestion?

What do you think, Glo? Find an anthill somewhere, tuck a napkin under my chin, and go to town?

She wondered if her little sister was out here in these same woods. Maybe she was miles away, maybe she was close. How was she holding up? Was she taking one for the team and roughing it?

Doubtful. Even in such dire circumstances, Gloria probably wasn't too far from a full bathroom. From a young age, Glo had luxuriated in long showers. It had driven their father nuts. He'd bang on the bathroom door and order her to shut the water off. Once she was old enough to say such things, she'd shout back, "You can afford it!"

She'd been a rebellious teenager. She'd gone Goth at one point, preferring black eye makeup and a black leather jacket to the long maroon jumpers required by her preparatory school.

She'd run away from school three times. When their father had found her and dragged her back for the third time, she'd gone ahead and gotten herself expelled.

It was true: Toth Prep didn't like it when you lit all your books on fire in the center of the student courtyard.

There were all sorts of reasons, then, that the nickname "Glo" was so appropriate.

First, her affinity for long showers. The water would dry her skin something terrible and so Gloria would apply globs of shea butter, making her positively shine.

Second, as an ironic moniker during her black-clad-and-perpetually-dour phase, "Glo" was a riot, at least as far as Katie was concerned.

And it was just icing on the cake that Glo finally touched a match to her gasoline-doused pile of books on a windy October day. The nickname took on a whole new level of meaning for Katie when she pictured Glo standing there in the firelight of her destructive streak.

Of course, fun and games and a big sister's nicknames were one thing, but their father, and the school, took it all quite seriously. Gloria went to counseling, saw a psychiatrist, and was prescribed Effexor for what was deemed her underlying depression.

Their mother had died when Glo was eleven years old, and it didn't take a shrink to deduce that Monica's death was about the time Gloria shifted from long, womb-like showers to a perpetual kind of funereal fashion.

In fact, Katie thought, it should've been obvious to anyone. But for some reason, when it was your family, when you were in the midst of it, it wasn't. You accepted things at face value and didn't dig too deep. You couldn't dig too deep, she figured, because you were a part of that picture, too. It was hard to see objectively.

It was hard to understand any other world where your mother hadn't been taken from you, or what it was like for people who still had both of their biological parents. You couldn't say, you didn't know, so you just went on.

Katie had coped by leaving the city. She'd found a remote spot, settled in, and now here she was.

Now she was truly removed from the situation, as removed as it got.

But not Gloria. Gloria had stayed in the city.

I'm so sorry, Glo.

The sound of the helicopters long gone, the woods were silent.

Katie stretched out on her back. She had to keep her right leg bent at the knee.

My big, fat leg.

What do you think about my big, fat leg, Glo?

Katie closed her eyes.

CHAPTER FIFTY-ONE

Katie's sister had a checkered past, Cross discovered. Her run-ins with the law were fairly minor — she'd been arrested for destruction of property as a juvenile (though charged with criminal mischief as an adult), and had a few parking tickets and moving violations.

But as he probed a little deeper, at first just surfing the net, the picture of a troubled woman became clearer. *New York Now* magazine had an article on Gloria's whole foods store, shut down for a health code violation two years prior.

He'd been aware of this from talking to David, but what he hadn't known was how news of the violation had spread through the surrounding community and an anti-gentrification protest had formed.

Cross found pictures of people with signs declaring, "Get out of our home," and someone had written "Scum" on the storefront. Protestors called the whole foods store a symbol of the inequality plaguing their neighborhood.

"These people come in with their money, they raise my taxes," one Brooklyn resident said in a separate article by the *Daily Post*. "There used to be a bodega here, where I could afford groceries. Now I have to take the subway just to get milk and bread. And this place has violated city health codes. It figures. The rich are always cutting corners to get richer."

The name Calumet, another protestor claimed, was synonymous with this kind of corruption.

"Jean-Baptiste Calumet is like a backward Robin Hood," the protestor said. "Taking from the poor to give to the rich."

The protestor didn't elaborate on exactly how, or the newspaper hadn't reported it.

Cross went through more articles, sitting at his desk in the Hazleton substation. He was anxious to be on his way to Brooklyn but wanted to finish brushing up first.

The charges against the store were: one piece of equipment which had expired; a single bottle of ammonium-based sanitizer which had been left uncapped in the supply closet; and an employee in the bulk-pack room observed assembling cartons while also packaging exposed, ready-to-eat quinoa cakes. Allegedly the employee hadn't washed hands or changed gloves in between tasks.

Compared to other health violations Cross imagined, the charges against Gloria's store were negligible; an oversight — a mistake anyone could make. It wasn't listeria, anyway. But Gloria Calumet followed all of the rules, shut down the store, updated all the equipment — even appliances not yet expired or even close to expiration, applied for a re-investigation, and passed it with flying colors.

Yet the renovations had come with a hefty price tag and the whole thing put the store out of business for over a year.

Gloria also owned a restaurant, a place two blocks from the whole foods store called Sorrel, presumably after the bitter herb.

Sorrel was high-end, a fusion of Asian and French cooking, according to its website. Its existence had surely added to the ireful anti-gentrification protests. In short, Cross figured, the yuppie hipsters loved Gloria Calumet, but she wasn't such a big hit with the other residents, the more working-class, those who'd called the area home for generations.

So what did it all mean?

Cross shut down his work station and grabbed a cup of coffee from the kitchen to go. He wondered how much of a financial hole Gloria Calumet had found herself in after the health code violations. Couldn't she have her father bail her out before she hit the skids?

Maybe not with Sybil, the stepmother, holding the purse strings.

Cross fired up the car and headed toward the interstate. He wondered if it was at all plausible that Gloria Calumet was behind her sister's abduction. Had she hired kidnappers to abduct her sister in order to extort money from her icy stepmom?

The organized crime thing seemed off the table. Not just because the feds didn't seem to think it, but because of how high-profile it all was. The mob took people in the night, weighted them down with bricks, and sank them in the lake. They didn't kidnap rich daughters for ransom. They had much more secure ways of making money.

And all the other leads were blind alleys: Henry Fellows, the ex-partner, or Lee Beck, the lawyer. The feds had called Eric Dubois, the chef who'd been fired from the Dobbs Ferry restaurant, a dead end. But recently he'd gone to work, according to the Sorrel website, for Gloria Calumet.

He'd even dated her, apparently.

Cross wanted to talk to the two of them.

Plus, he had something else he wanted to check out. Might be nothing, but it had been pinging around in his brain for a while now. The trip down to the city was two birds with one stone.

* * *

Five hours later, Cross sat at a table for one at Sorrel. It was early and the restaurant was empty except for a well-dressed couple in a corner booth and a bartender in a starched white shirt sliding wine glasses into the rack above her head.

The dinner rush loomed, scents of butter and garlic wafting from the kitchen doors and cutlery and china clashing. The chef barked at someone. Cross wondered who it was back there, if it was Eric Dubois. He planned to find out in just a few minutes.

A waitress picked her way through the tables and smiled at Cross. She held a black pad in her hands and explained to him that the kitchen wouldn't be open for ten more minutes, but he was welcome to wait and have a drink. He ordered a Scotch, single malt.

"Glenfiddich?"

"Please. Is Gloria Calumet here?"

The waitress, a pretty blonde in her thirties, gave Cross a little look. "No, she's not . . . Is there something . . . ?"

"No, it's okay. I'm a friend. She's probably over at the store, yeah?" He shook his head mournfully. "I don't know how she's keeping up, with everything that's going on."

The waitress glanced over her shoulder then back at Cross. She seemed to drop her guard. "I know," she whispered. "It's crazy. Are you . . . Do you know Ms. Calumet well?"

"I've come to know her a little, yeah. I'm actually wondering about Chef Dubois. Is he—?"

His phone rang, interrupting. The waitress looked wary again, but she pasted on a smile and promised to be right back with his drink.

Cross took the call.

"Hi, Dana."

"So, he's in surgery again. Not looking good." She meant Gebhart.

"You're in Albany?"

"Yeah. Just to check in with things."

"He was supposed to be released, I thought."

"Complications with his breathing. He has a collapsed lung."

"Jesus. Alright," Cross said, "Why don't you—"

"He talked to me."

Cross's mouth hung open for a moment. "What did he say?"

"He said he never dealt with Johnny Montgomery directly. He was renovating their house on Oak Street. His wife was the hirer. And she was the one to ask him about the hunting cabins."

Cross waited. "That's it?"

"That's it. You think he's talking about Janice Montgomery?"

"I do."

Dana sighed. "Well there it is."

"Thank you, Dana. You need to get out of there, get home to your family."

"Okay." She sounded ready to ring off but asked, "Where are you?"

Cross looked around the restaurant. He watched as the bartender poured his drink, the waitress standing at the bar, chatting, her eyes darting to Cross. The bartender looked, too.

Then a second waitress walked out of the noisy kitchen. She stuck her head back in the door, laughed at something, and stepped fully into the dining room.

Cross recognized her from pictures.

Quietly, he said to Dana Gates, "I'm looking at Janice Montgomery. Or, for all intents and purposes, Janice Connolly."

"Be careful."

"I'll call you back." He slipped his phone away. The place was dim, the kind of comforting lighting of a theater just before the movie begins, but he had good eyes and a clear view of the second waitress, Janice.

Eric Dubois could wait. Standing just a few feet away was the thing that had been pulsing in the back of his mind, personified.

She said something to the bartender, laughed, and walked away with a tray. She went about placing votive candles on the tables.

The blonde waitress returned and set down Cross's drink.

"Thank you."

"You're very welcome. I'll be back in a few minutes, okay? Tonight's menu is going to be good. Did you still want to—?"

He brushed a hand through the air. "No, no. Maybe after the meal."

She gave him a hundred-watt grin and swished away.

Janice Montgomery moved table to table, coming closer. His mind worked quickly — now he just needed to decide how to play it out. But that sort of depended on her, and whether or not she'd been watching TV.

She was around the age of the other waitress, only her hair was darker, her manner a bit rougher, like if the two waitresses were to arm wrestle, this one would be the easy victor.

She seemed disinterested in her work, distracted as she set out the candles.

Cross imagined a young life spent on the streets, where Janice Connolly had met all sorts of interesting people. People like Troy Vickers, or her future husband, Johnny Montgomery.

He took a sip of Scotch.

He waited.

When she reached his table, she paused, barely looking at him. "Do you mind?"

"No, I don't mind," Cross said.

She gave him a smile much less winning than her strawberry-blonde co-worker, and quickly set down the candle and made to leave.

Then she halted.

"You worked here long?" he asked.

He watched the recognition work its way into her eyes, form the tight line of her mouth.

He wondered how this was going to go down.

"Uh, been here a couple years," she said, recovering. She kept hold of the tray, a few candles left burning, and gave the front door a quick look. "Why? You writing a book?"

He pulled on a lopsided grin and acted guilty. "I am, actually . . . Well, not a book. I'm writing an article for the *Daily Post.*"

She showed him an unabashed look of disbelief but played along. "Uh-huh. Well, maybe you ought to think about that. I think the owner's been through enough, don't you?"

Janice started away.

"No, no," Cross said, raising his voice. "That's not really my angle."

"I don't really care what your angle is." She kept her back turned as she placed a votive on a table and moved on to the next.

He knew she wanted to run, was considering it — wondering if she was trapped.

"You should, Janice. When you applied here, did you use your married name or your maiden name? What do the paychecks say?"

She set down the next candle slowly. He watched the way her shoulders drew together. "You going through my trash?"

Cross stood, cautious. "My angle is about kidnapping, and how risky it is, how often it fails. My article is about why anyone would attempt it."

"I don't care about your article," she said, but she didn't budge.

"Like, in this case," he went on, taking a step closer. "It all went downhill. Troy Vickers, kidnapper number one — dead. Johnny Montgomery, kidnapper number two, also dead."

He let this sink in.

She performed well even under the immense burden of this information, he thought. No names had been released yet — the press didn't know; she likely didn't either. Maybe she'd been worried, suspicious, but this was confirmation.

At last she turned to look at him, candlelight reflected in her eyes. If she was nervous, she contained it well.

He drove the point home: "Kidnapper number three, we're pretty sure she works at a restaurant owned by Gloria Calumet. The victim's sister."

Janice slowly set the tray containing the last three candles down on the table in front of her. She untied the black apron covering her black slacks and set it beside the tray. Then she turned and started walking through the tables, toward the kitchen.

Cross pulled his badge.

There was more commotion from the kitchen. This time when the chef bellowed, someone shot back, "Keep quiet." It was enough that the sophisticated couple in the corner booth looked around, worried.

Janice was moving more quickly now.

A man in an apron stepped out of the swinging doors, looking angry about something unrelated.

The man quickly forgot his troubles and seemed to assess what was going on. He saw Janice coming; his eyes flitted to Cross.

Cross held the badge high. "Don't let her go in there, please!"

Janice turned away from the man and headed for the entrance. Cross changed course and wound through the tables after her.

"Janice?" The blonde waitress looked perplexed.

"It's alright," Cross assured the staff and guests. The kitchen crew crowded in the doorway behind the man in the apron, looking out with wide eyes.

Janice jerked into a run, slipping past the tables closest to the door, knocking a couple chairs to the ground as she left.

Cross scrambled out the door after her and burst out onto the sidewalk, just in time to see her running across the busy street.

Cross weaved through four lanes of fast-moving traffic. A bus slowed and blocked his view of Janice.

When he saw her again, she was turning down 7th, a narrower street less congested with traffic. She was incredibly fast, a real sprinter, and he was afraid he was going to lose her as he darted around a trio of kids on skateboards and a woman pushing a giant stroller.

Janice crossed the road again. He followed. Where was she going? Subway? There was nothing close. Just running blind?

She threw a look back at him and they locked eyes. She pumped her arms and legs but he was starting to gain on her. When she ducked into an alley, he was just a few yards behind.

The alley hosted a dumpster and a fire escape with the stairs retracted. It dead-ended. Nowhere to go.

Janice leapt for the fire escape and managed to grab hold of the rusted iron. She swung with its momentum, then hoisted herself up.

Cross reached her and jumped, his fingertips grazing her shoe at the last second.

Janice got to her feet on the first level just as an NYPD cop skidded into view at the mouth of the alley. "Hey!" the cop yelled.

Cross jumped for the stairs but it was no use. He had a load of adrenaline blasting through his system but he just didn't have the spring that Janice Montgomery had, and he only came away with a handful of rusty flakes.

She kept moving up the escape. She was either going to break into someone's apartment or take the stairs to the roof.

The local cop came running up. Cross intercepted him and gave a hasty, winded explanation about what was happening.

The cop got on his radio and broadcasted for backup, giving his location.

A window broke. It was hard to see Janice anymore through all the metal, but she'd gone into one of the top-floor apartments. Bits of glass sprinkled down.

"I'll go front door," Cross said. He pointed to the NYPD cop. "Back door, if there is one."

Cross returned to the street, thinking that if he got this close to Janice and lost her, it would be very bad.

Jean Calumet may have been dirty — he may have been unable to pay the ransom because his fortune was partly fraudulent and existed mostly on paper. And David might've been paid hush money for things he'd seen while working for Calumet. But it all boiled down to a woman who worked for Gloria, believed the family had money, and convinced her husband and his jailhouse friend to kidnap Katie, who lived close to where Johnny Montgomery owned a house upstate. They might've even pulled it off, but in the end it was Jean

Calumet's false fortune and Johnny Montgomery's greed which had screwed everything up.

Cross faced the entrance of the building with Janice possibly inside.

8544 7th Avenue, a residence with a glass front door, a vestibule filled with a bank of mailboxes, another interior glass door beyond. He had no key, no way in, and she had no way out.

Another one of the NYPD foot patrol came running up, his face beet-red.

His radio crackled. He held it out for Cross to hear. "Back entrance covered. No sign of her."

"Now it's a waiting game," the cop said, breathing hard.

But Cross didn't think so. Janice might hurt someone in there. He walked up to the apartment buzzers and started pressing buttons. He'd seen it in a movie once — a guy just hit a bunch of buttons and someone, perhaps expecting a visitor, buzzed the door.

Sure enough: "Who is it?"

"Police. Open up."

"Oh, gimme a break," the voice said.

No buzzer.

Cross pressed all the buttons again.

The voice came over, "You better knock it off or I'm gonna—"

They were cut off when the door buzzed open. Someone else had seen fit to open up.

Cross barged in and opened the next door before the buzzer quit.

He was inside. A wide hallway, several first-floor apartments, the stairs straight ahead, going up to the left.

There were five floors, according to the apartment numbers. Janice had gone in either the fourth or fifth. Cross got moving again, bounded up the stairs. He was tired from chasing her, but he felt good. He took the steps two at a time until he came round to the third floor and slowed down, listening.

A TV prattled away inside someone's apartment. The hallway reeked of cooking — a war of smells that didn't complement one another but formed a kind of food miasma. It was hot, too, the sweat running down his back, soaking his shirt.

He slipped his gun out. Third time now in his career he'd pulled his piece.

He thought of his daughters, said a small prayer. Then he heard a door open on the floor above him, the snick of the latch as it reengaged the housing.

Someone had just stepped out of an apartment.

Footsteps toward the stairs. Cross was on the landing between the third and fourth floors. Now he backed down a little so he was on the lower half of the stairs. He watched as someone stepped into view.

Running sneakers, not wait staff dress shoes.

He relaxed as the person casually descended. She stopped and sucked in a breath when she saw Cross, even though he'd pointed his gun down. A middle-aged woman wearing yoga clothes.

Cross showed his badge then held a finger to his lips and jerked his head, signaling that she keep going down the stairs.

She did, passing him with the whites of her eyes glowing in fear, and then she moved faster.

He continued up to the fourth floor.

More muffled sounds of apartment life; someone laughing.

A dog started barking — one of those little yappers, like a Yorkshire terrier.

Janice. Where are you?

Hiding. Maybe she'd gotten lucky and the apartment she'd broken into was unoccupied.

Cross oriented himself — to his left were the units which overlooked the alley. The fire escape had been almost at the very back. That meant apartment 4A, maybe 4B or C. Those were behind him.

He turned around.

Moving against the wall, he slid along until he came to 4C, and listened.

Nothing from inside, no giveaway. She could be in one of the three units or she might've reached the floor above him. At least from this vantage he had the stairs in view if she came down from the top floor.

The only remaining option was the roof. From there, he didn't know. Maybe other buildings abutted. Certainly the alleyway side was a no-go — even a track star couldn't jump that far from roof to roof.

He was almost positive this wasn't her building. For one thing, it was in too pricey a neighborhood for a waitress. For another, she hadn't exactly used a damned key.

Still, she could have a friend who lived here, even an accomplice. She might not have chosen the building at random.

The sweat dripped from his face and landed on the marble floor. He breathed and renewed his grip on the gun.

NYPD was creeping up the stairs. Two new faces, guys different from the ones he'd met so far. More backup had arrived.

Cross pointed to each of the doors, and the cops nodded. Then he pointed at the ceiling. They understood, and one of them continued up to the top floor.

The little dog kept barking. It sounded like it was inside one of the three end-apartments nearest to him. He moved to 4B, and the barking got louder. Either the terrier sensed someone outside in the hallway, or it didn't like an intruder in there with it.

Then the dog fell silent.

Cross snapped his fingers. The remaining cop came closer.

Cross stepped back from the door and kicked it.

The door didn't budge. Damn these Brooklyn brownstones, solid as shit.

He heard thumping, steps from inside the unit. Now both Cross and the cop kicked at the door, over and over, until it splintered around the deadbolt.

The door gave way and swung inward.

Straight ahead was a broken window overlooking the fire escape.

Cross rushed in, his heart rocketing in his chest, the NYPD cop right behind him.

Cross searched the living room first, gloomy in the failing light of day, then turned down a short hallway which fed a couple more rooms — he passed a bathroom, headed for probably a bedroom, door closed.

"She threw the dog out the window," the cop said.

Cross kicked the bedroom door.

Janice chucked something at him. He tried to duck the object, but it hit his head. Cross went down.

She charged past as he clutched for her legs, tripping her. She fell into the hallway, screaming, clawing at the carpet, trying to get away.

The NYPD cop showed up and pounced on her. Cross scrambled to his feet.

Janice thrashed beneath the city cop. Cross felt blood running from the gash on the side of his head. The thick ceramic ashtray she'd hit him with lay broken in two on the hallway floor.

"You have the right to remain silent," he said to Janice Montgomery, and she screamed again.

CHAPTER FIFTY-TWO

It had been a week since Brooklyn, and the maple leaves along the main road through Hazleton were turning red.

Cross was driving, David Brennan beside him, coming back from David's interview with *NBC Nightly News* at an affiliate station in Plattsburgh.

Cross slowed for David's driveway, glad to see no one loitering at the gate.

Reporters had been hounding Cross from as far away as Pennsylvania, calling him daily, asking about David once they'd sucked every last drop from the Janice Montgomery arrest. News vans could be seen outside David and Katie's gate as recently as the day before, but they were gone now, their thunder stolen by the interview, drawn off by other scents.

Including the sensational story developing around Jean-Baptiste Calumet, and the breaking news of his federal indictment.

Which meant they'd be back for David before long — as soon as they caught wind he was involved.

Cross turned into the driveway; David hopped out of the car and opened up the gate.

He had been out in the woods more consecutive days than any other searcher, including DEC and law enforcement.

Eleven days.

The feds had been itching to talk to him. There had even been rumors of a team prepared to go in and extract him like a fugitive.

Cross had convinced them otherwise. Finished with the week's worth of paperwork and internal investigations on the Connolly-Montgomery arrest, he'd driven down to Speculator and paid a visit to incident command.

There he'd contacted David via sat phone and talked him into coming out, giving the NBC interview to satisfy the media, and lawyering-up for a chat with the FBI.

When the helicopter flew David out of the wilderness, he was rank, gaunt, but completely energetic. He had a mostly-gray beard and looked leaner than when Cross had first met him.

As soon as he was done with the feds, though, David planned on going right back into the woods.

Cross hoped it all worked out for him. He pulled through the gate; David closed it up then jumped back in the car for the ride up the hill to the house.

Cross pulled up in front of the main entrance.

"Thanks for everything," David said, getting out.

"You going to be okay?"

David draped a hand on the open door. "Yeah. Glo should be getting here any minute. We're going to cook a nice meal."

"Good," Cross said. "You deserve it. No one's worked as hard as you."

David looked away then smiled wanly and shut the door. His wife would have no nice meal tonight, no warm bed to sleep in.

And things were not looking good. Despite the determination of her husband, Katie's chances of surviving this one were getting slimmer every day. Dr. What's-His-Face on the TV had been right.

A couple of the nights had dipped down into the thirties in the mountains, but that wasn't the worst of it. It was hard to imagine a water supply that would've lasted her this long. She had to have been drinking from creeks, lakes. Giardiasis was a likely problem, an intestinal infection caused by a microscopic parasite often present in those bodies of water. Even boiling didn't always get rid of it.

If she had it, she could be suffering abdominal cramps, bloating, nausea, diarrhea. Dehydration was almost certain.

Plus, she had heart trouble. And there was a high probability she'd sustained injuries from all she'd been through.

Unless she was hunting, food would be scarce. There were wild berries available, some edible plants, but she'd have to know which ones and where to find them.

Investigators at both cabins had deduced how much Katie would have brought with her on her attempt to hike out, and it hadn't amounted to much — just a few days' worth, well-rationed.

And it was too easy to get turned around in all those woods.

Over hundreds of square miles, dozens of campfires had been spotted, but most were along the main trails, which teemed with touring hikers as "leaf-peeper" season ramped up. Helicopter search crews repeatedly hovered over individuals only to verify they were hiking or camping. A prop plane pilot had spotted something reflective on the ground, circled, but come up empty.

The area would stay active like this from now until late October. In addition to the search for Katie, forest rangers and backcountry caretakers were working overtime just to keep all that activity under control. Two other people had gone missing since the search for Katie had gotten underway, but both had been found not far from the groomed trails.

Cross watched David walk into the house and then turned around, drove back down the driveway.

He passed Gloria on the way out, waved. She smiled and waved back. Katie's sister had been tied up all week, like Cross, dealing with the fallout from Janice Connolly.

Gloria was shouldering a terrible sense of responsibility, Cross knew. She blamed herself for Katie's disappearance. It was someone who had been working for her for a year, right under her nose, who'd orchestrated her sister's kidnapping. Janice had gleaned bits and pieces on Katie by listening to Gloria: where she lived, what she was like, right down to her propensity for morning runs. Aside from being surreal, and frustrating, it had shredded Gloria with guilt.

When Cross got back home, he opted for a glass of water rather than a beer. He'd been trying to drink less over the past week, keeping his head on straight for the marathon that had been wrapping up the kidnapping case, at least on his end. Bouchard was happy with how things had turned out for the department, and at least that was something.

Cross had also been talking with Marty almost every day, and that was something, too.

It was mid-week, and in two days, he'd get his daughters for the weekend. He couldn't wait to see them again.

That night he turned on the news and watched the broadcast of David's interview with Channel 5.

David had dressed in a dark blue chambray work shirt. His face was tanned from many days outside.

He was calm and direct.

The interviewer asked, "*What do you think your wife, Katie, is thinking right now? What is she feeling*?"

"She's feeling determined. She's thinking she can do it, she can get herself out."

"Does she have any experience with the woods?"

"Some. She's organized nature walks for children. She loves animals. She's an avid runner, hiker. She's got a lot of energy."

"What would you want to say to her right now, if you could communicate to her?"

David's eyes became glassy, and he pressed his lips together. Then he steadied and answered, *"I'd tell her I believe in her. I support her. And that I won't give up*."

"Thank you, Mr. Brennan. I know this—"

"*But she doesn't need me,*" David went on. "*She doesn't need me to rescue her. I'll be out there every day, there's no doubt about that. But what I mean is — Katie is the one doing this. I'm just there to keep her company.*"

The interviewer reached over the desk and touched David on the hand.

Cross realized there were tears rolling down his own face.

When the interviewer turned and recited the hotline for people to call if they had any information, had seen Katie, or wanted to volunteer for the search, Cross leaned forward in the chair. He put his face in his hands and cried.

He had no idea if he was crying for Katie, for David, for his wife, or his daughters. Or himself.

It all blended together.

* * *

A few minutes later, Cross sat back down with a fresh glass of water. The news had turned to Jean Calumet.

There was footage of Katie's father being led into a courthouse by federal officials. The reporter said Calumet was being investigated for tax fraud, along with three other prominent businessmen, including Henry Fellows and an unnamed accountant.

"While Calumet and Fellows are being investigated by both the IRS Criminal Investigation team and the FBI, Katie Calumet's kidnapping has been considered a separate matter."

The program cut to Cross himself, giving the press conference two days before. Cross tensed as he watched himself on camera. No nail polish this time — just a dark spot on his forehead from a flying ashtray.

"Our investigation has concluded that Janice Connolly-Montgomery developed the idea to kidnap Katie Calumet while working in a restaurant owned and operated by her sister, Gloria," said the Cross on screen. "*We allege that Connolly-Montgomery enlisted her husband and a felon, Troy Vickers, to perform the abduction. They watched her for a time, learned her exercise routine, waited, and then took her.*"

Cameras flashed and Cross, at the podium, cleared his throat and continued.

"It will be the intent of the prosecution to show that Janice Connolly-Montgomery considered the kidnap-and-ransom viable because of rumors involving the total worth of the Calumet family. It gave the kidnappers the confidence to proceed. They believed the Calumets would quickly try to solve the situation with money. But it didn't work out. And it's more proof that crime doesn't pay."

Watching himself, Cross winced at his own shopworn line.

Never again, he thought dourly. *Never let me do press conferences again. Please.*

His phone rang as soon as the news turned to secondary stories.

"Mr. Big Time," Marty said. "Aren't we popular."

"Stop," Cross said, grimacing.

"What are you wearing, Mr. Big Time?"

"Oh, you'd love it. Fifteen-year-old sweatpants, a T-shirt with a hole in the armpit."

"Mmm," Marty joked.

They flirted a bit more then talked about the girls, and Cross finished his water.

After the call with Marty, he got in his bed and stared up at the ceiling.

It had been two weeks since Katie's abduction. Out for a morning run, lured into a stolen minivan, taken deep into the woods.

He tried to imagine her alive in all that wilderness.

He wanted to believe.

CHAPTER FIFTY-THREE

When she heard the water, she thought it was another stream. An outlet from a pond. She'd encountered several, usually clogged with sticks and saplings collected by beavers.

This was different.

Katie took a step, dragged her leg. Took another step, dragged the leg again.

She'd come across plenty of rivers, too. One had been too big to cross. She'd spent three hours walking alongside it, moving southwest, looking for a place to get over. She'd called out as she'd hobbled along. Peered through the underbrush and tried to see a trail. The river had ended up winding away, an impenetrable thicket slowed her down, and then the water turned turbulent as it frothed over the rocks.

This wasn't loud like those rapids. This was the sound of an easy, babbling stream.

Ohh, yes. Get excited. This is exciting. For Christ's sake — are you kidding me?

—Fuck you. It could be something.

It's nothing. Just another stupid creek. In the middle of absolute nowhere. Why don't you try to follow it like you did the last one?

—Shut up.

The further she'd tried to follow the big river, the tougher the going. A scree of rocks she couldn't get past unless she crawled on her hands and knees — and she'd tried, and it was excruciating. She'd given up, gone around a large bushy swath, tried to find the river again.

She hadn't.

This is different?

—It might be.

She took a step. Dragged her leg. Took another step. Dragged her leg.

She was no longer carrying the bag with the pot in it. Her shoulders were covered in blisters. After using a rock to scratch her name into the wooden stock, she'd ditched the rifle. All she had left was the canteen, half-full of dirty pond water.

She pushed a lock of clumpy hair from her eyes. Took a step. Dragged her leg. Took another step.

A light rain was falling. The precipitation felt chilly. A couple nights had been so cold she'd barely slept.

Last night, the rain had fallen nonstop, and she'd thought she was going to die. The coyotes had howled in the distance. Without fire, she'd had nothing to scare them. She'd thought about them coming in, just low shapes in the dark. She'd imagined what it would feel like for the teeth to sink in.

She'd imagined what a relief it could be if she died.

The coyotes had loomed close but had never come for her. She wondered if it was because they'd smelled her, had known she was dying, and had just waited.

Nope. You're not dead.

Brain-dead, maybe.

Body still alive.

Both of us still alive.

—Maybe.

She put a hand on her stomach. Took a step. Dragged her leg. Stared into the trees.

Something was different.

Something looked really, really different.

Katie stopped moving. Peered through the pine boughs at an utterly alien shape. Geometric. Man-made. Rust-brown.

She moved faster, leg pain flaring, eyes blurring. No tears, really, not enough hydration for that, just a blur of semi-consciousness.

Is that a fucking truss?

It was. A God-blessed, mother-loving, load-bearing infrastructure. Triangular units of metal. Rusted, scrappy-looking metal.

But metal.

She shambled hurriedly along, nearly blinded by the pain, holding her breath.

She dropped the canteen. Took her thigh in her hands and half-jogged, half-skipped.

A truss. Not joined together on the top by cross braces, just on the sides, it looked like.

It was a bridge.

Had to be.

A fucking bridge.

Not a hiking bridge. Not a couple logs thrown down over the creek for tourists. A real bridge. She could see both sides of it now. Single lane . . .

Then she heard a rumbling engine. Saw a blur moving laterally across her field of vision, just flashes of it in between the pines.

"Hey!"

A croaky whisper. Nothing left to her voice — it had gone completely a day or so ago. Maybe longer. She'd been spitting up blood for a while now, too. Maybe her gums, her throat, her lungs. Who knew.

She broke into a run.

Today's target heart rate is 122.

"Hey! Hey!" A ragged whisper. She waved her arms as she ran. Her thigh was completely numb, like she was running with a leg on one side, a block of wood on the other.

She almost fell, caught herself. Saw the vehicle turn, cross the bridge, moving away from her. It sputtered down the road on the other side of the bridge.

Target heart rate is 220 minus age, multiplied by 6,000%, since kidnapping ideally increases a person's heart rate by that amount.

She was just up a ways from the road, on an embankment. The ground was a slick carpet of wet pine needles. She dropped onto her ass and skidded the way down. Dug in her fingers and raked the ground to slow her freefall.

And then she was down. Her feet were touching asphalt. Some old crummy road, running along the river, which turned onto the little pony truss bridge that spanned the rushing water.

The sound of the engine sank away.

Katie flopped back against the embankment, breathing hard, her heart thumping.

But steady.

Her heart was steady.

Got some problems with your ticker? Interested in homeopathic remedies? Try our patented—

The thought cut off abruptly — another vehicle was coming. Jesus, another one already.

Katie pushed herself up. Stumbled into the road.

Where was it?

Nothing.

It was the same truck she'd seen roll over the bridge. Must have crested a rise, the sound briefly rolling back to her, now it was gone again.

Everything was quiet.

She wandered back to the dirt shoulder, lowered back down. Looked at her feet.

Not bad for a pair of running sneakers. At least I had the proper footwear. Women are always in such terrible situations, running in the worst *possible footwear.*

She stared up at the sky. Listened to the water purling over the rocks. It made a kind of tympanic chattering as it passed beneath the little bridge.

Her vision swam. Where was her water?

Left it back there.

In the woods.

Something was wrong. She put her hands over her chest, felt her heart fluttering. She was too thirsty.

Things were turning black.

* * *

The hand touched her.

A finger poked her ribs.

"Ma'am?"

Katie opened her eyes.

She didn't comprehend what she was seeing. Couple of kids? A little too old to be the kids at Riverside. Sixteen, seventeen. Two boys. One with a cigarette stuck behind his ear.

"Ma'am? Can you hear me?"

"Can hear you," she rasped.

"I'm going to get you up, okay? Noah, grab her feet, man. No — wait. Here. Look at her leg, dude. Okay. Let's get her under her arms here."

They pawed at her, hoisted her up. She swayed on her one good leg. Leaned against the boys.

"Holy shit. She smells."

"Dude, she can hear you. Ma'am, I'm going to put you in my car . . ."

"Fuckin, Ryan. Oh my God, dude. You know who this is? I think this is that *lady*, dude."

They continued to jabber. They wondered about a reward. They put her in the back of their little beater car.

The car was moving. She smelled cigarette smoke. A window was cracked and wind thundered through the gap. She saw the smoke slipstream out into the air. Eyes in the rearview mirror, watching her. The vibration of the engine, the car jouncing over the old, broken road. Everything in her ached. Everything screamed. Like an orchestra, warming up, a beautiful cacophony of pain.

She felt a smile stretch across her face.

CHAPTER FIFTY-FOUR

How many days?

She tried to count them and kept losing track. She looked down for the wristwatch attached to the rope around her waist, but all that was there was a white blanket.

She felt for the rope pulling her through the woods. Grabbed it, moved her hand up it.

Someone took her hand and moved it away.

Katie focused her vision and saw a tube, not a rope. Going to a hanging IV bag.

* * *

David's face. David's arms around her. Lifting her up.

Where are we going?

Voices, murmuring. Talking about her. What was wrong with her.

Takotsubo cardiomyopathy. Stress cardiomyopathy.

No:

Dehydration. Hypothermia. Giardiasis. Torn quadriceps tendon.

Vocal polyps. Lacerations. Abrasions . . .

She waited for the word.

Baby.

Tell me about the baby.

* * *

The gurney moved swiftly; Katie felt a hand on her arm. David's face again, smiling down at her.

Beeping machines. People moving purposely about on the edges of her vision.

Katie asked what was wrong.

No sounds came from her but a small wheeze.

David was there again. He squeezed her hand. Leaned over and whispered in her ear:

"Just hang in there. Just hang in there, Katie . . ."

She felt heavy. Tried to keep looking at him but her eyes were closing. "You never put the caps on the bottles all the way."

Her words were slurred, her tongue too swollen.

Blackness. She didn't know how long.

Carson. Carson was going to come for her. Open the door to the back of the camper and rape her.

Her hips kept lurching. He was pulling on her, pulling on the rope around her waist.

He was on top of her. His hot breath in her ear.

His knee in her back.

I'll kill you, Carson.

I'll push you to your death.

I'll tear your skin from your body.

* * *

She rolled back her lids and daylight flooded in. Katie was sitting up, the bed at an incline. David slept in a chair in the corner.

Katie slowed her breathing, tried to ease her pulse back. She felt sweaty. She grunted as she moved to get more comfortable, and her efforts roused her husband. He first looked around in a daze, then he saw her.

David's face lit up. He rose from the chair and approached her.

"Hi."

She could only breathe the word. "Hi."

"How are you feeling?"

She thought about that. She went through a quick inventory of her various issues. Then she lifted her hand and stuck her thumb in the air.

He took her hand in his, laughed, and bent toward her. As he hugged her, she looked over his shoulder at the trees outside.

One red, one yellow.

He leaned back and followed her gaze. "Yeah. It's autumn, baby."

She mouthed, "How long?"

"You've been here a little over a week. They've taken good care of you. Your parents have been by a couple times; Glo was here . . . Everybody's been pulling for you."

She reached for him, grabbed him by the shoulders, pulled him close. Her eyes flooded with tears.

"I think I was pregnant," she whispered.

He pulled his head back to stare into her eyes. He laughed so abruptly a little bubble of spit popped on his lower lip. The tears rolled down his eyes and he laughed again, a spasm erupting from his chest.

"You still are."

* * *

She watched her husband as he came into the room with the wheelchair. It had been another two days, and her voice was returning.

"You're so friggin' handsome," she said. She arched an eyebrow. "Have you lost weight?"

He grinned at her as he helped her from the bed and into her chair. It had taken half an hour to get dressed because nothing fit her still-swollen leg. But the leg was getting better, and the old yoga pants were perfect — they just cut off one of the legs. Otherwise David had helped her into warm socks, hiking boots, a warm fleece shirt, and a sweater. They'd brushed her hair back and given her a topknot, both of them laughing their asses off about it for reasons she didn't even care to analyze.

A topknot was just funny, given the circumstances.

Now in the wheelchair, as he rolled her down the hallway and out of the hospital, the comedy continued to grow. These people watching her, like she was a celebrity. The looks on their faces . . .

Was that nurse crying?

It was beautiful, lovely, hilarious.

Surreal.

The reporters in the parking lot charged in as they emerged into the cool, crisp day. David was gracious, giving them a few good sound bites while the lenses trained on her. What a blessing, to have no proper speaking voice. No one expected her to say anything.

Except one reporter, who got a microphone past David and stuck it in her face.

"Katie, how do you feel?"

"Good," she croaked.

David helped her into the vehicle and handed the wheelchair off to a waiting nurse. People waved as David got in and drove away.

"That was it?" he asked. "That was your big moment? You say, 'Good'?"

She laughed at him. The laughing kept hurting her throat, but she didn't care. They found the freeway and headed back toward their home in the mountains.

* * *

In the night, their first night back in the bed, she jerked out of a fitful doze and found him looking at her, his eyes shining in the dim light.

He stroked her hair. “You okay?”

She wanted to tell him. About everything. But knowing where to begin was another story. She rolled over and tried not to let the emotions bubble over.

Breathe. Just breathe.

He spooned close behind her, his big arm wrapped around her chest. They lay like that for a full minute as she went through all the possible ways to start. But she wondered if she even could. If she could tell him she still saw them, in their masks, when she closed her eyes. That she didn’t like the darkness because it reminded her of the shroud. That she could still feel the bindings around her wrists. Could still hear Carson’s voice wailing up to her from where he lay mangled on the rocks.

Like he was still there, still down there calling to her.

Katieeee.

David was silent for a long time. She waited for him to say something, but she didn’t expect him to.

She was relieved, even, when he didn’t. He just lay there with her, keeping her company.

The next morning, she had her first cup of coffee in weeks.

“I drank coffee before my run that morning,” she said. They sat together at the stone-topped kitchen island. “Not supposed to do that.” She smiled and took a sip.

David grinned and then looked around. “You should have seen this place. Overloaded with people, at some points. There was this one woman, Laura Broderick, with DEC. She was something. You’d like her.” He took a sip of his own coffee then gripped the mug in two hands and looked into the liquid. “She drew a map. Want to see it?” He gave her a compassionate look. “You don’t have to.”

Katie took a deep breath. Let it out. “Yeah. I want to.”

He left to the study where he kept his musical instruments and came back a few seconds later with a topo map and spread it out over the island.

He pointed to a red line, sidewinding through squiggly contours. West Canada Lake Wilderness and Black River Wild Forest. "This is the best guess of your route. Since you came out, DEC found a couple of your campsites. And from what you've described, here and there, Broderick put this together."

Katie focused on a spot near Indian River. She'd described the rapids she'd come across at one point. It looked like the biggest river in the region, so that must've been it. Haskell Road was on the other side. Dotted lines indicated it wasn't a paved road. Likely just a logging road, no more than a couple of wheel ruts through the brush.

"And this is the marshy area you talked about," David said. "But this section here — see where it says 'wilderness boundary'? That's Little Rock Lake. They're pretty sure you were in here, and this is where you really got turned around." His eyes found her. "Broderick said anyone would have gotten turned around in there."

She blew out some air and rolled her eyes, attempting levity. But it was hard to shake the guilt. The guilt about approaching the minivan. Taunting Carson. What he'd done to her. What she'd done to Hoot.

"I should've just stayed at Hoot's cabin," she said. She looked at the red circle by Twin Mountain, and her heart broke. Both for Hoot — Barry Turner — and herself. And everyone. All the people involved, lives disrupted. She planned to write a letter to every single searcher who'd spent time away from their families to try and find her.

David was shaking his head. "The investigators found evidence that John Montgomery doubled back to the cabin before he walked off again into the woods and died. You would have confronted him."

They stared at each other over the map.

"No, things happened the way they did for a reason. You're alive."

He dropped his gaze. "And here is where you came out. Fayle Road. That little bridge is a restored bridge. The kids who found you, Ryan and Noah, they came to the hospital to try and see you. Couple of maniacs, those kids. Honestly, them driving you into Hoffmeister was probably the most dangerous part of the whole ordeal."

She laughed in the midst of drinking from her mug, and had to put a hand over her mouth. She blotted her lips with a napkin, gave the map one last look. "I gotta say, that was one hell of a run."

"Yeah," he said, folding up the map. "I think that's a record distance for you."

EPILOGUE

Justin Cross.

She'd heard about him dozens of times. Apparently, he'd been to the hospital, twice, but she'd been sleeping. Another investigator, a woman named Gates, had questioned her when she was more lucid, but she hadn't seen Cross yet. Not as a conscious human being, anyway.

From what David said, it was Cross who'd zeroed in on where she was. While they hadn't found her, it certainly wasn't his fault. He'd gotten them closer than anyone else had.

They turned into the small brown house where Cross lived and parked in the driveway.

David glanced over at her. "Ready?"

She nodded.

"I'll get the crutches."

He banged out of the vehicle, full of energy, opened the hatch, and retrieved them. Two months since the abduction, and she was still using walking aids. She had physical therapy three times a week. Ob-gyn visits once every two weeks. Two ultrasounds already.

Katie looked down at her stomach: just beginning to show.

David opened the door, helped her out, and she slid the crutches under her arms.

As they walked up to the front door, it opened. A man she'd never seen before, with wavy brown hair and a dusting of freckles high on his cheeks, walked out to greet them. He was dressed casually in jeans and a flannel shirt.

Katie smiled, shook his hand, and he led them inside. As she walked through the front door she glimpsed a couple of little girls watching from the window. Then a woman appeared, very pretty, wearing a nice-looking suit. "Hi, I'm Marie Cross."

"Nice to meet you."

Marie showed Katie to a couch and urged her to get comfortable. David sat beside her.

The little girls sat on the carpet, both staring.

"Did you get lost in the woods?" the elder asked. Katie knew her name was Patricia.

"I did."

"Wow. I got lost in the woods once."

"You did?"

"Yeah. Mommy was yelling for me, 'Petrie! Petrie!' I was hiding behind a rock."

"Oh. Hiding. So you weren't lost. You knew where you were."

"Yeah." Petrie grinned adorably and bobbed her head. Then she turned to a pile of beads and string and started working on a necklace.

The smaller girl, Ramona, just kept clocking Katie, sucking on her fingers.

Katie turned to Cross, who'd sat in a chair beside the couch. Marie came in with a tray of cheese and crackers. She set it down on the table between the couch and chair.

Ramona immediately went for it.

"Hey, those are for us," Cross said to her.

"Snack," Ramona said. She took a handful of crackers and hurried away.

Katie watched the girls. Ramona neared her sister, and Patricia snatched a cracker from the girl's hand. Ramona yelped then stuffed the two crackers she had left into her mouth.

Marie was talking, Cross was talking, David responding, but Katie just looked out the window a moment.

"You have a nice view," Katie said.

She stared off at the mountains.

"Yeah," Cross said. "I like it."

THE END

A LETTER FROM T.J. BREARTON

I want to say a huge thank you for choosing to read *No Way Out*. If you did enjoy it, and want to keep up-to-date with all my latest releases, just sign up at the following link. Your email address will never be shared and you can unsubscribe at any time.

tjbrearton.net

There's a little bit of me in each of the main characters in this book, and I bet you saw some of yourself, too. The way David fights for his spouse, the way Cross feels when he's missing his family, the way Katie persists — even the way she argues with herself. Both writing and reading a book, then, is partly cathartic; a journey — when Katie was in those woods, we were in those woods with her. Like David says, we were keeping her company.

I think there's some magic in that.

I hope you loved *No Way Out*, and if you did, I would be very grateful if you could write a review. It would be great to hear what you think, and it makes such a difference helping new readers to discover one of my books for the first time.

I love hearing from my readers — you can get in touch on my Facebook page, through Twitter, Goodreads, or my website.

Warm regards,

T.J.

ACKNOWLEDGEMENTS

Once again I need to thank Trooper Kristy Wilson, who likely had to let a few speeders pass while she responded to my endless texts and emails about state police procedure. Please credit her with technical accuracies. For any mistakes, look no further than yours truly.

I'd like to thank Leslie Brodbeck with New York's Department of Environmental Conservation. Leslie shared both her firsthand experience and in-depth knowledge of the Adirondack Wilderness, crucial to the writing of this book. Not to mention she knows how to turn a poignant phrase: "Unfortunately, it is usually not 'til disaster strikes that people begin to see and respect the power that is found in the wilderness."

Thanks to Corey Fehlner for introducing me to Leslie, and for his own contributions as an experienced outdoorsman and an interior outpost caretaker.

Thank you to Steven Lucas, who showed up in my life at just the right time to help me understand the intricacies of prison administration. Steven has twenty-five years of experience as a corrections professional with the Federal Bureau of Prisons. He's also a great guy to be seated next to at a wedding.

Many thanks to my editor, Abigail Fenton, who guided me through to the final realization of this story with her usual smart and judicious insights. Abi's good humor, her canny ability to take the sting out, are exactly what this emotional writer needs. Thanks to DeAndra Lupu for catching all the potentially embarrassing errors and shining up the manuscript; thanks to Oliver Rhodes, Lauren Finger, the illustrious Kim Nash, and all the talented staff at Bookouture, not to mention the gang of brilliant writers who are always ready to commiserate and offer words of encouragement.

Finally, I can never thank my wife enough for her contributions to this ridiculous obsession I have with writing books. And for this one, I have to be straight up: She really deserves credit for inspiring the whole thing. Every book starts out somewhere, and this one started in her mind. Then it was up to me to do the dirty work. Thank you, Dava.

Without these people, this book would not have been possible.

THE JOFFE BOOKS STORY

We began in 2014 when Jasper agreed to publish his mum's much-rejected romance novel and it became a bestseller.

Since then we've grown into the largest independent publisher in the UK. We're extremely proud to publish some of the very best writers in the world, including Joy Ellis, Faith Martin, Caro Ramsay, Helen Forrester, Simon Brett and Robert Goddard. Everyone at Joffe Books loves reading and we never forget that it all begins with the magic of an author telling a story.

We are proud to publish talented first-time authors, as well as established writers whose books we love introducing to a new generation of readers.

We won Trade Publisher of the Year at the Independent Publishing Awards in 2023 and Best Publisher Award in 2024 at the People's Book Prize. We have been shortlisted for Independent Publisher of the Year at the British Book Awards for the last five years, and were shortlisted for the Diversity and Inclusivity Award at the 2022 Independent Publishing Awards. In 2023 we were shortlisted for Publisher of the Year at the RNA Industry Awards, and in 2024 we were shortlisted at the CWA Daggers for the Best Crime and Mystery Publisher.

We built this company with your help, and we love to hear from you, so please email us about absolutely anything bookish at feedback@joffebooks.com.

If you want to receive free books every Friday and hear about all our new releases, join our mailing list here: www.joffebooks.com/freebooks.

And when you tell your friends about us, just remember: it's pronounced Joffe as in coffee or toffee!

Printed in Great Britain
by Amazon

57466109R00209